Love in the Middle Ages

A Time Travel Romance

Laura Virgo

Southway Publishing

For Rob,

BFF, occasional plus one, always the gallant knight.

Much loved and missed.

CONTENTS

CHAPTER 1

Friday 17 December

PATIENTS AND PATIENCE - she had one, but not the other.

When push came to shove, Maggie always preferred functionality over aesthetics; the detour she was currently being forced to take, reminding her why. She knew she ought to be more appreciative of her surroundings, when most people would give their right kidney to live in such a chocolate-box hamlet. Admittedly, the rippling stream weaving its way under a quaint stone bridge looked as if Monet had whipped out his paintbrush. And yes, the picture perfect backdrop did wonders for local postcard sales, but at this very moment, she'd gladly trade the narrow cobblestone streets for a decent, tarmacked highway, because the traffic in Pebble Heath was maddening!

It shouldn't have been at this time of day. The early shift was supposed to give her an easy drive to and from the hospital, but the florist van that had taken the corner too fast up ahead, promptly put paid to her stress-free commute. Cars crawled at a snail's pace past the accident, as the authorities attempted to clear the road of broken boxes, smashed vases and a multitude of colourful blooms strewn across their path.

Tapping her fingers irritably on the steering wheel, Maggie tried to temper her restlessness by focusing on trivia; her eyes drawn to the rivulets of liquid trickling down her windscreen. Typical English weather that she was well used to, but could have done without today - rain always tending to make the traffic worse, and probably contributing to the van's misfortune. As the crawl came to a complete stop, she bit her bottom lip in frustration; a habit of hers when things weren't going according to plan.

The phone rang, flashing a familiar caller ID. Maggie switched the radio off - muting an annoyingly festive Mariah Carey - and pressed the hands-free button to answer it.

"Hi Dad,"

"Hi love, you sound echoey; are you still driving? I thought you'd be home by now."

Welcoming the distraction of a chat with him, she explained the cause of the delay.

"Oh, that's a bugger," he sympathised. "I just wanted to check in with you about your sister's birthday and an idea I had for a present."

"Sure, fire away."

As he continued, she peered past the queue in front of her to see how far it extended; her automated wipers sluicing through the layer of water and her line of vision in a perfectly symmetrical arc. It made her think of looking through the arched window on Play School as a child. Then she frowned at the realisation her brain had chosen a 1970s image to illustrate the simile - God, was she that old?!

Bringing herself back to the present - in both senses of the word - she said,

"It sounds perfect, Dad. She'll love it!"

"Great. I had hoped so, but always appreciate your opinion. Thanks, love. You take care, and use the traffic jam as some downtime, Margaret. I know you don't get enough of it. In fact, given that you're surrounded by flowers, you could actually do what we've been telling you to for ages."

"And what's that?"

"Stop and smell the flipping roses!" he roared, signing off with a cackle.

Maggie grinned and gently pressed her foot down on the accelerator, as the snake of vehicles promisingly began to slither forward again.

Sometime later than anticipated, she arrived home to her townhouse set in a quietly inviting cul-de-sac, and eased down the driveway to a detached garage. She didn't usually mind the lack of internal access, but grimaced today as she stepped outside; her skin goose-bumping in response to the bone-chilling temperature.

As the skies darkened belligerently, she made a frantic dash across the gravel to avoid another impending downpour. Once inside, Maggie soaked up the cosiness of her sanctuary and kicked off her shoes; one of them nearly hitting the giant dog in the hallway who had been eagerly awaiting her return. He sniffed it, disappointed that it wasn't edible, but happily received a pat on the head instead. She briefly lamented his inability to greet her with a steaming cup of hot cocoa, due to the absence of opposable thumbs and reasonable thinking power. Pity really. If he'd had either - or perhaps both - he could have done the laundry and cleaned up his own poop as well.

She idly entertained a thought that somewhere in a parallel universe, the week might finish with her breezing into a tidy house, the delectable smell of coffee brewing, and perhaps a male other than her Great Dane showing interest in how her day had gone. It was a frivolous fancy though and not one to be taken seriously. She was just glad to put the weather and traffic behind her.

Maggie's relief to be home was short-lived, however. Walking into the kitchen to put the kettle on, a background noise seeped into her consciousness: a slow, repetitive plop, plop, plop that seemed to magnify in sound the closer she got to the sink. A sigh of resignation escaped her lips.

Clearly, it was going to be one of those days.

Wanting nothing more than to collapse into a chair after a manic Friday, she knew the incessant dripping would aggravate her to the point of self-combustion, so begrudgingly rolled up her sleeves. Compelled to determine the villain of the piece, here and now, Maggie knelt on the floor, opened the door under the sink and felt the dampness at the bottom of the cupboard. Her dishwasher was already on the blink, and now it seemed her plumbing problems were compounding.

"Dammit!" she muttered.

It was all very well getting down to ground level, but returning to an upright position was a different thing altogether. Her middle-aged muscles frequently deciding that a smooth transition from lying to standing was an optional extra these days, often only possible if accompanied by a great deal of grunting. Hopefully, her son would be home from high school soon to give her a helping hand back up.

"YES, JACK?" CATHERINE HOLDEN pointed to the fair-haired boy at the back of the class with his hand raised.

"Whippings, stonings, hangings, dismemberment, Ms Holden."

"That's right Jack," she praised. He had answered her question about punishments in the Middle Ages. "And you guys think you're hard done by if your mobile is taken away for a day."

The class groaned and rolled their eyes, to express that adults obviously didn't understand the debilitation of a phone-free day to a teenager. Catherine - or Cat - laughed. She was winding them up and enjoying it. Having lived with her own children's adolescent antics and survived to tell the tale, she'd managed those turbulent years between puberty and emotional maturity twice already, leaving her well-equipped to teach history to a room full of thirteen-year-olds. Of course, a monthly subscription to a wine club had helped, as had her penchant for retail therapy, neither of which she'd given up since her kids had left school.

Cat remembered her offspring going through this phase of life. As their brain synapses disengaged to make way for alternative neural pathways, any instructions given more than a minute ago were instantly forgotten, common sense seemed to be thrown out the window, and Oh My God, the bloody-mindedness! But there were laughs too, with generational differences pointed out by either side: the kids couldn't fathom a world without internet; she didn't understand memes that were apparently hilarious.

Now Samantha, her daughter, 19, was at university studying art, and Josh, 22, had secured a job in IT. Where had the years gone?

Cat looked fondly at her nephew and allowed herself a moment's thought, pondering how her sister would navigate Jack through his teens. Perhaps she ought to sign her up to the wine club too? Then she smiled, knowing Maggie would cope marvellously, given the practical, capable woman she was. Her only trepidation being; that because her sister was older, and had become a mother at the ripe old age of 41, as the teenage years approached for Jack, so did the menopausal ones for Maggie. There would be hormones raging everywhere. Ah well, she shrugged, them's the breaks.

Motioning for quiet, Cat resumed her teaching. She'd learnt from experience, the best way to engage children in learning was to pick a topic that held their attention. And what better way to pique her students' interest than to go into the gruesome details of torture in medieval times, with special emphasis on blood and death?

"And what was the average age people died in the 1300s?" she asked the class.

This time Rose volunteered an answer, "About 40, Ms Holden, largely due to the plague."

"Correct. If you lived in those days, you'd be on your way to a midlife crisis sooner than you think."

The class scoffed, their faces plainly saying, 'As if.'

On cue, the final bell of the day rang, signifying it was time for everyone to put away their books and devices.

"OK, that's us done for the term," said Cat, drawing the lesson to a close and wiping the blackboard clean, as cries of jubilation erupted from the room.

"Don't forget our Medieval Fayre on Monday. I expect to see you all in costume and ready to have fun."

A chorus of "Yes Miss" rang out in an automatic monotone, as 28 phones came out of pockets to take over their focal point. The students filed out into the corridor, filling the air with a general clatter of laughter, music and TikTok videos. Jack turned and waved, saying,

"See you Saturday night, Aunty Cat," - '*Ms Holden*' officially dropped for the end of the calendar year.

Jack put his headphones on and strolled out of class, lip-synching to songs on his playlist as he made the easy fifteen-minute walk home; seemingly oblivious to the arctic-like conditions. He kicked through leaves on the pavement; soft scuffs and crunches confirming the trees' seasonal state of undress. Turning the last corner and nearing his house, a deep, doleful woof permeated through the rap lyrics as a large black creature came loping up the path, wagging his tail at the sight of his master's arrival.

"Hey," Jack greeted, rubbing the dog's ears that were nearly level with his chest. "Been a good boy?"

Another woof in the affirmative.

"Yo, Mum!" shouted Jack, as he walked through the door; the Great Dane tripping over his feet behind him and living up to the breed's reputation of being notoriously clumsy.

"Hey, Bud," came a muffled reply, "I'm in the kitchen."

Jack found his mum lying face upwards under the sink.

"What are you doing?"

"The pipe is leaking, but I think I've got it. These new PVC pipes are much easier to deal with than the old copper ones." She accepted his outstretched hand for assistance and stood up, arching her back to straighten out the kinks. Drying her hands on a tea towel, she asked,

"How was your last day?"

"It was sick!" he enthused, eyes shining.

Maggie understood sick meant 'good', and mentally prepared herself to translate the teen-speak she knew was coming.

"Bro, it was nuts. I broke David's ankles so bad he fell on the floor, then I stepped back and splashed a three in Liam's mouth. My one-legged jumper is crazy good too; I can't miss!"

"Err, great?!" said Maggie, not understanding the basketball lingo one iota, but guessing that today's scrimmage had gone well.

Like most children in England, Jack had started out playing football at school, but after a growth spurt a few years ago, his PE teacher suggested he try out for the basketball team; a sport rapidly growing in popularity around the country. Taking to it like a duck to water, and discovering a natural talent, he'd developed an absolute passion for the game, including the jargon commonplace amongst the players, much to his mother's amusement.

"What about inside the classroom?"

"K," said Jack. Anything other than sports only warranted a monosyllabic answer, but as long as her boy had had a good day, that was all that mattered.

"Well, have something to eat, then we need to pop down to the costume store to pick up our outfits for the fair on Monday. Your cousins are going to come too."

Jack reached into the pantry for some Pot noodles.

"Serious? I can't see Sam wearing a dress; she never does."

"True. Knowing her, the most we can ask for is a dragon tattoo to go with the times, but Josh and his mate, Aaron are always keen to dress up, as you know."

"Are they kidnapping Pops again for Aunty Cat's party?" asked Jack.

"More than likely," answered Maggie.

CAT AND MAGGIE'S FATHER, Harry, lived in The Stables Retirement Village conveniently located behind the school. He and their mother, Grace, had moved in to make the most of their twilight years, but sadly, Grace had passed away since leaving Harry on his own. Jack only had a few memories of his grandmother, but he loved his grandad to bits, as did Josh and Sam.

It was a good base for Harry. He'd been withdrawn after Grace's passing, but as time lessened the pain of his grief, he gradually started making friends and participating in the activities on offer. The complex had been built on what was, long ago, an equestrian arena adjoining estate grounds, and named after the stables situated at the bottom of the garden. A competitive rider in his youth, Harry didn't think his body was up to galloping across the countryside any longer, but rated this area his favourite part of the village. He spent many a time wandering around the stables for nostalgia's sake; strolling through the empty stalls and abandoned storehouses, running his fingers along crumbling walls and exploring the structure's nooks and crannies. Never restored from its original state, the building had seen better days and was merely a historic preservation. The other village residents didn't take much notice, which suited Harry fine, as he often had the place to himself. His friend Doris came with him sometimes, but she was conscious of her daughter's warning that it could be unsafe.

Doris's daughter, Esme was a pain in the arse, Harry thought. They were older, not senile. And not children either. These senior homes were no longer waiting rooms for death, but provided a lifestyle that meant the occupants were usually fitter and healthier than their predecessors. If Esme wasn't so overbearing and over-protective of her mother, he was sure Doris would join him on some of his adventures.

He was very much looking forward to his next one tomorrow night. Despite liking where he lived, the village did try to enforce a curfew of 8 pm, discouraging any night-time activities outside of its walls, supposedly for the safety of its residents. But Harry still loved a good party and knew Josh and Aaron would turn up in one of their many disguises to spring him free. Previous successes included the boys dressing up as caterers for a village event, and smuggling Harry out under the tablecloth on the cakes trolley. Another time they came as gardeners, on the pretext they'd left some equipment there from the morning and were returning to collect it. Doris kept reception occupied with a bogus claim about her air conditioning not working, while Harry snuck out and was whisked away in a wheelbarrow covered by a tarpaulin.

"Good old Doris," Josh had said. "Next time we can come back as air conditioning repairmen!"

What would it be on Saturday night, Harry thought? Maybe something Christmas-themed as that was just around the corner.

CAT, HAVING LOCKED UP the classroom for the year, drove to get her hair done at Frankie Cooper's salon: *Curl Up and Dye*. She loved the humour in the name and the play on words, but more than that, trusted no-one else but Frankie to style her hair the way she liked it. A customer for years, their professional relationship had turned into a friendship, and much like a bartender, Frankie was a sounding board and confidante for Cat. She was always amazed at how many of her stories he remembered, given he had so many customers who would also share their troubles and triumphs at every visit.

Today, her hair needed a definite refresh. It was her 50th birthday on Saturday, and she was having a small get-together at her place. Hairdresser today and nail salon tomorrow. She took pride in her appearance, whereas her sister didn't care so much, usually in jeans and T-shirts, and rarely going to spas despite Cat's encouragement. Super organised, Maggie was always thinking ahead, and usually had a plan of some sort or goals to achieve, which didn't leave much room for titivation. Cat was more into style and presentation, embracing her femininity and enjoying the finer things in life. Her flamboyant friend greeted her as she entered,

"Kitty Cat, darling, you look knackered. Take a load off. I'll get you a cuppa."

Cat wasn't going to say No. It was a busy time of year, and although the academic side of teaching was done, she still had to finalise some last-minute details for the school fair. Trying to squeeze in a birthday party as well, a week before Christmas, just made her To-Do list longer.

"Thanks, Frankie," she said, "for the tea, not the '*you look like shite*' comment."

Frankie grinned mischievously, wrapping the plastic cape around her neck as she sat in front of the mirror.

"Looking forward to tomorrow?" he asked, mixing up the hair colour to hide those pesky greys.

"I guess so," replied Cat. "I'm not sure how I feel about turning 50."

"It's a gift, babe," responded Frankie positively, "not everyone makes it this far."

"That's true," said Cat, remembering Rose's answer to medieval life expectancy.

"Anyway, it's a great excuse for a knees-up. How's your sister doing, by the way? Found herself a man yet?"

"No," laughed Cat. "Her problem is, she's too bloody independent. She's worked since she was sixteen, travelled overseas and back again, built up a business and bought a house. Even had a kid on her own! She's so self-sufficient I don't think she needs a knight in shining armour. She's hardly a damsel in distress."

"Maybe not," said Frankie, "but Jack will be grown before she knows it, and then she'll be on her tod. She might not need a tall, dark and handsome type, but it wouldn't hurt to have one in the wings."

"Well, she's always got LeBron James to keep her company," said Cat.

"Excuse me?"

"LeBron James: their Great Dane - tall, dark and handsome, like you said."

They laughed as Frankie led Cat to the basin to wash her hair.

"And you and Tom are all good?"

"Same old, same old," sighed Cat. "Of course I love him, but after twenty-five years you get a bit stuck in a rut, you know? He's forever got his head in spreadsheets, and I'm just as bad. There's so much paperwork in teaching now; I'm as guilty as him for bringing it home. After working full-time, raising kids and restoring a house, we really don't have the energy or inclination for date nights."

"Sounds like you guys need something to spice up your life too," observed Frankie, squeezing the water out of her hair and wrapping it in a towel.

"How about you?" asked Cat. "Is business good?"

"Sure, but I ain't a millionaire yet," he said. "Trouble is, the rent's gone up, and the utilities are already so expensive; there's too much month left at the end of the money, honey. The other tenants in the building are struggling too, so we're all in the same boat. But we'll keep on keeping on."

Frankie appreciated he had a relatively good setup. The salon was well-established in a purpose-built block of shops, incorporating residential apartments over each commercial space. The tenants worked below and lived above, giving them a great sense of community. Frankie's friend Tallulah ran a dance studio to his left, and to the right was a café, sandwiching him agreeably between music and food. It worked well, and the residents were close, but everyone was feeling the pinch nowadays.

"Oh, Frankie," said Cat, commiserating, "you've worked so hard and have such a great reputation. I wish things were easier for you. Are you going home to your family for Christmas, at least?"

"Uh-uh," Frankie shook his head. "They're right across the other side of the country, and my credit card has a long-standing relationship with the 'insufficient funds' notification. But it's OK - we're having a 'waifs and strays' Christmas here with some of the others who are at a loose end."

"Well, come to my party tomorrow night. You're not working on Sunday, are you? So you can have a few drinks and a dance, and sleep in late the next day. Don't bring anything, just your gorgeous self."

"You know, Kitty Cat, I might just do that," Frankie smiled. "It's a date!"

RETURNING FROM THE COSTUME shop and donning their selections once more, Maggie tried to take a selfie of her and Jack dressed up to send to her sister, but as usual, she couldn't get the angle right.

"My thumb's not long enough to press the button," she moaned, moving the phone all over the place while trying to frame their faces.

"Give it to me," Jack cried, exasperated at how old people couldn't do the simplest of things. That was one of the bonuses of having a Gen Z around the house. Tech wasn't Maggie's forte, and she couldn't count the number of times she'd gone to Jack complaining there was no sound on her phone, whereby he'd flicked a switch somewhere, looked at her pityingly, and sorted it. She was just as bad with the remote control, never getting the hang of rewinding, and driving Jack to distraction with her attempts.

"Can I please do it for you, Mum?" he had asked last night when they were watching a movie.

"That was very polite, Bud," she teased, "what were you really saying in your head?"

"Honestly, Mum? For fark's sake!"

"Language!" laughed Maggie, mock scolding him and pretending to be shocked.

He was a teenage boy. They swore. There were too many other battles to fight at this age, so she wasn't going to be precious over that. Especially when she was hardly a saint in that department herself.

Nailing the selfie in one seamless snap, he stuck his tongue out at her to gloat. She playfully cuffed him on the side of his head and went into the kitchen to check what groceries she needed for the week. Jack - growing like a weed - was eating her out of house and home, and the dog wasn't much better. Plus, she needed to prepare for next weekend.

Maggie always hosted Christmas Eve dinner at her house; a low-key affair with a mish-mash of food. Not a brilliant cook by any means, she still wanted to contribute at this time of year, so it had become tradition to mix everyone's favourites, which fortunately, happened to be quite simple: toasted sandwiches for Jack, pizza for Sam, burgers for the boys (she always included Aaron, as he and Josh seemed to be joined at the hip), and cottage pie for the adults. Even the dog got a hard-boiled egg, which he loved, but was only allowed on special occasions because of the after-effects. Apple crumble with a dollop of cream for dessert got the thumbs up from everyone. Maggie could manage all of that, and there was something about comfort food on a cold, wintery evening that put everyone in a good mood. Afterwards, the others would immerse themselves in video games or play cards, as she and Cat watched trash TV from the couch, while LeBron James farted in front of the fire.

Cat - a gourmet cook and Christmas fairy - would put on a lavish lunch the next day, with silly jumpers and mulled wine and crackers and everything; but Maggie secretly thought to herself that everyone cherished the simplicity of the night before.

CHAPTER 2

Saturday 18 December

"CAN YOU MOVE THOSE baubles up a level, love?" Cat asked her daughter, not willing to touch anything as her newly polished nails were still drying out.

"For God's sake, Mum, what does it matter? Can we just get the decorating over and done with?"

Both her kids were home for the Christmas holidays, and Cat was adjusting to having their personalities back in the household again.

Samantha, ever the headstrong individual, insisted on the abbreviation 'Sam', and railed against the machine by wearing black all the time; her body adorned with tattoos and piercings. The only girl-next-door feature she deemed permissible was her curly red hair; akin to Victoria in the Twilight movies or Merida in Brave, which she usually tied up haphazardly. Genetics had flung sideways, with Sam inheriting her aunt's hair colour, rather than her father's brown or mother's blonde. And typifying the redhead trait, she had a 'balls to the wall' attitude that served her well in some respects and to her detriment in others.

Not a huge fan of Christmas, Sam preferred Halloween, where her goth presence fitted in better. Christmas was too schmaltzy. Everyone rushing around, trying to outdo each other with competitive light displays, extravagant gift giving, and making far too much food. Honestly, she didn't even like turkey. A pizza would be fine. But she was conscious that her mother adored Christmas Day and all its trimmings, and as it was her mum's milestone birthday today, she guessed she should cut her some slack. A point emphasised by her father's request:

"Do as your mother says, Sam, please. It's not going to kill you."

"Yeah, Samantha," her brother teased, using her full name to deliberately irk her, "you're the artist in the house, make the tree look pretty".

Josh had an irritatingly placid nature, was good with numbers like his dad, and tended to go with the flow in life. He hadn't attended university as his sister had; instead getting an internship at a games development company. Tom, who had a fairly conservative view of the world, was somewhat dismissive of his children's career choices to begin with, but as Josh started climbing the rungs of the company ladder - recently entrusted with developing a new app - and Sam had carved out a passion for photography, he realised that times had changed.

Sam glared at her brother, lounging on the couch without a care in the world, and threw one of the heftier Christmas ornaments at him. Untroubled by her malevolence, he caught it smugly with one hand. Snorting her disappointment that it hadn't connected with his head, she returned to beautifying the tree. Not that she'd ever tell him, but he was right. Other than the nail situation, she knew her mum had employed her assistance, because Sam had a knack of placing ordinary objects in such a way as to make an overall scene look stunning.

Despite her dark outer covering and prickly personality, through the lens of her camera, she was able to capture gems of joy in the world. When life was perceived as chaotic, she could uncover the hidden tranquillity; her creativity consequently earning recognition from tutors and peers. So much so that she had been invited as one of five selected artists to display her work in a New Year's Eve exhibition entitled The Secret of Love. And right now, her fuse was incredibly short, as she had less than two weeks to pull together a decent collection. She'd made a start with her immediate circle, capturing a great shot of Jack and his dog. No mistaking the love there. But she was lacking inspiration with everyone else:

- Mum and Dad were boring: an accountant and a teacher. How mainstream could you get? She didn't think they'd had sex since she was born.

- Aunt Maggie was alone and had been for ages. Nothing to report there.

- Pops had lost the love of his life and didn't ride anymore; his passions a thing of the past.

- Josh and Aaron were more interested in pranks and video games than girlfriends. Bros before hos they had charmingly told her once.

Well, there was her mum's do tonight and the Medieval Fayre on Monday. Maybe different settings would get her creative juices flowing. She'd keep her camera close by. Sam preferred using an old-school Polaroid, habitually printing out the photo as soon as she'd taken it, and pinning it to the top of her easel as a visual cue for her imagination. Using different techniques to paint the picture's mirror image with an innovative twist, had garnered her respect and acclaim, hence the exhibition invitation.

Noting the events her mum had committed her to on the calendar: - birthday bash, Jack's school fair, pre-Christmas shopping, Christmas Day and Boxing Day sales - she calculated she had a very limited amount of time to produce a portfolio of artwork by New Year's Eve. I better get a wriggle on, she concluded.

IN ADDITION TO IT being Cat's birthday, the 18th of December was the night for the Christmas shindig at The Stables Retirement Village. With most residents going home to their families for the big day, they always had their own celebration the week prior.

Harry placed his secret Santa gift under the tree, before helping himself to a glass of eggnog and piling nibbles on a plate to share with Doris. Catering was usually sponsored by a local business who took the opportunity to promote their services to a captive audience. This year, said business had provided two Santa Clauses to hand out presents halfway through the Christmas themed quiz, already underway. Bringing in sacks full of goodies and livening up the atmosphere with enthusiastic Ho Ho Hos, the pair mingled through the group. As the noise and laughter went up a few decibels, Harry felt a tap on his shoulder.

"It's me, Pops," whispered Josh, a wicked glint in his eye. "Follow my lead."

"Merry Christmas, everybody," Josh boomed in a faux deep voice. "We hope you enjoy your gifts. My fellow Santa will explain how to use them while I make a small pit stop. Could someone kindly show me where the bathroom is, please?"

"Oh - err, yes, I can," said Harry, cottoning on and quickly escorting Santa Josh into the hallway.

Excited chatter accompanied the rustling of wrapping paper as Santa Aaron drew the attention to himself. Their game company had developed a prototype gadget targeting seniors, as an increasing number of the elderly were becoming adept at using technology. Today's complimentary gift was a virtual version of bingo, which appeared to be a hit straight away.

In the bathroom, Josh quickly got out of his Santa uniform, already dressed in a T-shirt and trackies underneath.

"Put this on," he whispered. Harry stifled a giggle as he got into the outfit. With white hair and beard covering his face, and the quintessential red suit big enough to go over his clothes, Santa Harry quickly replaced Santa Josh.

"Perfect," said Josh, slapping his grandad on the back. "Go and join Aaron, pretending to be me, say your farewells, and casually saunter out the front door. I'm going to sneak out the bathroom window."

Harry did just that, winking at Aaron and joining him in shaking hands with the village staff, who were none the wiser. He couldn't resist blowing Doris a friendly kiss on his way out, which the others thought delightfully cheeky. Doris chuckled to herself, realising what was going on. Those kids, she thought - keeping her admiration quiet - came up with something new every time.

CAT AND TOM LIVED in an end-of-terrace Victorian house. They'd bought it as a doer-upper when they'd first married, and had renovated every inch of it, as and when time and money allowed; updating the décor, but keeping its vintage appeal. Besotted with the original features, Cat loved the elegant sash windows and intricate parquet flooring, amongst other things. Once again at odds with her sister's taste. Maggie, while able to put together an IKEA flat pack and apparently fix a leaky pipe, wasn't much cop at major renovations, so when it came to houses, opted for new builds, contemporary architecture and a ten-year warranty. But it was always nice to visit each other's homes for a change of scenery. The party was in full swing when Harry and the boys got there. Still in their Santa suits, Aaron sidled up to Sam and joked,

"And what do you want for Christmas, little girl?"

"Don't be a dick," Sam retorted, marching into the kitchen to get some crisps and dip. Harry's disguise wasn't fooling Jack, who ran up to his grandad as soon as he saw him.

"Looking good, Pops," he laughed, both going through their special handshake routine. The dog, however, wasn't so keen on these strange-looking men, and started growling to voice his displeasure.

"LeBron James," admonished Jack, "ssshhh!"

Tom and Sam came out of the kitchen carrying trays of food.

"Stupid name for a dog," Tom commented. "Should've been called Hans Christian Anderson."

"Why?" asked Jack.

"Cos he's a Great Dane!" Tom chortled.

Sam raised her eyes to heaven. "God. No, Dad, don't even..."

Maggie and Cat were in the lounge talking to Frankie, who had arrived wearing a tinsel halo, and was happily indulging in the punch. Harry took his hat and beard off to kiss his daughters.

"Hello, Margaret," he said, "you look lovely. And Catherine, you look more like your mother every day. Happy birthday, darling."

He hunted around in his fat suit until he located the package he wanted to give her. She smiled at him lovingly; her eyes welling up when she opened the box to find a gold locket previously worn by her mother. With pictures of Maggie and Cat inside, Grace often took it with her, when she and Harry had gone on holidays.

"I always want to keep my girls near," she would say.

Cat opened the locket and saw the photos of her and her sibling had been replaced by ones of Josh and Sam instead, continuing to provide the same comfort.

"Thanks, Dad," she said, "it's beautiful."

Music and laughter infused the evening as more people arrived. Later, on a big screen, Sam showed a montage of photos she'd put together of Cat, ignoring her mum's howls of protest. Frankie gave the birthday girl a pretty scarf, and the kids had clubbed together to buy her a Louis Vuitton handbag. Maggie had organised the cake, and would sneak into the kitchen from time to time; clearing away tables and loading the dishwasher, so Cat wouldn't have a big mess to clean up the following day. As the evening wound down, people started braving the cold to make their way home. Harry, who was staying the night, tried to get comfortable on the very end of the couch - as the dog had commandeered the rest of it - and was using a phone app to play online scrabble with Doris back at the village.

"C'mon, Bronny," said Jack, shortening the Dane's name and making it easier to roll off the tongue, "give Pops some room."

The four-legged behemoth obediently trotted over to his boy, who clipped a lead to his collar. As Jack and his mum grabbed their coats, ready to leave, Maggie said,

"Welcome to the club, little Sis. Now we're both in the same age bracket when we fill in forms. Or you know, when you have to put your date of birth in a box online, and there's a scroll down that you have to spin like a mother...."

"Mum!" interrupted Jack. "Language."

Cat hugged her sister, saying,

"Thanks, Mags, it's been a fantastic night. Oh wait, I have something for that animal of yours." She ran into the bedroom and returned with a regal-looking dog coat. A proficient seamstress, she'd made it herself and even incorporated the NBA colours of navy, red and white.

"I thought he should look the part at the fair on Monday."

"Wow, that's fire!" applauded Jack, using the updated version of 'cool', and draping the coat over Bronny. "It'll keep him warm too."

The Dane wagged his tail in approval, promptly knocking a glass off the table. Tom deftly caught it with a quick swoop of his hand before it broke on the floor.

Everyone said their goodbyes and shivered as they walked into the night air. There was a smattering of snow on the footpath and their breath formed misty clouds in front of their faces, but all sported a rosy glow from the good time they'd had that night. A storm was due in the next couple of days according to the weather forecast, but thankfully it hadn't arrived to spoil Cat's moment.

SUNDAY DAWNED, WITH EVERYBODY doing their own thing. Cat was at the spa getting a massage - Tom's gift to her while he promised to make the house spic and span in her absence. He really was a good man, she reflected. Josh and Aaron slept late, while Sam strived to come up with ideas for her exhibition. She sorted through some shots she'd taken last night and found a great one of her family convulsed with laughter over one of Frankie's hysterical anecdotes. It was a start, at least. The little snow that made an appearance last night had since melted away, so Jack's friends met him in the driveway of his house to practise their three-pointers in the basketball hoop fixed atop the garage door.

Maggie was working today, then had a week off before returning to the hospital on Boxing Day. Her schedule had panned out nicely, giving her time to attend Jack's fair tomorrow, with a few days up her sleeve to get some Christmas shopping done. Arriving in the neighbouring town of Aldacott, feeling a little jaded from last night, she adjusted her hair in the rear-view mirror and yawned. The vitality of her youth somewhat diminished in her fifties.

When she was an ER nurse - before Jack was born - Maggie could easily cope with early mornings, late nights and everything in between, but as the years went by, the demands of the job and ongoing stress took its toll. Looking for a change and observing distressed patients who didn't have support, she'd spoken to Human Resources and suggested the role of Patient Liaison Officer could be beneficial, leaving the medical staff to concentrate on repair and recovery, while she acted as a bridge in communication and patient welfare. Doctors and nurses didn't always explain things in layman's terms, and weren't necessarily as approachable as those on Grey's Anatomy. It wasn't their fault. She was well aware of the nation's current health crisis and how much pressure the medics were under. Those at the coalface worked ridiculous hours and prioritised diagnosis and treatment, meaning some of the gentler bedside manners often fell through the cracks. Her background and innate empathy gave her the resources to help manage patients' expectations, while remaining compassionate and understanding. The hospital board agreed to trial the idea, so Maggie returned from maternity leave with renewed energy and purpose.

Initially a pilot scheme, her new role was so well received, she started recruiting other people with medical backgrounds to help cover all shifts. Word got around and demand from other facilities increased, turning her little enterprise into a flourishing business. Tom helped her with the accounts, making the paperwork manageable. All in all, she was pleased with its success and enjoyed being her own boss.

Maggie took the lift to the third floor where she always checked in with Hayley, the receptionist, to get an update on new patients. Adam, the orthopaedic surgeon, was already there.

"Hey, Mags," he greeted. "How did the party go last night?"

"It was good, thanks," replied Maggie, trying not to strike up a conversation with him.

"Yeah?" continued Adam, "would have been better if I were there, no doubt. Shame I was on call, otherwise I could have come as your plus one."

Maggie smiled politely. These flirtatious remarks from Adam were cute from his point of view, but were growing tiresome from her side.

"I had a plus one, thanks. Jack was there."

"Ah well, that doesn't really count, does it? I was talking about a real man."

And what was the definition of a real man, thought Maggie? Someone who flaunted his status and wealth as if he were a coveted prize to be won? I don't think so.

"Maybe another time," she said, turning to face Hayley, who was finding it difficult to hide a smirk. Maggie glared pointedly at her.

"Who have I got today?" she said, changing the subject and deliberately ending the dialogue with Adam. He looked fleetingly dejected, but she doubted that would stop his attempts to hit on her later.

"Yes, best we get back to work," he said, admitting defeat for the time being and walking away. "I'll catch you later."

"He's not that bad," said Hayley, "why don't you give him a chance?"

"Cos I don't need a man. Not one like that, anyway."

"But he's easy on the eye, has an amazing job, and he drives a Porsche."

"Hayley, Hayley, Hayley," sighed Maggie, "those things aren't exactly high on my priority list. Although I do respect his skill as a surgeon."

"But don't you get lonely, being on your own?"

"On occasion, I do, but my family and friends are great, and Jack is good company now."

"And what about Jack? It must be difficult raising him by yourself."

"Sometimes it is. There's a lot of juggling when you're chief cook and bottle washer. And only having a female perspective makes it a bit one-dimensional. Especially at the age he is now. Having a bloke's guidance from time to time would be useful. But there are positives too: Jack hasn't had to go through the trauma of divorce like some of his classmates have, and I don't have a disgruntled ex in the background, who I have to share joint custody with."

"I guess."

"Honestly, I thought long and hard about having him on my own, but I knew what I was signing up for, and he's such a good kid, the cards have fallen very much in my favour. I've ended up with a beautiful boy to look after. No regrets from my end."

"I get all that; I just think it would be cool if you had someone to be there for you, too."

"I suppose, but I'm pretty set in my ways now, and it takes all my energy just to keep everything on track. If a man came into my world, he'd have to enhance things, not make them harder. You know what Adam would be like. He'd want all my attention, expect me to cook for him every night, and buy me clothes and jewellery that were his preference, not mine."

"Sounds alright to me," said Hayley wistfully.

"He likes to be in charge, and so do I - we would just clash," continued Maggie. "Then there's his antiquated outlook on the roles of the sexes - here, I'll give you an example."

Hayley listened expectantly.

"I was talking about things in the house breaking down. I'd worked out from YouTube how to fix the dishwasher, but then the pipe under the sink started leaking, and with one thing after another going wrong, it was beginning to piss me off. And do you know what he said?"

Hayley shook her head.

"He said, '*You shouldn't have to worry your pretty little head about things like that.*' I mean, Christ, what century does he think we're living in? Look, I'm sure he'll make a nice traditional husband for someone, but it won't be me. Besides, I really don't have time for dating, and to be honest, I can't even comprehend introducing Jack to a stranger, so any romantic liaisons are unlikely to be on the cards for the next few years."

Hayley thought that sounded like a lot of half-hearted excuses. Truthfully, Maggie's cavalier attitude towards love came from a place of self-doubt. Divorced a lifetime ago, she wondered why she hadn't been able to maintain a partnership for the long haul, like her parents had and her sister seemed capable of doing. She backed herself in most aspects of life: managing the house, parenting, building up a business; but for some reason, struggled with insecurity when it came to being in a relationship. Romance seemed like a distant concept - the stuff of fairy tales and movies - and Maggie was very much a realist. Dismissing the topic as usual, she said.

"Anyway, that's enough about my lacklustre love life. Where's my patient list?"

She began her rounds with people recovering from accidents. They were on the fourth floor, one level up, with issues as minor as a fractured finger, or as major as paralysis. She carried on to those suffering illnesses, which could take a while, subject to the complexity of the cases, then go to the next floor where the maternity ward was located. Finally finishing in paediatrics - always bittersweet as this area tended to be the most rewarding, but also the most heart-breaking, depending on the circumstance. Her days as an ER nurse had been physically demanding; triaging and dispatching patients to the appropriate departments. Now, not so hands-on in a treatment sense, the physicality of the job was less, but emotionally draining instead.

Today, the new arrivals included a dislocated shoulder, a pneumonia case, a seven-year-old due for a tonsillectomy, and an expectant mother who had been ordered bed rest for a week minimum (most likely a Christmas baby). All fairly manageable, and thankfully no heart attacks or cancer diagnoses, that were concerning at any time, but especially tragic in the lead-up to Christmas Day.

After she'd finished her duties, tired but fulfilled, Maggie headed home, picking up takeaways for her and Jack on the way. Indian was the choice de jour, as Jack currently had a thing for naan bread. She arrived, hands full, and shouted out to him as she entered the doorway. He'd put the fire on for her - good lad - which warmed her up immediately.

Not having any homework to do anymore, Jack was ensconced in building a Minecraft world online, in a multi-functional room next to his bedroom. When he was little, it had been a playroom where Maggie could put his toys and keep an eye on him from the kitchen. Over the years, it had evolved into a tech room containing a laptop, large TV and PlayStation console. A framed picture of Michael Jordan's buzzer-beater in the 1998 NBA finals hung on the wall. And while Jack could be incredibly loud when playing video games remotely with his friends, she got a kick from hearing his laughter, so it was an acceptable concession to make.

Maggie's bedroom was upstairs, tucked away against the north wall, making it cooler than the rest of the house; a quality she liked. With the UK not known for its sunny disposition, there didn't seem much need to escape from the heat, but the last few summers had included a few days of scorching temperatures, during which, Maggie was only too happy to retreat to her bedroom with a book and a chilled iced tea. When the weather wasn't quite so sweltering, she'd move to her favourite spot on the bench under the Japanese cherry tree in the back garden. Not one for pink decor or accessories anywhere else, she loved how the tree stood out like a ballerina's tutu when blossoming in the spring. It was her peaceful place when she needed some time out. She'd even learnt how to block out the sound of bumps and crashes when Jack's basketball missed the hoop, ending up on the garage roof instead.

After they'd polished off their butter chicken and lamb korma, Maggie pulled out Cluedo from the games cupboard, while Jack called through the door to the appliance on the kitchen counter.

"Alexa, play Jack's playlist."

"Really?" questioned Maggie. "I'm sure it was my turn tonight."

"Nuh-uh," said Jack. "You guys played your 80s crap last night at the party. I've had enough of Wham and Bananas in Pyjamas."

"I think you mean Bananarama," Maggie giggled, "but OK, you've got a point," and she resigned herself to listening to Kendrick Lamar and Stormzy for the evening.

That night, as she undressed and put moisturiser on her face, ready for bed, Maggie wondered how long Jack would be happy to watch movies and play board games with his mum on a weekend. She could feel the transition of her little boy turning into a young man already, and knew it was only a matter of time before he started to pull away. He did well at school, was into his sports and had a kind, caring nature. She couldn't be any prouder of him. But he'd mentioned Rose a few times recently; a girl in his class she thought he might have a crush on. And Maggie was very cognisant of the fact that, in the blink of an eye, she - his mother - was not going to be the most important woman in his life anymore. She tried not to think about him growing older and inevitably moving out, leaving her to return to a solitary life. Time was flying by so fast, it begged the question:

And then what?

CHAPTER 3

Monday 20 December

DESPITE BLACK CLOUDS GATHERING ominously in the distance, Cat remained optimistic that today's Medieval Fayre would be a roaring success.

Because her students were learning about Middle Age history, she thought it fitting to tie in the theme with their usual end-of-year celebrations. The school field had transformed into Ye Olde English Village, with marquees erected to house various old-fashioned activities, such as quoit throwing, skittles, and bobbing for apples. A maypole stood tall, dressed in the prerequisite coloured ribbons, and a sizeable rope lay curled on the ground, ready for a tug-of-war later. Hearty fare included a pig on a spit, corn on the cob, different cheeses and a variety of breads (ciabatta and focaccia weren't strictly medieval, but what the hell). A coffee cart for the adults and a candy floss station for the little ones were also onsite. Realism could be stretched a little if it made the day more enjoyable.

Tom was in charge of a display in the library showing the school grounds in days gone by. According to the documents, Baron Buford owned a large plot of land in the 14th century that spanned across the school field and the retirement village behind it. Ah, that would explain the stables where his father-in-law lived, Tom thought. He finished pinning up posters and blueprints; leaving his wife to oversee the final touches before popping home to get changed.

Cat walked the lengthy distance to the bottom of the field towards the archery area, where she would be based today. Perhaps her attire of a long flowing medieval gown, with elongated sleeves and a steeple headdress, was not ideal for this activity, but she didn't care. She loved her dress and too bad if it got a little mud on it. The other teachers were assigned to different activities closer to the school buildings. Everyone had turned up suitably clad, and were eager to get the fair underway.

Not so far away, Harry and Doris wandered through the retirement village walkways, enjoying a brisk morning stroll past multi-coloured flower beds nestled against meticulously manicured lawns. Wooden benches were dotted about in pockets of open space, for people to sit back and watch the world go by. Positioned on higher ground, the top gardens provided a great view of the township, and Harry could see the school adjacent putting on an event of some kind. Oh, that's right, it was Jack's end-of-year fair. He scanned the field but had no luck in spotting his grandson.

"Doesn't look like it's kicked off yet," he said to Doris. "Let's get some lunch and we'll see what's going on next door later."

They turned back from the path leading down a slope to the stables; the towering oak tree at the base casting shadows over them, as they headed to the village cafeteria.

TOM AND SAM PULLED up to Maggie's house in their Volkswagen.

"I'll get them," said Sam, running up the pathway just as Jack opened the door, brandishing a rubber sword in her face.

"Shit, Jack, way to greet your cousin!"

"Be gone, witch!" Jack countered, pulling out a fake knife from his belt in addition to his sword.

"Aunt Maggie, your son has issues," joked Sam.

Maggie followed him out the door wearing clothes of a serving wench, with Bronny on a lead, resplendent in his blue and red coat.

"The only way I could get Jack into tights was to let him have an arsenal of weapons," she explained.

Armed with a sword, a knife, and a quiver of arrows on his back, Jack got in the car. Bronny followed, turning round in one mandatory circle before planting his bum on the parcel shelf, which left a narrow space for Maggie to squish into; holding her skirts together, so they were all concertinaed in the back seat.

"What about my jousting stick?" said Jack suddenly. Sam, still on the path, ran into the house to get it.

"It's in the kitchen," shouted Maggie. "Look for a broom with a flag attached to the end."

Sam returned with the DIY lance and threaded it through the back window, so it went over Maggie's and Jack's laps, and under the dog's legs. Delighted that he'd been given a giant stick to play with, Bronny immediately started chewing it.

"You lot are a right sight," laughed Sam, who hadn't dressed up at all. She'd stuck to her black theme with Doc Martens, ripped tights, a denim mini-skirt, and a black vest emblazoned with a retro Metallica picture, over a short-sleeved top. She pulled her camera out of her backpack and took a picture.

"Are we good to go now?" asked Tom, adjusting his cap and robe. If Cat was going to be a lady, then he was going to be a lord. There was a unanimous cry of Yes, so he pulled out of the driveway. Not exactly built for four people and a Great Dane, the VW tottered down the road, heaving under the strain of a carload of bodies, with the brush of a broom and the Union Jack trailing in its wake.

Once at the school, Jack ran off with his friends, leaving Maggie holding his jousting stick in one hand and the dog in the other. Sam wandered around with her camera, looking for possible shots. Tom attempted to give her a jersey, which she'd blithely shrugged off. It's a wonder that girl doesn't have hyperthermia, he thought. Josh and Aaron arrived about an hour later in knights' costumes, riding non-existent horses and quoting Monty Python.

Pleased to see them, Bronny affectionately nosed Josh in the crotch.

"Oof Bronny!" he moaned, "Right in the nuts!"

"Did someone say nuts?" asked Maggie, passing around little bags of roasted chestnuts to whomever was in reach. Jack returned briefly to quash his hunger pangs and scoffed his down without pausing for breath. He licked his fingers quickly before grabbing Josh and Aaron's arms.

"C'mon, you're just in time for the tug-of-war."

After the competition, which the boys won, Tom whistled to pull his clan together.

"We can't leave your mum down the end of the field on her own. A few people tried archery earlier in the day, but it looks pretty empty there now. Let's have lunch and I'll pack some food up for Cat, then we'll walk down to keep her company. And Jack, you can have a go with your arrows."

"Don't forget me, lovelies," came a voice from behind.

And like a vision from yesteryear, Frankie arrived in a gown that looked like it had been plucked from Marie Antoinette's wardrobe.

Maggie kissed Frankie on the cheek.

"You look positively ravishing," she said. "Cat will be thrilled you've come to support her."

"Of course," said Frankie, whipping out a fan, "who doesn't love dressing up?"

"Are you warm enough?" asked Maggie.

"Babe, I ain't stupid. I've got Long johns on underneath."

After tucking into the barbecue Tom was helping to man, they sauntered en masse to the end of the field as the clouds circled menacingly above them. Jack used his plastic arrows and aimed at the target. He failed dismally, but Bronny thought this a great game of fetch and duly brought them back. Jack, still with the remnants of a sausage sizzle in his hand, offered him a reward.

"Sit Bronny."

"Now speak."

The Dane plonked his bum on the ground and woofed.

"Speak more!"

"Woof woof!"

It was the only trick his dog could do, and Jack always had fun putting it into practice. He tossed Bronny the hard-earned sausage, which was demolished in an instant.

HARRY AND DORIS RETURNED outside, ambling down the slope towards the stables and sitting beneath the oak tree.

"When's Esme coming to see you?" asked Harry.

"Soon," replied Doris, "she's taking me out for dinner. We'll be back by 8 pm, though."

"Of course you will," teased Harry. "Can't be breaking the rules, can we? I wonder if I can see Jack now?"

He got up and stood on tiptoes, craning his neck, but not able to get the same panoramic view as from the top garden. Using the tree for support, he stepped onto the seat of the bench to get a better look.

"Harry!" Doris exclaimed, "Do be careful."

"There he is," Harry said, indicating over the fence, "with the family too, by the looks of it."

He waved, and Doris instinctively grabbed his legs so he wouldn't topple over. From the school field, Bronny saw him first and barked, causing Jack to turn around.

"Hey, there's Pops," he shouted, and they all waved back.

"Please get down, Harry," Doris pleaded.

"OK, OK." he relented. "Here, let's be rebels and carve our initials into the tree for posterity's sake." He pulled out his pocketknife and handed it to her.

"You first."

"You are incorrigible," said Doris, but taking the knife anyway, she carefully marked a D on the tree at eye level. They were interrupted by a cry from the top of the slope.

"Mother, what are you doing out here? You'll catch your death."

"It's alright love, I've got a coat on," Doris said to her daughter, turning to face her.

"And what on earth are you doing with a knife in your hand?! For heaven's sake, do you want me to have a panic attack?"

"No, sorry, love," Doris said, giving the knife back to Harry. "I've got to go," she whispered, "will you come too?"

"And be subjected to Esme's frosty stare of disapproval? No, you go; I'm going to hang around here for a little longer. I'll see you later for a game of backgammon."

As Doris made her way up to her daughter, Harry pulled his jacket closer to him, doing up the buttons and putting his hands in the pockets; his fingers welcoming the warmth of the fabric and depth of the pouches. It was getting colder, that's for sure. He shivered as snow started to fall, but getting some protection from the tree's branches, he sat back, happily watching the stables and surrounding gardens turn into a real-life snow globe.

Across the fence in the field, Tom looked up at the snowflakes and declared,

"I think that's our cue to call it a day."

They were about to walk - perhaps jog - towards the refuge of the classrooms, where the rest of the fair attendees were, when the weather took a turn for the worse and it started hailing.

"Ouch," complained Sam, her minimal clothing now completely inappropriate.

"Double ouch," copied Josh, having removed his knight's helmet earlier, and now suffering the consequences.

Suddenly all hell broke loose, with the hailstones increasing in frequency, size, and painfulness. They could see people at the opposite end of the field scattering in all directions, and running for cover into the school buildings. Some distance away, out in the open and unprotected, the family had no such option.

"Son of a bitch!" yelled Sam, holding her backpack futilely above her head. "What are we going to do?"

Bronny started yelping and pulling on his lead.

"Over here!" shouted Harry, his hands waving above the dilapidated fence. He'd heard their cries and could see their predicament.

"You're closer to me and the stables are right here!"

Detecting salvation, the Dane let out a bark of recognition and lurched towards his voice. Unable to hold him, Maggie watched helplessly as nine stone of hairy determination rushed in Harry's direction. Launching himself upwards to his full height of seven feet - a sight to behold - LeBron James and his massive front paws crashed through the fence to escape the hail.

Tom wasn't going to look a gift horse - or dog for that matter - in the mouth.

"Quick, everyone - run through the gap and get to the stables!"

A flurry of dresses and chain-mail and swords and arrows bolted through the hole in the fence, to follow Harry undercover. The sighs of relief to escape the atrocious conditions, however, soon gave way to the reality that the building was not going to offer them much protection because of its age and the state it was in. They backed away from the open-air stalls where horses were once housed and piled into a small room with a dirt floor; most likely the stable hand's quarters many moons ago.

Through the gaps in the stone walls, they could see the storm in full throe, dumping thick swathes of snow all around. The youth reverted to their automatic default of phone-watching while sitting on the floor with their backs to the wall. They played games or Snapchatted to keep their minds off the cold, while their parents discussed what to do.

"We'll have to sit it out," said Tom. "It's getting too dangerous to go anywhere else."

"Could be a while," said Maggie, showing the weather report on her phone.

"Ugh," complained Cat, "it's freezing. We're all going to get frostbite."

"Unless you came prepared," Frankie chipped in, giving them a flash of his Long johns.

Bronny had discovered something interesting in the corner and was digging with gusto. They left him to it, figuring if he had something to keep him occupied, he was less likely to be afraid of the storm outside, which was currently ramping up into a blizzard; the strong winds prying their way through any crevice they could find.

Harry sent a text to Doris:

"Rain check on backgammon, sorry. Holed up in stables. Family here too. All safe. We'll sit it out."

A sudden crash in the stalls made everybody jump. Tom poked his head around the doorway to see what the commotion was. The weight of the snow on the roof had broken through what little there was left of ancient tiles and slats, leaving the remainder of the building exposed to the ever-darkening sky and tumultuous weather. An icy blast swept up through the open areas and into the room where everyone huddled, making the group gasp in unison.

Bronny didn't seem to notice, but became increasingly excited about his digging expedition. The noise of his efforts changed from a muffled pawing of earth to a distinctive thump of claws, scratching something solid. He whimpered in frustration that his hole wasn't getting any bigger.

"What's up, boy?" said Jack, going over to check it out.

"Mum," he said, "Bronny's found something. It looks like a trapdoor."

Maggie joined her son, crouched down, and brushed away more dirt the dog had done a very good job of dispersing. She uncovered a handle and gave it a good tug. There was a small movement, but clearly the door had remained in place for decades, if not centuries.

"I need some muscle, please," she requested.

"At your service, m' lady," offered Josh. He and Aaron squatted on either side of the door and grabbed the handle.

"On Three," said Aaron. "One, Two, Three!"

They gave an almighty pull to dislodge the years of mud and debris keeping the door closed. With success, they fell back on their haunches to see it open and reveal a set of stairs down into darkness.

"Awesome!" said Jack, treading on the first step.

"Oh, no you don't," said his mother, grabbing him by the scruff of the neck. "We don't know what's down there." She couldn't hold Bronny back, however, who'd already made up his mind to investigate and report back. Before she could stop him, the Dane ran down the steps and disappeared from view.

"Oh God," bemoaned Maggie, "how are we going to get him back?

"Still at your service, m' lady," said Josh again, "We, the knights of Ni, shall rescue the beast." He and Aaron switched on their phone torches and shone light onto the stairs below.

"They look in fairly good shape," said Aaron, who began tentatively stepping down.

"Be careful," said Cat and Maggie together.

"What is this, do you think?" queried Cat.

"It could be an old Roman aqueduct," suggested Harry. "If so, the construction is pretty robust. It wouldn't be a bad idea to hunker down there for a bit. Away from the elements up here."

"I don't know," frowned Cat, "I don't fancy sitting in the dark in a tunnel."

"But it's so cold, Mum," whined Sam.

After a few minutes, Bronny's head popped up through the open hatch, eyes gleaming and panting heavily, obviously enjoying his adventure. Aaron and Josh followed.

"It's much warmer down there," said Aaron.

"And it leads to another door," said Josh.

"Where to?" asked Cat. "A different part of the stables?"

"I don't think so," Josh replied. "It felt like we were going under the stables; the end of the tunnel likely coming out somewhere else. But the other door is wedged solid. There are no handles, just a bunch of gibberish carved into the wood."

Tom looked thoughtful.

"The gibberish wouldn't be Latin, would it? That ties in with the possibility of it being an aqueduct."

"Could be," said Josh. "I took a shot of it, have a look."

They circled around his phone as Josh zoomed in on the picture.

"Hopeless photo," said Sam with scorn, "you've chopped the bottom bit off."

"Whatever, Annie Leibovitz," her brother retorted, "do you want to go down there?"

Sam scowled as Tom took Josh's phone to study the picture closer.

"It does look like Latin, but I can't translate it. Can you, Harry?"

Harry put on his glasses to read the ancient words in front of him:

Quid Ho! Quicumque intrat hanc ianuam
In veritate mea, et in diebus antiquis
Mane quaeso, sed si valefacias
Cum Deo Spede, vale in Vigilia Nativitatis Domini

"Sort of," replied Harry, "definitely a reference to the door, and something about coming and going."

"Wow," said Jack, impressed, "when did you learn Latin?"

"At school, my boy," smiled Harry, "which was a long time ago, obviously. But I think I can work this out."

"Because you've got a great memory, Pops?"

"No, because I've got Google translate," laughed Harry.

He located the app and copied the words into his phone. An English translation instantly appeared and Harry intoned,

What Ho! Whomsoever enters this door
By my truth, you will happen upon days of yore
Pray thee stay, but if you must take your leave
With God Spede, fare thee well by Christmas Eve

"Who's a ho?" Josh sniggered. Cat clipped him round the ear.

"It's not *'What a ho'* dopey, it's *'What Ho!'* An old English way of saying 'Attention' or 'Warning'."

"But what does it mean?" asked Frankie.

Tom looked thoughtful again and offered a possible explanation.

"So, days of yore means the past. Olden days if you like. Could it be referring to archives in a library or something like that? Perhaps you could only access old scrolls or documents until the end of the year."

As they were talking, another deafening crash came from behind. More of the roof had fallen in. Instinctively, Maggie held Jack close while Bronny made for the trapdoor again. Josh caught his collar just in time.

"Look," he said, "the tunnel or aqueduct or whatever it is, is in much better condition than the building up here. Let's venture down there before our batteries run out and see if we can find a way of opening the other door. It's got to be worth a shot."

There was a general murmur of agreement and all used their phones to cast light on the space under their feet. Aaron and Josh led the way, the rest following in a single file. The group cautiously walked about thirty or forty feet to another set of stairs leading up to a second trapdoor. Now that the area had been completely lit up, they could see the tunnel forked off to the right in another direction, but it looked like it continued for a long way into the distance. Thank goodness Bronny hadn't gone down there. They would never have got him back.

Aaron and Josh tried to break the door open with brute force, but to no avail. Harry gave Maggie his pocket knife to jimmy the sides, but it still wouldn't budge. Tom, using his maths brain, wondered if they could find a prop of some sort to engineer the hinges out.

"Let me look at that Latin verse again," suggested Harry, "maybe the last bit chopped off in the photo is some kind of instruction."

He pushed forward to the front of the group, looking at the words inscribed in the wood, and deferred to Google once more, copying the extra two lines into the app. He read out loud what he saw, this time in its entirety:

What Ho! Whomsoever enters this door
By my truth, you will happen upon days of yore
Pray thee stay, but if you must take your leave
With God Spede, fare thee well by Christmas Eve
Damsels and Gents to conjure the light
Seeketh days end and return with the night

Unexpectedly, all four sides around the wooden hatchway lit up. Josh and Aaron pushed again, and this time, without much exertion, the door opened.

"Woohoo!" they shouted, running up the stairs to hopefully find shelter and warmth. Josh helped his grandad up into the mystery room. Aaron turned to offer his hand to Cat and Sam. Predictably ignored by Sam, but gratefully accepted by Cat. The others followed and were thrilled to find a building intact, with lanterns already lit and a disused log fire in the corner. Tom went straight to it, pulling out a box of matches from his pocket that he'd used to light the barbeque at the fair.

As he endeavoured to get a fire going, the others looked around.

"It's not a library, is it?" observed Jack, noting the arched architecture and another room with pews and a pulpit. "It looks like a church."

"Yes, maybe a chapel," agreed Maggie, her tone of voice quizzical. "But I don't remember anything like this being near the school."

"Me neither," agreed Tom, "but there is a familiarity about it that's bugging me."

Maggie wiped away the condensation on a nearby window with her hand; a coating of water clinging to her palm. Whoever had installed the windows had done a cowboy job. The glass was thicker than building code standards and inserted crudely into the framework; as if someone had grabbed a random sample and not even bothered to check the measurements. As a result, slivers of frigid air leaked into the room, but it was still their best option compared to the alternatives. Tom had mercifully got the fire going; the heat from the flames making a solid effort to usurp the draughts. She could see the storm was still going strong, with snow enveloping the landscape beyond - the topography now indistinguishable to the naked eye. And it had started hailing again. With the wind violently whipping up snowflakes and hailstones, visibility was virtually zero.

"Look, I know people from the school or retirement village will bring snow-ploughs to clear the way for us, but that's not really feasible at present. I think we have to accept that we're here for the night. Let's see what we can find to make things more comfortable."

The room they were in looked like a rectory. A basic single bed and two chairs were pushed up against a wall, with several faded, well-worn rugs on the floor. Perched on a shelf was a bible, sitting alongside a small rustic bowl and cup. And draped over a hook on the door leading to the chapel, hung what appeared to be a monk's cloak. Everything was dusty, like no one had been there for a while.

"My phone's not working," cried Jack.

"Nor mine," echoed Sam.

"It's probably the bad weather mucking the reception up," said Maggie. "You'll have to do without tonight."

There was a collective groan from the teenagers.

"How are we going to get out if no one knows we're here?" Jack asked.

"It's OK," said Harry, "I texted Doris from the stables. She knows we're trapped, but safe. She'll get the maintenance staff to dig us out when the storm settles."

"So let's see what we've got," Maggie said. "We're lucky that we pigged out on the barbeque at lunch. And I've got more nuts if you're peckish. Sam, do you still have water in your backpack?"

Sam rummaged around in her bag, offering up three bottles of water for anyone who wanted some, and poured a little in the bowl for Bronny to sup as well.

"Right then," continued Maggie, obviously in no-nonsense, organising mode, "thankfully, our heavy costumes are going to help us keep warm tonight, but Dad and Sam, you need something more."

Sam grabbed one of the rugs from the floor and wrapped it around her shoulders, finding it surprisingly effective.

"Here, Pops," said Josh, "why don't you have this monk's robe or whatever it is?"

Harry put on the brown hooded cape, making Jack laugh.

"You look like Obi-Wan," he giggled, drawing his sword upright as if it were a lightsabre and improvising the whooshing sound effects. Harry responded accordingly, holding out his water bottle in front of him; pretending it was a weapon fending off his foe.

Maggie smiled at their role-playing.

"All right, you two, let's save your Jedi powers by having an early night," she said. "You have the bed, Dad. Cat and Tom, do you think you could get some sleep on the chairs?"

They nodded.

"Jack, we can curl up on the floor on the other rug with Bronny - his body heat will be good for us. And maybe you kids could see how comfortable the pews are," directing her last comment to Sam, Aaron and Josh. Frankie had already settled in another spot on the floor, and was arranging the ample skirts of his dress as padding under his butt.

A huge wave of tiredness descended upon the group, so Maggie's suggestions were accepted without objection. Everyone settled into their allocated sleeping quarters, vaguely concerned about how the day had ended, but reassuringly huddled together.

Moving his chair closer to Cat's, Tom bent his head and spoke in a whisper.

"I've just remembered where I've seen documentation of a chapel like this."

She leaned in to hear the rest of what he had to say.

"In the display pictures I put up for the fair."

"Go on,"

"The blueprints of the land from the 14th century showed the school grounds and the retirement village were both part of one plot. Baron Buford owned the manor, which would have sat where the school buildings are now, and then halfway down the fields were the stables and a small chapel adjacent. The rest of the field above the slope was where they held jousting tournaments and suchlike."

"But the chapel's gone now, and the stables have just about collapsed as we've witnessed today."

"Yes," mused Tom, "it seems that...."

"I don't really have the headspace to ponder history at the moment," interrupted Cat. "Wherever we've ended up, must have been tucked away in a part of the village that we didn't notice before. Walking through tunnels is pretty disorienting, anyway. Let's be grateful we're out of that awful storm; I'm sure things will get back to normal tomorrow."

She blew out the candle in the lantern beside them, leaving a singular flame on the shelf to provide a hazy glow throughout.

CHAPTER 4

Tuesday morning 21 December

Come Tuesday morning, the hail and gales had dissipated. Snow started melting on higher ground but still blanketed anything in a valley. Doris put her woolly hat on and joined the maintenance crew, who had arrived early with extra equipment to clear a pathway to the stables. She'd voiced her concerns about Harry to the retirement village staff the night before, but the weather was so horrendous they hadn't been able to go out. She'd received a message from her friend saying he was safe, but hadn't heard from him this morning and that worried her.

In the chapel, as people stirred - a little worse for wear due to a fractured night's sleep - thoughts turned to getting home to a warm shower, a decent breakfast and the comfort of double glazing.

Maggie stretched, as did LeBron James, who rumbled with pleasure as she rubbed his ears affectionately. Jack had drawn a smiley face in the condensation on the window. She peered through the eyeholes, but wasn't sure what she could see outside. Still lots of snow and several buildings in the distance. Was that the school? She really couldn't tell. It should be, she thought, but her geography had come unstuck since their unplanned sleepover. Wandering around the room to get the blood flowing into her limbs - always a bit creaky in the mornings these days - she hovered near the Bible on the shelf. Flicking over the first page, Maggie read the notation: *"To my friend Baron Buford in the year 1380. Glad tidings from King Richard the 2nd."* The book was in remarkably good condition, considering how old it was.

"C'mon, you motley crew," she said, addressing the bodies stretched out on the pews and those curled up around her. A round of yawns, groans and head scratchings morphed into a slightly grumpy lined arrangement; ready to descend through the trapdoor again to the tunnel that led to the stables. As Harry had sounded the alarm to Doris, that's where they thought their best chance of rescue was. The two boys lead the way once more, with Maggie, Jack and Bronny bringing up the rear.

"STAND BACK, LOVE, IF you would," requested one of the men charged with clearing a path to the stables. Doris obeyed, positioning herself near the oak tree she and Harry had sat beside yesterday. She found where she had marked it with his knife and gently traced the D with her finger.

"OK, we're getting there," said the same man, breaking through the snow mounds to reveal the corridor to the room Harry and his family had sheltered in.

IT DIDN'T TAKE THE costumed group long to get through the underground passage. Josh glanced up to the underside of the trapdoor at the stables end and cocked his head to one side.

"Hey, I can hear something," he said, "they must have found us."

The maintenance crew put down their tools and strode down the corridor to the old stable hand's quarters.

The boys pushed open the trapdoor, with Josh's head the first through the hole. "Um, Aaron," he said, "you're not going to believe this."

The crew chief stepped through the doorway. "Ah, Doris," he said, "there's no one here."

Doris looked into the empty room, confounded, while the workers searched the rest of the building for any signs of life. With no refugees to be found, they returned outside. Somewhat baffled, Doris asked,

"But where would they go?"

The village receptionist, Nadine, coming to check on the crew's progress, had witnessed the lack of a reunion with Harry.

"Check out the fence," she said, pointing to the gap Bronny had created and walking over to it. On the ground through the hole lay a long, thin branch, which, upon further inspection, turned out to be Jack's jousting stick.

"They must have gone that way, through the school field," she said.

"But Harry hasn't contacted me and he's not returning any of my messages," persisted Doris.

"You know what he's like," said Nadine disapprovingly, "off on one of his escapades with his family, no doubt. Yet again, defying safety procedures and not officially signing out. They would have had a rough night, I'm sure, and will probably be at home sleeping it off. Let's go back Doris. It's still slippery out here."

Doris wasn't sure she bought that explanation, but compliantly followed Nadine back to the main building, in the hope that she would hear from Harry soon.

"Holy Cow!" said Aaron. "Or horse, to be precise!"

Because there in front of them, instead of broken down premises from centuries past, stood a fully intact stable, complete with horses in the stalls, who seemed fairly nonchalant at the arrival of their new visitors.

"Mum, Dad, you gotta see this!" shouted Josh down the tunnel. Tom and Cat, together with Sam and Harry, scrambled through the door; Aaron again offering his hand to assist and all accepting it, with the exception of Sam, who was being her typical contrary self. Once they stood up, they were equally shocked to discover their surroundings. Shock quickly changed to glee for Harry, though, when he saw the equine inhabitants. He immediately went to stroke one of the horses' heads and got an appreciative snort for his efforts. Sam walked down the corridor to the front of the stables and gasped when she looked out.

"Pops," she cried. "Your village is gone!"

"What's happening?" said Cat, a slight tone of panic in her voice.

By now, Frankie had surfaced, with Maggie, Jack and Bronny following close behind. Fortunately, the Dane still had his lead attached, as he was immediately spooked by the horses and started to back away towards the safety of the tunnel. While Maggie tried to calm him, Jack couldn't help but marvel at the upgraded stables.

"What the hell?" he said.

"What the hell, indeed," Maggie muttered under her breath.

"Flipping heck, I wasn't expecting this," chimed in Frankie. "Have the Christmas fairies revamped the stables overnight?"

He was joking to keep the mood light, but his eyes disclosed the same concern the rest of the adults were feeling. Bronny, also showing signs of discomfort, let out a woof, making them all jump with the tension. The horses - unsettled at the sound of the dog - started to whinny and pace in their stalls.

"He probably wants a wee," said Jack. "Can I take him outside?"

"I don't know," said Maggie.

"But I want a wee too, Mum."

"There doesn't seem to be anything out there other than a small tree," said Sam, still standing by the window.

"OK," Maggie relented. "To the tree, that's all. Josh, Aaron, can you go with them, please?"

The boys went out into what was now a very still day, with even the sun making an appearance. Sam remained at the window on watch, while the others stood together to talk.

In a hushed tone, Maggie said, "I mean, what the actual...! Where are we?"

"You might mean '*when*' are we?" Tom corrected her.

"What are you talking about?" said Cat, her voice getting higher.

"Look," continued Tom, "I know this is unbelievable, but we've only walked twenty yards or so; we can't have got lost. This is the stables at the bottom of your dad's village."

"It sure is," confirmed Harry, "I know this place like the back of my hand. It's just that now, it looks like what it would have done when first built."

"But where's your village?" asked Cat.

"Yeah, that's not here, but the tree is."

"That tree's tiny, Dad," said Maggie. "Yours is enormous."

"That's because it's young," explained Harry, as he and Tom exchanged knowing glances.

"Are you seriously saying we've somehow gone back in time?" asked Sam incredulously, who had been listening in. "No wonder the bloody phones don't work."

"The Bible!" Maggie remembered.

"What about it?" asked Cat.

"The dedication inside was from King Richard II and dated 1380. I thought it was in good nick."

"Who was it dedicated to?" asked Tom.

"Baron Buford," replied Maggie.

"The Baron who owned the manor and the land in the Middle Ages," said Tom with a sigh of realisation.

"But how has this happened?" asked Cat, a definite tremble in her voice.

"The poem?" suggested Frankie. "Perhaps it was a magic spell?" He laughed uncertainly.

"This isn't funny," hissed Cat.

"He might not be wrong," Harry said and repeated the first two lines.

What Ho! Whomsoever enters this door
By my truth, you will happen upon days of yore

"Jesus Christ! You mean we've literally gone back to days of yore!" Maggie exclaimed. "So how in God's name do we return to the present?"

Harry remembered the rest and recited it:

Pray thee stay, but if you must take your leave
With God Spede, fare thee well by Christmas Eve
Damsels and Gents to conjure the light
Seeketh days end and return with the night

Tom looked contemplative.

"I'm guessing the light we saw around the outside of the trapdoor when Harry read the verse wasn't coming from the lanterns on the other side, but was the key to the door opening. And in order to repeat that, we have to come back at night and read it out again."

"And," he surmised, "maybe we have to do that by Christmas Eve."

"Or what?" queried Maggie.

They lapsed into silence as the enormous implication dawned on them all at the same time.

"Tom!" cried Cat. "We can't get stuck here!"

Tom put his arm around her. "Don't worry. It's the 21st of December today, so if we return tonight, that's well before Christmas Eve."

"What do we do in the meantime?" asked Maggie. "The kids - and the dog - are going to get hungry. And the horses don't seem too keen on Bronny, either. I don't think we can stay here."

Tom gave it some thought.

"The info I gathered for the school fair said the Baron held annual Yuletide festivities in the week preceding Christmas, and that people would come from towns all around to partake. From memory, he sounded like an OK guy. Well, until he got a bit of grief during the Peasants Revolt, and they burned half the buildings down."

"What year did you say was in the Bible?" Cat asked Maggie.

"1380," her sister replied.

"Oh great," sighed Cat, "the Peasants Revolt was in 1381; they're probably already restless."

"That won't be our problem," argued Tom. "Given that most of us are in the right dress code, why don't we try to blend in for a day? Maybe find a place to get warm and something to eat. And then tonight, we'll be out of here."

"Sam doesn't have a costume," Cat reminded him, "and people were very superstitious in medieval times. They aren't going to take too kindly to tattoos. Especially on a female."

"OK, then!" Maggie said, resolute.

"Sam, Frankie, you're going to have to swap clothes. Frankie, you've got Long johns on underneath, so you can slip Sam's mini skirt over the top, turn her vest inside out, add the belt, and Hey Presto, you'll be some sort of serf or something. Sam, take your piercings out, let your hair down and wear Frankie's dress; it will cover your arms."

The pair immediately started to remonstrate, but Cat had gained her composure and agreed that her sister's idea wasn't a bad shout.

"Sam, for once in your life, pretend you're a lady," she ordered. "Ditto, Frankie, pretend you're a man."

"Ouch. Harsh, sweetie," said Frankie, feigning outrage.

"And less of the 'sweeties' please."

Grumbling to each other, Sam and Frankie went back into the stable hand's quarters to change. The boys returned inside and Tom explained what they thought had happened, filling them in with the plan. After cries of disbelief and a few questions, they understood what they had to do; all three adjusting their costumes as if to instil some extra authenticity. Frankie emerged from the room in his new outfit borrowed from Sam, looking pretty good. Good enough to fit in for a day, anyway. Then Sam walked through the doorway.

"Wow, Sam!" gasped Aaron, taken aback by what he could see. "You...look...amazing."

"Sod off," she snapped, bending down and brushing away the hay on the bottom of her dress, to hastily conceal the heat that had crept up her neck and onto her face.

"You do look lovely," smiled Tom. "I know it's not your style, but it's only temporary."

Maggie's organising resumed.

"OK, everyone, put all your modern-day gadgets in Sam's backpack. Phones, watches, etc. Dad - your pocket knife and glasses, please; they look too new, sorry. Sam, hide the bag in the tunnel, close the door and brush the dirt back over it. Hopefully, we're the only ones who know it's there."

Sam did what was asked of her, but covertly stashed her camera away in one of the deep hidden pockets she'd found in her skirt. Her most treasured possession, she wasn't going to let go of that for anyone. And as it wasn't digital, there was a chance she could still use it. Her photographic ambitions overrode any risk there was of it being discovered.

Suddenly, Bronny stood up on his hind legs, putting his front paws on the windowsill and started barking at something. This, in turn, set the horses off, prompting them to neigh and move around; unnerved by this noisy creature. Jack looked through the window and said with some urgency,

"Somebody's coming! Bronny, ssshh, you're upsetting the horses!"

"OK, show time!" said Frankie in a confident voice, as he grabbed Jack's hat and quiver full of arrows to wear himself.

"Hey!!" Jack objected.

"Needs must, Jackie boy," asserted Frankie, "you look like a kid, so be one. I, on the other hand, have a performance to put on."

"To be honest," added Maggie, "Frankie's got a point. We need the right people to have the right props. Sorry, Bud, but you'll have to give your sword and knife to our family knights."

"No fair!" said Jack petulantly, reluctantly passing his weapons to Josh and Aaron. Pouting, he turned his attention to Bronny. At least a boy and his dog fit the right narrative, and he wouldn't have to give him up. As Jack pulled Bronny from the window, the two men he saw drew closer, striding down the slope that used to be the path to Pops' village. Having heard a ruckus coming from the stables, they were naturally curious to see what their animals were complaining about.

Cat put her hand in Tom's and looked at him nervously. Frankie thought it best to front foot the situation, so he walked outside, standing tall, ready to meet the strangers. Jack followed with Bronny, their departure thankfully settling the horses down, but dialling Maggie's anxiousness up. Harry went too, motioning to his daughter that he would keep an eye on his grandson; with Sam coming along out of interest.

"Greetings, kind Sirs," said Frankie, tipping his hat and dipping into a small bow.

"Good Day," responded the shorter, stouter man. Dressed in heavy, multihued robes, he looked like a gentleman of importance. His taller companion wore brown britches, boots and a plain top, obviously the subservient of the two.

"What do we have here?"

"Begging thy pardon, Sir," apologised Frankie, "we are but weary travellers who hath no means of fleeing the storm last night. Please forgive our trespass of thy stables, whilst seeking our refuge."

Sam stifled a snigger and got an elbow in the ribs from her grandfather.

The brightly robed gent ran his eyes over the group, ostensibly determining they didn't pose any particular threat.

"Robin," said Frankie, introducing himself, "Robin of Loxley at your service."

Jack turned and looked at him with a raised eyebrow. Frankie, beginning to enjoy himself, decided to up the ante. Grabbing Sam's elbow, he said,

"Accompanying me is Maid Marian," - quietly whispering '*curtsy please*' in her ear, to which she obliged. Then putting a hand on Jack's shoulder - "and this is young Will Scarlett." Jack, who was getting the hang of the game, respectfully bowed his head without having to be told. Frankie looked at Harry behind him. "And with us is Friar ... err... Kenobi," he finished.

"Ah!" boomed the stranger, his eyes turning to Bronny. "And this fine beast must be one of the entrants in the race of the hounds."

"Err, yes," said Frankie, thinking that sounded like a good reason for them to be there.

"May I also present Lord Thomas and Lady Catherine, whom we happened upon in the forest. Miss Maggie, lady-in-waiting, and their security detail," referring to Josh and Aaron. The boys stood up straight, looking suitably knight-like. Tom stepped forward before Frankie had them play out a whole scene from a movie. He took a chance.

"Baron Buford, I presume," and to demonstrate reverence, he bowed deeply; bending his arm and pulling his hand into his waist. The Baron looked pleased to be recognised and bowed back. Tom continued,

"We extend our apologies as well. Alas, the weather got the better of us on our way north. When we paused momentarily in the woods to disembark our carriage, a sudden thunder crack caused our horses to bolt. Praise God for Robin here, who heard our cries and led us to shelter on thy property."

Frankie smiled in appreciation of the heroic picture Tom had painted.

"Egads! The winds of the storm have blown in friends of the manor. Welcome all!" Baron Buford's loud voice expressed his amusement at finding new and interesting people on his estate.

"Allow me to introduce Noah, my stable master," he said, turning to the good-looking man on his left. Noah bowed his head, acknowledging the group. Maggie gauged his age to be similar to hers: silver flecking his dark hair and subtle wrinkles around his eyes. Maybe a little younger - the stubble caressing his jawline reminiscent of George Michael from his Faith album. She also spotted a scar on his chin that was sure to have a story attached. A man who had real-world experience, she concluded. His eyes were a cobalt blue, and when they briefly glanced in her direction, her pupils dilated without warning. He caught her looking at him and smiled cordially, making her start and turn away; embarrassed that she must have been staring.

"We were in the midst of inspecting the grounds above," said Noah, diffusing Maggie's awkwardness and indicating the area behind him. "For they are to host the chariot racing and polo tournament; the highlights of Baron Buford's Yuletide Celebrations."

"Indeed," confirmed the Baron, "and then came to examine the horses. Pray tell, did thee note the welfare of the animals? How have they fared after the storm?"

"They are truly beautiful," volunteered Harry, "and seem in good health, all things considered. The palomino is stunning. Did she originate from Arabia? One of the smartest breeds of horses, I understand."

"Thou art well versed in equine knowledge," said Noah, impressed.

"Excellent!" said the Baron, his voice echoing in the still of the valley, "Henceforth, thou must stay for the duration of the games. Let us away to the warm and dry. There is an abundance of room for thee." He gestured for everyone to move from the stables and in the direction of the manor.

And with that, the Baron, his stable master, a group of nine visitors and a dog, started walking across a school field, to where the school wouldn't be built for another 600 years.

CHAPTER 5

Tuesday Afternoon 21 December

WITH THE SUN FINALLY making its presence known, the grounds became a patchwork of white snow refusing to melt, and green grass punching a way through. Fresh country air and the pungency of nature invaded their nostrils; devoid of any exhaust fumes, cigarette smoke or fast food aromas; all yet to be invented. The usual traffic noise was noticeably absent - disquietingly so. Maggie didn't miss the irony of wanting to clutch hold of the very thing that had driven her mad only a few days ago.

Harry and Noah discussed different breeds of horses as they ambled towards the manor. Tom had Baron Buford's ear, discreetly trying to glean any useful bits of information pertaining to their current predicament. The women stuck together; Maggie holding a firm hand on Jack's shoulder, not wanting to let him out of her sight.

In addition to the manor, now an imposing sight that appeared bigger with every step forward, there were several smaller wooden cabins scattered in ad hoc positions across the field, with what were presumably the local peasants going about their daily chores. When the group reached the centuries old mansion, Cat glanced behind to the stables - the portal to their real life - and wished they weren't so far away, in footsteps and in years.

Inside, the men made approving noises about the architecture and interior. Bedecked with artwork and sculptures, the grand entrance boasted a sweeping staircase to the upper level, at the top of which a striking stag's head stared vacantly from the wall. To the left of the stairs, a large ballroom doubled as a banquet hall, with a grandiose study beside it and a drawing room adjoining. And to the right, they could hear noise coming from a big bustling kitchen further down the hallway; the staff in the midst of preparing a bountiful welcome feast. After lunch, the hound race would commence - the opening event of the Yuletide Celebrations. Jack, taking everything in his stride, got quite excited about that. Maggie took pride in how he was handling things, and felt slightly jealous of his teenage fearlessness, compared to the menopausal anxiety she was doing her best to hide.

A tall, slim man came into view and approached the group.

"Ah, Egbert, my good man," acknowledged the Baron, "meet our new visitors, some of whom will be partaking in the festivities. They've had a bit of a rough night, so rustle up some bread and cheese from the kitchen, wouldst thou?"

His footman dutifully obeyed and returned with food and water, gratefully received by all concerned. Cat counted her blessings that, in travelling back in time, they had landed at a wealthy landowner's country residence where the water was generally safer to drink, unlike the oft polluted version found in poorer, urban areas of medieval England.

"Now," said the Baron, "I must take my leave and bestow greetings upon other new arrivals. Please busy thyselves by exploring the estate until the midday meal is ready. Afterwards, the hound racing will commence at the end of the field, and rooms for thy slumber will be ready anon. But Brother, could I speak with thee briefly?"

Harry nodded, following Baron Buford while the others gave a chorus of Thank Yous; the adults exceedingly relieved that their host gave all the signs of being a stand-up bloke. Noah also made his excuses, but said he would join them for lunch, which inexplicably pleased Maggie for some reason. They bunched together under a tree laden with apples in the courtyard, giving them some privacy to talk. Harry reconvened with the family after his chat with the Baron.

"What did he want?" asked Tom.

"He offered me the chapel to use as my own, and explained that their man of the cloth passed away some time ago and has never been replaced."

"Not of the plague, I hope," said Sam.

"No, good old influenza, it appears. From what I understand, the black death hasn't reached this part of England yet, touch wood,"

Harry put his hand on the tree trunk symbolically, so as not to jinx his words,

"He asked if I would do the honours of opening the games this afternoon. I couldn't see the harm, so I said I would."

"Are you going to try to speak the old English way?" checked Frankie. "I'm not sure I can keep it up with any conviction."

"No, bugger that for a lark," answered Harry, "we've enough on our plate without worrying about when to say thy, thee or thou. I fudged our background a little when I was talking to him. Dropped a few hints that we were foreigners from a far off land with a peculiar vernacular. I think he bought it."

Cat spoke up, "It might be useful to have you in the chapel, Dad. Maybe you could try saying the verse again by the trap-door to see if anything happens."

Harry nodded.

"Things seem to be going OK at the moment," noted Tom, "but we do need a plan."

"Wasn't there another tunnel that forked off in the direction of the manor?" asked Josh.

"Yes," Aaron concurred, "it looked like it could potentially travel all the way under the field. It must have an opening somewhere in this vicinity. If we can find it, that would be an easier way to sneak to the chapel tonight, instead of having to go above ground."

Having eaten something and feeling more positive, they discussed what they ought to do to get through the next eight hours or so.

They agreed to spend the morning familiarising themselves with the environment, and it was OK to split up as long as they all returned for the banquet lunch. Sam suggested she and Frankie - who, as Robin and Marian, were supposedly engaged - look around inside the manor; two people being less conspicuous than a group. Hopefully, the staff would be so preoccupied with their tasks, they wouldn't notice a couple of strangers poking their noses into places. Josh and Aaron were going to check out some of the outbuildings to see if they contained any hidden trapdoors in the floors, similar to those already discovered. Tom and Cat would walk down one side of the field in an attempt to interact with the locals, and Maggie, Jack and Harry would do the other. And so, feeling like they had some semblance of control, they began investigating their new - or rather, old - world.

"Thanks for being so cool, calm and collected," said Cat to Tom, as they squelched across the damp grass.

"Perks of being a boring accountant," he replied, squeezing her hand and winking, "we're so analytical, there's not much room for fearful emotions." Then, not wanting to minimise her feelings of nervousness, followed up with, "which are, of course, perfectly normal in these circumstances."

His wife smiled, appreciating the reassurance. They met a blacksmith, a tanner, and several gardeners - all in the employ of the Baron, but didn't get a terribly warm response when trying to engage in casual conversation.

"Just as well Frankie - or Robin, should I say - upgraded himself from serf to archer," she whispered, "otherwise he might have ended up out here gathering firewood."

They discerned the cabins they'd seen before were living quarters split up for males, females, and children. Cat didn't really like that. She could see some of the peasants were husband and wife, but understood this was probably the most practical way to house people using the resources of the time, unlike how the modern-day nuclear family lived. She also deduced the locals' reluctance to chat with them was probably because she and Tom were dressed as nobles; the class system very much alive and well in the 1300s. Perhaps Maggie was having better luck.

Maggie was, in fact, succeeding in mingling with the workers on the other side of the field. Less threatening in servant garb, and with a child and an elderly man by her side, she came across as more relatable. They said Hello to a basket weaver and a woman mixing herbs. Keen to see what natural remedies were used for healing in this era, Maggie stopped and chatted for a bit. Harry spotted what looked like a beehive further afield and started making his way towards the beekeeper.

"What's this guy doing?" asked Jack quietly as they came upon a strong man of portly presence, studiously bending metal into a curve to wrap around some timber.

"He's a cooper," answered Maggie, "he's fashioning wood into barrels which were, I mean are, very useful containers for everything from salt to wine. That's the original name for men in that trade."

"Like Frankie's last name?"

"Yes, somewhere along the line, Frankie would have had an ancestor who was a cooper, and the name stuck. There are a lot of common surnames that originated from people's professions. Like Mason, Hunter, Fisher, and Cook. Think of someone at school who might have a medieval surname."

Jack considered for a moment and then said,

"What about Carpenter? Our PE teacher is Simon Carpenter."

"That's right," praised Maggie.

"Oh, and Rose is Rose Weaver. Do you think she descended from the basket weaver we spoke to?" he suggested excitedly.

"It's very possible," said Maggie, humouring him and pleased that at the very least, this trip was teaching him something.

The cooper paused his work for a minute, his face opening up into a gap-toothed grin as Bronny took it upon himself to have a good sniff of his creations. Jack, who'd promised to tone down his use of modern teenage slang, apologised for his dog's behaviour and asked questions about the cooper's job. The man, known as Walter, indulged the boy; flattered to have someone show interest in his craft, and demonstrated the process while explaining it to him. As he was articulate - not all the peasants were - Maggie endeavoured to get some inside information on the Baron and his land. What she found out was quite disconcerting.

Walter, obviously taking what she was wearing at face value, and assuming her a servant or 'one of us', told Maggie in a gravelly Idris Elba type voice, that while he didn't dislike Baron Buford per se, he was still Lord of the Manor who taxed his workers heavily. And that was becoming increasingly difficult for the peasants on the estate, especially with a harsh winter looming. There seemed to be a general consensus that the Baron putting on his Yuletide Festival, and expecting his staff to cater to strangers in a lavish way, when they themselves, were cold, sometimes hungry, and had little to show for their hard work, was not a very popular move. Never one to ignore a pretty face and trying to impress the lad, he conspiratorially told her the feeling was the same on other estates, that there was an uprising coming, and his cousin in London was an associate of one of its leaders.

Maggie inwardly gulped. This was the start of the Peasants Revolt Cat had spoken about. On that note, she thought it time to join her sister again. She called out to Harry to come back too.

In the meantime, Josh and Aaron had used their knight status to get access to some of the outbuildings near the manor. One accommodated cows and calves; the bovines' attending milkmaids giggling at the arrival of two handsome men who wanted to look around. Staying in character was easy for the boys, and Josh wondered out loud to Aaron as they walked outside again whether this whole experience would give them any new ideas for kidnapping Harry. They determined another building to be a small warehouse, storing tools and suchlike. Neither had a trapdoor to speak of.

Fast becoming their rendezvous spot, the group reassembled under the apple tree in the courtyard. Frankie and Sam shook their heads, implying they hadn't stumbled upon the end of the tunnel anywhere. Maggie repeated what she had learnt from her chat with Walter.

"He might have been showing off to you," suggested Tom.

"Did he say the name of his cousin's contact in London?" asked Cat.

"Yes," said Maggie "Someone called Wat Tyler."

"Lordy," gasped Cat, "That's him! He's the leader of the revolt. To be fair, most of the action took place in London, but if one of his henchmen is Walter's cousin, I can imagine a bit of rabble rousing happening down here. Didn't you say the Baron's manor was burnt down as part of the retaliation, Tom?"

Tom nodded. "I guess that could be a matter of months away."

"Not really our problem," said Frankie. "Our priority is to get home ASAP."

"I know," agreed Tom, "but the Baron seems to be one of the good guys. He'll just be going along with the King's request to tax everyone to the hilt. It's a shame to think of his demise."

"Or anyone else's," murmured Maggie, thinking of Noah, Egbert and the people she'd met that morning. They cut their conversation short as Baron Buford came out of the manor, heading in their direction. With a beaming smile, he said,

"If thou art satisfied with thy exploration of the grounds, come forth into the banquet hall where lunch will be served presently."

The Baron went on ahead to speak to Egbert, and as the search for the other entrance to the tunnel had proved fruitless, the group quickly whispered a Plan B to each other. They presumed their accommodation would be upstairs, so after supper, when dismissed for the night, they'd go to their rooms together, and then sneak out individually a few minutes later to meet under the apple tree again. Once regrouped, they planned to cross the field as fast as they could, preferably without disturbing the sleeping peasants in their cabins on the way. As Harry was going to use the chapel as his lodging, he would light the lanterns so they'd have some illumination at the end of the field to aim for. It was risky, but all were keen to give it a shot, with the potential of the 21st century being within reach after dark.

In the meantime, they would make the most of their host's hospitality, and partake in the games to keep their minds off worrying. They entered the banquet hall and took their seats. As long as they stayed together, everything would be alright, Maggie thought.

Egbert signalled to the heralds, who blew their trumpets to announce the start of the banquet. Bronny's nose began to twitch uncontrollably at the smell of an assortment of meats being brought into the room, in addition to bread, cheese and nuts already laid out. Various dogs lay under the tables, as was the norm in those days, waiting expectantly for scraps to be dropped on the floor. The kitchen staff went from diner to diner, offering jugs of ale and aromatic salads to each. Tom and Cat had been invited to sit with the Baron as he seemed to have taken a shine to the couple. Noah returned from his stable master chores, and to Maggie's secret delight, joined her table.

Savoury and sweet dishes were all served at once on pewter plates: poached pears swimming in white wine next to sticky chicken drumsticks; thick, gooey honey from the hive beside juicy slabs of beef. Jack's eyes grew wide, as did Bronny's, when the culinary showstopper arrived: a magnificent wild boar presented whole, with an apple in its mouth (presumably sourced from the tree outside). Its placement in front of the Baron triggered a spontaneous round of applause from the room. Baron Buford turned to Harry, also on the grand table, and asked him to bless the food. Harry coughed and stood up.

"Blessed are we to receive the food before us.
May we thank the Lord for such abundance.
Blessed are we for our host's benevolence.
May we be considered grateful and worthy.
Blessed are we for strangers to become friends.
May our time together be fruitful and fun.
And blessings to all in your spirited competitions,
May the Force be with you."

He looked at Jack with a wry grin as he uttered the last line. Baron Buford sealed his approval by banging his fist on the table, shouting,

"Hoorah! Let the Yuletide Celebrations begin!"

The feast lifted everyone's spirits, and as they filled their bellies and quenched their thirst, just for a moment, those from the future forgot they were trapped in a time that wasn't theirs. Afterwards, as everyone finished eating, the heralds trumpeted again.

"Hear Ye," announced Egbert. "Would all hound competitors make their way to the bottom of the grounds, ready for racing."

Maggie and Jack coaxed Bronny from under the table and took him outside with Egbert. As they headed down the field, the others slowly filed outside to position themselves within view of the finish line, directly in front of the manor.

"Now, lad," instructed Egbert, "when prompted, announce the name of thy dog, his breed, purpose and provenance."

Back in the banquet hall, Baron Buford voiced his dilemma between watching the race, and his ongoing hunger detaining him from doing so. Josh and Aaron offered to help.

"Where we come from," said Josh, "we can make food portable."

He took the knife from his belt and roughly split a round loaf of bread in two. Aaron lay some lettuce and a slice of tomato on one side, followed by a thick cut of beef. Then Josh used his knife again to slice off a hunk of cheese. Lastly, he placed the other half of the bread on top and handed it to the Baron.

"We call this a takeaway," he explained, "because you can take it away and eat while still watching the race."

"Bravo!" exclaimed the Baron. These newcomers really did have some interesting customs. They joined the crowd and went outside with Josh's new invention in the Baron's hand; a clumsier version of McDonalds, but nevertheless, effective.

Meanwhile, Bronny's nose bobbed in the air. Not satisfied with his food quota either, he could tell a tasty morsel had made its way outside, but was some way off in the distance. He was further distracted by a cute little spaniel by his side, currently showing her affection by licking his shins: the highest part of his anatomy she could reach. Jack pulled the lead taut, trying to get Bronny to concentrate, but without much success.

"Behold," shouted Egbert above the noise, "Thy hounds are at the ready. Please present and introduce thee canines forthwith."

The first competitor stepped forward with a tall, elegant Irish Wolfhound:

"Bannonbrig Squire Brightside, Irish Wolfhound, Hound from the Forest of Dean."

The next person moved up, standing alongside a thickset, drooling dog:

"Koolwaters Duke Warrington, Mastiff, Working Dog from Colchester.

Then it was the spaniel's turn:

"Plumhollow Sunset, Cocker Spaniel, Gun Dog from Littlehampton.

And lastly, Jack, virtually dragging Bronny along.

"LeBron James, Great Dane, Point Guard from the NBA Lakers."

"He's not French, I hope," said Egbert to Maggie, noting the masculine 'le' and the Dane's coat colours of red, white and blue.

"Ah no - he was born in the...err...New Brunswick Area," said Maggie, creating an acronym off the top of her head to cover her son's literal interpretation of his dog's moniker.

"Oh," said Egbert, "and they have nice lakes there?"

"Yes. Yes, they do," she stammered.

Bronny, still focused on having fun with the spaniel, displayed no signs of competitiveness whatsoever and didn't look like he had a hope of beating the Wolfhound, who was patently raring to go; his owner holding him back by the collar to contain his dog's restless anticipation.

At the other end of the field, Baron Buford deservedly secured a prime viewing position in front of the crowd. Noah stood beside him on one side, with Josh and Aaron on the other, extolling the virtues of takeaway dishes such as pizza and hotdogs; embellishing their descriptions with medieval equivalents to make them relevant. In the distance, Egbert raised his hand.

"On thy dog's mark..." he began.

"And what doth thou call this specific concoction?" asked the Baron, happily biting into the transportable food the boys had kindly put together for him. Josh glanced down the field to Bronny - noting his complete indifference to racing - and figured a way to entice the canine into action.

"This is a hamburger!" he advised the Baron in a louder than necessary voice.

Bronny stopped fidgeting; his cropped ears turning in Josh's direction, like two rotating satellite dishes. That was a word he knew and liked.

"But there's no ham. How splendidly silly," boomed the Baron. "Hoorah for the hamburger!!"

That was all Bronny needed...

"And Go!" proclaimed Egbert.

Pulling away from Jack with a jerk, Bronny's clumsy day-to-day plodding transformed into a glorious gallop. As his coat of many colours flapped open with the breeze - the black fur underneath shining like sheet metal in the sunlight - his lean, powerful limbs propelled him towards the object of his desire: a burger. Almost as big as a horse, even Noah had to admire the dog's strength and speed; comparable to the best of his animals in the stables. The Wolfhound's equally long legs were no match for a Great Dane's appetite. On a mission to fill his stomach, Bronny passed his competition in full flight; his momentum drawing admiration from everybody in the crowd. They cheered noisily when - with a final burst of speed, like an unstoppable locomotive - he flew across the finish line; ultimately winning the race.

Thoroughly entertained, Baron Buford felt a dog treat was in order. Not that he had much choice, as Bronny made an immediate detour towards his host, plonking himself at his feet with tongue hanging out; his expectations unmistakable. The Baron chuckled and rewarded him with the remainder of the burger. A little way behind, Jack came running across the field whooping with joy, while Maggie struggled to keep up with him.

"LeBron James," mused the Baron, "what an unusual name."

"Yes," said Tom, unable to resist, "he should have been called Hamlet."

"Hamlet?" queried the Baron.

Cat kicked Tom in the shins and rasped,

"Shakespeare hasn't even been born yet; you can't make one of your Dad jokes."

"Ah yes," said Tom, furtively shrugging to Cat and trying to cover his tracks, "he was born in a little hamlet."

Egbert also arrived to congratulate the winner.

"A little hamlet by the lake in the New Brunswick Area," he finished off, sounding very knowledgeable to the confusion of the others. They all smiled awkwardly, but Baron Buford didn't seem to notice Tom's stumble, and with the excitement over, the crowd dispersed. Maggie looked up at the sky and over to the hills, ascertaining the sun's position. Harry read her mind.

"It's about 4 o'clock, I'd say. Sunset around 6."

She nodded and draped her arm around Jack's shoulders.

Soon, she thought. Soon.

The day turned chilly again, forcing a return inside, where Egbert advised the sleeping arrangements for the night. Tom and Cat had been allocated a room upstairs to the left of the staircase, with Frankie and Sam next to them. Josh and Aaron were given a bedroom on the right, over the other side of the landing. Then Egbert turned to Noah and said,

"Noah, if you please, when it's time to retire, wouldst thou escort young Will to the children's cabin and Miss Maggie to the servants' quarters on thy way back to the stables?"

Maggie's stomach dropped. According to the class system, she and Jack wouldn't be allowed to sleep in the manor with the gentry. Why hadn't she thought of that? She could cope, but the thought of Jack being on his own with a group of children he didn't know, in a very challenging environment, made the colour drain from her face. Once again, her dad came to the rescue.

"Actually, if permissible," he said to Egbert, "I'd like the lad with me. My old eyes, you know. Makes it tricky to read the Bible. He would be a great help."

"As thou wishes," accepted Egbert.

"Thank you," said Harry. "We'll take our leave now, if you don't mind. It has been a tiring day for the boy and dog."

"Of course," said Egbert, "Please help thyself to food now, if thou doth not intend to return for supper."

Harry nodded and salvaged some cold meats and grapes from the kitchen. This was a good idea, he mused. Without his glasses, Harry's eyes weren't the best, anyway. He wanted to make sure he was reading the poem on the trapdoor correctly, and suspected Maggie would feel better if Jack was with his grandad. The look of relief on his daughter's face confirmed his thoughts, so taking Jack under his wing and Bronny by the lead, the trio walked across the field again to the chapel, knowing there were only a few hours to kill before the conclusion of a very eventful day, and their ability to return to the 21st century.

CHAPTER 6

Tuesday Evening 21 December

INSIDE THE MANOR, THE Baron invited the men to join him in the study for a few ales. They mixed with other guests, and there was talk of a knight returning from France tomorrow. Tom calculated that England was smack in the middle of the 100 Years' War and enquired more. Noah advised they were expecting Sir Sebastian to arrive in the morning. Tom got the feeling that the two of them didn't get on. Noah - who was very down to earth - gave the distinct impression that Sebastian was a show pony (Tom's words) and, as Noah put it himself, liked to 'curry favour' with the ladies.

The female guests were directed to the drawing room to while away a few hours doing lady-type things. Seated on a chaise lounge, Sam looked over her mother's shoulder, attempting to copy her embroidery technique. Maggie performed her lady-in-waiting duties, separating and sorting the different coloured silks for easy selection. The other women in the room were either sewing, reading, or chatting to each other; the topic of conversation gravitating towards Sir Sebastian again, instigating much simpering and sighing.

"Are you OK going to the servants' quarters tonight?" whispered Cat. "I can always make an excuse about needing you in our room, like Dad did with Jack."

"No, it's OK," said Maggie, "I'd rather be closer to Jack, and that means three of us are down that end of the field already."

"Plus, you get a yummy chaperone," Sam interjected with a grin on her face.

"Be quiet, you," Maggie retorted.

"But he is lovely, isn't he?" Cat asked, also grinning.

"Oh, for God's sake," said Maggie, "Yes, Noah is very nice, but there's no future in that, is there?"

"You could always have a smooch behind the apple tree for the hell of it," Sam teased.

Maggie picked up a brightly coloured cushion and playfully hit her niece with it.

"Ouch," said Sam.

"Ooh sorry," Maggie apologised. "I didn't mean to hurt you."

"No, it wasn't the cushion. I've pricked my bloody finger with the embroidery needle. Stupid pastime. Mum, I can't do this all afternoon. I feel like I'm in the friggin' Handmaid's Tale. I think I'll go to the kitchen; there are girls of my own age there. Do you want anything?"

They shook their heads, and Maggie took Sam's seat as she left to find something more inspiring to do. As Sam walked out the door, she tapped her pocket, comforted to know her camera was still there. She wondered if she could take any sneaky photos while they were here. It would be quite something to capture the essence of the era.

The atmosphere in the kitchen was certainly more lively than in the drawing room. On a break, the mostly female kitchen staff were noisy and animated, with some girls mimicking the nobles and mocking their conduct. Sam could see the funny side and laughed out loud spontaneously, startling the girls into silence. They stopped what they were doing and respectfully curtsied, hoping they had not insulted one of the Baron's guests.

"Don't mind me," said Sam, picking up an apple. "I'm bored with that behaviour, too."

The girls relaxed a little, pleasantly surprised to find a noble willing to talk to them. This visitor to the kitchen had an unusual way of speaking and was more outgoing than other ladies in fine dresses.

"What are you making?" asked Sam, looking around the kitchen.

"Nothing at present, m' lady," said a young girl with a shy smile. "We're supposed to be practising a dance for the last day of the festivities."

"Ooh, let me see," said Sam eagerly, hoisting herself up onto one of the recently cleaned preparation benches. There was an audible gasp from the room. Who was this pretty woman from the upper class acting most unusually?

"Alas," said the girl, twirling her blonde hair around her finger, "Mistress Edith isn't here to lead us. She be out foraging mushrooms for tonight's supper."

"And what's your name?"

"Ivy, m' lady,"

"Hmmm, like the vine," mused Sam. "I bet you can weave and wind your way around the kitchen without Mistress Edith."

Ivy and the other girls giggled. As subservient staff, although a little self-conscious, they felt obliged to obey a lady who technically outranked them. After moving some of the benches against the wall, they began to dance in a very formal, synchronised way that Sam was sure she had seen before in period dramas. Pride and Prejudice, maybe? Or perhaps the more recent Bridgerton? For a second, she allowed herself to think of life at home with Wi-Fi, internet and streaming. Endless channels of entertainment and connection across the miles at the press of a switch. Technology she had taken for granted and was missing deeply. Reverting back to reality, she clapped politely at the girls' performance.

"Well, I think you're all terrifically talented, but do you like that sort of dancing? Ever want to step it up a notch?"

The girls looked confused.

"Sorry, m' lady?" questioned Ivy.

"Please call me Samantha," she said, choosing to disclose her real name and allowing the full version for once (appreciating the masculine alternative would bewilder them completely). She finished her apple, throwing it in a composting pile close by, and jumped off the table.

"Follow my lead," she said, standing in front of the group with her hand in the air. "Five, six, seven, eight."

In a rebellious mood, Sam demonstrated some high-spirited moves she'd remembered from a TikTok clip. Totally bemused, the girls chattered in excitement. They had never seen such a dance! As she repeated the steps, Ivy and some of her friends tried to copy what she was doing.

"How may we see thy feet?" came a cry from the back, and to everyone's surprise and amusement, Sam hitched up the long skirts of her dress and tucked them into the sides of her knickers; putting her Doc Martens on display. She repeated the sequence once again. As interest gathered around her, the chatter ramped up to hollers and cheers; those in the room getting used to the new rhythm and quickly picking up the choreography. Just as they were getting the hang of it, their laughter was interrupted by the return of Mistress Edith: an older woman with greying hair and crow's feet etched at the sides of her eyes and mouth - clearly a matriarchal figure in the manor. Her severe countenance may well have been Medusa's doing; the permanently pissed-off look, seemingly cast in stone. Annoyed by the commotion in her kitchen, she made her presence known.

"Glory be! What is this hue and cry?!"

Everyone stopped at once and bowed their heads. Sam - puffing from the activity - smiled broadly, brushed her hair out of her eyes and introduced herself.

"We've just been trying something new," she explained breathlessly.

Mistress Edith raised her eyebrows at the girl's impudence. "We?!" she questioned. "Tis inappropriate for gentry to mix with kitchen staff."

"Oh, I don't mind; it's more fun here than with those pretentious pollies in the drawing room," said Sam, expressing her malcontent.

Again, the girls had to suppress their giggles, but Mistress Edith was having none of it.

"What undignified utterances fall from thy tongue?" she berated. "Take caution in thy tone, young lady, and don't let youth betray thy breeding. We all have a place in this world - yours is not in ours."

"You'd be surprised," countered Sam.

Mistress Edith ignored her brazen backchat, clapped her hands and said to the room,

"Come now, return the benches to their rightful positions. We have supper to prepare."

The girls scurried about immediately, but Sam wasn't giving up.

"Let me stay," she pleaded. "I'll keep out of everyone's way and won't distract them. I'd just rather be here doing something other than decorating a boring cushion."

Mistress Edith didn't know what to make of this disruptive stranger, but she knew better than to go above her station and risk the ire of the Baron. She would teach her a lesson another way.

"Very well," she said, apparently conceding, "you may fetch me the golden goblets from the storage room at the end of the hallway."

Ivy had been listening and swallowed hard when she heard this. Nobody went into the old storage room, as it was believed to be haunted. An exterior building constructed well before the manor was built; it had stood isolated on the land without many clues to its history, giving rise to the rumour of it being possessed. Ceding to superstition, the storehouse remained largely untouched, so as not to disturb the ghostly occupants. There were stories of suffering from those who dared to enter, like the wood-turner and the cook who had snuck in together for a moment of privacy, with the couple becoming sick in the days after. Or the knight looking for his jousting stick who subsequently died in the tournament. The golden goblets were undoubtedly there, but had never been used, as everyone was too afraid to retrieve them.

"Sure," said Sam, and unable to warn her, Ivy looked on in horror as Sam started to walk down the hallway.

In the drawing room, with the evening fast approaching, Sam's mother and aunt were talking about their anticipated departure from the Middle Ages.

"So after supper, you think?" asked Cat.

"Yes," Maggie concurred. "I'll let Noah take me to the servants' quarters at the end of the field. After he drops me off and goes to the stables, I'll slip out to the chapel to join Dad and Jack."

"I'm not keen on running that distance in the dark to meet up with you,"

"I know, but it doesn't look like we have any other option. Let the boys lead, hold on to Tom's hand, and run for your life. Just think about getting home."

The men had come to a similar conclusion in the study, which they'd fleetingly discussed when Baron Buford and Noah were out of earshot.

Sam opened the closed door at the end of the hallway, coming across a detached stone outbuilding, she assumed was the old storehouse. It looked like it had been there forever. The wooden door was latched shut with a heavy board across the front. She grunted, needing all her strength to lift it. Expecting an equally strong resistance to push the door open, she was surprised when it yielded with minimal force, creaking like something out of a horror movie. Unaware of the superstition attached to the building, Sam walked in, brushed a few cobwebs away, and scanned the room. Seriously, it looked like nobody had been there for ages. It smelt dank and musty; there was a green, moss-like substance on the walls, and any items sitting on the shelves were covered in dust and grime. The wind whistled through gaps in the stone walls, turning the room into an icebox. She wrapped her arms around herself, rubbing her hands rapidly up and down her limbs. Getting some warmth from the friction, and feeling her fingers again, she pushed a table out of the way so she could get closer to the shelves. She'd spotted the golden goblets on the top one and wanted to collect them and get out of there as soon as possible.

"Yuck," she said to herself, "these will need a damn good clean before they're usable." Sam reached up, managing to get five out of six goblets down and onto the table. As she extended her arm a tad further to retrieve the final one, a mouse unexpectedly popped out from a hole in the wall and looked her square in the eye. She screamed, accidentally knocking the last goblet to the floor.

"Shit," she cursed. Regaining her balance, she knelt on the ground to pick it up and felt something hard beneath her knee. A splinter of moonlight was enough to illuminate the floor at the right time, revealing the culprit to be a handle. Giving it a good tug, she was amazed to see the open door expose a staircase leading down into a tunnel, just like those in the stable and chapel.

"Oh my God!" she exclaimed, "It's the other end!"

Gathering the goblets up, she put them in her skirt pockets, and exited the door backwards. A familiar voice whispered in her ear,

"Hope you're not stealing the Baron's treasures."

Sam jumped what felt like a foot high.

"Hell's teeth, Frankie! You scared the bejesus out of me!"

"Sorry, hon," he apologised. "Nature called, so I nipped out and then saw you emerge from this derelict piece of crap. What on earth is so interesting?"

"You won't believe it," she whispered while looking over her shoulder to check no one else was listening. "I've stumbled across the other end of the tunnel. Quick, before I board this up again, have a look." She led Frankie to the spot under the table, having to feel around with her fingers this time, as the light was no longer cooperating. But she managed to locate the handle and pulled the door open to prove her point.

"OMG, Sam, you little star! Now we can go back to plan A for tonight."

"You let the guys know, yeah?" said Sam. "I'll tell Mum and Aunt Maggie on my way to the kitchen." Frankie quietly fist-bumped Sam in appreciation of her discovery, and helped her board the door back up. He returned to the study while she brushed dirt off her dress and cobwebs out of her hair. After a quick detour to the drawing room, putting long-awaited smiles on Cat and Maggie's faces, Sam skipped the rest of the way to the kitchen.

Ivy, noting Sam's levity instead of the expected doom and gloom, greeted her with much enthusiasm. Mistress Edith looked a little disappointed that this intruder had found the gold goblets and returned without some misfortune happening along the way. When the lass pulled the chalices out of her pockets, she was equally stupefied to get a glimpse of a rather strange contraption that Sam hastily concealed. There was definitely something odd and bothersome about this girl, she thought.

THAT NIGHT, AS THE diners finished their supper and retired to their rooms, Noah and Maggie braved the cold night air to cross the field - her to the female servants' quarters and him to the stables. He offered his arm to escort her through the grass, which she gladly accepted, as the clouds were covering the moon, making it hard to see. Thank goodness Sam had located the third trapdoor; a much easier route for the rest of the group to take tonight.

"Ye young lad and his dog performed gladly today," said Noah, initiating a conversation.

"Yes," replied Maggie. "I'm very proud of Jack."

"Jack?" queried Noah, "I thought his name was Will."

"Ah," hesitated Maggie, realising the mistake she'd made and quietly cursing Frankie for portraying them as fictional characters. Well, they would be gone soon, and she was tired of keeping up the pretence, so didn't think it would hurt to reveal some of the truth.

"Um, yes, his name is Jack, not Will. Robin and Marian have become friends and Will is a nickname they gave him. Sorry, it's a bit complicated to explain."

"Worry not," placated Noah, patting her hand. "I need not be privy to your private arrangements." He felt the tension in her body recede and, not wanting her to feel uncomfortable again, directed the discussion to himself.

"I have a son also."

"You do?" said Maggie, genuinely interested. "Where is he?"

"Fighting in France," replied Noah. "I know not if he is alive nor dead, but nary a night goes by without me lighting the lanterns in the chapel afore slumber, in the hope he will find his way home one day."

"That must be hard. I can't imagine Jack going off to war."

"But the day will come when he is of an age to defend the land."

"The part of Britain we come from is very peaceful. I do not expect Jack to become a soldier."

"Indeed, your home doth sound charming from what I've heard. Strange dialects, interesting meals and no fighting. Certainly intriguing. Whilst I enjoy my place on the Baron's estate, I fear trouble is brewing amongst the serfs."

Maggie nodded understandingly. She wished she could tell him about the Peasants Revolt, but how could she? They walked in amicable silence for a while, then as they approached the servants' quarters, Maggie said,

"Thank you so much for escorting me across the field. And also for lighting the candles in the chapel. If we hadn't seen them shine, we wouldn't have been able to get out of the storm." That, at least, was a true statement.

"The pleasure is all mine," said Noah, "Even though the lights have yet to guide my son home, thou is a very enchanting alternative." He bowed slightly to kiss Maggie's hand. She blushed, thankful he couldn't see her cheeks colour in the dark.

"I look forward to the honour of thy company again on the morrow."

"Of course," said Maggie, feeling hideously guilty that tomorrow she'd be 650 odd years away. Which, in turn, made her feel a little sad. Noah continued to the stables, and once she could hear the horses acknowledge his entrance, she snuck out from behind the servants' quarters and quickly ran to the chapel.

"Mum!" greeted Jack, thrilled to see her.

"Hey, Bud," she responded, ruffling his hair with her hand, "how are you coping?"

"I'm alright," he said. "Pops and I have been playing noughts and crosses in the dirt. It's not the same as Fortnite on the PlayStation, but it passes the time."

Maggie smiled at her father, indebted to him for his help.

"I have good news. Sam found the other end of the tunnel in a small outbuilding behind the manor. So the others should be able to get here without disturbing the Baron or his staff."

As she spoke, the rest of the group crept from their respective rooms and down the stairs. Led by Sam, they were able to see their way down the hall, thanks to a few torches lit on the walls. Tom grabbed one on their way, and they worked quickly to get out of one door and open the next; keeping their fingers crossed that any creaks and groans their footsteps made would be put down to random noises buildings of that age tended to generate, anyway. Sam and Frankie pushed the table to the back of the room and pulled the trapdoor open. With barely concealed excitement, they descended into the tunnel.

Upon reaching their destination, Tom passed the torch to his wife and pushed the underside of the chapel door open, to be greeted by Harry, Jack and Maggie. Bronny contributed to the welcome by licking his face as he climbed into the room. Those behind followed in a happy and hopeful frame of mind.

"Well, no time like the present," smiled Tom as they regrouped. "Pun intended. Are you ready with the verse, Harry?"

"I am," he said.

"We need to be quiet," warned Maggie. "Noah's back in his quarters now."

They moved stealth-like, underground, in the direction of the stables. On arrival, Harry took a deep breath before reciting the poem once more:

"What Ho! Whomsoever enters this door
By my truth, you will happen upon days of yore
Pray thee stay, but if you must take your leave
With God Spede, fare thee well by Christmas Eve
Damsels and Gents to conjure the light
Seeketh days end and return with the night"

Nothing happened.

Harry said it again, waiting for the light to shine around the door as it had done last time.

But it didn't.

"What's wrong?" asked Cat.

"It's not working," said Josh. "Unless it doesn't light up this way round. Let me have a look." With great care, he cautiously pushed the door open a smidge; peeking through the gap, whereupon his worst fears were confirmed. Josh could see Noah's back as he slept facing the wall, and could smell the horses in their stalls.

They were still in 1380.

Quickly and quietly, he closed the door and told the others in a hushed voice what he had seen. They were instantly deflated. Tom motioned for them to backtrack to the chapel, so they did; heads down, shoulders drooping - body language that only a moment ago had been the opposite.

In the stables, Noah stirred. He thought he'd heard something behind him, but when he looked, there was nothing there. He felt restless, though. Maggie was on his mind. Since his wife had died some years ago, he really hadn't been interested in any other women, but there was something about

Maggie he couldn't define. She appeared friendly, but had a mystifying quality he hadn't previously encountered. Her red hair made him think she had Celtic blood, and Lord Thomas had mentioned they were travelling north. But she didn't have a Scottish accent. He couldn't really hazard a guess where she was from. Noah stretched, pulling his knees to his chest and straightening them again, before standing up. Perhaps a breath of fresh air would clear his head. He walked past his horses, patting each one as he went outside.

He thought he heard some noise coming from the chapel, and briefly wondered why Friar Kenobi and Maggie's boy, Jack wouldn't be asleep by now, then dismissed it. They were a strange group with strange ways. He was about to go inside when the chapel caught his attention again; the light giving way to shadows and movement. There seemed to be a number of people there - more than two anyway - and a muffled discussion taking place.

In the rectory, a panicked debriefing ensued. Having interpreted the verse to mean the portal would open again at nightfall; now that it hadn't, they were at a loss as to what to do next. Voices became strained and hasty suggestions were made as the anxiety in the room lifted to an all-time high. Then there was quiet. A dump of cortisol - in tandem with the hope-crushing fear of being stuck in the past forever - flooded through their bodies. Fatigue had set in from the charade they'd been playing in the 1300s, and their unsuccessful attempt to leave it. They were emotionally spent, and rightly so.

Gradually simmering down in order to think straight, the group conceded Plan A had failed. So what the heck was the poem going on about? But tired, stressed heads were not going to come to a speedy resolution, and given no one at the manor knew they had ventured outdoors, they agreed the best thing to do was to return from whence they came, and slink back into their rooms. Tomorrow was another day, and as Tom reminded them, they still had Wednesday, Thursday and Friday before Christmas Eve presented itself.

Keeping his distance from behind the oak tree, Noah heard the overture of voices stop abruptly and saw the flurry of movement in the chapel disappear. Then a lone figure came out, sighed deeply, and sat on the small bench outside. It was Maggie! But he had left her at the servants' quarters, hadn't he? To his dismay, he saw her put her head in her hands and start to weep.

Cat, holding her husband's hand in the tunnel, was also in tears. In an effort to stop the group's depression spiralling, Tom tried to keep the mood upbeat.

"It'll be alright, love," he reassured, "we just need a good night's sleep to figure it all out."

In the chapel, Harry recognised Maggie needed some time alone, so challenged Jack to a game of I Spy. Out of the group, they were probably the least perturbed. Jack - as a child - didn't fully understand the gravity of the situation, and while Harry was very mindful of the devastating blow they'd just been dealt, he felt more philosophical. Perhaps at his age, resilience went hand in hand with experience. He'd been through a number of challenges in his life that had felt insurmountable at the time, and yet somehow survived each one, eventually moving onwards and upwards. Harry was still hopeful they were close to finding the answer. He reflected on that while Jack tried to guess something beginning with B.

"Bed,"

"No,"

"Bible,"

"No,"

"Beam,"

"No,"

Clearly, the poem unlocked the portal to go back in time, and gave the impression there was a way to return. We just aren't seeing what that way is, he thought. Sometimes if you looked too hard, you couldn't see the wood for the trees, so maybe a reset was required. Like turning a computer off and on again to get it working properly, Harry felt sure all they needed was to switch their brains off for a bit and revisit the riddle again the next day.

"Bollocks,"

"Haha, where?"

"Bronny! Bronny's bollocks."

The pair had a much-needed cackle and continued the game until Jack guessed 'bowl' as the correct answer.

Noah didn't know whether to approach Maggie or not, but while he was thinking about it, she pulled herself together, wiped her eyes and returned to the chapel. Noah went back inside the stables, deciding to keep his observations to himself, despite the way they had unnerved him.

"Hey, love," said Harry, concerned, "are you OK?"

"I am now," said Maggie, managing to smile. "I just needed a minute."

"Are you going back to the servants' quarters, Mum?" asked Jack.

"Nah," she said, "I think I'll sleep here with my favourite men."

Jack grinned and gave her the same rug they had used on the first night. She sat on the floor with her legs crossed, patting down her skirt in the middle. Bronny viewed her lotus position as an invitation, reversing up to Maggie and plonking his butt in her lap. They couldn't help but laugh. Man's best friend - if only briefly - had successfully vanquished the stress from the room.

Bronny didn't care where or when he was, as long as his humans were with him.

CHAPTER 7

Wednesday Morning 22 December

WEDNESDAY MORNING WAS AS gloomy as the group. Maggie and Jack joined the others for breakfast in the banquet hall; an informal affair, with leftovers from the previous night's supper on offer. Jack asked Josh and Aaron if they would be on his team for the tug-of-war competition at the children's fayre that afternoon. It was pretty surreal they'd participated in the exact same activity only two days ago, in a pretend medieval village, and would now be living it for real. A cloud of despondency hung over them all and despite the food available, no one had much of an appetite.

Harry stayed behind as he had a problem of his own he needed to sort out. The fact that they hadn't managed to get home last night was troubling him, because he knew Doris would be worrying. The others had finished work and school for the year, so weren't particularly expecting to hear from friends or colleagues this week. But as he and Doris spoke every day, he knew she would be agitated if he made no contact at all.

With zero possibility of communicating across the centuries, Harry had one inkling that he thought might be worth a shot. He ducked down into the tunnel to retrieve his penknife from the hidden bag and went out to the young tree he knew was going to grow into a stupendous oak. Bending down, he carved a D into the trunk, as Doris had done when they were in the garden together. He carried on scraping the bark to write: "D IM OK C U 24TH H"

Wishful thinking, perhaps. Hope, for sure. Success, who knew?

Little did Harry realise that Noah had seen the whole thing, which only left the stable master more perplexed. As well as the questions nagging in his brain, Noah's hungry stomach made itself heard, so he went to breakfast; quietly monitoring Maggie and her companions. Not quite understanding what had gone on last night, but noting the general air of malaise among the group, he wondered whether he could alleviate it. The horses needed a good run prior to the polo match on Friday, so he approached the boys to ask if they could ride. Josh and Jack confirmed they could. About to say it ran in the family, Josh bit his tongue, remembering they were all playing different parts in 1380, with Noah unaware that most of them were related. Aaron hadn't ridden a horse before, but the chariots also needed an outing to ensure they were in good shape for the exhibition race the next day, so Noah suggested he drive one of those. Perking up from the morning blues, the boys eagerly agreed to meet him at the entertainment arena beyond the stables. Jack told Maggie about their plans and she managed to catch Noah's eye to give him a grateful smile.

To keep their minds off their worries, Maggie took Cat, Frankie and Sam outside to introduce them to Nancy, the herbalist, and Agnes, the weaver. Walter the cooper waved them over after. He was easy to talk to and obviously enjoyed their company. While he was chatting up her mum and her aunt, an idea popped into Sam's head. She picked up one of the steel rings waiting to be a barrel component and asked Walter if he could spare a couple for the children's fayre. Happy to oblige, he gave her two unused circular parts. She thanked him and then sprinted in the direction of the stables. Frankie stayed with Walter, keen to discover the history of a person with the same surname as his.

"Noah!" shouted Sam, her breathing uneven as she caught up with him. "Do...you...have a...jousting stick?"

"That I do, Miss Marian. They are located at the rear of the stables."

She slowed down and wheezed sporadically. Sam hardly ever exercised at home. Running across fields in a full length dress, holding two metal rings was not something she'd anticipated doing this week, but she wanted to catch Noah before he went off riding. Harry, too, had joined the men; needing no arm twisting to hang out with his favourite four-legged animals.

A generous sized storeroom attached to the stables housed two chariots, more riding gear, and several lances. Noah passed one to Sam, not knowing what she was planning to do with it, as well as some thin rope she had also spotted and requested. He led four horses out into the open; saddling up three. Then he turned to Harry and inclined his head towards the fourth.

"And the palomino for thee, Brother Kenobi?"

Harry's eyes gleamed.

"What's her name?" he asked Noah.

"Perfect Grace," came the reply.

Harry inhaled deeply...

Of course it was.

Josh helped attach the chariot harness to the horse, then Harry and Aaron stepped onto the platform, adjusting their stance to balance themselves. Noah led Perfect Grace up the slope to the vast pastureland used as an arena for sporting events; with Josh and Jack behind, walking the other three horses. When they got to the top, the boys mounted their animals and started a slow trot around the open paddock. Harry and Aaron steadied the chariot and soon found their feet. In his element, Harry encouraged Perfect Grace to accelerate as she went. They got into a rhythm and picked up speed to a canter, passing those in front. The other riders, realising they were being overtaken, started to cheer them on and launched into a gallop to keep up.

In the meantime, Sam used the rope she'd acquired to tie the barrel ring onto the bottom of the jousting stick. Ensuring it was secure, she turned everything upside down and jammed the pointy end into the earth. Impressed with the result, she ran back down to the stables and grabbed another lance to repeat the process. But before returning, she paused, and - as she was alone - surreptitiously opened the hidden tunnel door to retrieve the bag she had stashed away. A nostalgic sigh escaped her lips, as she saw all the mod cons they'd abandoned, including their mobile phones - batteries well and truly dead now. Just touching them made her feel good and within reach of their normal life. She half thought about putting her camera in the bag for safekeeping but changed her mind, as it was one of the few things keeping her sanity intact. At the last minute, on impulse, she grabbed Maggie's small bottle of perfume: - Playing With The Devil by Kilian. Described as fiery and flirtatiously fierce, she felt the Eau de Parfum needed to see the light of day. Aside from the fact that none of them had had showers for several days, and were getting a bit whiffy, her aunt could do with a push to be flirtatiously fierce, and this might do the trick. What the hell, it smelt good, she thought, spraying a quick squirt on her wrist. Sam stowed the perfume and the camera away in her very useful pockets, and threw the bag down into the tunnel again, but in her haste, did not see one of the handles get trapped between the door and the floor.

When the men had finished exercising the horses, they raced each other back to the stables, hurtling across the field at speed; the sound of thumping hooves and screams of wind exaggerated to such a degree that neither encouraging cries nor competitive jibes could be heard above the noise. Sods of earth dislodged by the sheer force of the animals' velocity, spewed mud in all directions. Rising to the challenge and ignoring the scattergun of soil stinging their bodies; the riders relished the pandemonium of pursuit. Hair whipping into knots, faces flushed and hearts pounding; the unexpected thrill of the morning had stimulated all of their senses, banishing the despair piled upon them the previous night.

Sam met the men, as they pulled up in a storm of dirt and sweat, to help still the horses while they dismounted.

"Hey, hotshot," she said to her cousin, "wanna shoot some hoops?"

Jack looked behind her to see the DIY basketball hoops she had constructed and shouted, "Shot!!" in gratitude and affirmation. She'd also come by a pigskin ball in the storehouse, and while it didn't really bounce, it was enough to give Jack a taste of home.

As they attempted to indoctrinate Noah into the rules of hoopball (a necessary name change for simpler explanation), they saw another horse dart out of the forest and advance in their direction. Looking like a Harlequin book cover, the majestic black stallion threw back its glossy mane in sync with its rider, who wore a full silver suit of armour minus the helmet; his raven coloured hair tumbling down the back of his neck. Both animal and human could only be described as spectacularly handsome. The horse came to a halt beside Noah, nostrils flaring - his rider jumping to the ground with a flourish and slapping the stable master on the back.

"Hail to thee, Noah, ye old rogue!"

"Sebastian," said Noah, somewhat muted in his response, "war didn't kill thee, then?"

Missing the sarcasm and removing his steel plated gloves, Sebastian replied,

"By God's will, I have returned."

Then he turned to Sam and asked, with thinly veiled desire,

"And behold, who is this bewitching creature? A pleasurable sight to be certain."

Josh cringed.

Aaron bristled.

"May I introduce Miss Marian and her fellow travellers. They are here for the games."

"This is very good news," smirked the knight. Bending to kiss Sam's hand, he smelt her perfume - the sensual aroma making his eyes crinkle with lust.

"Alas, she is already spoken for," said Noah, pre-empting Sam's need to make excuses. "Betrothed to one of the greatest archers in the land."

Sam blinked at Noah with a wry smile and thought, *Silver fox, loves horses, protective, and a sense of humour. I've got to get Aunt Maggie hooked up with him.*

Sebastian, far from being deterred, smiled again provocatively before introducing himself to the men. She noticed Josh and Aaron intentionally puffing their chests out to display a proprietary right over her. Jack copied their stance, to look like an adult. Sam could take care of herself but knew very well that women's rights were non-existent in the 1300s, and while her every instinct was to tell Sebastian where to go, she was happy today to let the men postulate as necessary, so as not to cause a scene.

"Away with thee, Sebastian," commanded Noah. "Baron Buford - and the ladies in the house, I'm sure - will be joyous at thy arrival."

Sir Sebastian grinned, failing to note the disdain in Noah's voice. Another leer and bow to Sam, then effortlessly climbing onto the stallion again, he galloped across the estate grounds to the manor. The unspoken hostility between the two men was evident to all.

"He's very full of himself," observed Aaron.

Noah agreed. "An interesting turn of phrase, but aye, the man holds himself in high regard."

With their appetites returning after expending so much energy, all were ready for the midday meal at the manor. Before the boys set off, Josh whispered to Harry,

"Any more ideas on what the verse means?"

"Not yet," Harry whispered back, 'but I'll stay here to poke around while you guys are at lunch. Save me some bread and honey if you would. I'll keep you posted."

Noah also remained, inviting Harry to help him feed the horses. As they distributed the hay, Harry casually conversed with Noah about the history of the land, hoping to pick up a clue about their current predicament. Noah was happy to talk. He liked Harry. And Jack. And Maggie, of course. He was even fond of that mountain of a dog of theirs. He, too, was subtly trying to get information from Harry about the goings-on of last night, but they were both too polite to push the point, and only received vague generalisations that didn't help either man. Harry thanked Noah for his hospitality as he returned to the chapel, saying the fun they'd had that morning had meant a lot.

Noah finished tidying up, then sauntered into his room in the stables for a bit of peace and quiet. While sitting on the floor, chewing a piece of hay and contemplating things, something dark caught his eye. He reached over and pulled at the strap Sam had carelessly left poking out of the trapdoor. Opening the door, he yanked the bag from below and emptied out its contents. Staring open-mouthed at the weird and wondrous things that lay before him, his enjoyment of the morning turned into concern. These newcomers were evidently hiding something, and he worried that if they were not who they said they were, then why were they here? What was their objective? But, if anything nefarious, surely they wouldn't involve a young boy and his dog. As puzzled as ever, he inspected the phones, water bottles, spectacles, watches, and penknife - things completely alien to his existence - then put them away in the bag and under the trapdoor again. Noah was well aware of the tunnel that went underneath the estate grounds to the manor. He had stumbled upon it when first setting up his living quarters, but understood the other end led to a haunted building. He'd always ensured he kept the door in the floor firmly shut, lest any wayward spirits elected to pay a visit. But how did the others know about it?

IN ANOTHER WORLD AWAY, Doris also had more questions than answers. Worried that she hadn't heard from Harry since the storm, and with the weather better now, she went to the stables looking for any sign that her friend had sheltered there. Finding nothing of relevance, she sat on the seat beside the oak tree, feeling very ill at ease. Remembering their rebelliousness a few days ago, she stood up to look for the D she'd carved into the tree trunk before Esme had interrupted them. She spotted it, but unexpectedly, there were additional letters. Her jaw dropped as she read the message that Harry had ingeniously sent her:

"D IM OK C U 24TH H"

What on earth....??!! Doris couldn't quite grasp what she was seeing. Not doubting that it was from Harry and relieved that he was OK, why the 24th? Where was he now, and why this bizarre form of communication? Had he marked the tree prior to leaving the stables after the storm? No - she thought - because I touched my finger to the D yesterday, and that's all there was. So, if he'd come back to carve the message, why not just tell me face to face? Her mind was racing, and she didn't know what to think. Her only consolation being that wherever he was, and whatever he was up to, Harry was alright.

Sebastian's arrival in the manor caused quite a stir. The men; congratulating the knight on his return to England, and encouraging him to regale his war stories. The women; fluttering their eyelashes and tittering, trying desperately to make eye contact, which he was all too willing to reciprocate.

After lunch, everyone went to the top field with Jack, including Tom, who had been elsewhere that morning. Cat wasn't sure what he was doing, but knew it involved an in-depth meeting with Baron Buford. She had seen her husband with parchment, quill, and abacus, illustrating something to him. The Baron had looked interested, and while she didn't understand accounting - now or in the future - if Tom had found a kindred spirit, that wasn't a bad thing at all.

At the entertainment arena that had served as an equestrian racing ground earlier, various games were laid out for the children to have fun. A big sign stood in the middle announcing: '*The Children's Fayre*', to give the young ones a sense of importance, even though half were illiterate. Much like the staged fair at Jack's school, there was a rope for tug-of-war, croquet hoops and mallets, a makeshift football field with sticks for goals, and now, thanks to Sam, a new sport to play called hoop-ball. She'd shifted the hoops to the northern end of the field, to spread everything out. The children ran around with plenty of zeal, wanting to do everything at once. Finding it difficult to get them to stand still for a minute, Egbert struggled to contain the high octane energy. Child wrangling was not one of his specialties, but he got there in the end with the help of Aaron and Josh, who sorted the kids into teams and offered their services as coaches. It was a good opportunity for Bronny to stretch his legs too, and after they'd cheered Jack on in the football game, Noah asked Maggie if she wanted to walk the dog in the forest.

As they strolled amongst the trees, light snowflakes began to fall. Only a smattering, not like the heavy dumping from Monday night, but enough to decorate the ends of the branches so they twinkled like fairy lights on a Christmas tree. Maggie paused to take in the snow-kissed surroundings. They were breathtakingly pretty. If she was genuinely living in this time period, she would have been thankful to be part of the Baron's Yuletide Celebrations, and in the company of lovely Noah. But the truth was, her heart belonged to modern day England with all its busyness and chaos. There were pros and cons for either era, but Maggie opted for the 21st century with its flushed toilets, career options, and little fear of Jack being sent off to war. Noah picked up on her pensiveness and took the opportunity to delve deeper into the maiden's past.

"Doth Jack have horses at home?" he enquired. "To bear witness to his skilful riding was a privilege."

"Not his own horse, no," answered Maggie, "but his grandfather taught him how to ride, as he did me."

"Thou and thy companions are very accomplished."

"Thank you. I think we can be quite competitive and try to outdo each other sometimes."

"Will thee stay til Christmas Eve and partake in the week's activities?"

"Ah well, that wasn't our plan," Maggie said, almost apologetically. "Initially, we were northward bound, but the storm put a stop to that."

"This I see," said Noah understandingly. "I sense a strong desire to return home."

"Yes," Maggie agreed, "we were hoping for... some, um... alternative transportation, but that hasn't transpired yet."

Noah hesitated, wondering whether to risk mentioning his discovery in the stables. However, his burning curiosity overrode his discretion, and moreover, if Maggie was going to leave sooner rather than later, what did he have to lose?

"Home provides different offerings for thee?"

"I'm sorry, I'm not sure what you mean," said Maggie, slightly unsettled at his odd question.

"Forgive me for what mine eyes have seen."

Feeling queasy, she cast her eyes downward, trying to stave off his line of enquiry. But Noah continued,

"The rucksack hidden in the tunnel under the stables. It belongs to thee? Or thy friends?"

Maggie stopped walking and looked up at him.

"You know about the tunnel?"

"Aye. But it is not to be trifled with. The end location lies within a haunted building."

"Oh," said Maggie, not acquainted with the superstition, "and what did you find in the bag?

"Cylindrical containers made of a material I have not seen afore. Metal rectangular objects for which I do not know the purpose...I have fears as to what this doth mean...rumours of the peasants' unrest spring to mind... and troubles stem from the north, where thou claim to originate from...I beseech thee..."

"Noah." Maggie stopped him and put her hand on his arm.

His whole body surged with heat in response to her touch.

"We are different," she admitted, "and we are lost. But we are not coordinating a rebellion, I promise."

Wanting to take her at her word, he allowed his mind to ease a little.

"Although you are right to be worried," she continued, causing his anxiety to resurface.

"Noah, I can't explain it to you completely, but your apprehension about a peasant uprising is valid. Some people of our ti..., I mean of our land, know about others who will lead a revolution in months to come. I too, suspect there is a connection with this estate, but it's not us, I swear."

She looked at him earnestly.

"Promise me this," she implored, taking hold of both of his hands. "If troubled times arrive, use the tunnel to lead the Baron and his staff to their escape. The outbuilding isn't haunted like you think. Trust me. Please."

He looked into her eyes, partly in confusion and partly not caring what she said, his feelings for her strengthening with every minute they spent together. Noah looked down at their hands and then back into her eyes. She spoke with sincerity and compassion, but there was so much he didn't know about her. The snowfall had started to get heavier, so perhaps this was enough for the moment. While questions ricocheted around his brain, his heart felt full to the brim, and that was something he hadn't experienced for a long time.

"So it will be," he said. "By my oath, I will heed thy words."

Maggie smiled, hoping she'd avoided a potentially difficult discussion, and allayed his fears in one go.

"Bronny," she called to the Great Dane, who bounded back good-naturedly, having enjoyed the excursion to the woods to sniff and explore. She slotted her arm through Noah's as she had last night, and together they ambled back to the field, full of frenzied children running around and playing. Their companionable silence and subtle smiles were not lost on Cat and Sam, who nudged each other when the couple came into view.

Jack had scored a goal in football, won his tug-of-war, and was currently teaching the children how to play basketball. As if he hadn't seen him for days, Bronny ran boisterously up to his boy, accidentally knocking him down with his exuberance. Jack chuckled as he fell to the ground, and making the most of being flat on his back, started to wave his arms up and down; forming snow angels in the ever-thickening icy layers beneath him. The other children joined in, while their parents made louder and louder noises about absconding to the warmth of the manor. Finally, the youngsters acquiesced, having had a fun afternoon and now intent on filling their stomachs. LeBron James barked in agreement and cavorted up the field. The kids hooted and cheerfully bounded after him, with the adults actively encouraging the Pied Piper effect he'd created.

CHAPTER 8

Wednesday Evening 22 December

As the sun began to set, the kitchen grew busy again with preparations for supper. Sir Sebastian had ensconced himself in the banquet hall already, in anticipation of a hearty meal. Not remotely interested in children's competitions, he had spent the afternoon imbibing far too many pitchers of ale, and was unsurprisingly plastered. That didn't seem to put the ladies off, however, with several clinging to his every slurred word and giggling at his garbled jokes. Noah glanced at him, unimpressed with his tawdry behaviour, and ushered the men into the study for a more civilised glass of wine that the Baron had imported for the occasion. The ladies went into the drawing-room and it took Cat and Sam all of ten seconds before they started quizzing Maggie on her get-together with Noah.

"Soooooo?" Cat enquired.

"So nothing," Maggie stated.

"Aww, come on, Aunt Maggie, you were positively glowing when you got back from the forest," insisted Sam.

"Well, we did hold hands for a bit," grinned Maggie.

"Ah hah!!" said Sam exultantly.

"But we do have a bit of a problem," Maggie continued. "He knows about the tunnel, and he saw Sam's bag along with everything in it. Apparently, the handle was poking out of the door."

"Oh my God!" exclaimed Sam. "I was feeling homesick and looking through our things when I was alone in the stables. I must have left it sticking out when I put the bag away again. I'm so sorry."

"It's OK. We talked, and even though I didn't tell him the whole story, he gets that we are an unusual group but aren't in any way threatening to the estate. In fact, he comes across as refreshingly objective and non-judgemental."

"And clearly enamoured of you," added Cat. "Are you blushing?"

"Don't be silly, just having a hot flush, that's all," responded Maggie, grabbing her sister's fan to keep up the pretence.

In the study, Noah was trying to concentrate on what the men were saying, but all he could think of was Maggie. He liked her a lot. She was engaging and interesting and had an alluring aura about her.

"What say thee, Noah?" asked Baron Buford for the second time.

Noah snapped himself out of his reverie and stammered,

"Apologies, m' lord, what was thy query?"

"The morrow," repeated the Baron. "Doth thou think it wise to stay indoors for a change? I fear the snow and rain will remain with us."

"Aye," agreed Noah, "let us do away with the chills and bask in the fire's warmth for a day. Tis satisfactory to delay the chariot race til Friday hence. Although, what can we offer our guests as an alternative recreation option for Thursday?"

Josh conferred with Aaron, who bobbed his head in assent.

"We've got an idea," he said. "Can we have parchment, ink, pebbles, and a bowl, please? We can set up a game in the morning and entertain everyone in the afternoon."

"Hoorah!" cried the Baron, lifting his glass. "If thy game is as innovative as thy food proposition, it will surely enthral the people."

"Tis an appropriate prelude to the ball in the eve," Noah concurred.

With plans sorted for the next day, they toasted to the success of the games so far, and for the triumphs to continue. The schedule change was music to Egbert's ears. Already with his hands full organising the masquerade ball, it was a great relief to have someone else take over entertainment for the afternoon. That would give him plenty of time to furnish the banquet hall properly, turning it into an elegant, opulent ballroom.

THAT NIGHT, THE MANOR was a hive of activity.

Under Egbert's advisement, Mistress Edith stood with him in the banquet hall, taking note of the food requirements for tomorrow. In her absence, Sam risked visiting the kitchen once more. Ivy was delighted; first to see Sam again and second, that no disaster had befallen her. Although she was still nervous that the trip to the haunted outbuilding would eventually bring bad luck into being. Sam encouraged the girls to try her TikTok dance again. Little did she know, they'd been practising the steps in secret while she'd been otherwise occupied, and were keen to show her the outcome. She clapped her hands in approval.

"Encore!" she cried. And this time, as the girls did the bit where they turned around to face the far wall, Sam pulled out her camera and quickly took a few clandestine photos. The noise of dancing feet muffled the sound of the clicks, but when she heard familiar clomping footsteps from behind, she hurriedly tucked the camera back into her pocket.

"Just helping with the salad," she fibbed to Mistress Edith, picking up a head of lettuce and smiling sweetly.

The kitchen supervisor forced a smile, but was unsuccessful at hiding her displeasure in finding Sam in her kitchen again. Evidently, the evil spirits had yet to punish this rebellious girl. Sam decided not to push her luck and waved the girls goodbye. Bumping into Frankie in the hallway, she playfully pinched his bum.

"Hi, darling," she said cheekily, "how's your day been?"

"Well, hello there," responded Frankie, "up to no good?"

"Always," she laughed.

They entered the banquet hall together, and with their entrance immediately piquing Sebastian's interest, he staggered across the floor to kiss Sam's hand again. She reluctantly let him do so; his alcohol fuelled breath fogging over them. Frankie wrinkled his nose in distaste, which didn't go down too well.

"Thou dare insult me," growled Sebastian. "Thou is a pathetic image of a man, and not worthy of this woman."

Sebastian believed his solid build made him more attractive and desirable than Frankie's slender frame, but Frankie wasn't putting up with that malarkey.

"Settle down, Sunshine," he retorted, pulling Sam away curtly; the sharp movement making Sebastian lose his balance and fall to the floor.

"Why you...," he cried.

Noah came into the room and immediately saw the state Sebastian was in. He lifted him from the floor and put the knight's arm around his own neck.

"Will thou desist, blighter!" said Noah to his drunken appendage. "Quarrels will not serve. But methinks the night air will. A walk in the cold will sober thee."

Egbert draped a heavy cape over the pair as they stumbled out of the hallway and through the door.

Tom and Cat came down the staircase - Cat listening to her husband intently as he brought her up to speed with the meeting he'd had with the Baron that morning. Something about parcels of land and monetising the games. She didn't quite get it and couldn't understand its relevance to their own problems. But before he could finish his update, Tom noticed the two men floundering outside, and went to help Noah; taking Sebastian's other arm to share the load. Zig-zagging down the field unsteadily, they reached the stables; depositing the knight onto a hay bale. He burped loudly and let his head loll to one side, endeavouring to sing a song that sounded more like grunts and mumbles. They left him to it and chatted on their way back to the manor.

"I thought you didn't like Sebastian," questioned Tom.

"He is a braggart and a blighter, but verily, he has gone to war for our sire. For that, I respect the man."

"Were you in the military, Noah?"

"Fighting against our French foe, that I did for some time. Unfortunately, a slice of a sword's blade ended my service." He looked upwards, stretching his neck to show Tom his scar was not merely a nick on the chin, but travelled all the way down to his collarbone.

Tom was horrified; realising that in combat, someone had tried to slit Noah's throat.

"But for my evasion and God's good grace, I would be no more. I credit my quick reactions to my work with the horses. The culprit's fate, however, was more final." He coughed awkwardly and changed the subject, not wanting to dwell on the past. Deep and meaningful talks were not one of Tom's strong suits, either. Shocked at the sight of Noah's wound, and the thought of him killing his attacker, he was stunned into silence and also glad to move on to a new topic.

As darkness descended, Harry lit the torches in the chapel. He'd taken over the nightly ritual Noah had started, which served twofold: - still a beacon of safety should Noah's son return; and as a guiding light for his family if they had to dash across the land for any reason. Once the torches were aflame, he took a minute and closed his eyes. Knowing the cryptic message by heart now, he dissected it line by line, trying to unlock the code that would lead them to their sanctuary.

What Ho! Whomsoever enters this door

Literally translated to: Attention, to those who walk through this door. That's fairly straightforward. I can't see that I've missed anything there, Harry thought.

Next door in the stables, Sebastian's singing got louder and increasingly incomprehensible

By my truth, you will happen upon days of yore

So the truth or reality, maybe, is that you will see - no - be in the past. OK, that is the truth. That's exactly what happened.

Sebastian lay on his back, still singing and now clapping his hands, totally out of time.

Pray thee stay, but if you must take your leave
We seem to have the choice to stay in this time or return to our own. Ergo, there must be a way to get home.

The horses snorted their disapproval of this disruptive interloper.

With God Spede, fare thee well by Christmas Eve
Yes, this is the bit everyone's worried about. It's now the evening of 22nd December, giving us only two days to work this out and skedaddle. Or what? Harry didn't want to think about it.

The singing diminished as the drunken man forgot the words, and levered himself up from the hay bale to look out the window.

Damsels and Gents to conjure the light
This must be referring to the light surrounding the trapdoor, somehow casting the spell to conjure up another dimension. Surely, we have to repeat this to get back.

His bladder ready to burst, Sebastian felt the urge to go outside.

Seeketh days end and return with the night

The day's end is the evening, right? Or did we time it wrong? Does it have to be midnight? But there wasn't a specific time for us to come through in the first place. That was during the day. What am I missing?

Then Harry stopped his scrutiny of the rhyme, as to his bewilderment, a bright light surrounded the trapdoor in the rectory.

What??!! He'd read the same words last night in vain, and now, without changing a thing, they were mysteriously working again. But nobody's here. They're all at the manor. Harry had seen Tom arrive at the stables and leave again, so rushed out the door, calling to him loudly. Recognising the urgency in Harry's voice, Tom convinced Noah to go on to the manor for supper, saying he would be there shortly. Harry stood outside the chapel, wildly waving to his son-in-law as he ran towards him.

Sebastian, only just managing to hold in his ale, staggered outside to the tree; relieving himself with a great groan of satisfaction.

"What is it?" Tom asked.

"The light," said Harry excitedly, "It's back!" Grabbing Tom by the arm, he pulled him inside the rectory, but when the two men stared at the trapdoor in the floor, the magical illumination had disappeared.

"Dammit!" exclaimed Harry, "it was here, I swear. I read the poem out again, very carefully, and the door lit up."

"I believe you," assured Tom. "Did you do anything differently? You don't think you previously misread a word, and then corrected it?"

"No," said Harry, genuinely mystified. "I've read the verse aloud so many times when I've been here. Even Jack checked that I'd got it all right. Nothing has happened until tonight, but where has the light gone now?"

"Quick, say it again," encouraged Tom.

Harry recited the poem once more, but this time it had no effect.

"OK, let's report what happened to the family. It's no good unless we're all here, anyway. At least we know it works, which is a good thing. We just have to figure out the trigger."

A short time later, Tom and Harry burst through the manor entrance, looking startled but exhilarated, and excitedly told the group about the light. A rapid brainstorm ensued, with everyone agreeing to give the plan a second shot. Repeating the movements of last night, Harry, Jack and Bronny would go to the chapel first. Then, after dark, Maggie would walk with Noah. Assuming they were going home tonight, she wanted to make the most of the time she had left with him. The others would sneak out of their bedrooms and down through the tunnel again.

This time....

At the other end of the field, Sebastian had thrown up behind the tree and was feeling much better. Having had enough of his exile and in need of some food, he returned to the banquet hall, giving Frankie and Sam a wide berth. He selected another table with several ladies present - easily morphing back into his rapacious self.

LATER THAT NIGHT, THE intrepid travellers journeyed underground again.

Noah and Maggie had already crossed the field, with him supposedly dropping her off at the servants' quarters, but knowing she would secretly skulk off to the chapel. He felt like they were getting better acquainted, but obviously Maggie wasn't ready to share the reason for her deception just yet. Behind her enigmatic smile were thoughts impossible to guess.

With no explanation as to what the paraphernalia in the bag was for either, Noah couldn't resist having another look. As he sat on the floor of the stables with the trapdoor open, a dim light shone in the distance below, that seemed to be moving progressively closer. Emboldened by Maggie's assurance the building at the opposite end wasn't possessed, he bravely trod down the stairs to investigate. Not having previously realised the tunnel forked off in two directions, Noah cautiously walked along the left passage, curious to see what was there. Upon finding the second trapdoor under the chapel, he squinted; trying to make out the engraving, but it was too difficult to read in the dark. Giving up, he retraced his steps to the longer part of the tunnel he knew. He crossed himself as a precaution, hoping the action would protect him from the bearer of light - whatever, whoever it was.

Frankie, at the front of the line and holding the torch, bore right around a corner and nearly jumped out of his skin.

"Jesus, Mary and Joseph!" he shouted at the sight of a man in the tunnel.

Cat screamed, not knowing who or what Frankie had run into, which sparked a round of expletives from the others.

"Bloody Hell,"

"Shit a brick,"

"What the fu..."

Noah, also startled, cried, "Gadzooks!! What is this which I see before me?"

Immediately relieved it was someone they knew, and trying to downplay their fright; Josh and Aaron imitated and modified his cry with a rendition of Macbeth's famous quote. Aaron held his plastic dagger out in front of him to clarify the reference. Sam thumped him on the arm in annoyance.

The disturbance underneath their feet was noticeable to those in the chapel too, who were patiently waiting for their family to arrive. Maggie opened the rectory trapdoor, dashing downstairs to witness the melee in the tunnel. Shocked to see Noah, but thankful it wasn't anyone sinister, she instructed assertively,

"Oh, thank goodness it's you lot. Get inside, everybody."

Noah - a little rattled - stood to one side as the group ascended the steps. Visibly shaken, Cat accepted Aaron's hand for assistance, while Sam, as usual, stubbornly refused to take it. Tom and finally, Noah were the last through. Once their nerves had settled and Maggie had had a quick word with her dad, she began cautiously telling Noah of their real origins, and why they were all congregating together in the middle of the night. The others watched his reaction apprehensively, wondering if the revelation might scare him. Instead, he started nodding, in an attempt to comprehend their situation, and let out an audible sigh of relief.

"I could not have dreamed of such an explanation," he said. "Forsooth, I tarried with my thoughts back and forth, as to thy intentions."

"You believe us?" said Sam in surprise. If the situation had been reversed, and someone in the 2000s had told her they'd travelled through a portal from the Middle Ages, she would have laughed in their face. But as Noah pointed out, the evidence corroborated their story: a group of strangers turning up out of the blue in his stables, speaking eccentrically, and introducing unique inventions like hamburgers and hoopball. Not to mention the outlandish objects he'd found in the hidden bag. Although mind-blowing to process, the likelihood of these newcomers coming from the future, now seemed entirely within the realm of possibility.

"Yea, indeed I do; pray tell me more, so I can grapple with my understanding."

Jack didn't need to be asked twice, enthusiastically diving into vivid descriptions of cars, planes and space shuttles.

"Whoa," said Maggie, gently reprimanding her son, "that's too much for Noah to take in right away. Perhaps just some of the basics to start with, like hot water, electric lights, and supermarkets."

The atmosphere warmed with everyone offering titbits of information, and feeling a huge sense of relief that Noah wasn't going to publicly denounce them as some sort of evil entity. Noah, in turn, glowed with the trust his new friends were granting him. Having lost his wife and son, his devotion had transferred into steadfast loyalty for the Baron. And while he appreciated his sire's generosity, there were occasions when he craved kinship. Like a lone wolf in the woods, he sometimes yearned to be part of a pack. Trying to take in the chatter and laughter that surrounded him now, he felt accepted and included - a fine feeling indeed. The buzz of excitement slowed to more serious matters, as Maggie described their process of travelling back in time, but how they'd been unable to replicate the conditions to return.

"In some way, I am glad," said Noah, "for your early vanishment would have created upset."

"Not merely for myself," he clarified, noting all eyes were on Maggie. "The Baron and Egbert are fond of thee fellows," he said to Harry, Tom and Frankie, "and I have heard of Maid Marian's sway with the kitchen girls."

"It's actually Samantha, not Marian," said Sam, putting her hand up.

"Frankie here," said her companion, jumping on the bandwagon and raising his hand too.

"And Harry," continued the roll call. "It's complicated."

"Ist thou even a friar?" asked Noah.

"No," admitted Harry, "but I do love horses."

"Nor an archer?" Noah queried, turning back to Frankie.

"Hardly old chap," said Frankie, taking an arrow out of his quiver to reveal a rubber suction tip at the end instead of a sharp point. Firing it across the room, the arrow hit the wall with a dull thwack, making the shaft judder on impact.

Everyone collapsed into hysterics at the ridiculousness of it all.

As the night progressed, Harry recited the poem once more, and they watched as absolutely nothing happened; again scratching their heads. Tired from the emotional roller coaster and unsuccessful escape plan, all but four returned to the manor. But the discussion between those in the tunnel on their way back was hopeful. Now that they had a real medieval person within their fold, he might offer a different perspective to their plight and, in time, see what they obviously couldn't.

Not that they had much time anymore...

"C'mon, Noah," Maggie said, taking him by the hand. "Let's go to the stables, and I'll explain what our bag of goodies are."

Looking over her shoulder at Harry and Jack, she said, "I'll be back soon, guys."

They took the short walk outside to the stables, rather than use the tunnel again. Sitting on the hay bale that Sebastian had previously lounged on, Maggie went through the items they had hidden.

"These hold water," she said, showing him the bottles, "and the snazzy lid keeps the liquid in until you want a sip. In our time, we don't need wells and buckets. Our water is taken from its source by a series of pipes and filtered, so it is safe to drink. Those pipes end up in our houses and finish with what we call a tap. So we can fill the bottles and take them with us to use whenever we get thirsty. We can even chill the water in a refrigerator - like a big cupboard that has an icing mechanism." She also told him about toilets, drawing a picture in the dirt on the floor with her finger, explaining that pipes were again used to remove the waste, and that people washed their hands afterwards to improve hygiene. She briefly touched on how simple practises had changed over the years to prevent sicknesses like cholera and dysentery.

"Egads," said Noah, fascinated, "and these?" He pointed to the two digital watches.

"Timepieces," advised Maggie. "I won't go into the mechanics of how they work, but they're like miniature clocks you wear on your wrist."

Noah picked up Harry's reading glasses.

"Ah, I have seen eyeglasses afore," he said, putting them on his nose. "But by cripes, what power!"

Maggie laughed.

"And these trinkets?" he asked, scooping up Sam's jewellery.

"Earrings and suchlike. You wear them as a fashion statement, like a necklace or bracelet."

"But how do the prongs serve?" he queried, touching his finger to the protruding pins.

"You pierce your skin, and put them through like this."

She demonstrated, guiding an earring through the hole in her ear and attaching the butterfly to the back. He looked appalled that humans would deliberately impale themselves for the sake of wearing a piece of metal. Maggie laughed again, taking the earring out to show it didn't hurt.

"Then there's our phones," she added, retrieving hers. "Probably the most evolved and useful thing of our time. They were only invented thirty years ago. Well, you know, my thirty years ago. They need charging...err... power to work, so I can't show you, but in these tiny handheld gadgets lies access to so much information and the ability to communicate with anyone, anywhere in the world.

"Zounds, it does sound like witchery."

"I know. That's why we needed to keep them hidden. People wouldn't understand in this era. But it's not black magic. It's creative inventions and the progression of technology that constantly improves. You think about what changes have been made in your lifetime that the previous generation wouldn't have been able to comprehend. Imagine what develops over six or seven centuries."

Noah nodded thoughtfully. "In two score years and ten, I have seen the Black Death, poverty, famine and conflicts. A king no older than your boy. But also advancement by way of agriculture and farming, building techniques, and healing elixirs. Despair and betterment are friends who often travel together, I feel."

Maggie was touched by his philosophical view of the world. Rivers ran deep with this man.

"Do you mind me asking, Noah, what happened to your wife?"

Noah gazed into the distance as if the image of his spouse might appear on the horizon.

"Her name was Eleanor, and she was a fine woman. We escaped the plague by coming to the country, but not the coughs and sneezes from people we met on the way. I believe they called Eleanor's condition tuberculosis."

"Oh, I'm so sorry," commiserated Maggie, putting her hand on his.

"'Twas troubling times, but Baron Buford took in myself and young son, Henry, and gave us work and shelter. I fought the French in days gone by and Henry followed after me. Lo, I returned to England in one piece...mostly...," he semi-joked, while lifting his head to reveal the scar from chin to collar-bone.

Maggie's hand unconsciously went to her mouth in shock, but she stopped it en route and instead, reached out with her fingers, gently touching his neck in sympathy. Noah quickly lowered his head again, not wanting to make a big deal of his injury and disconcerted by his internal reaction to her touch.

"By some miracle, I survived. Alas, I know not what hath become of Henry."

Maggie contemplated what it must be like to be in Noah's shoes. For all the nuisances of the contemporary world like commute times, leaky pipes, and VAT, they were nothing in comparison to the hardships of the 14th century. Noah patted the top of her hand congenially, not wanting the conversation to be weighed down by seriousness. They continued to talk about each other's lives. Noah, naturally, had a multitude of questions.

"In the 21st century, are there no wars?"

"I wish I could say there weren't, but the human race hasn't changed much in that regard. There always seems to be something to fight about. And the weapons are more destructive. No swords, but a man can be killed by the press of a button."

"I don't mean a decorative one," she added, noting his confusion, "something far more lethal. It depends on where you live, though. England now is pretty peaceful. We're even friends with France."

Noah arched his eyebrows at this disclosure.

"And it's easy to visit other nations in our time, with the flying machines Jack was describing. I've just realised, you don't even know about America being discovered."

"Who is America?" Noah asked.

"Not who," chuckled Maggie, "but what. It's a very big, powerful country. They speak English - well, sort of - but have their own customs. I've been there. I think you'd like the Midwest. Lots of horses in that area."

"And what is life like for thee?"

"Busy, but I like it. I run my own business and work in a hospital. Umm ... a building where they look after the sick and injured. Doctors and nurses tend to the ill, and scientific research means people live much longer. There's no plague and no smallpox anymore. Even tuberculosis is treatable."

"Intriguing."

"Jack goes to school nearby. Most children can read and write. He's studying the 1300s now. That's why we're dressed like this. These costumes were for the fair he had at his school." Maggie briefly bent her head in sorrow; the longing for her normal life suddenly hitting hard. More than a pat this time, Noah put his hand firmly on hers and left it there.

"Life for thee, is there," he said understandingly. She nodded.

"But Jack's father is absent? Deceased? Forgive me, I do not mean to pry."

"It's a long story," said Maggie, not for a moment intending to elaborate on her unique foray into motherhood. "But not a sad one. We are happy, just the two of us."

"For now," said Noah, "when Jack is no longer a lad and makes his own way, what then? Are there no gentleman suitors?" He dropped eye contact with this last comment, not completely sure he wanted to know the answer.

"No gentleman suitors," replied Maggie coyly. "I have family and friends nearby. And my work. And there are things I plan to do when I'm not responsible for Jack anymore, like travelling."

"By thyself?"

"Naturally, it would be nice to have a companion, but in our time, it's not necessary to be part of a couple. Women, especially, are free to do what they choose."

She could see Noah's cogs ticking over, and hoped he wasn't too overwhelmed with all the information he'd received tonight. He was reassuringly accepting of their bizarre circumstances. Far from scoffing at what sounded like outrageous scenarios, he had quietly taken it all in to mull over. She wondered, with his open-minded outlook on life and curiosity for the truth, if he was better suited to modern times than the restrictive ways of the past. Suddenly remembering the Peasants Revolt was due soon, and not knowing how Noah would fare in the skirmishes, she impulsively asked him a question of her own.

"Noah, are you happy here? It's just that, if you weren't, you could always come back with us."

He was caught off guard by her candour, and wasn't sure how to respond. The estate was all he knew. He was comfortable tending to the horses, and indebted to the Baron for providing the necessities of life. Admittedly an introvert, he didn't see solitude as an enemy. He had, however, valued the company of these outsiders, and felt their insights and outspokenness had brought out the best in him. This year's festivities had been the most enjoyable yet. He would miss his new friends once they were gone. And Maggie in particular.

His deliberate, unspoken understatement did little to conquer the dread he was trying to keep at bay. In truth, he feared there would be a substantial hole in his heart when Maggie returned home, but could he leave his entire life behind to follow her to the 21st century? That was a big ask.

Because he couldn't give an answer - and with the rhythmic pitter-patter of rain on the roof adding to the ambience - his gallantry deserted him, and giving in to his instincts, Noah leaned towards Maggie for a kiss. She intuitively understood his dilemma and was not complaining about the response. She, too, felt the moment was right and softly kissed him back. He closed his eyes as their lips pressed together - his mouth slowly and seductively parting hers open; tentatively exploring with his tongue to elicit the passion he suspected they were both trying to suppress. Complying willingly, she ran her hands up his arms and along the breadth of his shoulders; her fingers skimming across taut muscles, and reaching the nape of his neck, then tousling his hair. The physical intimacy and rush of endorphins made her spine tingle - a sensation she hadn't felt in years. In a similar heightened state, Noah's long laid dormant desire came alive with a vengeance. He wrapped his arms around her torso and hungrily pulled her close, feeling the contours of her body crush against his chest - not a modicum of space left between them. She yielded to his strength as his kisses became more insistent; the stubble on his chin roughly grazing hers. Body against body, mouth against mouth; longing, yearning, craving. The world tilted on its axis for an instant, but suddenly and just as intentionally, he released her from his embrace - his breathing ragged and coarse. Afraid that he'd overstepped the mark, Noah got to his feet and apologised, politely suggesting they return to their separate sleeping quarters. Maggie stood up too, facing him square on, and held his hands again like she had in the forest.

"It's OK, Noah, really it is, but you're right, it has been an eventful night."

She'd felt the intensity of the moment too and knew he'd retreated because he wanted to remain a gentleman. Probably just as well, she thought, as she wasn't sure she had the willpower to resist, anyway. And if they'd acted on their impulses, it would only be more painful when they inevitably went their separate ways.

More than likely, the evening had overloaded him. She shouldn't have suggested he leave his life here. It was selfish of her and, realistically, could cause all sorts of complications. As she'd told Hayley, she didn't need a man to fulfil her life, and even if she did, it was an absurd notion for it to be someone she'd only just met. What was she thinking? She squeezed Noah's hands and said she would see him in the morning.

Outside, even though the rain was heavier, and the night was colder, a contented smile formed on her lips as she deliberated over the way the evening had turned out. In the rectory, Maggie found Jack and Harry top and tailing in bed, fast asleep - emotionally exhausted from the happenings of today. She made herself comfortable on a chair and stroked Bronny's ears, who'd lay down beside her. For the first time in a long while, she felt soothed and nourished. What was it about Noah that gave her butterflies when he was near, and feel incomplete when he was not? She'd gotten used to his old English way of speaking, and detected under the medieval prose, he was methodical and thoughtful like her. He appeared to be genuinely interested in her life and happy to talk, even though she wondered if she was too direct at times. Not one for diplomatic niceties, Maggie tended to get straight to the point, but Noah rallied back with easy exchange and intelligent conversation, making her feel relevant. There was a subtle strength and independence about him that seemed to complement, not overshadow, her own. Not to mention the inherent masculinity that had certainly shown itself tonight.

But for goodness' sake, girl - she said to herself - you're living in a fairy tale, and this is a welcome distraction to alleviate your anxiety about being stuck in a foreign world. That's all he is - a distraction. Get a grip!

Noah, too, attempted to settle in for the night, but his head hurt from trying to soak up everything he'd heard. Travellers from the future, a land with mechanical transport, and cures for all types of maladies. Even chilled water in abundance! It truly boggled the mind. And he didn't know what to make of Maggie's invitation at the end. He'd known this woman but for a trice, yet she was firmly entrenched in his thoughts. With his body aching in agreement, he doubted that sleep would be easy tonight.

CHAPTER 9

Thursday 23 December

THE WEATHER WAS AS expected: heavy rain turning the snow into slush. Those at the end of the field arrived at breakfast in various states of dishevelment. Harry's heavy robe with hood gave him some protection, but Noah, Maggie and Jack decided to make a run for it; all holding hands and laughing as they splashed through puddles. Sam heard them, and standing behind one of the columns at the entrance, discreetly took a Polaroid snap as they reached the manor. That was a goodie, she thought, smoothing her pocket down as she hid the camera away. Despite the answer to the riddle remaining a mystery, everyone was feeling positive; largely because they had been able to share their secret with Noah, and didn't feel they were deceiving him anymore.

After breakfast, Jack joined the other children to decorate the Christmas tree Egbert had installed in the entrance, adding to the hall's stately splendour. Aaron and Josh were working away in the study, putting together an era-appropriate version of bingo. Understanding that some of the attendees would be numerically challenged, they drew simple pictures of various animals, food, and tools of the age, in a grid on parchment paper. Then duplicated the drawings onto stones; mixing them up in a bowl. Instead of bingo, they were calling the game Hoorah, in honour of the Baron's usual catch cry, whenever he made an endorsement of something he liked.

Harry and Noah stayed in the banquet hall after breakfast, sitting close to the open fire. Partly to dry out their wet clothes and partly to get some privacy to talk. The latter didn't last long as the Baron soon came to join them. Not that they had any objection to his inclusion. He was good company and had plenty of stories to tell. The warmth of the flames and camaraderie made for a casual and carefree climate, completely devoid of rancour, with Sebastian sleeping late elsewhere. Bronny and his spaniel friend lay curled up by their feet, taking advantage of the heat emanating from the hearth; blissfully unaware of what date it was.

By contrast, Egbert was running around like a headless chicken, making sure arrangements for the masquerade ball that night, and final activities for the next day were in place; the Yuletide Celebrations coming to an end tomorrow. The exhibition chariot race was set to run in the morning, followed by the annual investiture, also conducted in the entertainment arena, where everyone would already be assembled. Every year, Baron Buford had the option to bestow a knighthood on whomever he felt was deserving of the honour. Sometimes he did and sometimes he didn't, so the ceremony wasn't a guaranteed occurrence. But rumour had it, he definitely had someone in mind this year. Afterwards, the week of festivities would culminate with its last event: the highly anticipated polo match. Noah would captain one team and Sir Sebastian the other. That should be interesting, thought Egbert.

Cat and Tom were in their bedroom, together with Sam and Frankie, comparing the intricately bejewelled masks each had been given for the ball that night. Maggie shared their admiration but didn't have a mask of her own, as invitations were for the aristocracy only. Not that she minded. She'd heard the Baron was breaking with tradition this year, and while the gentry were dancing in the ballroom, a second soiree would be held in the kitchen for the staff and serfs of the estate. Noah wasn't a noble either, and she would much rather be there with him.

After lunch, the established cliques of people that joined together in the morning split up and merged into different groups, like the unpicking and reattaching of broken chain-mail. Tom wanted a second opinion on the idea he'd been sharing with Baron Buford and called upon his son.

"But I'm doing the bingo calls with Aaron," Josh protested.

"I'm sure your sister can take over that role, can't you, Sam?"

"I suppose," said Sam, seemingly reluctant, but secretly pleased that an opportunity had arisen to delay the necessity of getting dolled up for a ball she didn't want to go to, anyway. Aaron was agreeable to the alternative pairing and showed her what he and Josh had created. Josh followed his father into the study and respectfully bowed to their host.

"Ah, my boy," greeted the Baron, "I thank thee for thy presence. Thomas here tells me thou hath a good head for mathematics, too."

Egbert arrived soon after, somewhat flustered as he had so much to do. But the Baron had requested his attendance, citing it as an important meeting, and by the tone of his master's voice, Egbert knew better than to try and get out of it. He was summoned to the table, where all manner of drawings and calculations were laid out for discussion.

Harry offered to fill in for Egbert while he was indisposed, and with the Christmas tree looking dazzling in the entrance, he turned to supervising the decoration and transformation of the banquet hall, in readiness for the ball. Floors were polished and windows were cleaned. Flower pots containing pansies, cyclamen and winter jasmine supplanted the usual plain ferns and grasses. Sprigs of holly, mistletoe and decorative candles were placed around the outside of the room, leaving the middle to operate as a bingo hall for the time being. It was all looking very elegant.

"Bingo's not my jam, Mum," complained Jack, pausing at the door, "it's for old people."

"Cheeky bugger," said Maggie, pretending to be offended.

Noah - about to feed his horses - heard Jack, and as there was a brief break in the weather, asked if he wanted to help him with the fodder, and the tidying up of the arena from the children's games yesterday.

"Can I?" asked Jack enthusiastically.

Maggie consented, "OK then, I'll go in with the others. If my decrepit old bones can get me there," she joked.

Noah and Jack laughed, and off they went like old mates who'd known each other forever. Maggie watched them leave, taking pleasure in the way they'd bonded.

Aaron and Sam stood at the front of the room, explaining to the guests how bingo worked. Maggie, Cat, Harry and Frankie split themselves up, sitting at different tables to help people understand this new game. While they waited for the general chitter-chatter to die down, Sam asked Aaron about the calling out.

"I guess we can't do the normal stuff. You know: *'Knock at the Door, number 4, Clickety Click, 66'*, cos we're not using numbers. So what do we say instead?"

"Make it up as you go along," he replied. "You can see the pictures we've drawn on the paper and pebbles, so link them with something that rhymes." He picked up a pebble with a picture of a pheasant on it, to use as an example.

"Lucky peasant, caught a pheasant."

"Oh, OK," said Sam, thinking this might be fun after all, and selecting a pebble on which a pig had been drawn.

"Not too big, this little pig," she suggested.

"That's it!" said Aaron, stoked that she was getting into it, and not her usual cantankerous self. The game began, and as the kitchen staff were serving drinks throughout, it didn't take long for the room to turn into a cacophony of noise. Chuckles became howls of laughter, and it was a wonder anyone could hear the increasingly inventive calls from the front.

"A spinster's lot, pan and pot," shouted Aaron, nudging Sam as if it had some relevance to her.

Feigning outrage, she followed with, "Ignore the buffoon, find a spoon."

He carried on, "Don't ask me how, such a cow."

Thoroughly enjoying herself, Sam whispered to her co-host,

"Pity we don't have a duck."

Aaron guffawed loudly at her remark. Sam laughed with him, pleased that he'd immediately understood her sassy insinuation. Maggie and Cat looked across the tables at each other, then back at Aaron and Sam; not exchanging any words, but knowing exactly what the other was thinking

It was Sam's turn, "Off with his head, for stealing the bread."

"Hoorah!!!" came the cry from the back. One of the ladies she'd seen in the drawing room yesterday waved one hand in the air, while pointing to her completed card with the other. Sam ran to her table, checked the card, and confirmed she had won. There were cries of 'Again' from the rest of the room, so Sam skipped back to Aaron, mixed up the pebbles, and they started from the beginning.

AT THE STABLES, NOAH and Jack fed and watered the horses.

"I know this one is called Perfect Grace," said Jack, patting the palomino. "What about the other horses?"

Noah stroked the nose of a lean, strong stallion with silky black hair.

"This is Carbonel, which means black coal."

"And this is Pegasus," he continued, feeding a horse with a coat the colour of white marshmallow."

"Like the winged horse from Greek mythology?"

"That is so," confirmed Noah, impressed by the child's knowledge.

"And this fine filly is Autumn Haze," he said, turning to a beautiful chestnut-coloured horse with a white blaze down her nose.

"Mum would like that one," commented Jack. "Autumn is her favourite season. She loves the colours of the leaves at that time of year - all the reds and rusts and golds."

Noah looked thoughtful. Another simple thing he shared with Maggie. It was his favourite season too, for similar reasons. He often wandered through the forest in September and October, when the skies were clear and the trees provided a kaleidoscope of orange hues. It made him feel as if he were part of an oil painting; his silhouette small in comparison to the majesty of nature.

"And the horse has the same colour hair as Mum," Jack observed.

Noah had noted that too, but thought his daydreaming about Maggie and her soft red tresses might be best left for another time.

"Let's tarry not, young Jack. By my lead, we shall scale the hill and see what remains of yesterday's fun."

Together they hauled the tug-of-war rope to the stables and removed the sticks that had been used as goalposts. Then they split up, collecting bits and pieces on the ground that were in danger of getting stuck in horses' hooves the next day. Noah didn't mind leaving the hoops where they were, as they wouldn't impede the chariot race. Lastly, on their way back down the hill, they pulled out the sign for the Children's Fayre, adding it to the rest of the equipment in the storehouse. They returned to the manor just before it started raining again.

"Noah!" called out Tom, inviting him into the study to include him in the discussion with the Baron.

"Jack!" Maggie shouted, beckoning her son to join her.

She, Cat, Frankie and Harry sat together now, as the other guests had learnt how to play the game without assistance. Aaron and Sam were still going. Running out of inspirational calls, Sam noticed her cousin's arrival and waved to him,

"Jack's back. Hessian sack," she said triumphantly.

Jack waved back and sat down. She looked unusually happy, he thought.

"How'd ya go, kiddo?" asked Harry.

"Good," replied Jack. "We fed the horses and picked up stuff. Noah's dope."

"Aunty Cat," he continued, in a tone preceding a question, "you know the sign that was up yesterday? Why does it say Children's Fayre spelt with a y, when we know it as Children's Fair with an i? It was the same at school, too."

Willingly switching to her teacher persona, Cat responded,

"It's an alternative way of spelling from the different ages. I wrote it as 'fayre' back home to give it a more authentic feel. As you can see, that's how it's written in real life here. It still means the same thing, but words can change over the years, and now we spell it f.a.i.r."

"English is confusing," said Jack, shaking his head.

"You're right," agreed Cat. "I hate to say it, but French and many other languages are a lot easier. The English language has words that are spelt differently, but mean the same, like fayre and fair or gaol and jail. Then some sound the same, but mean different things like their, there, and they're..."

"I still get those wrong," Jack confessed to his grandfather.

"You and me both," said Harry.

"...or words that are spelt the same but have different meanings, like minute as in time and minute as in small..."

Cat continued the lesson, and while Jack was still listening, Harry suddenly went quiet. He was staring off into the distance and watching the last piece of an imaginary jigsaw slot into place.

"That's it!" he shouted.

People looked around, and someone called out,

"You have to say Hoorah if you've got them all."

"No, sorry," said Harry, "my mistake, carry on."

Then he leaned across the table to kiss Cat on the cheek.

"What's that for?" she asked.

"You've solved it, Catherine," he said excitedly. "It's all in the spelling; you said so yourself."

Cat and Maggie looked at each other, slightly bewildered. Jack just shrugged, as teenagers do.

"The spelling, girls. Of the poem. On the door." The penny had suddenly dropped so hard Harry was having trouble getting his words out.

"Dad, what are you talking about?" said Maggie, worried that the stress of the situation was getting to her father.

"The last line," persisted Harry. "It's not *Seeketh day's end and return with the night.* It's *Seeketh day's end and return with the knight!*"

His voice croaked, hoarse with insistence.

"With a K!" he said, frantically drawing the shape of the letter in the air with his finger to emphasise his point.

"What makes you think that?" asked Cat, still confused.

"Because," Harry replied, feeling like Hercule Poirot summarising the ending to one of Agatha Christie's whodunits, "Sir Sebastian was there last night. Drunk in the stables, while I was reciting the verse from the rectory. That's when the door lit up. While he was in the other building connected to the chapel by the tunnel. When he went outside - away from the building - it stopped working. His presence in the stables made the difference. He's the knight. He is the key to our return!"

Harry continued his explanation.

"And I think 'days end' refers to the end of our time in these days, not that we have to return at nightfall. Which means, as long as we can get Sebastian to float around in close proximity to the trapdoor when we're all gathered together, it should work, whatever time of day."

Cat and Maggie looked completely dumbstruck, their mouths agape. Jack said nothing but high-fived his grandad. Frankie was the one to break the silence with an appropriate quote for the epiphany:

"By George, I think he's got it!"

They moved to the drawing room to talk more in private. With the rest of their group still busy and unable to be interrupted, the five of them hashed out what they could do with their important discovery.

"So Sebastian has to be in the stables or the chapel for the rhyme to work?" asked Maggie, double-checking she understood correctly.

"That's right," confirmed Harry. "The tunnel connects the two buildings, so I'm pretty sure the magic works either way. We need to get him there under some false pretence at the same time as the rest of us, without arousing his suspicions."

"How do we do that?" said Cat.

"He likes Sam," contributed Jack.

"Does he?" Cat asked. "How do you know?"

"When we finished riding yesterday, he turned up from the forest, got off his horse and kissed her hand straightaway."

Frankie nodded in agreement. "That's right, he made a beeline for her last night too, when he was smashed."

"Yeah," said Jack, "he's a bit of a creep."

"But that could be useful," suggested Maggie, "if she was able to sweet talk him down the other end of the field."

"Oh," said Cat, not sure she wanted her daughter to be bait for that letch.

"They'll both be at the ball tonight," said Maggie, her mind formulating a plan, "and you guys will be there to keep an eye on things."

"He'll probably get wasted again," said Jack with a sneer.

"Yes," said Harry, "and we'll be separated; some in the ballroom and some in the kitchen. It could be problematic, trying to coordinate a hasty departure for nine, whilst luring a drunken boor to go with us in that environment."

Maggie considered this for a moment and then said,

"What if Sam used the ball tonight to have a dance with him, suggesting they meet in the stables tomorrow morning after the chariot race? People will be milling around anyway, so we'd be safer to hide in broad daylight, rather than trying to make a break for it tonight."

"But tomorrow is literally Christmas Eve!" exclaimed Cat. "Isn't that leaving it til the last minute?"

"We have all day, Catherine," said Harry, placating his daughter. "Plenty of wiggle room if there are any hiccups. But I don't see why there would be. We know the answer now."

"I'm still not sure about using Sam to tempt Sebastian," said Cat nervously. "She doesn't even want to go to the ball tonight, let alone flirt with a..."

"Douchebag," volunteered Jack.

Harry sniggered and winked at his grandson.

"Don't encourage him, Dad," scolded Maggie, but Frankie was also affirming Jack's estimation, slapping his hand and saying,

"Damn, you know it, dude!" - his opinion of Sebastian, as low as Jack's.

Aaron and Sam were feeling pretty chipper. The afternoon's fun and games had wound up, and having successfully introduced bingo to the Middle Ages and won the people over, Aaron was keen to tell Josh how well it had gone. He headed upstairs while Sam stopped by the drawing room to join her family.

"What are you guys gabbing about?" she teased. "My ears were burning."

"You're not wrong there," replied Maggie, laying out the plan to her.

"Uh-uh, no way!" protested Sam. "I'm not cosying up to that dick."

"But it might be our only chance, love," said Harry gently. "You don't need to do anything, just convince him to meet you tomorrow morning. Perhaps tell him you'll be in the stables, but instead, we'll be in the chapel. Once we see him go inside, I can quickly recite the pöem. The light will appear, and we'll scoot down the tunnel, open the other door, and be back in the 21st century before you know it."

"But, Mum..." Sam pleaded.

"I know," sympathised Cat. "I'm not happy about it either. I can see why he fancies you, though. Your beautiful copper-coloured hair looks gorgeous when it's not tied back."

"Actually..." Cat looked thoughtful, then impulsively turned to Maggie.

"You do it Maggie. Instead of Sam."

"What?" said Maggie, confused.

"It's a masquerade ball, so your face will be hidden. You have the same hair colour and build as Sam. You could swap dresses and go to the ball in her place."

"Oooh, I like your thinking, Mum," egged on Sam, seeing a way out of not just flirting with Sebastian, but attending the ball altogether.

"Now wait a minute," said Maggie, putting her hand up in a stop position.

"No, you could do it, Aunt Maggie," said Sam. "I didn't speak to Sebastian either time he approached me, so he doesn't know my voice. You and I are pretty much the same height and build, and we're both redheads."

"And fiery and stubborn," added Frankie impishly.

Harry looked over at Maggie and shrugged in a 'why not' way.

"You're a grown woman, Margaret; you can handle this guy. Surely that's better than sending in your vulnerable niece."

"Hmmpph," scoffed Maggie, "I would hardly call Sam vulnerable. She's perfectly capable of looking after herself."

Sam dramatically put the back of her hand on her forehead, and with a superfluous Southern American accent, cried, "Oh, mercy me, Miss Maggie, please come to my aid."

Then, reverting to her normal voice and reaching into her pocket, she continued.

"Oh, and I forgot. When I was looking in the bag in the tunnel for old times' sake - I mean new times' sake - I grabbed your perfume. I sprayed some on my wrist and I know Sebastian smelt it. That would seal the deal, as it were," she smirked.

"But... you've forgotten two things," said Maggie, "A: I'm old, and B: My hair is straight while yours is curly, so that would give the game away."

"Aww, honey," commiserated Frankie. "You're only as old as the man that you feel, and besides, the mask will cover your wrinkles."

"Charming," said Maggie, as the others snickered.

"And as far as your hair goes - did somebody call my name? Cinderella, get thy butt upstairs and let the transformation begin. You shall go to the ball!"

Cat clapped her hands together, happily drawing the discussion to a close.

"Well, that's settled then. The boys are still in their meeting with the Baron, I think, but we'll fill them in on the details later. One more sleep, ladies and gentlemen, and then we're off home."

Cat reached out to grab Maggie's hand as they stood to go upstairs.

"Thank you," she said gratefully.

"I hope this works," Maggie said warily, quietly terrified about getting her game face on. She hadn't chatted anybody up in years. It was different with Noah. Their relationship had blossomed organically and hadn't felt forced. Then it dawned on her she wouldn't see him this evening, as she wasn't going to be at the kitchen party as intended.

"Dammit," she muttered, that hadn't occurred to her before. Nonetheless, they could still walk down the field together at the end of the night. A bittersweet thought that gave her comfort on the one hand, as she imagined linking arms with him again and feeling his body close to hers, but also sadness on the other, that tonight was probably their last opportunity to be alone together.

CHAPTER 10

Thursday night 23 December

In the bedroom upstairs, Frankie got to work. The manor staff had lit the fire earlier, so the room was lovely and warm. He picked up a poker and held it in the flames until the steel turned red from the heat. Seating Maggie on a high-backed chair, he pulled her hair loose from the bun she had worn it in since dressing up on Monday. He let it flow down the back of the chair, keeping it a good distance from the flesh on her neck. This was going to be a delicate procedure, and he did not want any scorching incidents. He picked up the poker in one hand, and a long toothed comb made of bone, in the other. With patience and precision, he took a section of Maggie's hair, curling it around the hot poker and leaving it there, just long enough to bend the tresses into waves, similar to Sam's style.

Completely in his comfort zone, Frankie's artistry came to the fore, and Maggie relaxed into it. There was a gentle rap on the door, already slightly ajar. The lady who had won the bingo game asked if she could come in. She was looking for Sam to thank her for a wonderful afternoon, and saw what they were doing.

"Forgive me, but pray, may I inquire as to the nature of thy work?"

"He's curling her hair," explained Sam.

"My, my," exclaimed the lady with her hand on her heart. "A wondrous sight. Wouldst thou be able to fashion my hair alike?"

"Sure," said Sam, "why not? But come back a little later if you would."

The lady bowed her head in understanding, leaving them alone; and so began Frankie Cooper's fan club. Word travelled fast. Once he'd finished creating Maggie's new hairdo, she and the girls moved to Cat's room to get ready for the ball. Within minutes, Frankie found himself with a queue of women outside in the hallway, waiting for his services.

Next door, Maggie swapped dresses with Sam, put her masquerade mask on, and dabbed some of the perfume behind her ears and on her wrists. Likewise, Sam pulled on Maggie's frock, totally comfortable wearing servant's clothes, as that meant she could go to the kitchen tonight instead of the ball, and hang out with Ivy again. Copying her aunt's style, she put her hair up in a bun, and the metamorphosis was complete. Tom walked in the door and did a double take at the sight of his daughter and sister-in-law. Cat took him to one side to report on their finding of today, and the subsequent plan to put it into action. On the other side of the landing, Josh returned to his room and found Aaron quietly grinning to himself.

"What's up with you?" he asked.

"Oh, nothing," said Aaron, forcibly adopting a neutral expression. "I was just pleased that our bingo game worked so well today."

"That's cool," said Josh, "I hope Sam wasn't too much of a pain"

"Nah," said Aaron, his grin returning, "she was good, actually."

Josh looked at his friend, somewhat perplexed, but chose not to push it.

"Obviously, I would have rather been having fun with you guys, but the meeting with the Baron was pretty important. Dad's got a great plan for the estate," he said, proceeding to elaborate while they got ready for the ball, too. Embracing the festive fever that was beginning to envelop the manor, the boys donned their masks - black and sleek - always keen to dress up for the fun of it. Not yet briefed on today's breakthrough and the deception that was about to transpire, they casually sauntered towards the stairs and noticed the queue of ladies outside the room across the landing. One woman came out, patting her new curls, evidently very happy with the result.

"Oh God, looks like Frankie's hairdressing again," laughed Josh. "Well, if he's going to be late, and Sam comes down by herself, you'll have to dance with her. It'd be weird if I did it, being her brother and all."

"Sure, bro," said Aaron.

There's that grin again, noted Josh. What the hell was up with his mate?

The Baron was still in the study, and now that he and Noah were alone, he sought the stable master's confidence.

"What doth thou think of Lord Thomas's proposal?" he asked. "He is insistent that it will make the estate more convivial, and quell any thoughts of unrest."

Noah nodded his head slowly. Aware that the yet-to-be-called Peasants Revolt was fast approaching, he knew there was a likely connection between one of the manor workers and the ringleader in London. While it was in his future, it was already in Maggie and Catherine's past, and they had told him their history books had documented the downfall of Buford Estate.

"Tis an unusual suggestion to move yon the feudal system," the Baron continued. "I trust thee, my friend. Should we have concerns?"

He looked at Noah in such a way to imply he had guessed there were things not being said, that the stable master might be privy to.

"Aye, Sir," confirmed Noah, "I too, have heard of a displeasing rumour. Tis conjecture, but we would be wise to do what we can, nay it becomes the truth."

He hoped that vague, but assertive, statement would be enough to convince Baron Buford to change direction in the handling of the peasants' affairs. Noah was keen to talk to Maggie about the future again, amongst other things, and was keenly anticipating her presence at the servants' soiree tonight.

Shortly thereafter, both shindigs got underway. A formal quartet of stringed instruments played traditional music in the ballroom for waltzes and suchlike. In the kitchen, several mistrals provided up-tempo beats for the servants to dance to.

Noah went straight from the study to the kitchen, and chatted to the cooks, complimenting them on their food presentation. As people began trickling in, he observed the excitement of the lower class: manor staff, gardeners, milkmaids, woodcutters, farmers and everyone else who worked on the estate; eyes agog at the food, ale and music that was theirs for the taking. Never before had they indulged in any hospitality during the Yuletide Celebrations. They'd always been there to provide for the aristocracy, so this was a rare treat indeed. Ivy and the kitchen girls had always worked hard, but today, their invitation to the party tonight was great motivation to top the quality of any preceding meal. And they had done themselves proud, making lots of tasty dishes available. Even Mistress Edith had sung their praises. Officially off the clock now, Ivy couldn't wait to get started.

Suddenly, she squealed at the unexpected sight of Samantha entering the room. But what was she wearing? No longer a lady's dress but what looked like a servant's frock, and her normally free-flowing hair, tied up tightly in a bun on the top of her head. Not that Ivy cared. Samantha was like no other girl she had met. The energy around her always seemed boundless, and her frank way of speaking, simply fascinating; endearing her to anyone near. Apart from Mistress Edith. Ivy knew the kitchen supervisor thought Samantha's behaviour was unbecoming and interfering, but tonight was all about fun, so surely she'd go easy on her.

To his surprise, Noah saw Sam too. Why was she here? In Maggie's clothes, no less. Before he got the chance to ask her, she uttered an equally delighted squeal to see Ivy, and ran off in that direction. Jack followed in the slow strut that teenagers usually adopt, providing a second option for Noah's query,

"Where's your mother, Jack?" he asked.

"Oh, she and Sam have swapped, because Sam didn't want to go to the ball."

"And Maggie did?" Noah questioned.

"Yes," said Jack absently, breaking a small bun in two and giving one half to Bronny.

"She wanted to see Sir Sebastian or something."

"For what purpose?" pursued Noah. "I didn't think she'd even met him."

"Cos he's a knight," answered Jack, which made no sense to Noah at all. But Bronny was tugging on his lead to see his spaniel friend on the other side of the room, and dragged Jack away before he could get any clarification.

Noah's first feeling was disappointment. He had so wanted to spend the evening with Maggie. But that quickly turned to hurt, as it sounded like she had blithely chosen to go to the ball instead. Surely she wasn't interested in Sebastian simply because of his status. Maggie didn't seem that type. Unless their moment of intimacy had scared her off. She had made it very clear that in her day, women were independent, and it wasn't compulsory to pair up with a man. Or was this flippancy on her part? Achieving closeness with him and now seeing if she could work her charms on another. Noah realised he was getting angry.

Of all people.

If Maggie, for some reason, no longer wanted his company, he couldn't force things. But to court his rival was just too much. He'd suddenly lost his appetite.

In the ballroom, instead of noise and laughter, there were pleasant murmurings around the room. Lords, ladies, and knights showed the decorum expected from their class, and the respect that the Baron warranted. Not a hair out of place, the women glided into the room with poise befitting that of the gentry. The men courteously bowed; some politely asking for a dance. Moonbeams shone through the windows like strobe lights, casting white shards of translucence upon the doorway; ensuring every guest made a grand entrance. Josh and Aaron leant against a shelf that acted as a bar, talking to each other and drinking wine. Sebastian was at the other end, on his third ale already, but relatively quiet and happy to people-watch for the moment.

Then Tom, Cat and Maggie walked in, and all three men stood to attention.

Moving forward to welcome them, but mistakenly thinking she was Sam, Aaron bowed exaggeratedly, held his hand out to Maggie, and said,

"Might I have the pleasure?"

Caught off guard, Maggie uttered a small cry of "Oh", but before she could respond, Sebastian, in only a few long, determined strides, showed up by her side and took her hand out of Aaron's reach. Justifiably pissed off, and about to object, Aaron was equally surprised when Cat hastily put her hand in his, saying,

"I'd be delighted."

Not knowing what the heck was going on, he had no choice but to follow Cat onto the dance floor. Tom, seeing that Josh also needed to be distracted from the temptation to deck Sebastian, slapped his son on the back, and suggested they get another drink from the bar.

"Alone at last," said Sebastian, with an unapologetic smile, "and nary a showing of thy other half?"

"Err, no," said Maggie, sure that her voice was trembling. This was all happening way too fast. "He has some business matters."

"Excellent," leered Sebastian, "a dance with thee it is, then."

Whisked away with no chance of protest, and watching Cat watch her, Maggie shook off her nervousness, remembering what she was here to do. And that there was no option to fail, despite how much it repulsed her being a lure for a lothario like Sebastian. If this was what she had to endure to get everyone home tomorrow morning, then she would pull up her Bridget Jones knickers and get on with it.

Baron Buford made his way around the room, talking to his guests. Expecting them to leave at various times the next day, he wanted to make sure he articulated his thanks for their attendance of the games, lest he miss any goodbyes tomorrow. As the consummate host, he laughed at the men's jokes and complimented the ladies, remarking on a new trend of hairstyle that seemed to be popular.

Although Aaron was supposed to be leading, Cat engineered their way across the room to a dark corner. Aaron, already feeling uncomfortable to be dancing with Sam's mum, now looked positively embarrassed. And he couldn't help but notice that Sam was lapping up Sebastian's attentiveness, which, in turn, added to his puzzlement.

"It's not Sam," whispered Cat.

"What?"

"It's Maggie. Frankie curled her hair, so she looks like Sam."

"Why?"

"Harry worked out the riddle today. It's the spelling of the last word. We don't go back to the trapdoor with the night. We go with the knight!"

"Sebastian?"

"He's the only knight here, isn't he?"

"Josh and I are supposed to be knights."

"Yes, but you're not real ones, are you? The only battle you've fought in is Call of Duty on the Xbox."

"So what's Maggie doing?"

"Jack told us Sebastian had taken a shine to Sam, so she's pretending to be her, under the guise of seducing him into meeting up with her at the stables tomorrow morning."

"Eeeeeww!"

"I know, but she only has to set up the meeting. Then we'll sort it so that we're all in the chapel when he goes into the stables. Harry knows the poem off by heart and can say it straight away, the door will light up, and... Hey Presto. Besides, would you rather it was Sam playing the part of temptress?"

"No!" said Aaron a little too quickly.

"I thought not," said Cat, a knowing look on her face.

"How do you know this is going to work?" asked Aaron, getting back to the point.

"Because it happened last night. When Tom and Noah left Sebastian in the stables to sleep off his alcohol intake, Harry was reciting the verse. The door lit up, but he didn't make the connection until this afternoon."

"I see," said Aaron, understanding. "Alrighty then, that sounds very encouraging."

At the same time, Tom was relaying the identical information to Josh. His face, too, went from confusion to clarification, and he had to admire his aunt for taking one for the team.

"Well, I better rescue Aaron," he said. "You know Mum. I'm sure her explanation is twice as long as yours."

"Very likely," agreed Tom, "and as this might be the only chance I get, I think I'll ask my wife for a dance."

Sebastian's hand was planted firmly on Maggie's back, but gradually inched its way downwards. When it had travelled far enough for her to feel uncomfortable, Maggie reached behind her and moved it back up.

"You are a rapscallion," she said flirtatiously, wanting to be in control of the situation but also feigning her interest.

"And thou is positively captivating," Sebastian responded, his hand already beginning to move again.

Dear God, thought Maggie, how I must love my family.

Baron Buford finished his affable small talk in the ballroom and bid his temporary departure.

"I shall return anon," he waved to his guests. "There are words I must share with the rabble." It was a term of endearment, referring to those in the kitchen, and his noble guests tittered politely at the joke. Walking out of one doorway and across the hall to the other, the Baron bumped into Harry, intercepting his path to the kitchen.

"Friar Kenobi, thy timing is auspicious. Wouldst thou quieten the crowd on my behalf so they may listen to my speech?"

"My absolute pleasure," said Harry obligingly. Being held in high regard by the Baron and manor staff gave Harry a feeling of importance he hadn't had since he retired. Not that he wanted all that responsibility anymore, but he wished every senior citizen had the occasional opportunity to act as if still in their prime. The inquisitive children from his end of the field also looked at him with wonder and curiosity. In his late seventies, Harry understood that reaching this age was a rarity for the era. Surviving so many decades gave him an almost magical status, befitting of his Obi-Wan Kenobi alter ego.

Noah saw the two men enter the kitchen and walked directly towards Harry, hoping he could shed some light on Maggie's disappearing act. Harry saw and acknowledged Noah, but made signs with his hand that the conversation would have to wait, as the Baron's speech was more pressing. The Baron hoped he had timed it so the peasants were tipsy enough to be in a jovial mood, but not so drunk as to cause a ruckus. They stood at the front of the room, and Harry picked up one of the goblets, tapping a silver spoon against its side. It reminded him of when he'd done the same thing at Tom and Cat's wedding as father of the bride. Thankfully, he was only doing the introduction this evening, and didn't need to prepare for a whole monologue.

"Welcome all, guests of the Baron," he started, "we hope you are enjoying yourselves and glad to be out of the inclement weather."

There was an effusive cheer from the crowd.

"May I ask you to hush a little, so that your host can speak of glad tidings to come."

The noise died down instantaneously; everyone facing forward to hear what the Baron had to say.

"Thank you, Brother," Baron Buford said, nodding in appreciation.

"Good evening, everyone. Hearken, one and all, with good news to come! Such is the success of this year's festivities, a proposal has been thought upon and agreed to. The games will not only be held at Christmas, but become a seasonal event, occurring four times thusly in one year."

There were sounds of consternation, as this could only mean more work for the peasants. How was this glad tidings or good news? But Baron Buford had predicted their reaction, and spoke at speed to reassure.

"Yea, though the preparations will be fourfold annually, there will be rewards aplenty."

Those complaining to each other stopped mid-sentence, to give the Baron a chance. He glanced at Noah for support, who duly stepped forward and stood beside his master. People settled down a bit. Seeing Noah - one of them - standing approvingly by the Baron's side, made them want to hear more. The Baron coughed and continued.

"From New Year's Day, all workers will be designated a small portion of the estate to become landowners."

His audience gasped. Were they hearing correctly?

"Thee hath the right to cut timber in the woods to build dwellings for thy families."

Another gasp.

"And no taxes will be sought for this."

There were cries of disbelief once more, but this time with elation, not sorrow. Harry raised his hand to request calm again.

"Loyal subjects, thou have proven thy worth and deserve stability in these uncertain times," the Baron pressed on. Walter the cooper was not the only one with his mouth open, but he could have sworn the Baron looked at him specifically, when alluding to the rumoured discord on the estate.

"Generous praise regarding the festivities has been laid at my feet by our guests; in no small part due to thy hard work. And hail to thee, Egbert, for exhaustive assembly of each event."

There was a spontaneous round of applause for the Baron's manservant, who did not expect recognition for his services, and was taken aback by the reaction.

"And so, whilst there will indeed be more work to execute the games each quarter, we plan to administer a fee for the attendees to pay forthwith. Thanks to unique insights from some of our friends, we can offer experiences no other in this country can. Accommodation, partaking of activities, and the consumption of meals will no longer be complimentary."

Still not understanding how this was going to make their lives easier, the serfs waited with bated breath for the Baron to get to the point. The kitchen so quiet now, you could hear a pin drop.

"Our noble guests depart on the morrow, and with them take memories to speak of and crow about. Word will travel, and Buford Estate festivities will be hailed as a joyous experience. From the monies accrued each quarter, a tally will be made and a share of the surplus distributed to thee."

Someone dropped a glass in astonishment. Unfathomably, it was Mistress Edith.

Nobody noticed. They all stood still, immobilised by what they had heard.

Harry broke the stunned silence by reaffirming what Baron Buford had said simplistically.

"By my truth, your benevolent master values you all. You deliver the games in spring, summer, autumn, and winter, and he will reward you with land to call your own and a share of the profits."

To show his agreement with Harry and to validate the Baron's strategy, Noah lifted his glass.

"What ho! A merry Christmas announcement. A toast to our beloved Baron Buford!"

Hearing the endorsement they needed, the room exploded into cheers for the Baron. Hats were thrown into the air, lads spun around lasses, and the mistrals started the music up again, for there was definitely something to celebrate now. The Baron's satisfied smile spoke for itself. This was going to work. But there was one more thing to do, to make sure all the peasants were on board. Harry raising his hand to motion for quiet again, didn't have the desired effect this time, so he resorted to putting two fingers in his mouth, emitting a loud whistle.

"Furthermore," shouted the Baron, pausing until the din subsided, "Egbert shall hold charge of the finances for these activities, so we seek a willing soul to orchestrate the games. Walter, would thy be of a mind to take up the challenge?"

Walter, dumbfounded, pointed his finger to his chest, silently asking: *You mean me*?

Harry nodded, confirming the man's selection was correct. Having heard his daughters voice their concern that Walter's cousin was a known associate of Wat Tyler's, they'd sought to put into practice the old adage: '*Keep your friends close, but your enemies closer.*' What better way to distance Walter from his relative, than to have him head the team of staff whose work would benefit them all? The responsibility to make the events a success, and his own monetary gain, would surely be an incentive to discourage his cousin from ever bringing the revolt to the south. With an encouraging smile and a nod in the Baron's direction, Noah beckoned Walter to approach, whereby the cooper responded by bowing to his sire, saying,

"It would be a privilege, m' lord." The crowd around him applauded. Harry, Noah and Baron Buford discreetly exhaled, relieved their gamble had paid off.

Tourism at Pebble Heath had begun.

"Gadzooks, hear ye another announcement," hollered the Baron, elated his news had been taken so positively, and wanting to get to the part of the evening he had been looking forward to the most.

"On the morrow, this year 1380, there will be a knighthood proffered."

Another roar of exultation filled the room, followed by impatient catcalls from those who couldn't bear the suspense.

"For this man is a courageous soldier, hard worker, and loyal friend. All speak so well of him."

Jack was standing with Sam and had been swept up in the exhilaration of the night.

"Who is it, who is it?" he croaked, almost beside himself with excitement.

"I don't know, I don't know," said Sam, on tenterhooks herself.

"It would be a tragedy to dismiss his contribution to the manor as mere duty; such is his heart and passion. And so," the Baron turned to his right and raised his glass, "Thou are as noble as the steeds you tame, Noah, and much deserving of the honour."

The crowd went wild. Of all the cheers and applause that night, the hullabaloo for Noah topped everything else. Jack - cock-a-hoop at the proclamation - ran up to his friend, loudly expressing his adulation. Sam and Harry followed immediately after. The Baron stood back with Egbert, letting a throng of Noah's estate colleagues come forward to congratulate him. Noah, having no previous warning of the Baron's intentions, became quite overwhelmed. And as much as he appreciated everyone's compliments and good wishes, the one person he really wanted to share the moment with was in another room, apparently with another man.

As the frenetic energy in the room died down, those in the kitchen split up into mini groups to absorb everything shared that evening. Sam and Jack joined Ivy and her friends to dance around in a circle. Harry stopped to talk to the Baron once more, praising him for his brave move and reaffirming that - while Tom's plan might have been an unorthodox approach in this current age - it would sow the seeds for reform; ultimately making the estate and surrounding townships prosperous.

Noah needed some space, and easing his way through the mass of bodies in the kitchen, he stepped outside, welcoming the chill in the air and respite from the noise. Then, out of the corner of his eye, he spied two figures standing under the apple tree. It didn't take him long to work out they were Sebastian and Maggie. Yes, she was wearing Sam's dress and her hair was different, but her stance and gestures, even in the dark, were unequivocally Maggie's.

Straining to hear their whispers - to Noah's dismay - he discerned they were planning to meet in the morning. Even more troubling was her suggestion to use the stables as a rendezvous point.

The sense of betrayal was devastating.

The very place where he and Maggie had talked and laughed - and even kissed - was now the one she chose to meet his adversary.

An upcoming knighthood should have filled him with pride and pleasure, but what he bore witness to now tore him apart. Sebastian had adroitly produced a sprig of mistletoe from nowhere and was holding it aloft, suggestively leaning in close to Maggie. Noah had to look away. He couldn't bear it anymore. With head down and heart breaking, he left the pair behind in the darkness, as he quietly crossed the field to seek solace from his much-loved - and loyal - horses.

CHAPTER 11

Thursday night continued 23 December

INSIDE, THE HOLDEN FAMILY moved from the ballroom into the hallway, curious at the racket coming from the kitchen. Noting the cheerful look on people's faces as they tumbled out into other areas, coupled with the applause they'd heard before, Tom guessed the distribution-of-wealth plan had gone down well. Baron Buford arrived; his business matters complete and his cheeks pink with success. He grinned broadly upon seeing Tom and marched over to give him a giant bear hug.

"Thomas! Thy superior notions are beyond the realm of our paltry imaginations. The people are rapt as to what the future holds, for the games and for their lives. Thou is surely a wizard, conjuring up this unification."

"Glad to be of service," Tom replied, tipping his hat in a gentlemanly manner. The Baron responded in kind, then returned to the ballroom, ready to resume socialising.

"Nice one, Dad," said Josh, shaking his father's hand.

They were interrupted by LeBron James and Plumhollow Sunset running between their legs, intent on getting from one room to the other. Jack came tearing after them and saw his family congregating in the hallway.

"Uncle Tom, Aunty Cat, where's Mum? Did you hear the news? "

"Yes," said Tom, "it sounds like everyone is in favour of the new format of the games."

"No, I mean about Noah. He's going to be a knight. Isn't that cool?"

"My goodness! Yes, very cool indeed," Cat said, looking meaningfully at her husband.

"In more ways than one," Tom concurred. "Where is Maggie? She hasn't been in the kitchen looking for you?"

"No, I haven't seen her," said Jack.

"We need to find her tout de suite," urged Cat. "With that knowledge, her duties for tonight can come to an abrupt halt."

As she spoke, Maggie and Sebastian reappeared from outside. Not expecting to bump into her family, Maggie looked a little sheepish; knowing how fond Jack was of Noah and not fully understanding why her chicanery with the creepy knight was necessary. On the contrary, Sebastian looked like the cat who'd got the cream. Having set up the rendezvous with the knight for the following morning, Maggie now wanted to get away from him as soon as possible. As luck would have it, Frankie came downstairs, finally finished with the ladies who wanted waves in their hair, and hoping to be part of the fun before it got too late. Giving her the perfect opportunity to make her excuses, she said,

"Robin, my dear, how lovely to see you at last!"

She moved away from Sebastian, glancing at him briefly and pretending to confirm their arrangements with her eyes. Sebastian was satisfied he'd won his prize, and knew he just had to be patient for a few hours before he could claim it. Flashing a salacious smile at Maggie, he deliberately sauntered in front of a glaring Frankie, and back to the ballroom to see if anyone else could tickle his fancy in the interim.

"What's the goss?" asked Frankie. "Mission accomplished?"

Maggie nodded, but before she could provide an update, Jack blurted out his information again.

"Noah's going to be a knight!"

"Is he really?" said Maggie. "That's fantastic! Where is he now?"

"I'm not sure," said Jack.

"Oh, that's strange; I would have thought he'd be celebrating. Has anyone actually told him we've solved the riddle?"

Tom shook his head. "He stayed with the Baron when I came to our room, but I didn't know at that point."

"We didn't find out until Mum and Dad told us," Josh contributed.

"I've been stuck upstairs," said Frankie.

"He did ask me where you were, Mum," offered Jack.

"And what did you say, Bud? Verbatim."

Jack's brow puckered, and he looked at his Aunty Cat.

"Word for word," she clarified.

"OK, I said Sam didn't want to go to the ball, so you two swapped."

"And?" Maggie prompted her son.

"And when he asked why you wanted to go to the ballroom instead of the kitchen, I said you wanted to see Sebastian because he's a knight."

"Good grief," sighed Maggie, "I love you, Jack, but your diminishing adolescent brain cells leave a lot to be desired at times."

Maggie didn't mean to be blunt, but this evening had been stressful for her. Cat tried to salvage the conversation.

"It's OK, Jack," she consoled, "you didn't do anything wrong. What your mum means is, because Noah didn't know about the relevance of the 'knight' thing, he might have interpreted her absence from the kitchen differently."

Nonetheless, Jack's earlier excitement evaporated. He and his mum had the best relationship, and he didn't want to do anything to disappoint her. He looked crestfallen, hanging his head in regret. As they were talking, Harry and Sam came to join them. Maggie hurriedly asked,

"Dad! Did you tell Noah what happened today?"

"No, sorry, I didn't have time. The Baron whisked me away as soon as I entered the room."

She looked at Sam, who shook her head too.

"Do you know where he is?"

"Oh, he stepped outside for a breather. Poor guy, he just about got mobbed when Baron Buford announced he was going to knight him tomorrow."

"When was this?"

"About ten or fifteen minutes ago."

"Shit," said Maggie, mentally calculating where she was then. "If he was outside, he might have seen Sebastian and me under the apple tree. Without knowing the reason why, I can't imagine what he's thinking. I've got to find him."

Hitching up her lady's dress to avoid the mud, she ran out the door and across the grass.

"Oh dear," said Cat, "what have we done?"

An ominous thunderclap reverberated overhead, as Maggie ran as fast as she could to the stables. The accompanying lightning cracked open the night sky above, but there was no rain yet; merely a warning of what was yet to come. Maggie's own storm of emotions had already arrived. Chiding herself for getting together with Sebastian before Noah had been told of the plan. And for being sharp with Jack, when he was the only one who'd tried to inform him of what was going on - albeit with a typical teenager's explanation in half sentences. Her body pounded with self-reproach, trying to work out in her head how she could make everything right again. A few hours ago, she was in a brilliant mood; jubilant that Harry had unlocked the key to getting home, and anticipating a lovely evening with Noah. But that had all gone to hell in a handbasket. She hadn't even been there to congratulate him on his impending knighthood! Worse, when the glory should have been his to bask in, she was faking admiration of another man.

She didn't want to admit it, but had she followed her heart over her head, she wouldn't have gone to the masquerade ball, and instead, would have been cheerfully laughing and dancing with Noah in the kitchen. Then, when the Baron made his announcement, it would have given them a completely different opportunity to enact upon Harry's discovery. She fully expected that once Noah became Sir Noah, he would have gallantly offered himself to activate the portal, and maybe, just maybe, come back to the 21st century with them. Now, with the misconstrued execution of her scheme, making him angry and disillusioned by her behaviour, that seemed highly unlikely. She knew she was a bit of a control freak and felt compelled to organise things to get the best results. She also knew that her fear of letting people down sometimes did just that, in ways she hadn't expected. It was difficult for Maggie to trust in fate and let things unfold as they were meant to.

She reached the stables, and sure enough, there was Noah by himself, looking miserable.

"Noah!" exclaimed Maggie, simultaneously relieved to have found him, and mortified to think she was the cause of his obvious distress. "Whatever you think happened tonight, didn't. And wasn't. Going to, I mean. Nothing was going to happen."

In a rush to expound on the matter, she was tripping over her words.

"Look, can I sit down and tell you what was really going on?"

"No need," said Noah haughtily, "with my own eyes, I saw him kiss thee."

"No, you didn't," she implored. "Look." She reached into her pocket and extracted her fan, fluttering it coquettishly in front of her face, with only her eyes peeking out over the top.

"He tried to, but I blocked his path with this." She chuckled at the memory of Sebastian's attempts being thwarted. Hearing that appeased Noah a little, and the lines around his eyes deepened a touch, as the faintest of smiles emerged.

"Noah, it was all a ruse." She removed the fan, took a deep breath, and said, "Let me start from the beginning."

Setting the scene, she described being in the bingo hall with Cat, discussing different spellings, and how the answer to their conundrum had gradually dawned on Harry. She went on to explain how Sam was meant to set the trap, but as Maggie was older and better able to handle a tricky situation, she had been talked into swapping with her niece and deceiving Sebastian.

"I thought Harry or Sam might fill you in on what was happening, but I understand they didn't. And Jack's account probably got lost in translation. I'm so sorry Noah. I should have spoken to you before the charade started, so you weren't left in the dark."

Noah's self-protective, icy demeanour began to thaw. He wanted to believe her, but the hurt he had felt was so real that his walls remained up for the time being.

"But now," she moved closer to him and clasped his hand, "I don't even have to go through with the pretence of meeting him tomorrow. With you about to be a knight and all, if you join us by the trapdoor, the portal will open without Sebastian's involvement."

Noah clenched his jaw, pulled his hand away, and stood up. Maggie was shocked. He looked upset. But she had cleared everything up, hadn't she?

"I see," he said. "Verily, I shall assist thee and thy family homeward bound. Thy first priority, naturally."

Maggie realised she'd put her foot in it again. It sounded like she wanted to use Noah purely for the purpose of escaping the 1300s.

"No Noah, I didn't mean it like that. I mean, of course we want to get home, but ..."

Noah put up his hand to silence her.

"Thou need not justify thyself. I understand completely. Thy life seven centuries away is of most importance to thee. I shall oblige accordingly."

He walked to the door, implying their conversation was over and it was time for her to leave. Engulfed with remorse and bereft at the turn of events, but not trusting herself to say anything else in case she made things worse, she reluctantly followed him. Another thunderclap from above, and Maggie felt as if a greater power was berating her in surround sound. She turned to face Noah one more time, unable to stop a tear from escaping.

"I'm so sorry," she said again, gently touching his arm and stepping into the darkness that felt as empty as her insides.

Hoping to get some consolation from her family in the chapel, she arrived to an equally frosty reception from her son. Jack sat sulkily in the corner, and had resorted to cuddling LeBron James for comfort, not wanting to talk to anyone. She didn't think she could feel any worse, but this was an actual dagger to her heart. How had she gotten herself into a position where she was being rebuffed by two of the most important people in the world to her? Clearly, the cunning plan she had suggested that afternoon had spectacularly backfired.

Harry picked up on her misery.

"C'mon, love," he said compassionately, "let's have a chat in the other room." And with his arm around her shoulder, he guided his daughter through the door to sit on the front pew.

"Oh, Dad," she said with a sob; her fortitude dissolving, "how have I messed everything up?"

"You haven't, Margaret," placated Harry, "it's just misunderstandings galore at the moment. Both your boys are licking their wounds right now, because they love you to bits, but neither knows where they stand."

Maggie sniffed while listening to her father.

"Jack has coped marvellously this week. You should be so proud of him."

"Of course I am!" Maggie asserted, aghast that her father might think any differently.

"I know, I know," he said soothingly, "not purely for his resilience, but his maturity as well. He hasn't complained once about us being stuck here, and if anything, was more worried about you than himself. He thought he was doing the adult thing by telling Noah what was happening tonight. Even though the wording wasn't quite right, it was more than the rest of us did. We were the ones that failed. Jack didn't see you all night, and only partially understood why you were somewhere else. He wanted to provide you with valuable information so you'd be pleased with him. For his words to be discarded as a problem, and for you to disappear again, was pretty hard on the lad. He might be verging on adulthood, Margaret, but for a few years yet, he's still just a kid."

"I didn't mean to hurt him. Or Noah," said Maggie, her voice cracking with emotion.

"I know you didn't," said Harry, trying to assuage her guilt, "but you've been so flipping independent all your life, you don't even recognise when someone's trying to help you. And then when they do, half the time you dismiss what they say, only to take over anyway. Even your first full sentence when you were little was: *'I do it myself.'*"

He smiled affectionately and continued,

"Because you've had to do most things in life on your own, I get that you're spinning several plates at any given time, and it takes every effort to keep them going. But you're so focused on what needs to happen next, you sometimes miss the magical moments of now."

Maggie looked down at the floor, knowing there was some truth to this.

"Jack will come around. He's an amazing boy, and that's all credit to you. As for Noah, did you broach the subject of him coming back with us?"

"Yes, I did," said Maggie. "I said his outlook on life and open-mindedness would suit the modern world."

"Uh-huh."

"And that if he wasn't truly happy here, we would welcome him to join us."

"Uh-huh."

"And I even mentioned the horses in Midwest America."

"Uh-huh. And did you tell him that you love him and couldn't imagine life without him?"

She shook her head. No, she hadn't said anything like that to Noah. It was ludicrous to think she could have that level of affection for someone she'd only known for a few days. That didn't make sense.

"But that's how you feel, isn't it?" enquired Harry, "even if it doesn't seem logical in that rational mind of yours." She nodded silently.

"Well, sweetheart, as the wise philosopher Lieutenant Commander Spock once said, *'Logic is the beginning of wisdom, not the end of it.'* You're so fearless when it comes to running a business and a home and raising a child by yourself; why does having a relationship terrify you?"

It was a rhetorical question, not meant to be answered.

"I know you, my girl," Harry continued with fondness. "If you open yourself up to the possibility of love, there are any number of reasons it could end in anguish. You've already experienced divorce and seen me lose my one true love. And I detect an underlying dread about Jack growing up too. You're bracing yourself for his departure when he's older, and that too will be heart-breaking."

Maggie nodded again. "He's my world, Dad."

"Agreed," said Harry, "like you and Catherine are mine. But trying to protect yourself from hurt by being busy, and breaking everything down into nicely ordered compartment boxes, isn't going to cut it. One day, one of your spinning plates will fall and smash to the ground, and there is nothing you could have done ahead of time to stop it from happening. That's life whether we like it or not. And maybe that crash is Noah. If you take the risk of telling him how you feel, you'll be insecure and scared of his response. Then, if you did get together, it might not even work. You've had entirely different life experiences, that's for sure. You may not be compatible; he may not feel comfortable in different surroundings; there are all sorts of variables."

"Exactly," confirmed Maggie.

"But that's your head talking when it's filled with trepidation," continued Harry. "What does your gut say? What if you took the plunge and found you were both on the same page? What if he felt completely at home in our day? Wouldn't that be the most terrific thing in the world? You took a huge risk in having Jack on your own. I know there were naysayers, and those who disapproved, but that was the one time that you trusted yourself and your intuition. And hasn't that been the best decision you've ever made?"

"Yes, absolutely," affirmed Maggie.

"So trust yourself again, Margaret. Trust that whatever happens, you'll be able to handle it. Tomorrow morning, before the chariot race, tell Noah how you feel. After that, it's in fate's hands. And sometimes that's not a bad thing. You can't control everything."

He wiped away her tears, and once more she felt so very grateful he was here.

"Now go and give my grandson an enormous hug."

Maggie stood up and squeezed her dad's hand. She returned to the rectory, walking over to her boy and his dog.

"Room for three?" she asked contritely. "I'm sorry I snapped at you, Bud; you've been incredible throughout this whole thing. And I love you so much."

Jack looked up, gladly accepting his mother's apology and echoing the sentiment; both embracing as if their lives depended on it. Bronny wanted part of the action, pushing his snout between their faces, to plant big, slobbery kisses on their noses. The sombre mood in the room lifted, and Harry looked on at his daughter and grandson. Then he glanced upwards to confer with his wife in spirit.

"Well, Grace, it's been one hell of an adventure, but I think it's time I got your girls home."

Tom and Cat sloped off to their bedroom, yawning, leaving the younger ones to party on their behalf.

"Darling, I'm so proud of you," Cat said to her husband. "I didn't quite get what you were doing with the Baron, but now I understand. By compensating the serfs for their work and giving them somewhere to live, garners their loyalty. They're likely to be more productive and have an incentive to stay on the land, rather than rebel against the aristocracy."

"Got it in one," said Tom.

"But if the estate is making more money, won't the Baron have to pay the King more taxes?"

"Ah, well, because of my accounting expertise," said Tom, stroking an invisible moustache in a Machiavellian way. "I've shown Egbert how to denote the profit distribution as a legitimate expense before recording the surplus, so it should all work out for everyone. And Josh used his marketing nous to put a plan in place for promoting the games as a seasonal event."

"You are so clever!" enthused Cat admiringly.

"Capitalism at its finest," joked Tom.

"So, if the income from the games gets shared around the peasants instead of lining the king's pockets, perhaps Frankie wasn't too far off with his Robin Hood reference, after all. And if it keeps the Baron and the other lovely people we've met safe, then I'm all for it." She gave him a big smacker on the lips.

"Mmmm," responded Tom, "I'm going to have to talk about profits and expenses more often."

He kissed her back, and they giggled their way towards the bed.

Sam, Frankie, Aaron and Josh were still downstairs, dancing with the kitchen staff. Mistress Edith was not amused. Not only was this girl mocking the working class by dressing up in a servant's frock, but now she'd brought three of the upper class into the supervisor's terrain, which just wasn't right, as far as she was concerned. The lass was also a bad influence on Ivy, who had been speaking back lately. Thank goodness the guests were leaving the festivities tomorrow. They needed to stick to their own kind and had no right to disrupt her routines.

After a few more drinks and dances, the four decided to call it a day and retire upstairs for what they now felt confident would be their last night in the manor. Buoyed by the revelations of the afternoon, even though there had been some miscommunication between Maggie and Noah, they felt sure that after the investiture tomorrow, he would help them get home. As they neared the splendid sweeping staircase, Sebastian lurched out of the ballroom, three sheets to the wind as usual, but just managing to make out Marian through his blurred vision. She was with that insipid fellow, her husband-to-be, he observed, but it looked like she had changed her clothes. How odd. Even so, the sight did little to dampen his ardour. No matter, he thought, he would get his time with her tomorrow.

Sam had seen Sebastian too and quickened her pace in the opposite direction.

"Let's step it up, chaps," she prompted, encouraging the others to quickly climb the stairs.

Sebastian paused and looked at her again. Her voice was different, too. Or was he imagining things? He shook his head to clear it and then looked up once more. His third scan was too late, as the group had reached the top of the staircase and were now out of sight on the landing. Sebastian shrugged and thought maybe it was time to hit the hay himself. He had a romantic liaison planned for tomorrow morning, and a polo match to win in the afternoon.

CHAPTER 12

Friday morning 24 December

THE PREVIOUS NIGHT'S THUNDER and lightning proved to be an empty threat from Mother Nature. Performing a complete U-turn, she'd chosen to put on a sparkling display of sunshine this morning instead. The grass was still wet from the rain during the week but not completely sodden, so the Baron's wish for a fantastic final day of celebrations had been granted.

Maggie had hoped to talk to Noah first thing, but Egbert - being his usual efficient self - beat her to the punch; arriving early to confer with the stable master about which horse should be used for what event. Shortly after, the Baron turned up; all three men diving into a deep discussion about something important, and looking like they shouldn't be disturbed. She thought it inappropriate to interrupt, so changed tack, and walked with Jack and Harry to the manor for breakfast. Perhaps Noah would join them soon.

As it happened, he didn't. Still smarting from last night's conversation, Noah did what he always did when upset: put every energy into his animals. Concentrating on each stroke, he brushed the horses' coats until they glimmered in the sun's rays, all the while feeling conflicted. Trying to reconcile the reality of Maggie going home generated a nauseous feeling in the pit of his stomach. And to make matters worse, with only a few hours left, they'd had an argument and weren't even together. Struggling to mollify his emotions, he reasoned that he'd been through loss in his life before and survived. This too, he told himself, shall pass.

The revamped ballroom had reverted back into the practical banquet hall, to host the last meal of the week. Guests strolled in and out to consume what was on offer, and nattered away convivially. Some worse for wear after the merry-making of last night, but all in a cheery mood.

Apart from Maggie.

Cat noticed her sister talking animatedly to Jack about what they would do when they got home, but detected a sadness behind her eyes, and deduced Noah would not be joining them. Such a shame, she thought. She couldn't remember the last time she'd seen Maggie light up around a man. Pity that the one who'd ignited that spark already had an established life in an entirely different world. Maggie would cope, of course, but it still pained Cat to see the love her sibling deserved, had finally arrived in the most unexpected and promising way, yet seemed unlikely to result in the happy ever after of storybooks.

Once everyone had finished breakfast and given the scraps to the dogs, they proceeded across land towards the entertainment arena, eager to watch the final events of the festivities. A rudimentary viewing stand had been erected to one side of the field. At the base of it, Egbert silently offered a prayer of thanks that the sky was clear, and the ground rideable. Carbonel and Pegasus were already harnessed up for Noah and Sebastian's exhibition chariot race. The horses nibbled on the grass contentedly as the stable master checked their hooves. People wandered around chatting to each other, before finding a suitable spot to watch the race. The centrally placed viewing stand was reserved for the Baron, lords and ladies, with the peasants scattered either side on the flat. Ivy and her friends were grouped together; nervous but excited at the thought of presenting a dance soon to such a large audience. Mistress Edith had woken them early this morning for one more rehearsal; making sure their performance today would go without a hitch.

Walter the cooper joined his fellow workers with a newfound air of confidence. Never expecting the promotion Baron Buford had afforded him last night, he was beginning to see the estate in a new light. No longer a place to toil for a few meagre pennies, it was going to be a collective of sorts, where productivity would reward the serfdom financially. He liked the idea of the games generating a sustainable source of revenue. And to have your own piece of land as well. What joy! The gossip floating around suggested that Lord Thomas was the one who had proficiency in these matters, and was responsible for encouraging the Baron to agree to a unique way of thinking. He had to give Lord Thomas credit for having the inspiration, and Baron Buford, the mettle to put it in place. His employer had definitely gone up in his estimations.

Tom and Frankie came to congratulate Walter on his new position, making him feel even more important. As Tom had hoped, a new loyalty to the Baron was forming, and that - fingers crossed - would avert any calamity instigated by the uprising. Although the odds of the gamble paying off had been on their side, because of the type of person the Baron was. If he'd been the sort of aristocrat to only care for himself and his treasures, this wouldn't have worked at all. Baron Buford was a kindly gentleman who took the time to talk to his employees and ensure they always had food and shelter. Tom was going to miss his company and sincerely wished the very best for the Baron's future. Imagine if Sebastian had been the lord of the manor - a scenario that didn't bear thinking about.

As if Tom's thoughts manifested the man himself, Sebastian arrived at the arena looking cocksure of his goals for the day: his amorous meet-up with Marian, and winning the polo match against Noah. He rode in on his black stallion Onyx and with self-assured hubris, did an arrogant lap of honour to announce his presence; waving to the crowd and revelling in their response. Despite the personality traits that would not be tolerated in the future, in 1380, for the most part, he was lauded by men and adored by women. Baron Buford was mindful of the tension between Sebastian and Noah. Perhaps elevating Noah's status would put them on a more level playing field.

Noah wasn't bothered by Sebastian's overconfident display. They had always been two completely different breeds of men. He didn't feel the need to compete against the knight to validate his worth to the Baron. He'd done his bit in France when he was younger and had contributed to the estate by ensuring the welfare of his sire's horses. That was enough for him. He was comfortable in his own skin and wanted for nought. I am content, he told himself.

But a little voice inside his head challenged him: is contentment enough? This week had been a whirlwind of emotions for Noah. Meeting Maggie and her travelling companions, finding out their true origins, falling in love with her, and then having his hopes dashed; no longer being sure of anything. He had misgivings about where he stood with her, whereas the Baron consistently expressed his support. And now, a knighthood to affirm the respect between the two men, surely showed where his loyalties should lie.

Jack came running up to him, interrupting his incertitude.

"Hey, Noah!" the boy called out. "Good luck for today. You'll slay! I know it!"

With nary a dragon in sight, Noah smiled; his stoicism faltering upon hearing Jack's unconventional terminology. He would miss the boy's lively energy and zest for life. It had been nice to have a youngster look up to him and spend time with again, as he'd done with Henry years ago. Harry and Maggie approached too, at a slower pace.

"Congratulations, Sir Noah," Harry said, bowing with deference.

"Thou is ahead of thyself, Brother," corrected Noah, "for the moment, I am still a lowly worker."

"You were never lowly to me," insisted Harry. "Thank you from the bottom of my heart for everything you've done for my family. It's an honour to have met you, and I can't think of anyone more deserving of the title." He offered his hand to shake and when Noah took it, Harry placed his other hand over the top, in a gesture of true friendship. Then, pulling his counterpart close to him, he whispered,

"Go easy on her. Misunderstandings can have terrible consequences."

The comment only served to increase Noah's disquiet. Harry led Jack away to leave Maggie alone with the stable master, who was busying himself by tending to the undercarriage of the chariot.

"Noah," she began hesitantly.

"Mmm," he muttered, not looking her in the eye.

"I wanted to talk, if that's OK?"

"The race is about to start."

"I know, it's just that... I don't want to go back to our time with this unease between us."

Sebastian finished his circuit of the arena and tethered Onyx to the tree, intending to save his steed for the polo match later. He didn't object to Carbonel leading his chariot for the exhibition race. It was only a demonstration, anyway. He'd tried to catch Marian's eye before, but she was too busy talking to the kitchen girls. Why, he did not know. She had a mystery about her that was both appealing and unsettling, but also signs of a fire he was counting on setting alight soon. He couldn't care less about Noah being knighted, and the stables would be empty while everyone else was occupied - ripe for a passionate liaison.

Noah stood up, wiping his hands on a cloth, satisfied that everything was in order with the horses and chariots.

"Fear not," he said brusquely to Maggie. "After the polo match, when the people disperse, I will escort thy family to the chapel as a newly invested knight, and thou shalt go home as thou desires. I do not renege on my promises."

"Noah, that's not what I mean and you know it," said Maggie, getting frustrated.

"I thought I knew what thou meant, but now, not as such."

"It's my fault," Maggie confessed. "I didn't tell you what we were up to ahead of time, and I didn't say how I feel about you."

"And how doth thou feel about me?"

Sebastian sauntered over to where they were, catching the tail end of the conversation.

"Well, Noah, I dare say the wench will be feeling most favourably towards thee after the knighthood," he interjected.

Maggie immediately turned away from Sebastian, hoping he wouldn't figure out her duplicity from the previous night.

"Although, thy standards will need raising, and thou will have to start courting a noblewoman henceforth."

"I better go," said Maggie, walking past Sebastian with her head down; her teeth grazing her bottom lip in disappointment.

For a split second, he looked bemused - like someone with amnesia getting a flashback. There was a familiarity of something he couldn't put his finger on. Casting his confusion aside, he opted to insult Noah further as the most satisfying measure to take.

"Thou art such a hypocrite. You chastise me for pursuing the women, yet thy conduct is exactly the same."

"Only if the feeling is mutual, Sebastian. I don't make unwanted overtures on ladies betrothed to others."

"Tis thy loss, Noah. And that feeling will be paramount anon. Because losing is all thou will be doing today."

If anyone had overheard their antagonistic exchange, it may well have been interpreted as the beginning of trash talk; the vocal sparring that would become commonplace before sports games in centuries to come. Noah knew he should be impervious to Sebastian's goading, but the man irritatingly got under his skin. Precisely his opponent's aim.

At that moment, the heralds trumpeted, proclaiming the commencement of the Yuletide Celebrations' last day, and the imminence of the first event. Baron Buford waited for the crowd to settle, then welcomed them all and signalled to Egbert, who walked into the middle of the arena to officiate.

Sebastian and Noah took their marks, standing in their respective chariots and containing the horses who were itching to run. In response to their drivers glaring at each other, and sensing a heightened competitiveness, the animals shook their heads and snorted; both champing at the bit. Egbert raised a small flag as Carbonel stamped his foot in impatience. With a swift downward motion, Egbert dropped the pennant and shouted,

"And Go!!"

The arena erupted as the horses immediately launched into a gallop, tossing their manes and unwelcome restraint simultaneously. The air was thick with the sound of pounding hooves, puddles splashing, and the roar of spectators. Noah and Sebastian added to the din with yells of their own, urging the beasts to go faster. They sped past Egbert in a tornado of lithe limbs and spinning wheels that caught him by surprise. Originally meant to showcase techniques in an amiable collaboration, Egbert - and the Baron - could tell there was something more at stake here.

Jack, Josh and Aaron pumped their fists and cheered loudly for Noah. Maggie tried to cheer too, but her heart wasn't in it. Her face bore a wounded expression, distraught at the thought of Noah being angry with her still. Cat saw her sister's angst, and trying to make herself heard above the noise, leaned in close to say,

"Don't worry. You'll still have time to talk to him properly. After the polo match, the Baron will be mingling and fare-welling his guests, the workers will go back to the manor, and Sebastian will be preening himself like a peacock. We'll make some excuse about tidying the chapel before Friar Kenobi's departure, and no one will notice our escape from the Middle Ages. It won't be rushed, so you and Noah will be able to have some time in private before you say goodbye."

Maggie clutched her sister's hand in gratitude and hoped she was right.

As the horses reached the end of the field, the hoops that Sam had created now stood in as poles for the chariots to circle around. With only inches separating the two, as they neared the turnaround mark, Sebastian shook his reins and yelled louder. Carbonel responded, and coming out of the curve, put in an extra effort to pull away from his stable mate. Pegasus wasn't about to accept defeat though, and accelerating without warning, started to make up ground. Noah had to steady himself as the surge of speed knocked him off balance. For a moment, it looked like his waver had put them off course, and Sebastian cackled as he left them in his wake. But Pegasus wasn't named after a flying horse for nothing. Head down, nostrils flared; he hauled the chariot and its rider over the uneven ground, with a resolve fit for a warrior. Despite the cold, droplets of sweat dripped down the horse's flanks; the muscles of his hindquarters digging in and pushing off to lengthen his stride. Noah, too, had found his rhythm again, and matched Sebastian's shouts with his own. Neck and neck, the steely focus of man and beast centred on the finish line, where Egbert stood nervously to receive them. Like volcanic lava, all of Noah's pent-up emotions overflowed, giving him the final impetus for one last push. Masterfully navigating Pegasus to harder ground nearby, the horse gained traction and powered forward with fierce tenacity; propelling them towards the end of the field. By a very narrow margin, Noah and Pegasus crossed the finish line first, much to Sebastian's chagrin.

After the horses had slowed to a stop, the two participants disembarked, wheezing with exhaustion, to the sound of exaltation from their audience. Egbert, not willing to take on the role of adjudicator, was quick to congratulate both men in an attempt to head off any ill will. Sebastian, blatantly furious, stormed off to the stables without saying a word. Noah stayed put, inhaling deeply while gently caressing the heads of each horse, so very proud of their athleticism.

Egbert helped Noah lead the horses to one side, giving them water to quench their thirst. Their recovery was swift, and their placid manner restored as the chariot harnesses were removed. Noah, too, willingly supped on the water provided by Egbert, which helped steady his pulse rate. Several people came by to express their thrill at witnessing him win. Maggie remained on the side-lines watching Noah from afar.

Next on the agenda were the formal proceedings and Egbert once again took control of coordinating the investiture. Walter - taking his new role very seriously - assisted where he could, instructing some of the younger labourers on how to set up the stage where the ceremony was to take place. Baron Buford wore a black and gold robe, denoting the importance of the occasion. Noah pulled a smart purple tunic over his brown work clothes to cover up the mud. He felt he should look the part at least; aware of how much this meant to the Baron. He wished he felt more enthusiastic about being knighted, but could only associate it with Maggie leaving. The trumpeters sounded their horns again, declaring the start of the ceremony. Sebastian heard them too and knew that was a cue for Marian to join him in the stables. He waited expectantly, with high hopes of more sweating bodies and heavy breathing. This was one physical activity he indisputably excelled at, and was assured of a winning finish.

Baron Buford stood on the stage in front of his people, holding an imposing sword. Egbert placed himself supportively by Noah's side at the base of the steps; each man looking up at their sire. The Baron's usual baritone voice sounded even richer as he announced,

"To all here present, know ye that Noah, having been recognised for long and honourable service on the battlefield and the estate, is hereby admitted as a Distinguished Knight in the Order of Saint George."

Egbert held out his hand, palm open, to indicate the time had come for Noah to ascend the steps to his destiny. Maggie realised she was holding her breath. With humility and reverence, Noah walked up to the Baron, knelt before him, and dropped his chin to his chest. The Baron raised his sword; gently but firmly placing the blade flat on Noah's right shoulder, and then left.

"I, Baron Buford, in the name of King Richard II, do hereby dub thee, Noah. May your courage and devotion become a shining example to the people. Arise, Sir Noah."

Noah stood, bowed, and said respectfully, "My Liege."

All the spectators of the ceremony applauded with relish. Noah turned and looked over to the crowd, barely able to take in the accolade he was being given. As he ran his eyes along the lines of supporters, he spotted Maggie clapping and smiling broadly at him. He couldn't help himself and smiled back. She felt like a small firework had exploded in her heart. That smile hadn't shown itself for longer than she cared to admit.

Noah waved to his audience, treading down the steps again, to have his hand shaken by Egbert. But the Baron didn't move. In fact, he looked as if he had further business to attend to. He held his hand up for silence, but thinking the formalities were over, the onlookers continued to talk amongst themselves, unwittingly ignoring their leader. Remembering Friar Kenobi's tactic at the party last night, the Baron put two fingers in his mouth and whistled loudly, causing people to stop in their tracks and face forward again. He followed through with,

"Ladies and gentlemen, the ceremony is not yet at a conclusion. For I, as Lord of this manor, have the prerogative to bestow more than a single knighthood today. And that decree is my wish and my right."

Everyone went quiet, intrigued by this additional, unexpected proclamation.

"To all here present, know ye that Thomas, having been recognised for creative and robust financial solutions, for the benefit and wellbeing of all on the estate, is hereby admitted as a Distinguished Knight in the Order of Saint George"

Cat emitted an involuntary squeak as Josh and Sam, eyes wide with disbelief, turned to their father together and called out,

"Dad!!"

Tom appeared to be paralysed by the shock announcement and couldn't move. Until the peasants, supremely grateful for what he'd brought to the table during his brief stay here, started chanting his name in persuasion:

"Thomas! Thomas! Thomas!"

Sebastian heard the noise and wondered what on earth was going on. And where was Marian? Even if she'd stayed to watch that irrelevant fool Noah get knighted, that should be over by now.

Tom was broken out of his stupor by his wife shaking his arm and saying,

"Tom, it's for you. The knighthood. It's really for you."

She took him by the hand and led him down the viewing stand, to pass him on to Egbert. Also waiting by the stage, a beaming Noah, by way of encouragement, said,

"I think thy phrasing is: '*You got this,*'" as he indicated the way forward, showing the path he had previously walked himself.

With his ears ringing from the acclamation, and his head spinning with incredulity, Tom made his way up the steps and across the stage to the Baron. Compliantly bending down on one knee - which he hadn't done since he proposed to Cat - he, too, bowed his head to accept his fate.

"I, Baron Buford, in the name of King Richard II, do hereby dub thee Thomas. May your wise words and foresight be an inspiration to the people. Arise, Sir Thomas."

Tom stood up, bowed respectfully, and uttered the same words Noah had minutes before. They came out in almost a whisper, but still with genuine allegiance,

"My liege."

The Baron broke into a wide grin, very satisfied with his choices for today.

After the applause died down, Tom left the stage to join Noah on the grass. The newly knighted men soon found themselves encompassed by admiring well-wishers. With the ceremonies being cause for celebration, the mistrals started playing, and it didn't take long before the field was abuzz with noisy nobles and chattering commoners. Maggie, on the outskirts of Noah's focus, resigned herself to the fact that she would not be able to talk to him until later. Her woefulness, however, had been replaced by pride - for both Noah and her brother-in-law. Good, kind, decent men who deserved to be the centre of attention for once.

Meanwhile, Sebastian, who thrived on being the nucleus amongst a cloud of electrons in any given situation, was suffering from severe FOMO. He could hear fun times were being had on the higher ground above, but not only had Marian stood him up, it now seemed she felt mixing with the riff-raff was preferable to a private meeting with his good self. Actions that were inconceivable and infuriating! He was not accustomed to being spurned. Seeing the polo sticks in the storehouse, he grabbed one, plus a ball lying on the floor, plainly in the mood to hit something. Still fuming, he strode purposefully up to the entertainment arena and towards the tethered horses. Untying Onyx, he mounted the animal in one fluid motion, and slowly, but surely, trotted around the accumulation of people searching for Marian. One did not tease and then snub a man of his standing. Cutting an intimidating figure, Sebastian was going to remind her of that.

After giving her dad a huge hug, Sam returned to hang around with Ivy and the kitchen staff. Once the euphoria of the moment had settled down, the girls were due onstage to perform their dance, as a prequel to the final event of the games.

Egbert enlisted Josh and Aaron to take the chariots to the stables, so they weren't in the way. Harry proposed harnessing the chariots back up to the horses, and riding them down the hill would be the easiest way to achieve this, but as Pegasus and Carbonel were spent, he suggested using Perfect Grace and Autumn Haze instead.

"To warm them up before the polo match," he reasoned.

Josh felt pretty sure this excuse was more about Harry's desire to interact with Perfect Grace one more time than any practicality, but who was he to spoil his grandad's last opportunity to do so? Harry stepped assuredly onto the base of the chariot and took the reins. The experience of living in the past, although stressful in a lot of respects, also made Harry feel younger than his years, and he'd certainly welcomed that aspect. There was life in the old boy yet, he thought. Josh and Aaron followed suit, harnessing Autumn Haze, and the two horses casually trotted down the hill, comfortable with their drivers.

Noah went with them to the sanctuary of the stables, wanting to decompress for five minutes after the happenings of the morning. The fractured conversation with Maggie, war of words with Sebastian, and pomp and circumstance of the knighthood, had all taken a toll on his headspace. He needed to gather his thoughts.

Almost ready to take the stage, Mistress Edith rounded up her girls to give them a pep talk, as Egbert and Walter encouraged the crowds to clear the field; directing them back to the viewing areas. Sam was still clinging like a limpet, she noted.

"Stand back now, m' lady, and join thy family," Mistress Edith said sternly.

"But can't I stay here to watch?" pleaded Sam.

"Tis not thy place," insisted Mistress Edith. "The upper classes have the privileged view of the performance from above. At thy behest, I ask thee to honour thy position."

She turned her back on Sam, making it very clear her words were not a request. Sam moved away, sullen and moody, but soon spotted Egbert and Walter stationing themselves close to the stage. Egbert's slim frame was unlikely to provide much coverage, but she thought Walter's bulkier physique might enable her some camouflage if she unobtrusively stood behind them. She winked at Ivy, indicating where she would be.

As he tapped the ball along the ground with his polo stick, Sebastian scanned the masses, trying to locate Marian, but to no avail. Was the girl intentionally avoiding him?

Once again, the trumpets sounded, and the spectators took their positions, ready to continue with the festivities. Sebastian didn't care and continued to the northern end of the arena.

Stupid Carbonel! Obviously not as hardy nor as speedy as his own fine beast. That was the only reason he had lost the chariot race. But he would ride Onyx for the polo match and lead his team to victory, beating Noah in the most prestigious contest of the week, and regaining the idolisation of the guests. He lifted his chin and sneered. Sweet redemption was his to take.

In the centre of the field, Ivy and her friends stood ready to perform onstage. A single musician with a lute started playing a sweet melodic tune. On Mistress Edith's cue, after eight beats, they began. Their practice paying off; each girl danced with grace and poise, floating across the floor in well-rehearsed moves. The performance reminded Sam again of watching historical TV shows that featured old-fashioned dances. All very proper; the most important considerations being elegance and self-control. This was a big deal for Ivy and her workmates, and Sam was thankful to be able to watch it first-hand. She knew Ivy would also be pleased as punch to have her newly confirmed friend from the gentry, quietly cheerleading in the background. The audience was suitably receptive to the display, applauding graciously at the end of the presentation.

Sam clapped loudly, moving out of her hiding place, safe in the knowledge that it was too late for that old trout to reprimand her now. The dance had been pleasant enough, but she thought the people might be up for a livelier encore. Before the girls had time to follow Mistress Edith offstage, Sam ran over to the mistrals, ardently begging them to segue into the more upbeat tempos provided at the party the night before. Hypnotised by her impassioned plea, the musicians duly accommodated, and with a wicked smile, she leapt onto the stage to the amusement of the dancers. Whilst the music playing was definitely of the times, the beat reminded Sam of Madonna's song: Express Yourself - very apt for the occasion. Repeating the songstress's iconic first line, she cried out,

"Come on, girls!" skipping to the front of the stage and counting them in - five, six, seven, eight! The girls knew what to do, and discarding their conventional teachings, threw themselves into the TikTok routine Sam had taught them.

In the stands, Cat and Tom roared with laughter. That was their daughter, alright. She had done well pretending to be a lady this week, but let's face it, Sam's true nature was anything but. Instead of dainty steps and perfectly positioned hands, the dancers shimmied their shoulders, stamped their feet, and clicked their fingers in time to the rhythm provided by the mistrals, who were thoroughly enjoying themselves, too. Maggie, Jack and Frankie, standing on the ground, joined in the revelry.

"You go, girl!" shouted Frankie.

Sam's antics, however, did not impress Mistress Edith. Affronted by the gall of the girl, the scowl on her face represented her thoughts on the matter. She could tell the Baron and his guests were warmly receiving this crass interpretation of dance, so didn't think hauling Sam off stage would be supported. But once it was over, she intended to tear a strip off that wilful upstart; something that had been a long time coming.

Sam, feeling the daggers projected in her direction by Mistress Edith's glare, recognised she was in trouble. As with most TikTok dances, the performance was short and sweet. The girls curtsied to rapturous applause as Sam snuck through the middle of them and jumped off the back of the stage; running up the field with the view of eluding her nemesis. She wasn't as slick as she'd hoped, though. Mistress Edith had caught the movement in her peripheral vision, and was in hot pursuit, albeit at an uncomfortable plod, rather than a jog.

Cat had also seen her daughter's getaway, but noted that Sam was now putting herself between a rock and a hard place. Ahead of her: Sebastian, who was probably still riled at being lured to the stables on the pretext of a tantalising tryst that was never going to happen. And behind her: the kitchen supervisor who'd reached the limit of her patience, and wanted to punish Sam for influencing her staff. As her sister was in a more accessible position, Cat waved to Maggie, pointing out the predicament Sam was getting herself into. Maggie understood and immediately started running in support of her niece; Jack, Frankie and Bronny in tow.

With his back to them, Sebastian dismounted his horse to retrieve the polo ball that had become firmly wedged in a divot in the ground. At the sound of running feet behind him, he turned to see Marian. At last, he thought. This was his chance to confront her. He moved swiftly to get into her line of sight, but she was so busy looking over her shoulder to check on her pursuer; she ran right into him, tripped, and landed on the ground. Some of her photographs and her aunt's perfume tumbled out of her pocket and into the surrounding mud. Maggie caught up in an instant, offering a hand to help her niece, but Sebastian brushed it away, leaving Sam in the dirt.

"I think not," he commanded. "The lady has some explaining to do first." He dropped the full weight of the stick's mallet heavily on Sam's skirt; effectively pinning her to the ground.

"Don't be a prick," hissed Maggie.

Not taking kindly to being sworn at, especially from Noah's wench, Sebastian obstinately stood his ground and didn't budge.

"Let her up, for goodness' sake," demanded Maggie. "I thought knights were supposed to be chivalrous." She ran her hand across her brow in exasperation, and one long, wavy tress of red hair unlatched itself from her bun, to fall languidly over her face.

A lightbulb went off in Sebastian's brain. Her voice, her hair, and...he grabbed her wrist and turned it upward, smelling the scent still lingering from last night.

"Twas you!" he shouted, incensed. "At the ball. Pretending to be her!" glowering menacingly at Sam. "Thou dare make a fool out of me!"

The wind had picked up a little, and his words carried down to the stables. Noah, recovered to some degree now, pricked up his ears. As did Josh, Aaron and Harry. They were partway through putting the chariots away: Autumn Haze free from her harness, but Perfect Grace still hitched up, having given Harry one last enjoyable ride. In readiness for captaining the polo match, Noah was in the midst of prepping Autumn Haze anyway, so he hopped into the saddle and ascended the hill, to see what the commotion was about. As he reached the top, Cat came running towards him, with Tom not far behind.

"They're in trouble," she shouted, pointing to the other end of the field.

CHAPTER 13

Friday morning continued 24 December

FRANKIE AND JACK ARRIVED at the scene, with Mistress Edith trailing at the rear.

"Let's not do anything silly," Frankie cautioned, noticing Sebastian's grip on his polo stick had tightened. His stance was formidable; knuckles white and face red, suggesting he was considering what other uses the mallet might have.

Mistress Edith was overjoyed to see Sebastian had downed her quarry. Still puffing, with hands on hips, her words came out disjointedly as she spoke.

"Prithee, Sir... I said these newcomers weren't to be trus ted... Begging thy pardon... but I'll take this one... if thou so permits." She marched round to Sam and put her hands firmly on her shoulders. Sam tried to shake her off, but discovered she was stuck in an unfeasibly powerful hold. Sebastian removed the force of his polo stick, allowing Sam to scramble to her feet, and her captor to take charge; smugly satisfied that this manipulating maiden would receive the retribution she deserved.

It was then that Mistress Edith noticed the items scattered in the mud. She picked up the perfume bottle and nearly choked when she saw what was written on it: 'Playing With The Devil'.

Vindicated, she handed it to Sebastian and cried,

"An evil potion, Sir, surely to induce the trickery thou endured."

He opened the lid and smelt the contents, confirming a match to the scent that had enticed him into Marian's arms the night before. Only it hadn't been Marian. It had been Maggie. Nothing but a servant who'd had the audacity to dress up as a noble and deceive him. Sebastian seethed. The disrespect and treachery were tantamount to a declaration of war, of which he was determined to be the victor. He grabbed Maggie's wrist to compare the aroma again, more aggressively this time.

"Ow,' she cried, her arm twisting uncomfortably.

Jack, looking on at what was unfolding, yelled, "Mum!" in concern.

Noah definitely heard that and kicked his heels in his stirrups; Autumn Haze immediately picking up speed.

"The brat belongs to thee?" Sebastian laughed derisively. "My, my, the plot thickens. Not only has the stable master got himself involved with a dirty peasant, but one who has baggage too."

"Get off her!" shouted Sam, wriggling one shoulder free, and reaching over to protect her aunt. But Mistress Edith was still holding onto her other arm, and the two opposing forces had a breaking point; ripping Sam's sleeve open and revealing her tattoos underneath. Mistress Edith recoiled and shouted,

"Behold! The mark of Lucifer!!" Crossing herself and adding in full volume, "Lord have mercy on us all. The girl is a witch!!" She bent down and retrieved a second item from the ground.

"A witch, I say. Look, Sir." She showed Sebastian Sam's photo of the dance troupe practising in the kitchen.

"Stolen the souls of my girls, she has, with a devilish device in her pocket."

And then she understood why Sam had been able to go into the haunted storeroom, and not suffer any consequences.

"Witch, witch, witch!!" she screeched hysterically, pointing to Sam.

In the middle of the field, the multitude started to surge forward to see what all the fuss was about. Ivy felt a looming dread that something disastrous was about to happen.

"Oh my God, Tom, did you hear that?!" Cat asked her husband. "We can't let them get to Sam. Superstition runs rife in medieval days. If, for a moment, they think she really is a witch, they could stone her before there's time for an explanation."

Tom couldn't ride a horse like Noah, but he was ready to sprint down the field to save his only daughter. However, Josh intervened and stopped him. Signalling Aaron to bring Perfect Grace up the hill, he said,

"Wait! We need to get out of here as soon as we can, don't you think? Dad, you're a knight now, so you can unlock the portal key. And Pops knows the poem by heart. You have to stay here with Mum to get the mechanisms in place. Go to the chapel now and tell Pops. We'll get Sam."

Cat looked unsure.

"Mum, Dad, trust me. We can do this."

And before his parents could object, he'd jumped on the back of Perfect Grace, while Aaron shook the reins from the chariot, screaming "Haaaa!" to instil some urgency into the mare.

At the northern end, the situation was unravelling. Mistress Edith had gotten over her shock discovery, and having grabbed Sam by the hair, was pulling her towards the mass of curious onlookers, ready to substantiate her claim. Sebastian could see Noah advancing from the south, and still holding onto her arm, dragged Maggie in the opposite direction. She winced in pain, inciting LeBron James to come to the rescue. Growling and baring his teeth, the giant dog sprang into action, lunging at Sebastian to bite him. But the man was too quick, and with a deft twirl of the stick in his hand, clipped the Great Dane on his back haunch. Bronny yelped from the impact and snarled at his attacker. Now Jack was really upset.

"You arsehole!" he yelled, trying to run to his mum and dog's aid, but Frankie held him back as Maggie instructed forcefully,

"Take him away, Frankie, please. Try to help Sam."

Sebastian laughed with scorn, only too aware that Frankie would not be a match for a crowd fearful of dark magic. As part of that crowd, Baron Buford and Egbert were horrified to see the competitiveness of today had escalated into something more sinister. Unbeknownst to Sebastian, the point of Noah's meeting with them that morning had been a briefing on Maggie's family's plight. Baron Buford had always had an inkling there was something magical about the travellers he'd come across on Tuesday, even alluding to it when he'd met Tom in the hallway last night. He'd questioned Noah about them earlier, but doing the honourable thing, Noah had kept their confidence. But the Baron persisted, and in the end Noah thought it prudent to elucidate - as best he could - should these valued friends suddenly disappear without a word of goodbye. With their precarious position hanging in the balance, and hastening the necessity for departure, that scenario seemed highly likely now.

Frankie felt terrible about strong-arming Jack away from his mother. The kid was overwrought with emotion, but there was no telling what Sebastian was going to do with that mallet, and Maggie would never forgive herself if her boy got hurt. Hearing hooves thundering along the ground had convinced Frankie that salvation was on its way for Maggie, and heeding her words, tried to distract Jack by moving the spotlight to his cousin.

"Jackie boy, listen," he said encouragingly. "You're the coach. It's the fourth quarter with ten seconds to go, and you're taking a time out to talk to your star player. We need LeBron James for a counter-offensive. Call him over now, Jack. I know he's been hurt, but he's tough and he's got a job to do."

Jack sniffed, nodding ascent, and coughed, trying to stop his voice from cracking.

"Bronny!" he called out with as much authority as he could muster. "C'mon, boy!"

As keen as Bronny was to protect Maggie, hearing his master's voice made him duty-bound to follow it. With one final bark at Sebastian, as if to say, "This ain't over mate, I'm coming back for you," the Dane limped along to Jack, who quickly checked the state of his beloved pet.

"I don't think anything's broken," he reported.

"Great," said Frankie, genuinely relieved. "We need to create space between Sam and that mob, and I think an intimidating black beast, the size of a small house, barking his head off could be the answer."

By way of explanation, he motioned down the field, drawing Jack's attention to his other cousin on horseback, and said, "Cos the cavalry is coming."

On the other side, Noah's heart burst out of his chest as he flew across the landscape; his trusted steed accelerating to high gear. The chaotic thump-a-thump of hooves hacked up the earth below and spat it out behind them - the imperativeness of the mission throwing measured rhythm into careless disregard. Autumn Haze's terracotta coat glistened with sweat and friction, casting a brick-red shadow beneath her rider's feet. Noah veered left towards Maggie; both man and horse united in their determination.

Not far behind them, Josh sat astride Perfect Grace, egging her on to match Autumn Haze's commitment. His sister could be a pain in the butt, but there was no way he was leaving her to fend for herself in these circumstances. His best mate Aaron, in the driver's seat, was also fuelled by a fervour he'd not felt before. Equally intent on getting Sam to safety, the two friends dug deep to become the saviours they'd dressed up to be. Steering the chariot purposely to the right, the boys rapidly closed in on their destination.

Mistress Edith was remarkably strong as an ox, Sam bemoaned silently. Still being forced forward, her arm held in a vice-like grip, she knew she was running out of options. Although partially blinded by the sunlight, she could just make out a horse and chariot racing in her direction. And to her right, Frankie and Jack were coming to help. But what exactly were they doing?

Frankie stood solidly, legs apart, and reached back - arm over shoulder - to pull out one of the arrows from his quiver. He lined it up in his bow and set his sights on Mistress Edith.

The rubber tip was unlikely to do any damage, but he needed the woman to loosen her hold on Sam.

"Now, Jack!!" he ordered.

Jack obeyed, running in between the two combative females and the group of people drawing nearer. He called his dog to follow him,

"Speak, Bronny!" he commanded.

"Woof, Woof!"

"Speak more, boy!!"

"Woof, Woof, Woof!!"

The loud, persistent barking from the canine, combined with his imposing presence, was enough to make the horde hesitate. They stopped walking, and some even took a few steps backwards.

At the same time, Frankie called out to Mistress Edith,

"Leave her alone, you belly-aching battle-axe!"

Firing the arrow, it struck her squarely in the chest, and the shock of the bullseye hit together with the hurtful insult, brought about a stumble backwards, causing her to let go of Sam.

"Well, I never...," she exclaimed.

Frankie loaded up another arrow for good measure.

"If the shoe fits, honey, lace that bitch up!"

Sam saw her opportunity and ran into the space created by Jack and Bronny, just as Josh and Aaron arrived. Hardly slowing down at all, Josh expertly manoeuvred Perfect Grace into position, allowing Aaron to put the reins in his left hand and reach out with his right.

"For God's sake, Sam, this time bloody well take my hand!"

She didn't need to be told twice and clutched his outstretched palm, which closed firmly around hers, as he hauled her confidently into the chariot. She fell against Aaron's chest and held on for dear life. Her brother led them away from the crowd, circled around and reduced speed briefly, to pick up their other passengers. The bystanders watched in awe as Aaron duplicated his previous movements; managing to hold the reins and Sam with his left hand while scooping up Jack with his right. Having all three in the chariot was a bit of a squash, but with safety in sight, they gratefully stood on each other's toes and clung together. Meanwhile, Josh leaned almost horizontally off the side of Perfect Grace, locking arms with Frankie, and with a concerted effort from both men, heaved him up onto the horse. Josh looked back at Aaron to make sure everyone was on board and mouthed, "Time to go."

Tom and Cat craned their necks, fretfully looking towards the horizon; trying to determine what was going on and waiting for what seemed like an interminably long time for the return of their children. Cat clutched the pendant Harry had given her for her birthday, symbolically doing what she could to keep them close.

Some of the kitchen girls went to Mistress Edith's aid to console her.

Ivy didn't.

She'd spotted the photograph that had fallen to the ground and picked it up. She didn't understand what was going on, but not for a moment did she believe Sam was a witch.

She was her friend.

Around the same time, Noah reached Maggie. Leaping off his horse with a singular objective, he stormed up to Sebastian and took a swing at him. Sebastian parried with his stick, which Noah artfully grasped, pulling it out of his enemy's hand and casting it aside. This was going to be a fistfight, and Noah wanted all potential weapons out of his opponent's reach. Putting his fists up to protect his face, Sebastian released Maggie. Rubbing her arm - now with bruises, courtesy of his hold - she moved away from the men intent on exchanging blows in front of her. The onlookers, who had lost the melodrama of the first spectacle, hurried over to see what looked like a second. They had expected to be entertained today, and were beginning to wonder if this was some sort of finale performance to showcase the end of the games. Baron Buford and Egbert knew very well it was not, and were quite alarmed to see their two gallant knights trying to knock each other's blocks off. Breaking into a run and reaching the site of the confrontation, they tried to reason with Noah and Sebastian before the masses arrived. But the men were oblivious to pleas for moderation.

"What is thy problem, Noah?!" growled Sebastian, as he dodged a fist for the second time. "I'm the one who should feel aggrieved. It was thy harlot who humiliated me, besmirching my good name."

He paused to take a shot of his own, but Noah ducked just in time.

"Silence, Sebastian! Manhandling Maggie is crossing the line."

"Why so agitated? Did I spoil thy chances of bedding her last night?"

Noah realised he was being baited deliberately, but he'd seriously had enough of Sebastian's taunts. He let out a roar from deep within his diaphragm that sounded like a war cry and lunged at his opponent; arms encircling his waist, head down and grunting, using his full force to tackle his foe to the ground like a rugby player. Sebastian landed with a thud, the wind knocked out of him; proving the theory that the bigger the man, the harder the fall. But reacting quickly, he used his feet to kick out Noah's legs from under him. Both now rolling around in the mud, the scuffle rapidly intensified into a full-on brawl. Bare knuckles connected with solar plexus; dirt-filled fingernails scraped down skin; bodies heaved, noses bled, eyes were blackened. Sebastian finally gained some leverage and scrambled to his feet, towering over Noah who still lay in the dirt, vulnerable. Breathless for a moment, but then finding his voice for one more barb, Sebastian snarled,

"Thou art nothing but an old dog, Noah, who deserves a good kicking."

He drew back his foot to put his words into action.

"And then I shall tame thy bitch!"

But Noah had more fight in him than Sebastian gave him credit for, and as the boot came his way, with the same lightning reflexes that had spared his life in Lyon, he spun his body around; taking hold of Sebastian's ankle, twisting hard and bringing the oaf of a man crashing to the ground again. Finding traction in the momentum, Noah hauled himself off the floor, gaining purchase with his feet, and immediately used the weight of his own body to pin Sebastian down. Straddling his adversary, Noah drew his arm back to its full extension. And then, without hesitation - bicep strained, fist clenched, and letting loose like a catapult - he punched him in the face as hard as he could. Noah's right hook connected - and akin to the sound of a whip snapping - the loud crack of knuckles against cheekbone left no room for misinterpretation. Sebastian's head jerked acutely to one side, a dark crimson welt appearing, as his body shuddered and went limp.

"Noah!" Maggie gasped,

Baron Buford advanced towards his stable master and pulled him off of Sebastian.

"Be gone now! Both of thee, before he comes around."

Noah took a brief moment to make an assessment. Looking around the field, he could see the chariot in the distance heading to the chapel, and concluded Sam was out of danger. He also noted the shocked expressions of those who had been watching - some confused, some angry, some eager to see more fighting. Their beloved Sir Sebastian, out for the count, had seemingly suffered some injustice. And crying foul, their eyes turned to Maggie; looking for someone to blame.

Noah ran over, grabbing her hand, and pulling her in the direction of Autumn Haze. A seasoned rider, Maggie easily slipped her left foot into the stirrup and climbed onto the horse unassisted. She shuffled back as Noah followed, quickly settling himself in front of her and taking control of the reins. Sensing her master's emotional potency, Autumn Haze whinnied and reared up on her hind legs before launching across the field like a burnished fire bolt. Maggie clung tightly to Noah, her arms wrapped around his chest, and her head buried into his shoulder to escape the wind.

At the southern end of the arena, Josh and Aaron pulled Perfect Grace to a halt and jumped to the ground, helping Sam, Jack and Frankie down. Bronny, while still limping, had managed to follow them at a good rate and was pleased to be reunited with his boy. Jack hugged him devotedly, still concerned about his mother, but taking some comfort from his dog's arrival.

Cat and Tom embraced Sam and Josh intensely, then over their shoulders, Tom mouthed silently to Aaron, "Thank you."

"Inside, everyone, come quickly," ushered Harry. "I'll wait for Margaret."

"No, Pops," said Jack assertively, "You need to read the verse. Take Bronny and I'll wait outside for Mum."

Harry was going to refuse, the responsibility too big for a child, but then he studied his grandson's face and realised Jack had done a lot of growing up in a week. The most important person in the world to him was his mother, and he wanted to be the one on lookout duty to ensure she wasn't left behind. Harry nodded and put a firm hand on Jack's shoulder, signifying his agreement and pride.

Egbert was doing his best to disperse the crowd and take back control of the narrative. Mistress Edith was not making it easy, as she continued her loud accusations about Sam being a witch to anyone who wanted to listen. When Noah told them beforehand that the travellers were from the future, while it had taken The Baron and Egbert some time to get their heads around the concept, they knew the current accusation was false, and were trying to play down the incidents of the morning. Walter, now unswervingly loyal to his superiors, supported them even though he didn't know the whole story. Taking on the characteristics of a bodyguard protecting his VIPs, he stood dauntlessly facing the crowd, with his arms folded and a 'nothing to see here' attitude, while Sebastian, for the moment, remained motionless.

The heat between Noah and Maggie's bodies would have been welcome in any other circumstance. However, right now, they had but a single goal: to get to the chapel in one piece, and God - please God - let Harry's hypothesis be right. With a long expanse of pastureland to cover, and not in a position to talk to each other, Maggie allowed herself to recall the special times she'd had with Noah. From the moment she'd first met him - was it really only four days ago? - to strolling together that first night, her arm linked through his; to the chat in the forest where she'd held his hands and looked into his eyes; to the night on the hay bale - learning about each other's lives and ending the evening with an exquisite kiss. She shut her eyes at the thought, wishing that night had been the first of many. But for her recklessness with his feelings, and the inability to express hers, in all honesty, it was probably the last. Her thoughts became painful with images of Noah's hurt and disappointment. Even more so, when she knew it was her actions that had inflicted his suffering. Barely able to hold the tears back, the sound of her son's cry of relief on seeing his mother being brought to safety mercifully interrupted her remorseful introspection.

Harry, upon hearing Jack's shout to his mother, breathed easier inside the chapel and began to recite the poem - slowly and carefully - making sure he said every word correctly. The others stood silently around him, fingers and toes crossed.

SEBASTIAN STIRRED. EGBERT AND the Baron had their backs to him, directing the crowd to the stage, where they hoped they could make up a believable explanation for what their guests had witnessed today. Dismissing his injury as nothing - he'd had worse in France - Sebastian marched over to the basketball hoop Sam had concocted. Pulling out the base, he was astounded to see it was exactly what he needed - a jousting stick. He tipped it upside down and made quick work of untying the rope and disposing of the hoop. With a new vigour in his step, he took the few strides necessary to retrieve Onyx from behind a tree, who had been waiting patiently for his master to wake up. Baron Buford heard movement from behind and turned just in time to see the knight on his black beast; his face contorted with fury, jousting stick at the ready. Horrified, the Baron screamed,

"Sebastian! Noooooo..."

RESPONDING TO NOAH'S SHARP pull of the reins, Autumn Haze slowed to descend the hill and came to a stop beside the oak tree. In her familiar neck of the woods, the filly calmed down; standing still while her riders dismounted. Jack ran up to them and squeezed his mum tight with relief. She hugged him back with the ferocity of a mother's love, planting a kiss on the top of his head.

"Buddy, am I glad to see you."

Jack grasped his mum's hand on one side, and Noah's on the other.

"Let's go," he said, turning towards the chapel door. But Noah remained in place, and Jack's arm stiffened as there was no give from behind.

"Jack, love, go inside with the others; I just need a few seconds," said Maggie. She smiled warmly, trying to convince him there was no problem. Although a tad confused, Jack did as she asked, stepping into the chapel as Harry finished the verse.

Maggie turned to Noah,

"Please come with us," she begged.

"Thou doth not need me any longer," Noah said, nodding at the rectory window, where a luminous intensity could be seen in the room. "Thou hath Thomas. He is a knight now and will accommodate thy return."

"I do need you!" Maggie insisted. "Not for the portal, not even to rescue me - no, that's not true. I did need you to rescue me. From Sebastian and my own pig-headedness."

She choked back her tears.

"I need you so much, Noah. In my life, in my world. Please, Noah!"

Her voice cracked, a sob escaping from her throat, knowing that her desperate plea was probably too little, too late.

Jack stood in the doorway, beckoning them to come over.

"Mum, we have to go. Now."

Noah looked at Maggie with the love he knew he'd felt since the very first day they'd met. Still torn between the possibility of a life with her, and staying in the world that he knew, he wished there was more time to contemplate. He mourned the waste of a night and a day. Instead of cementing their relationship, they'd ended up swimming in a sea of uncertainty, and had squandered the chance to talk properly. And now there was no time left. But before he could respond to the woman standing in front of him, Sebastian's unmistakable voice sounded in the distance.

"Sir Noah, I challenge thee for once and for all. Come, fight like the knight thou pretend to be!"

Noah's stance immediately changed; his fight-or-flight reaction automatically kicking in.

"Mum," pleaded Jack, "you have to come. Now!"

Although there was a big part of Noah that desperately wanted to join Maggie, he couldn't just leave without a trace.

It wasn't in his nature. If he did, he would forever be known as a coward who'd hid from Sebastian, and he couldn't in good conscience let that happen. He wouldn't flee; he had to fight.

"Go," he said to Maggie, "Be with thy family. Make haste. My place is here."

And he pulled her close, kissing her firmly on the lips; hoping it would convey how much she meant to him. Above them, they could hear the sound of a galloping horse getting closer every second. Unable to restrain himself any longer, Jack rushed over to Maggie and tugged on her arm emphatically. She reluctantly released her embrace from Noah to comply. Realising he wasn't coming with them, Jack impulsively hugged Noah too, then turned to accompany his mum to the rectory.

Inside, the glow around the open trapdoor offered them a promise.

"It's worked, Margaret," said Harry, trying to turn her focus back to her real life. Understanding the torment she was going through, Cat squeezed her sister's hand.

"C'mon, Sis, you've got Christmas Eve dinner to make."

Maggie smiled through her tears. They were all together, and they were going home. That was the most important thing, she reminded herself. Already in the tunnel, Frankie attached Bronny's lead to his collar, while the dog waited for his owners to join him. The boys held torches, and Sam reclaimed her bag from its hiding place, putting her arms through the straps and securing it on her back.

"Your turn," Cat encouraged her sister, "with Jack. And then Dad. We're going to go last, in case Tom's knight thing prevents anybody descending after him."

Jack put his foot on the top step, offering his hand to his mother as they descended. Maggie held it tightly and took one last look through the window to see the back of Autumn Haze and her rider beginning to climb the slope up to the field again.

Harry walked down next, and then Cat. Tom, the last in the room, lowered his body through the trapdoor, placing his hands flat on the underside. He took a final glimpse around, at the place that had hosted them for the week before Christmas, in the year 1380.

And then he shut the door.

Noah stroked the side of Autumn Haze's neck as he ascended the slope to the top. He could hear Sebastian getting close, the echo of the horse's hooves reverberating around the arena. Expecting another slanging match or physical fight, Noah prepared himself for whatever altercation Sebastian had planned. Only, he couldn't have predicted the sight awaiting him as he emerged to higher ground. With eyes as dark as the horse he was riding - exuding resentment and revenge - Sebastian charged forward, thrusting his lance outwards, every ounce of his being pulsating with anger.

Noah looked up a fraction too late...

And then everything went black.

CHAPTER 14

Friday afternoon 24 December

IN THE TUNNEL, NINE people and a dog stood in silence. All sound from the outside receded into the background, then completely disappeared when the trapdoor closed. Just beyond, an orange brilliance, like an underground sunset, floodlit the path that led to their refuge. Reaching the underside of the stables' trapdoor, Harry had one more thing to say:

"Nunc aut nunquam est."

"Another Roman quote, Dad?" asked Cat, "Sicero? Or Seneca?"

"Elvis, actually," her father replied, "it's now or never."

He turned to Josh and Aaron.

"Boys, if you would be so kind..."

Crouching on the steps either side of the door, with their fingers at its edges, the best friends looked each other in the eye, hopeful but apprehensive. They tentatively pushed, not daring to breathe, until Josh could peek through the small gap that slowly eked open. The last time they'd got this far, he'd seen Noah sleeping in the stable master's quarters; the historic habitat remaining firmly in place. He prayed that wasn't the case this time.

The first thing Josh noticed was the smell. Or rather, lack of. Gone was the stench of horses, hay and manure. Nodding to Aaron, they pushed the door open further, steadily increasing Josh's line of sight as the gradually expanding view revealed an old, empty room. Emphasis on 'old'. He grinned and boldly thrust the door a full 90 degrees upwards. Climbing a few steps so that his upper body fully emerged from the hole, he looked around, then hurriedly ran up the rest of the stairs to confirm his suspicions. Confronted with a broken down building - slats and stones missing, the roof virtually caved in - Josh's relief to stand in such disarray washed over him like a wave.

"We've done it!" he cried triumphantly.

A beaming Aaron relayed the good news to the others in the tunnel.

"Are you sure?" Harry called out, not wanting to tempt fate.

"Come see for yourself," Josh shouted back.

Harry told the others to stay put for a minute. If, on the off chance, they'd travelled through time incorrectly, they were better to return to the 14th century, which by now held some familiarity, rather than venture into another unknown environment. Harry scaled the steps as fast as he could and marched straight to the window. Peering out, he was elated to see the sapling of the Middle Ages had grown into the magnificent oak he knew so well. He'd never wanted to hug a tree so much. Proceeding with caution, he wandered outside to put his hand on the bark, wanting the sensation of touch to confirm what he could see with his eyes.

There it was.

The message he had carved for Doris. How bloody good was that? And sure enough, the path to the right led to the retirement village up the slope; the modern accommodation and landscaped gardens, replacing the open-air entertainment arena Harry and his family had stood on only moments ago. He turned to Josh and Aaron, giving the thumbs up, and they helped the others through the trapdoor back into the 21st century. There were hugs all around, and the sun shining brightly through the window in a place they finally recognised, elevated their mood even higher.

"Doesn't seem to be much activity up there," Cat noted.

"That's not surprising," Harry commented. "It is Christmas Eve. Everyone will have gone home to their families for a few days."

"Everything feels a little surreal," she continued. "I mean, I can't quite believe we've made it. I just want to be certain that we've come back to the date we think we have."

Outside, the air smelled different. Good, but different. Less mud, sweat and fears; more safe haven sweetness. A very comforting hum of traffic sounded in the distance, and the hole in the fence they'd run through to escape the hail was still there. Good signs, for sure. Then Jack spied his broom, aka jousting stick, lying on the ground, on the other side of the fence on the school field.

"Look!" he pointed, running to fetch it. Surely this proved they were picking up where they'd left off. Tom also pointed, but beyond the expanse of the grounds, to the school buildings at the other end - no longer the manor that had been their temporary residence.

"Best we cross the field one more time to see if the cars are still in the car park," he said. They followed him away from the stables, through the hole in the fence and past the empty ground the chapel once stood on. Harry felt a pang of sadness that his lodgings for the last week no longer existed. Bronny - evidently recovered from Sebastian's thwack, and sensing the humans' change of state - caught a case of the zoomies, and raced backwards and forwards across the grass. They should have been ecstatic, but each had mixed feelings for different reasons. Sam felt bad that she hadn't been able to say goodbye to Ivy properly. Frankie wished he'd had time to farewell Egbert and Walter with a shake of hands at least. Tom and Harry quietly mourned the positions of respect they'd held in 1380, and secretly worried about returning to a humdrum lifestyle.

Maggie's profound regrets felt cavernous.

As they got closer to the school, she couldn't stop herself looking back at the stables several times; ever hopeful that Noah had changed his mind and would suddenly come into view. But no such luck. Her fairy tale was over.

The walk gave them time to adjust to a present-day mind-set, and talk of all the things they'd longed to come home to, allowed the memories of their unintentional visit to the past, drift into the recesses of their minds, with gratitude and optimism coming to the fore.

"Well, well, well, what do we have here?" announced Tom as they reached the car park, amazed to see the Volkswagen and Josh's car were still there, untouched other than some remnants of snow on the bonnets.

"Please tell me you've got the keys, Sam."

She fossicked around in her bag, and miraculously produced two sets of keys that she threw to her dad and brother.

"Friar Kenobi, can you say a quick prayer?" quipped Tom.

"Geez, it'd be a bummer if we got this far and the cars didn't start," Jack said, verbalising what everyone else was thinking. But luck was on their side today, and despite a couple of hesitant sputters, the two vehicles thankfully coughed into life. After discussing options, they decided to go to Maggie's and chill out for the afternoon. It was her day to put on dinner anyway, and Cat didn't want to leave her yet, knowing how much she'd be missing Noah. They'd been in the same clothes for five days, another few hours wouldn't hurt. And if they came across anybody on their way, Tom suggested explaining their costumes, by saying they were actors in a Camelot pantomime. It was as good an excuse as any, and certainly more believable than crossing the time-space continuum from 650 years ago. Cat still felt a little on edge, not having proof that today was, in fact, Christmas Eve in their own era. She'd seen time travel movies before, and wondered if they'd arrived exactly five days after they'd left, or if their calculations were a little off.

When they arrived at Maggie's house, the recognition of familiar markers gave everyone a bit of oomph: the crooked number on the letter box; the basketball hoop upon the garage; and the glimpse of the cherry blossom at the back. They were all there! As they were supposed to be. Crammed into two small cars, ten bodies clambered out, stretching cramped limbs and readily anticipating their entrance to normality. As soon as Maggie opened the door, Jack shouted out,

"Alexa, what's the date?"

"The date is: Friday, 24 December." came the response.

Just what Cat wanted to hear.

"Thank goodness!" she said. "Now we can relax. I bag's the loo!"

"Shower!" said Sam.

"Phone chargers," chorused Josh and Aaron.

"Biscuits," requested Jack.

"A cuppa for everyone, I think," proposed Maggie, heading straight for the kitchen and praying her pipe repair was still intact. LeBron James followed, confident of a bone being tossed his way, which he felt most deserving of, given his assistance in saving the humans today. Tom asked Jack if he could borrow his laptop and sat at the dining room table, wanting to use the internet. Harry sat beside him, also with something in mind. Frankie flopped into one of the chairs in the lounge, physically and emotionally drained from the drama of the morning, and so very pleased to be in a warm, dry house with these lovely people. Friendly with Cat and Maggie previously, their adventure together had now bonded them for life. With none of his relatives living close by, Frankie felt the Holdens and their extended family had officially adopted him, and he certainly wasn't complaining.

"Whoa! Check this out!" Tom exclaimed. He'd opened up Google Chrome and searched 'Buford Estate, 14th century' out of curiosity. To his surprise, the info that appeared on the screen included descriptive details about the Baron's quarterly festivities, apparently the talk of the town, and what the estate had become famous for. He read what he could see to the others:

"*Popular with locals and visitors alike, Buford Estate hosted spring, summer, autumn and winter events every year, promoting a collaboration of the upper and lower classes, very unusual for the time. The jewel in the crown was the week of Yuletide Cel-*

ebrations, held just before Christmas, where participants partook in innovative games such as Hoopball and Hoorah, while dining on an exotic dish called a hamburger."

Everyone burst out laughing, and Josh and Aaron congratulated each other on their contribution to history. Tom continued,

"It also says Baron Buford passed away in 1393, which would have made him about seventy. That was a pretty good innings in those days."

"That's nice," said Cat, "So he didn't perish in the Peasants Revolt after all."

"Does it say anything about anybody else?" asked Maggie.

"No, sorry," Tom replied ruefully, acutely aware of who his sister-in-law was referring to.

Maggie wasn't sure she wanted to know Noah's fate, anyway. Maybe ignorance was bliss under the circumstances. Tom passed the laptop to Harry, who immediately signed in to his Scrabble game. Everyone was patiently taking turns to charge their phones, but he wanted to contact Doris as soon as possible. This idea, he hoped, would be as effective as his tree carving, although he knew Doris would be mystified once again by his cryptic approach. He refreshed the screen until he got the letters he wanted, then placed them on the digital scrabble board.

H O M E

A few miles away at her daughter's house, Doris had settled into a recliner chair after a leisurely lunch, and was reading a magazine. Her phone beeped with a notification. She put on her glasses and opened the Scrabble app. Recognising Harry's nom de plume and understanding the word's relevance, she paused for a second before using the 'e' to attach a word of her own:

W H E R E

Harry, elated to get a response almost immediately, smiled to himself, thinking what a smart woman Doris was to understand his quirky way of communicating. Linking his next word to Doris's last letter, he added,

M A G G I E S

A few seconds passed, then Doris cleverly positioned three additional letters to the 'w' already laid down to let Harry know her thoughts.

W H E W

Not only had Doris somehow worked out that he'd been trapped in a place that prevented him from contacting her directly, she'd picked the exact right word to put in the puzzle that summed up the feeling from both parties. In addition, by using a triple word square, she'd scored an impressive 39 points. Clever lady, thought Harry.

Cat returned from her ablutions - which she'd enjoyed very much - with a new appreciation of the facilities. Previously underrating the joys of a flushing toilet, hot water, and flowing soap, she'd used the bathroom in her everyday life without giving it a second thought. Never considered a luxury, it now ranked as precious to her as her Louis Vuitton handbag. She and Tom went into the kitchen to help Maggie with tea and coffee. They cobbled together some sandwiches and opened a packet of shortbread biscuits for everybody. Maggie, coming to terms with her separation from Noah and trying to be philosophical, decided to go with the '*It's Better to Have Loved and Lost than Never to Have Loved at All*' mantra.

"Well," she said to Cat, "for a little while anyway, we both had our very own white knights by our sides."

"I don't think we were the only ones," Cat replied, looking over at her daughter.

Fresh from her shower and wearing her aunt's bathrobe, Sam leant against Aaron on the couch, shoulder to shoulder - the two comparing funny videos on their phones. Tom followed her gaze.

"When did that happen?" he asked, genuinely surprised.

"It's been building up all week, darling. Right under your nose."

Josh walked in on their conversation.

"I didn't see it either, Dad. I guess we were too preoccupied with our business meetings," he teased, nudging his father with his elbow. Helping himself to another sandwich, he mumbled with his mouth full,

"Hey, Frankie, do you play video games?"

"Does a one-legged duck swim in a circle?" Frankie replied.

"Great," Josh said, dropping crumbs on the floor, and immediately receiving a reprimand from his mother. "Let's go kick Jack's arse at NBA 2K."

Harry looked warmly at his family, so glad everyone was getting back to normal. It would take a while to adjust, he reckoned, but no one seemed worse for wear from their exploits, and if anything, were closer than ever. He wondered if they'd be able to slot back into their usual routines, or whether their experience would irrevocably change their outlook on life. If the latter, then surely it would be with a new appreciation of all they held dear.

They moved in slow motion for the rest of the afternoon - the release of anxiety reducing them to half speed - and did what they could to catch up with the week. Tom downloaded some of his cherished spreadsheets and knocked them into shape so he could send out a report to his clients. How he would have loved to include his work at the manor - surely the crowning achievement of his career - but that would forever remain a secret accomplishment. At least the Baron had endorsed him with a knighthood, and you couldn't get much better than that.

Josh and Aaron checked in with their boss by Zoom. They'd received good feedback from the retirement home about the bingo app, so could truthfully say they had been making successful sales calls this week (instead of riding chariots in the 1300s).

Frankie was getting a number of messages from other tenants in his building, saying they'd paid their rent online, and wishing him a happy Christmas. This baffled him, as he didn't understand why they were telling him about their financial transactions. It was none of his business. Hey Ho, he would catch up with them later, after he'd had dinner at Maggie's. They usually had Christmas Eve drinks at the cafe in the complex, and he was looking forward to seeing his colleagues again. A stiff gin and tonic or two wouldn't go amiss either.

Maggie switched the TV on to watch the early news. There were shots of the Oxford Street Christmas decorations, and reports that credit card spending was through the roof. No surprise there. Near the Thames, a Banksy original had materialised, adding to the increasingly merry mood. On the other side of the world, Australia and New Zealand were in the middle of record-breaking heat waves, and the UK and US politicians were serving up their usual seasonal tripe.

She turned it off again, returning to the kitchen to start her traditional meal mash-up, and requesting easy listening music from Alexa. Later, everyone came to the table as she dished up pizza, burgers, toasted sandwiches, and cottage pie (not forgetting Bronny's hard-boiled egg). As expected, there were oohs and aahs of appreciation; all devouring their favourites. Although the food they'd eaten at the manor had been plentiful and satiating, tonight's humble offerings seemed like restaurant quality meals by comparison. They talked and laughed congenially, remembering some of the lighter moments of their adventure and choosing not to bring up the more uncomfortable ones.

After they'd had dinner and washed the dishes by hand - Maggie's dishwasher malfunctioning again - Cat, Tom and the kids made their departure, dropping Aaron and Frankie home on the way. Jack excitedly returned to his video games, connecting with mates who hadn't heard from him in days. His mum told him to say they'd spent the week in the country with distant relatives and no phone reception. A little white lie to explain why he'd been missing in action, and the limit of her inventiveness right now. His friends didn't really care. They were just happy to have him back online, slipping into their banter without missing a beat.

Maggie and Harry settled in for the night. He'd taken off his friar's robe, the only souvenir they'd brought home with them. She'd unclipped the bun in her hair and scooped it up into a ponytail, feeling more like herself again. In the mood to be distracted, she selected a Hallmark Christmas movie on Netflix, and although keen to watch a predictable, feel-good story that had nothing to do with the Middle Ages, they both started yawning as soon as the opening credits rolled.

Across town, even though tiredness was setting in for Frankie too, his eyes lit up when he saw his salon, as Tom pulled the car into the kerb.

"Are you sure you'll be alright on your own?" asked Cat.

"Yeah, babe. Don't you worry. I'm going to catch up with Tallulah and the others. Thanks so much for the lift. And next time you have a school fair, I think I'll give it a miss, if you don't mind."

"I promise, I won't even invite you," assured Cat.

Frankie could see the party had already started next door, but was desperate to get out of his medieval clothes and freshen up. He quickly climbed the stairs before anyone noticed and turned the key in the lock of his apartment. About to walk into the entrance, he hesitated, stepped back into the hallway, and shut the door. He looked up and down the corridor and stared at the number in front of him. It was his flat, but it couldn't be. Opening the door again, he stared at the high-end furniture, lux rugs, and artwork on the walls. He surreptitiously took a few paces inside, feeling like an imposter.

Whose stuff was this?

Frankie entered the bathroom and clocked his favourite cologne sitting on the shelf; at least that was still the same. Then in the bedroom, lying pride of place on his pillow; his tattered teddy bear that he'd had since childhood, smiled back at him reassuringly. OK, this was definitely his apartment, but already knackered, he didn't have the bandwidth to work out why the decor was not as he remembered. Jumping into the shower, he let the hot needles of water massage his skin; his second wind arriving and preparing him to join the throng of people downstairs.

At the Holden household, Tom and Cat let the intoxicating pleasure of being back home sink in. Reaching into their drinks cabinet, Tom poured two single malt whiskeys. Neat.

"Aaaaah," he exhaled, taking a long swallow and savouring the medicinal bearing qualities of the drink. "Home sweet home. What a ride, eh, love?"

"I'm not sure I want to do that again in a hurry," Cat responded, taking a sip herself.

"No, but you can add an extra paragraph to your CV under Practical Experience now."

"I prefer my history knowledge to be theoretical from here on in, thanks very much. Going forward, I plan to have all my hands-on experiences in the near future, not the distant past."

"I like the sound of that," laughed Tom, raising his glass. "Cheers!"

They clinked glasses and went over their thoughts for the next day. A late Christmas lunch seemed like a good idea. Firstly, to allow everyone a long, leisurely lie in. The tsunami of emotions brought about by their shared encounter had caught up with them, flooding their bodies with exhaustion, and they expected to sleep like the dead tonight. The teenagers especially.

Secondly, to allow the turkey to thaw out.

Retrieving it from the freezer was Cat's first priority. Or maybe, second. Still not quite believing they'd got home just in the nick of time, she felt the need to touch everything to make sure it was real: the leather couch with the soft knitted throw; the photo of her mother on the mantelpiece; the newspaper on the coffee table that had been there since Monday. Even the silk tassels on the curtain drawstrings.

As Sam and Josh headed to their rooms, also on the hunt for peace of mind, Cat went to the master bedroom and let her body collapse onto the bed; her hands scrunching the duvet cover under her palms as her head sank into the pillow. Oh, the bliss of lying on a comfortable mattress and breathing in the scent of fresh linen. She'd changed the sheets at the beginning of the week, and still untouched, they were calling out to her with an invitation of cool, crisp Egyptian cotton.

Turkey first, she reminded herself, making a supreme effort to sit up as Tom came into the room.

"Do you think we'll ever think of bedsheets and electric ovens as ordinary again?" Cat asked her husband.

"I doubt it," he replied, sitting beside her. "I don't know about you, but I'm kinda seeing everything through rose-coloured glasses now."

"Yes, I know what you mean," she said thoughtfully. "Do you think Maggie will be alright? Without Noah, I mean."

"In time. She has a great life here. When the dust has settled and people get back into their routines again, she'll be OK. Bugger that he couldn't come with us, though. I quite liked the bloke."

"Me too. He was good for her. Brought out her softer side, which was nice to see."

Their ruminations were rudely interrupted by Sam's cry from the hallway.

"Mum, where are my earbuds?"

"Wherever you left them!" they called out in unison.

Some things didn't change.

FRANKIE WALKED INTO THE cafe, warmly welcomed by the other tenants of the building: his fellow business owners and workmates.

"Here's the Guv'nor!" came a cheer from the back, with a tone that said they'd been awaiting his arrival. The expression again puzzled Frankie, but he ignored it, just pleased to be home.

Tallulah ran up to him for a hug.

"Where have you been?" she enquired. "I couldn't get hold of you to firm up tomorrow's Christmas lunch arrangements."

"Oh my God. I haven't had time to get the desserts," apologised Frankie.

"What are you talking about?" she asked. "Aren't you using your usual catering service? I was just checking what time your parents were arriving, and whether they needed the limo." Now Frankie was completely confused. His family wasn't coming for Christmas. He hadn't been able to afford their train tickets this year.

"Anyhow," she continued, "while you've been wheeling and dealing in the big smoke - with your phone switched off, obviously - we've confirmed the refit of the salon, which is booked for next week. It'll be all bright and shiny for the new year!"

"Big smoke? Refit?" Frankie stuttered. "I'm not sure I understand."

"It's your complex, Frankie; it's only fair that your workplace gets the same treatment as you've given us. We're so thrilled you bought the building; you're the best landlord ever!" And she sashayed - as a dancer would - over to the bar to get him a drink.

Frankie didn't know if he was suffering the equivalent of jet lag, but he felt a little lightheaded and disoriented. Tallulah's comments didn't make any sense at all. Needing some air - and before he got waylaid by anyone else - he stepped outside again; steadying himself against a lamppost, his legs feeling weak. The colours from the neon sign on the roof cast a reflection in the puddles on the street, catching his eye. Not quite making out what it said, he looked skyward and read the words bold and bright above him:

Cooper's Landing.

The entire establishment was his...??

But how...???

CHAPTER 15

Saturday 25 December

On Christmas morning, the turkey remained in a stubbornly solid state. Choosing to be in denial, Cat proceeded to peel the potatoes and chop up the pumpkin. She was glad to have nagged Sam into decorating prior to their departure. The lounge looked suitably festive with stockings hanging from the mantelpiece, tinsel pinned to crown moulding, and the Christmas tree proudly showing off its baubles and twinkly bits.

Sam pulled on the reindeer jumper her mum had laid out for her; the crackling of static and weight of the wool enveloping her into a state of contentment. Having previously regarded traditions as stupid and naff, she'd had a change of heart. Stroking the worn, faintly tatty felt antlers on her top and catching the remnants of her mother's perfume, Sam basked in the comfort of certainty and sameness. A far cry from the fear and helplessness she'd felt during her harrowing brush with danger yesterday. Her feelings towards her brother had softened as well. Also previously classified as stupid and naff; his gritty display of determination to get her out of trouble made her appreciate him in ways she hadn't been inclined to before. They bickered constantly as siblings do, but in her hour of need, he had been there for her.

And then there was Aaron. Maybe she'd always liked his cheesy jokes. Maybe her subconscious had secretly fancied him. Very apparent now, however, was the warm and fuzzy feeling she got whenever he was near. The dynamics had undeniably shifted between them. Tapping into her thoughts, her phone delivered a text message.

> "Hey S, Happy Christmas. Can't wait to see your art exhibition next week. A xx"

She sent him a heart emoji back. Was that too presumptuous? No, he'd put two 'x's; that must mean something. Or was he the type of person to put those at the end of every message? Some people did, but she hadn't had a text from him before, so there was no precedent. Maybe that was his way. It wasn't her style, but then neither was sending a heart emoji and she'd just done that.

Honestly, messaging could be so open to interpretation!

She was still clueless as to whether romance was brewing or not. Having been literally thrown together in a panic to escape the mob at the estate, he had naturally held her close, with his arm wrapped around her in a protective manner. But there was something more, she thought. Even when hosting the bingo together, she'd felt a connection beginning to form, and after the daring rescue from Mistress Edith, it had definitely changed the way she looked at him. She was pretty sure the feelings were reciprocated - recalling how he sat close to her on the couch last night - but was it a temporary intimacy born out of the heat of the moment? She really didn't know.

Josh also got a text from Aaron.

> "Dude! Have a great Christmas. Still on for Operation Popsicle this Friday."

Josh grinned, glad to see that Aaron's interest in his little sister was not distracting him from their next Harry Houdini escape plan.

HARRY SAT IN MAGGIE'S kitchen, messaging Doris best wishes for the day; relieved to have a normal conversation with her at last, albeit by text. Still, much easier than tree carvings or scrabble tiles. He would go back to The Stables Retirement Village soon for a few days, and couldn't wait to catch up with his friend to finally play the backgammon game they'd put on hold. Then he'd join the family again on New Year's Eve for his granddaughter's art display at the gallery. He was very proud of all his grandchildren, each showing courage under fire and maturity beyond their years. As well as Margaret and Catherine - what a turbulent end of the year they'd had to endure. They too had handled things well, facing challenges he could never have prepared them for. Some day they would look back and laugh about their unexpected detour to the 14th century, but for now it was still raw, and there were a lot of things they needed to mentally unpack before it was business as usual.

LeBron James strolled past, eternally hopeful of snacks appearing for no particular reason.

"You've been a good boy too," praised Harry, ruffling the dog's fur. Always keen for scritches, Bronny sat down and put his head in Harry's lap, asking for more.

Harry loved being with his family at this time of year, but always missed Grace. Of course, he missed her every day, but Christmas brought back distinctive memories of their time together when the girls were little. Squawks of glee as the sisters ripped open Santa's presents, the smell of logs burning on the fire and a roast in the oven. Then, when Catherine and Margaret were all grown up, it was time for round two with the grandchildren. Just as thrilling, Grace took great delight in watching their little faces mimic those of her daughters at the same age. It was a special time when the kids believed in magic, and the adults indulged in their own childhood fantasies, always leaving milk and biscuits out for Father Christmas before the kids went to bed. Tom would - as Harry had before him - create fake footprints from the fireplace when the children were asleep, then bite into the biscuits and drink the milk; perpetuating the notion that the big man in the red suit had indeed visited overnight.

But now, even Jack was too old to believe in Santa Claus. And Grace wasn't here. The last few Christmases had been a poignant reminder of the passing of time, but today felt special again. Their nerve-wracking experience of the literal past made him cherish the present. Perhaps because they'd only managed to get home by the skin of their teeth, the family's bond was tighter than ever. Even his wife's presence seemed stronger. The spirit of Grace was unquestionably with him on Buford Estate and surrounded him still. It was a comforting feeling he hoped his daughters shared.

"Happy Christmas, Dad," greeted Maggie; joining him in the kitchen, giving him a peck on the cheek, and taking a hugely satisfying gulp of coffee that he'd made her. How she'd missed her daily ritual. The distinctive taste and gratifying jolt of caffeine was her favourite way to get the morning going.

"Morning, love, Happy Christmas to you too. How are you feeling today?"

"Better thanks. I do like being around my own stuff again. And knowing Jack is safe and sound has removed a considerable amount of stress. Today will be fun, I'm sure. Cat will put on a feast, Tom will tell his dad jokes, and the kids will fight over the remote. It'll be a bit of a reset, I think."

Harry nodded, noting she'd deliberately omitted any mention of Noah, and understanding her need to cling to current-day reality.

"Although there won't be any presents because none of us did any Christmas shopping. I might give Jack some money and let him go to the Boxing Day sales while I'm at work tomorrow. He's old enough to pick out his own clothes, and I think he's planning to hang out with his mates at the mall, anyway."

"Good idea," Harry agreed, "so, while Rip Van Winkle is still asleep, I'm going to monopolise the bathroom. Why don't you sit by your cherry blossom while you've got the chance?"

It was a good thought on her father's part. She topped up her coffee before walking into the backyard and sitting under the tree. A red-breasted robin joined her, perching on the wooden arm of the bench. It twitched its head back and forth, scoping out the area, then finished on a tilt, tipping the scene into a diagonal.

Maggie's mind wandered to the crazy times her family had been through. Pretty unbelievable, to be honest. If only they hadn't been down the end of the school field practising archery, none of this would have happened. Even if they'd tried that activity in the morning, and moved further up towards the classrooms in the afternoon, to give quoits or skittles a go, they would have been within striking distance of the school buildings to evade the hail storm. Instead, they'd run in the opposite direction to the stables and then…well…she shivered involuntarily at memories that would be permanently ingrained in her mind. Thank God everyone had returned unscathed. Although she couldn't deny that meeting Noah had been an unexpected bonus in the midst of the chaos. She sighed, trying to keep her 'if onlys' at bay.

On the plus side, Maggie had a very special reason to celebrate Christmas Day. That was the day, 14 years prior, when she knew she was pregnant. With a failed marriage already behind her, and the clock ticking louder every year, she'd made a decision just shy of her 40th birthday to proceed with the anonymous donor program at the fertility clinic. Having gone through the form-filling, blood testing and counselling - all compulsory for such a major life change - and then been wait-listed for six months, it came as a rude shock to discover that it wasn't as easy as she thought. After 40, the statistical likelihood of a woman becoming a mother was less than ten percent. IVF gave better odds, but was incredibly invasive and expensive. She didn't think she could go through with that particular process, so decided to stick with the more straightforward approach. With the staff tracking her cycle and calling her into the clinic at the optimal time, together with daily hormone injections to stimulate the growth of follicles on her rusty old ovaries; it was surely only a matter of time before the arrival of a bouncing baby boy or girl. She wasn't prepared for it to fail - six times! Disappointment took its toll on her every month, and in the end, taking a break seemed like the sensible thing to do.

Exhausted from her nursing work, and concluding that motherhood might pass her by, Maggie took a sabbatical; spending a couple of months in the Cotswolds to write in a journal, hike in the woodlands and read Marian Keyes novels. She did her best to remain positive, but the thought of being childless was a hard reality to accept, just the same. Then one night, while eating triangles of Toblerone and watching an episode of Sex and the City, she listened as Carrie and co asked Samantha how her life would be if she never had children.

"Not too shabby," came the reply, and Maggie realised that was true for her, too. As much as she wanted a child with all her heart, if becoming a mum wasn't her destiny, she still had a life to be thankful for. There were her gorgeous niece and nephew, of course, whom she adored spending time with. A loving family and great friends. The peaceful neighbourhood that she lived in; safe for walking the dog (although not so safe for the squirrels he chased). And the pretty park nearby - one of her happy places - where the rustling leaves of the beech trees whispered sweet nothings in summer, before putting their bling on in autumn and dotting the skyline with colour. And now, thanks to having some time out, she'd come up with an idea for a new role at the hospital, that she planned to pitch to HR. All enjoyable and fulfilling prospects to look forward to. She'd given her plan of parenthood her best shot, and if it wasn't meant to be, then C'est la vie.

Accepting her fate, she returned to Pebble Heath, rejuvenated from her break and ready to face the world; whatever it wanted to throw at her. Christmas music played on the radio and the streets glittered with fairy lights, some criss-crossing above her head as she drove progressively through each town. When she passed the gigantic tree in Aldacott town square, adorned with colourful ornaments and topped with a shining star, Maggie could have sworn she smelt a whiff of magic in the air. She arrived home in good spirits and eager to tackle the new year.

The next morning, she noticed a circle around the date on her calendar: Day 1 of her cycle.

She hesitated. Bit her lip. Mulled over her thoughts:

I haven't been taking my shots. It didn't even work when I was. And I'm effectively another year older than when I first started this whole thing!

But on a whim, and perhaps as a form of closure, she rang the clinic to give it one more go; under no illusions that her chances of success were slim at best. But, she reasoned, if she was going to walk away, she wanted to have given it her all.

Two weeks later, on Christmas Day, Maggie knew she was pregnant. With the shops shut and the clinic closed, she couldn't test.

But she just knew.

Call it intuition, call it serendipity, call it a Christmas miracle, but she was absolutely sure she was carrying a baby. As soon as the public holidays were done, she got a pregnancy kit from over the counter and a blood test to be sure, proving beyond doubt her hunch was right. Maybe some time in the country had helped, but as it transpired, the seventh time was the charm, and all became right with her world. Jack arrived nine months later, and Maggie's life was turned upside down, very much for the better. December 25th had a momentous meaning for her, and that would always be the case.

A cheery cry interrupted her reminiscing, startling the robin, who flew away.

"Merry Christmas, Mum!" sang Jack, revitalised after a decent night's sleep. Dressed in the interesting combination of basketball shorts over leggings, with a silly jumper on top (an ice-skating penguin), and a pair of Crocs on his feet, Maggie radiated with warmth at the sight of her son; ever grateful for not giving up her quest 14 years ago.

"I've got a present for you," he said, sitting down beside her and handing his mum a wrapped package. Not expecting any gifts today, she was touched by his gesture.

"Thank you, Bud, I didn't think any of us had had time for Christmas shopping."

"Didn't buy it. Made it," he grinned, "in carpentry at school."

Maggie tore open the wrapping paper to find a perfectly constructed wooden frame, sanded superbly, and stained a pretty maple colour.

"It's beautiful, love!" she said, hugging him fiercely. "I'm going to find the perfect picture to put in here."

Jack was stoked at his mum's reaction. She deserved something nice after the kerfuffle with Sebastian. And if Noah couldn't be here to have his mother's back, then he would be!

Today also marked a significant date in Jack's life. When he was seven, his mother had brought home a puppy for Christmas. The creature with feet and ears too big for its body, immediately became Jack's best mate, following him wherever he went. With no siblings to speak of, the companionship and adoration he received from his new four-legged friend proved invaluable. Naming the pup after his favourite basketball player, LeBron James grew quickly, and for a time, was nearly bigger than his boy. But Jack had grown too in recent years, and their sizes had levelled out once again.

There were some habits they'd had to temper. Bronny took great delight on a Saturday morning, in running down the stairs to throw himself onto Jack's bed as a wake-up call. But as the dog's weight increased to a massive eight stone, one particularly exuberant bounce had thumped the bed against the wall, cracking the bedhead and two of the legs underneath. Not to mention knocking the stuffing out of Jack as a giant black lump landed on his stomach. Jack kept his bedroom door shut these days to discourage a similar mishap, but often woke to puffs of air being snorted through the gap at the bottom from an impatient Great Dane wanting to play. Six years old now, Bronny was as ungainly as ever, but loved by his boy no matter what: as much a part of the family as the human kind.

Moving inside from the garden, Maggie cooked breakfast while Jack shot a few baskets and Harry completed his shower. After they'd eaten, they walked Bronny to the stream; pausing on the bridge for a moment to take in the picturesque sight of Pebble Heath dressed in her winter whites. Under their feet, a gentle flow of water meandered towards the woods. Silvery currents bounced casually over smooth stones; the banks of the stream curving into a self-satisfied smile, waiting to be immortalised on film or canvas. They played Pooh sticks with the twigs scattered on the floor; the dog barking every time one was thrown into the water on one side of the bridge, and again when he saw it emerging on the other. With clear skies above, it was the first leisurely, stress-free morning they'd had all week.

Meanwhile, at Cooper's Landing, Tallulah's dance studio had been transformed into a Christmas lunch venue, with a long table in the centre of the wooden floor - Hogwarts style - and the room festooned with balloons and bunting. Fake snow decorated the floor-to-ceiling mirror on the far wall and coloured ribbons wrapped themselves around the ballet barres. Delectable aromas wafted through the building from the café, where the caterers were doing their prep work. Frankie was tidying up his apartment, breathing in the deliciousness, when a knock on the door interrupted him. He opened it and was almost bowled over by a rush of hugs and kisses from his parents.

"Franklin Theodore Cooper," shrieked his mum, "you are a scamp!"

"You sure are," agreed his dad, "but we're not complaining about the upgrade. Thanks son, it made the flight much more enjoyable," and he gave a throaty laugh that reminded Frankie of Baron Buford. Overwhelmed by the unexpected arrival of his visitors who, it appeared, had flown across the country on his dime, Frankie was unable to utter anything other than Merry Christmas. Whatever was going on in the world he had returned to seemed to be to his advantage, and pumped to have his family with him, he opted to roll with it until an explanation was forthcoming. After depositing their luggage into the spare room, and throwing on his halo headdress for the hell of it, the Coopers went downstairs to join Tallulah and the other tenants for the start of a special day.

THAT AFTERNOON AT TOM and Cat's place, a hubbub of happy family members playfully teased and joked with each other, thankful to be part of their own Yuletide Celebrations, rather than the Baron's in 1380. Cat had put together a succulent array of food, despite the turkey not defrosting in time. That would have to be another meal in a few days' time. Instead, she'd pivoted and grilled some lamb chops, combining them with the vegetables she'd prepared earlier. Fluffy Yorkshire puddings covered in lashings of gravy accompanied the meat and veg, garnering rave reviews from those seated at the table.

Through the pouring of drinks, passing of plates and theft of the crispiest roast potatoes, Tom looked across to his wife and with a subtle smile, raised his glass the merest of fractions in acknowledgement of what the day meant to them.

27 years ago, Tom had asked Cat to marry him on Christmas Day. They had met at university, sitting in the stands on Athletics Day. Neither of them sporty; both had retreated to the relative obscurity of the spectator area. She; cheering on her friend Lisa, who was Fosbury flopping over the high jump; he; pretending to watch the field events but really not taking any interest. Tom would much rather have been in the maths room or the library, but attendance out in the open was mandatory on Athletics Day, with no lessons or lectures in the offing. To relieve the boredom, he'd bought a big punnet of chips smothered with tomato sauce and ended up sitting next to Cat. He immediately thought she was out of his league - pretty, petite, and more than likely, popular - but despite not

knowing each other, she gave him the hugest of grins when he sat down beside her.

It turned out she was after his chips.

Blessed with a high-functioning metabolism like her mother, Cat could eat anything she liked without gaining weight. Tom assumed, with her model-esque looks, that she'd prefer nibbling on carrot sticks and drinking water, but she had no qualms about asking if he would share his snack. When he agreed (quietly adding up the time he was spending with this total babe, so he could boast about it later), he was shocked to see her wolf the chips down in less than a minute - beating his own personal best. They got talking about their studies, and he was impressed to learn that she had taken on English literature and ancient history, both pretty meaty subjects, unlike the frothy topics he thought she might lean into. You definitely couldn't judge a book by its cover.

Later that night at the after-party, they bumped into each other again and she bought him a beer as a thank you. Her bubbly personality attracted him to her even more, and when she asked him to dance - before he could say he had two left feet and zero rhythm - she'd dragged him onto the dance floor, and began boogieing on down to Everybody by the Backstreet Boys. The ragged edges of his shyness gradually smoothed out, and as his confidence grew, he came to the unforeseeable conclusion that this girl might actually be into him. By the time the All Saints song, Never Ever, came on, he'd plucked up the courage to ask her for a slow dance. She accepted, and 18 months later they were engaged.

To this day, Cat steals Tom's chips whenever she can.

Today was turning out to be just as memorable. Polishing off the Christmas pud after a long, enjoyable lunch, and before the sun reached its zenith, the family went outside to play a game of corn hole, supposedly to burn off a few calories. Harry's shots were well on target, beating the younger generations. He justifiably gloated; teasing his grandchildren that there was no beating experience (or luck for that matter, but he didn't need to point that out). As it got chilly, they returned to the lounge to watch the King's message on TV; commenting about his age, and agreeing that they much preferred having an older, experienced Head of State, as opposed to the junior version that ruled in the late 1300s. The afternoon merged into evening, with mugs of hot cocoa plonked on the coffee table, and wrappers of individual chocolates discarded indiscriminately.

Everyone's cup - and stomach - was full.

A competitive game of Monopoly kept them occupied well into the night. Josh won, amassing houses and hotels on Trafalgar Square, Fleet Street, and the Strand, ultimately bankrupting everyone else. As he took Sam's last penny and counted up his pretend money, he reflected on recent events. Christmas Day was Christmas Day to Josh. He didn't hate it like his sister, or love it like his mother. Other than the religious reference, the date didn't have any special meaning to him, either. Laid back as usual, he was happy to have a few days off at the end of the year. But considering their close shave yesterday, that could have had them spending an entirely different Christmas altogether, he decided from here on in December 25th would symbolise the full stop at the end of a very unusual chapter in their lives.

As the night closed in and yawns could no longer be stifled; goodbyes were exchanged, hugs shared, and an excellent day came to an end. Maggie, Jack and Harry headed home before the clock struck twelve, and then in both households within minutes of each other, lights were switched off and bodies crashed into beds. Even the empty space in Maggie's heart couldn't stop her from sleep.

Christmas Day was complete.

CHAPTER 16

Sunday 26 December

JACK HAD ENERGY TO burn on Sunday morning. Having arranged to meet David and Liam at McDonalds - pancakes for breakfast being the order of the day - he was positively bouncing off the walls. Maggie, who admittedly felt a little flat when she allowed herself to think about Noah, found her son's uncontainable enthusiasm infectious. Her mood perked up at the thought of seeing her friends at the hospital, and getting back to doing what she did best. She dropped him off at the mall on her way to work; transferring some money to his account for a belated Christmas shopping spree.

Harry stayed at home, content to dog sit and potter around the garden. A people person in the normal scheme of things, he welcomed some time to himself, given the week that was. There was a talkback show on the radio he wanted to listen to, plus a crossword and today's Wordle to do. Having a lazy day and doing not much of anything suited him down to the ground.

Maggie arrived at Aldacott Hospital, parked up, then entered the lift, pressing the button to the third floor. Dressed in black pants and a white top, handbag slung over her shoulder, she clasped the clipboard in her hand; transferring herself into working mode. As the lift door opened, she copped an eyeful of Adam on the wrong side of the desk, whispering something in Hayley's ear that made the receptionist blush. Ready to take him to task for hitting on another staff member, Maggie checked herself when she saw Hayley turn to kiss Adam on the cheek.

Alrighty then, a lot can happen in a week, it would seem.

The pair jumped at the sound of the lift doors opening and looked sheepishly at her, not unlike children caught with their hands in the cookie jar. She wasn't sure if Hayley's embarrassment was because she'd seen her act of PDA, or because she knew Maggie would think she could do better. Ah well, each to their own. If Adam was less likely to pester her, it was a win, as far as Maggie was concerned. The surgeon looked very pleased with himself as he walked away from the reception desk. Hayley looked self-conscious but happy.

"Welcome back!" she said, her full attention on Maggie now, "did you enjoy your time off?"

"It was a week to remember," replied Maggie truthfully, "but I'm glad to be back now."

"Good to see you, Mags," added Adam. "I would chat but have to run, I'm afraid." He turned and headed to the lift, giving a small, awkward wave as the doors closed.

"I know, I know," said Hayley, anticipating Maggie's grilling, "you don't have to say anything."

"It's alright, Hayley," Maggie placated. "You're a grown woman; you can hook up with whomever you like, but how did that come about?"

"We bumped into each other at the pub last Wednesday. I'd annoyingly been stood up by a Tinder date, and Adam was grabbing a drink after an intense surgery. We consoled one another and ended up enjoying each other's company. It was just the two of us, and well... we kinda clicked. He walked me home and kissed me, but that was all. He was quite the gentleman."

Maggie recalled her Wednesday night with Noah, which had followed a similar pattern, and didn't have the heart to admonish Hayley.

"Well, good on you," she said instead, "I've always been one for meeting someone in real life rather than swiping right, so well done for doing it the old-fashioned way. Now, what's the latest with the patients?"

"So, the dislocated shoulder, tonsillectomy, and pneumonia case got discharged last week. But Sarah, our expectant mum, is still here."

"So not a Christmas baby, then? New Year's, maybe?"

"Yeah, I think they are going to induce if she doesn't have it by New Year's Day. Anyway, here's your list for today: Sarah, of course, in the maternity ward. Then four people who came in yesterday: a food poisoning case who's been throwing up all night - he's done his dash I think and is recovering with fluids; a suspected case of appendicitis that we're keeping an eye on; then on the fourth floor, a couple of injuries from falls and stuff. It's a wonder we don't have more, given the snow that's been around."

Maggie attached the notes to her clipboard, thinking she might go to maternity first and work her way down.

HUNCHED OVER A BIG trestle table, Cat was helping Sam decide which of her works to display at the exhibition on Friday. With a blend of photographs and different painting techniques, the collection was evolving quite nicely. She'd used some candid moments whilst away in the Middle Ages, as well as images captured before and after their escapade. The result was an eclectic compilation of pictures that Sam was truly proud of. The theme of the show - The Secret to Love - asked the artists to finish the title, with their own interpretation of what the word meant. Sam didn't have that part worked out yet, but was confident the artwork would tell the story; the definition of love bound to come clear in due course.

Cat's phone rang. It was Frankie, sounding a little agitated.

"Kitty Cat, how was your Christmas Day?"

"It was great, thanks, Frankie. How was yours?"

"That's why I'm ringing, hon. It was a bit strange, to be honest. Don't get me wrong, it was a brilliant day, but strange nevertheless. Is Tom doing anything this morning?"

"Not really, as far as I know. Are you OK? Do you want me to ask him to pop round to yours?"

"Yes, thanks, that would be great. I'd like him to run his eyes over my books if he doesn't mind working on Boxing Day."

"You know Tom, that's his idea of fun. He won't mind at all. I'll send him a text. You're still coming to Sam's thing on Friday, aren't you? I promise there aren't any time travel portals at the art gallery."

"For sure, babe. Wouldn't miss it for the world."

Tom got Cat's message and was more than happy to help Frankie out. He'd been twiddling his thumbs this morning, Christmas being done and dusted and everyone else having things to do; he'd let his thoughts roam to the demands of the 14th century. With no cars or phones or internet, there had been a lot of walking and talking and doing. In the current day, with all its creature comforts, he could envisage himself getting complacent again if he wasn't careful. Frankie's cry for help was just what he needed - a project would do him good.

Tom packed up his laptop, got in the car, and drove to the Curl Up and Dye salon. Also surprised to see the signage on the roof, he asked Frankie about it when he got inside. Frankie rewound to the night before, telling him about the unpredictable developments in his private and business life, since he'd come home. Fortunately, his mum and dad had gone for a walk, giving them some privacy. Tom opened his laptop and logged into Frankie's files. Setting up a new folder, he dragged and dropped documents for comparison's sake, looking for clues as to what had changed while they had been living in another era. He tried to correlate the Frankie of a week ago with the Frankie of today, and was coming to the most astonishing conclusion. After a few more minutes, and plenty of *hmmm's*, *fancy that's*, and *goodness me's*, Frankie's patience ran out; his edginess getting the better of him.

"What is it?" he asked with an intensity in his voice.

"All right then," said Tom, "it seems like all your Christmases have come at once, my friend. You're rich! And have been for some time by the looks of it." He smiled agreeably, turning the laptop in Frankie's direction, to show him the very healthy numbers on the screen.

"I don't understand," said Frankie. "I was virtually broke a week ago. You don't think something happened while we were away, do you?"

"Maybe," mused Tom, "but - here's a crazy thought - perhaps your situation has changed *because* we were away. What if Walter having the same name as you was more than just a coincidence? What if he's actually a bone fide ancestor of yours? Originally, his destiny might not have amounted to much, but we did manage to turn the peasants' financial prospects around. Perhaps that had a flow-on effect throughout the centuries. I'd say your parents will be well off too, if prosperity has trickled down the ages, but as your investment portfolio shows, you in particular have risen from comfortable to nauseatingly wealthy. Frankie was gobsmacked,

"My investment portfolio?" he repeated, hardly daring to believe his ship had finally come in. He silently offered a prayer of gratitude in appreciation of Walter Cooper's efforts back in the day; the man he'd met two weeks - or seven centuries - ago. The two men sitting in front of the laptop continued to pore over the details. Not being very financially savvy, Frankie did his best to keep up with Tom's explanation of stocks, bonds, and property. They wondered if any other changes from the past might show themselves in the now. It was an interesting premise. But Frankie had some ideas of his own to make up for the disconcerting week they'd been through.

"So, Tom," he pondered, considering his new position, "if I'm as flush as you say I am, I think I'd like to share the love. What do you think about this...?"

AT THE HOSPITAL, MAGGIE finished her rounds on the upper floors, then grabbed a bite to eat at the cafeteria on the third level, next to reception. She was enjoying getting stuck into her job again; it kept her mind off other things. Jack had messaged her saying he had bought some 'drippy' clothes that looked 'cold' and thanked her for the injection of cash. He and his friends were off to the cinema to see the latest Marvel movie, the timing of which worked well with Maggie's schedule. She'd pick him up after work as the movie finished, and they'd dine on leftovers with Harry at home. That sounded perfect, she thought, sipping her takeaway coffee. She went back to Hayley's desk, needing the details of the injuries on the floor above.

"A slipped disc in room 10," informed Hayley, "came in yesterday after sliding on some ice outside his home. And several crushed toes in room 12. Apparently, as a result of dropping a leaf blower on his foot. Not a great Christmas present, as it turns out."

Maggie nodded, jotting notes down on her paper.

"Oh, and one fella who came in on Christmas Eve with broken ribs and a fractured arm. He was concussed and not making a lot of sense. Adam said it looks like a blunt force trauma to the chest. Poor guy didn't seem to know what day it was."

"OK," said Maggie, heading towards the lift again.

"To be precise, he did know what day it was...just confused about the year."

Maggie's feet stopped moving. She enquired tentatively, "Do you know what happened to him?"

"Not in detail," answered Hayley, "but he did say he fell off a horse."

Now rooted to the spot, Maggie's heart leapt to her throat.

"Which room is he in?" she asked hoarsely.

"17," came the reply. "He was sleeping when I checked before. Not your typical middle-aged dad type. He's pretty cute - got gorgeous blue eyes."

Inexplicably, the song Lose Yourself by Eminem started running through Maggie's head: *palms are sweaty, knees weak, arms are heavy*. Exactly how her body was reacting to the ridiculous thought crossing her mind. Telling herself that it couldn't possibly be who she thought it might be didn't help. Hope ripped through her like a tidal wave, crashing through all her preconceptions. Her pulse raced - to go with the sweaty palms, weak knees and heavy arms.

Breathe...she told herself...breathe. And take the stairs to pull yourself together. You're being silly.

Sam had ninety percent of her display sorted. The only thing missing was a frame for her favourite creation: a painting of Maggie, Noah and Jack running hand in hand through the puddles across the estate field from a few days ago. She'd frustratingly lost the original photo taken behind the column at the manor, but using individual shots of each subject and showcasing her skill as an artist, she'd managed to transfer the scene in her head onto the canvas. Wanting to remind her aunt of the spontaneity and pure joy of the moment, she was pretty chuffed she'd been able to capture and hold those emotions, in paint at least. Sam was also working on a special picture for her grandfather, using a different approach that would further demonstrate her talents. Having felt discouraged at her lack of inspiration a couple of weeks ago, she was now overflowing with ideas, and very much looking forward to the exhibition. Cat smiled in admiration of her daughter. Worried that their time in the past might have affected the children negatively; instead, the opposite seemed true. All had gained a confidence she doubted could have been attained elsewhere. Silver linings, absolutely.

Look, if you had one shot, or one opportunity to seize everything you wanted, in one moment, would you capture it or just let it slip?

The lyrics of that sodding song mocked Maggie as she climbed the stairs. Yes, she'd let it slip. Her ability to handle most aspects in life with pragmatism and common sense, had seen her right for the majority of the time. But as her father had pointed out, love doesn't lend itself to logic. For all intents and purposes, finding Noah, someone with depth and sensitivity, had been a special kind of wonderful. An enhancement to her life - a quality she'd specified to Hayley - not a hindrance. Like two pieces of a puzzle, they'd slotted in beside each other, as if that was always the way it had been. But instead of rejoicing in the strange twist of fate and embracing every second, she'd been preoccupied with what might go wrong, until it actually did. Like the luxury of latter-day plumbing, she hadn't realised how much she needed something - or someone - until they were taken away.

Good God, what was wrong with her? She'd just compared spending time with Noah to the workings of a sewage system. No wonder she'd never solidified a meaningful relationship. Well, it didn't matter, anyway; there was no chance of that now. She'd absolutely scuppered her chances of love. Her one shot had passed her by, and now her responsibility was to tend to the injured patients in this very hospital who needed her assistance.

She knocked back the last dregs of her coffee with conviction, throwing the paper cup in the bin. Maggie opened the door to Level 4 and looked down the corridor. She was tempted to go straight to room 17, to prove that her laughable daydream was just that, but quelling the urge, and being a creature of habit, she visited each room in chronological order. Room 10 was feeling more comfortable thanks to the heavy-duty pain relief, and they sat down together to discuss physiotherapy options and what support was available. Number 12 was pretty chipper, considering he'd broken his toes and his leaf blower. Maggie ascertained he was a graphic designer who worked from home on a laptop, so having a cast on his foot, while inconvenient, wasn't going to jeopardise his ability to do his job. She helped him fill in various NHS forms, and they shared anecdotes of foolish things they'd done in their lives. If only he knew, she thought.

There was always a multitude of paperwork required for ongoing treatment, and listening to the back stories of what led people to be hospitalised was part of Maggie's duties, so she could write a report on their individual circumstances. She took copious notes: on who else lived at home, what medication the patients were on, and whether they had support and equipment to help them rehabilitate. Essentially filling in the blanks to complete the full picture, so the medical staff could put into place an effective and appropriate recovery plan. On her clipboard, she marked a big tick by number 10 and number 12.

Finally, her last patient. Feeling much more level-headed, she proceeded to Room 17. It would just be some guy who'd been mucking around on Christmas Eve. Perhaps he'd been drinking with his mates. Or fallen off a motorbike, not a horse. Hayley had said he was confused. She paused near the doorway, gauging whether the man had woken from his nap, and casually scanned the room for any signs of movement.

Then she saw it.

Her gaze was inexorably drawn to a purple silk tunic, folded neatly and placed on the shelf as part of the patient's personal belongings. Now wearing a hospital gown, he was lying on his side with his back to her, but there was no mistaking who that belonged to. A knot tightened in her stomach. Much like Frankie, with his shocking discoveries yesterday, Maggie felt the need to put her hand against the wall to steady herself. Taking a couple of quiet steps into the room, one barely perceptible word came out of her mouth.

"Noah?"

The man turned at the sound of her voice, and those familiar wrinkles around his sea-blue eyes deepened with pleasure. With one arm in a cast, he cautiously reached out with the other and responded,

"Maggie? Do mine eyes deceive me?"

Overcome with emotion, Maggie rushed to his side, clasping his good hand with both of hers, tears trickling down her face.

"Noah!" she cried. "Oh my God! You're here! But how? And what happened? You're so badly hurt."

He looked at her with affection, then cupping her face with his right hand, and gently wiping away her tears with his thumb, he began to replay his story...

...After Maggie's departure with her family, Noah - despondent but resolute - ascended the hill on Autumn Haze. As he reached the top, he heard Sebastian and Onyx thundering towards his end of the field, but did not comprehend the ferocity of the scene that lay before him. With barely seconds to register what was happening, he managed to brace himself and turn his filly out of harm's way, but knew he was unlikely to avoid the impact that was coming. An almighty blow to the chest from Sebastian's lance knocked Noah clean off his horse, with the momentum forcing him to roll back down the hill; tumbling into a misshapen heap that smashed against the oak tree at the bottom. The final crash rendering him unconscious.

He woke minutes later in the stables with Nancy, the herbalist, waving smelling salts under his nose. Bloodied, bruised, and broken, Noah had been lifted from the ground outside by Egbert and the Baron into the haven of his stable master quarters. The herbalist had been called upon to help rouse him and apply poultices to his wounds, but they all understood he was in pretty bad shape. The Baron asked Nancy and Egbert for some privacy, so he could talk to Noah alone. They obediently left the stables, deeply troubled by the plight of their colleague. Egbert's angst about the chaos that had developed that morning burgeoned considerably, but he trusted the Baron would have Noah's best interests at heart. Egbert's next priority was to help Walter. He and some of the stronger workers were delivering Sebastian to the manor's singular jail cell, where the Baron had insisted he spend the night to cool off.

In the stables, Baron Buford bent down next to the forlorn figure of his friend.

"Noah," he said softly, "gallant knight thou art, there are not many that would be a match to Sebastian when he acts in such a brutish manner. He will be reprimanded, that I promise, but I fret about thy state. Both physical and spiritual."

Noah could barely respond, but was alert enough to listen.

"Thou art a loyal servant, Noah, and hath fulfilled thy duties on this estate one hundredfold. If the future can heal as thou hath told me it can, and it offers solace for thy heart as well, thou hath my blessing and understanding to follow its call."

Noah shook his head as if to protest, but the Baron had one more thing to say.

"Look inwards for an answer, my dear friend. This treasure left in haste might sway thy decision," and he handed Noah something he had picked up from the ground at the northern end of the field, where the antagonism between the two rivals had exploded. Baron Buford stood up and bowed, showing his respect for the man who lay slumped and in pain.

After the Baron left, Noah looked at what he'd been given. A wave of despair rolled over him, and he leant his head against the wall, endeavouring to find relief from his physical and mental anguish. But everything hurt, and he felt so helpless; his left arm unable to move, and his breathing laboured from his chest injury. He was of no use to anyone if he couldn't recover from his injuries.

Noah drifted in and out of consciousness several times. In moments of lucidity, he tried to weigh up whether the limited knowledge he had of the future was enough to take the risk into the unknown. Would providence be merciful? But in the end, his unbearable pain, coupled with the Baron's declaration of permission, tipped the balance in favour of going. And so, with an almighty undertaking on his part, he gingerly crawled down the steps under the trapdoor, read the verse aloud as he had seen Harry do, then hauled himself up the stairs again.

NOAH'S FIRST IMPRESSION OF the 21st century was one of dejection. Seeing the stables in such a state of disrepair saddened him. But his melancholy was quickly superseded by awe, as he stumbled outside to take stock of the magnificent growth of the oak tree and the contemporary architecture of the building above. He could faintly discern the footprints from the recently returned group, going in the direction of the manor. Although it wasn't the manor anymore, it was Jack's school. That he remembered. He couldn't catch sight of anyone in the distance, but attempted to follow the footprints, anyway. However, the strain of physical activity was too much, and he collapsed again in agony, passing out near the fence.

What happened next was much of a blur. Noah came around in a moving vehicle, lying on a narrow bed of some description. A man in uniform told him they were on their way to a hospital, and because of Maggie's previous clarification, he understood. His pain did not feel as intense; and looking down, he saw a peculiar tube-like device sticking out from the skin near his elbow. He found it worrying to have a foreign object embedded in his body, but was too groggy to complain. His left arm was numb and bandaged in a way to restrict movement. He was scared and bewildered, but more than anything, exhausted. Despite having a myriad of questions, he gave in to his overwhelming fatigue, and did not awaken until he was transported to Room 17 on Level 4 of Aldacott Hospital.

NOAH PAUSED THE DESCRIPTION of events that had brought him to the present day, as Adam popped his head around the door.

"Ah, Maggie," he said, fortunately not noticing her high state of emotion, "I see you've met our wounded soldier." Then he turned to Noah and announced,

"Well champ, whatever disagreement you were a part of, it must have been one hell of a fight!"

Maggie and Noah glanced sideways at each other, telepathically acknowledging Adam's remarks were closer to the truth than he knew. He continued to speak directly to his patient, while pinning imagery to the high-tech, backlit panel on the wall to show his findings.

"The X-rays have confirmed a broken left arm and two broken ribs, but luckily, all your vital organs have been spared. There was some internal bleeding, but we managed to stem that when you first arrived."

Noah looked at the pictures in consternation.

"Those are my insides?" he asked.

A little bemused by the question, Adam nodded and continued his assessment.

"There's not a lot we can do for broken ribs. Other than rest and some breathing exercises I can give you. You'll need to take it easy for a good month or so. We'll keep you here this week for observation, especially as you had a nasty bump on the head too, but all things going well, I should be able to discharge you by Thursday or Friday. Then you'll need to come back to get the cast on your arm removed. Do you have someone at home to take care of you? Is there anyone we can call?"

Noah started to respond by saying, "Nay, tis a vexing state of affairs…" but Maggie interrupted before his old English way of speaking completely gave him away.

"I'll take down the details," she promised Adam, "and bring you a report later." She smiled cooperatively, which seemed to satisfy the surgeon, and he went on his way; leaving them alone again, oblivious to their connection.

The two talked for another hour or more, but Maggie could see Noah's energy beginning to fade. She understood the injuries inflicted, in addition to coming through the portal, would have taken a lot out of him. The nagging question she hadn't asked yet loomed like an indeterminable shadow - was Noah intending to stay? The words had to be uttered at some stage, but she didn't want to press him now. She kissed his cheek, assuring him he was in the best place with the most capable medics, and would see him again the next morning.

As she left, Noah felt lighter, a little more sanguine. Demoralised and battered to within an inch of his life, he had asked God for a sign as to what to do, and the Baron had given it to him. He slipped his right hand under his pillow, pulling out the memento that had convinced him to come to this strange new world.

CHAPTER 17

Last week of December

IT WAS THAT TIME of year; between Boxing Day and New Year's Eve when nobody knew what to do with themselves. Everyone stayed in their PJs past midday, ate too much cheese, and had no clue when to put the bins out. A kind of limbo where indecisiveness was the name of the game, and impromptu get-togethers randomly occurred.

Just about ready to explode with his news, Frankie suggested the latter, proposing a reunion dinner on Thursday for those who had traversed through time. Cat thought it a great idea. As Frankie and Aaron had gone home alone on Christmas Eve - not getting the same opportunity to talk about their weird experience - this would give them a safe space to offload any thoughts or concerns they might have had since. Still with a turkey to cook, she offered to host. Frankie asked Tom to keep his newly minted status to himself and bought his parents tickets to a show to free him up for the night (hardly a problem these days).

Maggie had concerns of her own. Did she tell her family about Noah, or should she wait until he revealed his intentions? For all she knew, he had followed the Baron's advice to travel to the 21st century, solely for the purpose of accessing superior medical know-how. Once his injuries were healed, he might want to return to the Middle Ages. After all, his lifelong friends, precious horses, and beloved son were still in 1380. She remembered how much she had wanted to get back to her own time; Noah may very well feel the same. Mindful that her family thought highly of him, and not wanting to get their hopes up - or hers for that matter - she decided she would sleep on it tonight.

OVER THE WEEK, VARIOUS preparations were put into place for different activities. Sam took her display pieces to the gallery, apart from the two she was still working on. The other artists were putting their exhibits together - their titles all sorted out.

The Secret to Love is:

- Kindness (sweet)
- Never Having to say You're Sorry (cliché)
- Putting the Toilet Seat Down (funny)
- Understanding what the Silences Mean (obscure)

Sam didn't have a completed title yet, but as she carefully positioned her pictures, a theme started to present itself. She took a minute to reflect on the images; all telling their individual stories to any observers, but having so much more meaning to those involved. Despite the recent difficulties they'd faced, she took pride in her re-creation of some of the special moments that had emerged amid the angst.

Josh and Aaron fell back into their natural habitat of jokes and prank planning. Needing a specific mode of transport for Friday, they sought the advice of an event organiser. Of a similar age, she showed Josh pictures of what was available - casually tossing her hair back and smoothing it out with her hand - all the while smiling up at him. Grateful for her recommendation, the boys paid the hire fee in advance. She handed out a business card with her mobile number on it. "...so you can call me to confirm the pick-up time."

As they thanked her and walked out the door, Aaron pushed Josh's shoulder with his.

"Bro, she was totally flirting with you!"

Josh laughed and shoved his mate into a nearby hedge.

"Shut up," he said, half embarrassed, half flattered. "Priorities man, aren't we well overdue for a decent kebab?" With the two mates in agreement, they headed in the direction of the food court, still punching each other in the arm intermittently.

Cat, excited about their reunion dinner, pushed her trolley around the supermarket, relishing the choice and abundance of food at her fingertips. Obviously, it had always been there, but now she was so much more appreciative of the variety. She definitely needed some cranberry sauce, new potatoes and Brussel sprouts. This was going to be the proper Christmas dinner they should have had on Saturday.

Frankie recruited Tom to go shopping too, but not for groceries. Like a kid in a candy store, he was having the time of his life in retail outlets and department stores, buying gifts for his friends. Tom gave guidance on what was good value for money, but mainly sat back, letting Frankie enjoy the novelty of his new financial freedom.

Harry went back to the retirement village on Monday, as did a lot of other residents, including Doris. They embraced, instantaneously launching into easy conversation.

"So, I guess you've been busy," she said with a noticeable hint of sarcasm.

"You wouldn't believe it, Doris, honestly. Shall we finally get on with that backgammon game?"

"Oh no you don't. That can wait. You don't disappear on me for a week, leaving mysterious messages on tree trunks, without following up with a thorough debriefing. Sit yourself down. I'm getting us a good, strong cup of coffee, and then I want a blow-by-blow account of what on earth has been going on with you."

Maggie naturally spent as much time as she could with Noah, without it being detrimental to her work. She purchased a mobile phone after she'd dropped off Harry, and gave Noah a quick tutorial, putting herself on speed dial in case he needed her at any time. She also downloaded her Spotify playlist, thinking he might like some music to bide the time, but avoided Google - knowing what a minefield the internet could be, and not wanting Noah's mind to be completely blown in this new environment. They discussed his recovery, and she, of course, suggested he recuperate at her house. He agreed because he didn't have anywhere else to go, but she sensed some reluctance, and was a little disappointed that he wasn't more enthusiastic at the thought of living with her. But there was a lot of water under the bridge, and he wasn't in a fit state to make any commitments at this stage, so she let it slide.

Putting her business hat on, Maggie embellished the details in her notes to read as a plausible scenario and handed her report to Adam. He mulled it over and commented.

"Hmmm, this is quite the tale, isn't it? Participating in medieval cosplay, you say?

"Yes, you know, like those American Civil War re-enactments, where they dress up in old officer uniforms and hold muskets. Except this was for a different era, and the idiot who was supposed to charge Noah with a fake jousting stick stupidly brought a real one."

"That explains how he was dressed, I suppose," said Adam, still not convinced.

"It sounds like the medieval re-creation happened in the woods next to Jack's school," Maggie continued. "The other guy thought he'd merely winded Noah, and carried on with the show. And Noah didn't appreciate how bad his injuries were either, until he staggered onto the school grounds, only to pass out close to Dad's retirement village. The maintenance crew from The Stables who came to fix the hole in the fence, fortunately stumbled across him."

She brushed away a bead of sweat, knowing she was a terrible liar.

"Well, he was lucky somebody found him collapsed in a heap. If he'd broken his sternum too, that could have punctured a lung. He's obviously no stranger to conflict. Did you see that long scar down his neck?"

"Ah no, I didn't," fudged Maggie, hoping she'd done enough to distract him from the truth. Adam closed the report decisively, happy for Hayley to write up a recovery plan. Maggie took the ring binder back again quickly, before he noticed the patient's home address was hers.

That night, she was in a quandary. Again, she wanted to keep Noah's presence confidential, justifying that it was to protect her family from any false assumptions.

But she was utterly fit to bust!

Jack could tell something was off and called her out on it.

"You all good, Mum?" he queried.

"Yes, love, just tired after a busy day."

"But you seemed a bit strange last night, too. Is it Noah?

Maggie squirmed uncomfortably, shocked at her son's intuition.

"What do you mean?" she said.

"Well, I know everyone is trying to get back to normal now. We're so relieved to be at home and with the people we care about - even Sam and Aaron are vibing. Noah was important to you, but he stayed behind. That must make you sad."

"How did you get to be so wise, Bud?" smiled Maggie, appreciative of his thoughtful words. "Yes and no is the answer. It's just that... I don't know how to...."

She was struggling to keep the burden of knowledge to herself, and Jack saw his mother biting her lip.

"Mum, if you need help, you only have to ask."

Remembering the speech her father had given her after the misunderstanding at the ball, and listening to her son being so empathetic, she couldn't help but think they were right. She didn't have to work everything out by herself. The people in her life loved her and wanted her happiness. Bottling things up only made them worry, and that wasn't fair.

"OK, Bud, I'll tell you."

She took a deep breath.

"He's here. Noah's here."

"What?!" cried Jack, "you mean in the 21st century?"

"Yes."

"Holy shit!"

"Jack!!"

"Sorry, but what the hell? Sorry again."

Maggie laughed at her son's reaction.

"He's at the hospital. And badly injured. After we left, Sebastian decided the fight wasn't finished and hit Noah hard with his lance."

"I told you he was a douchebag!"

"That you did, Bud. In any case, Sebastian flew down the field in full force on his stallion, and Noah was caught off guard, without any form of protection. So he's broken his arm and two of his ribs, and is covered in cuts and bruises. He managed to crawl through the portal, and one of the repairmen from your grandad's village found him and called an ambulance."

"OK, so that's great then!" said Jack, "Not that he's hurt, but great that he's staying here in our time."

"Well, I don't know if he is. Things got complicated before we left. I think the Baron has sent him here, so he'll recover, but I don't know if he's going to stick around afterwards. That's why I wasn't sure if I should tell anybody."

Jack put his hand to his chin, plainly contemplating her dilemma, and looking so grown up.

"It is what it is, Mum. We don't know what's going to happen next. But we do know Noah's here now. He'll be as frightened of this new world as we were of his. But he made us feel safe and included. I think that's what we should do for him."

Maggie was amazed at how Jack, at thirteen years of age, had somehow plucked the simplest and most appropriate course of action out of nowhere, when she'd been inhibited by indecision. It made perfect sense. She needed to get out of her own way and prioritise Noah's well-being. If him staying turned out to be a temporary thing, she - and the family - would deal with it. Her mother had once told her in her final days that it's not the things you do in life that you regret; it's the things you don't do.

"You're so right, Jack. How would you like to come to the hospital with me tomorrow and keep Noah company while I do my rounds?"

"You betcha!!" confirmed Jack, super excited at the thought.

"But it'll be our secret for the moment. He's got so many things to learn, I think a flood of visitors might be too much for him. Adam thinks there's a possibility he can discharge Noah by Thursday, and I said he could stay here to recuperate properly."

"Sweet!" responded Jack. This was getting better and better. He liked Noah a lot too, and felt certain that once he'd got used to the ways of the modern world, he'd be sure to stay.

"Alright then," said Maggie, feeling like a giant weight had lifted from her shoulders. "Let's take Bronny for a walk and pick up some chocolate on the way back. I need a sugar hit."

Jack wasn't going to argue with that; throwing on his jacket and shoes straightaway. Bronny - having heard the word 'walk' - was already dancing by the front door in anticipation. Maggie breathed in the evening air, inhaling the wintery smells of chimney smoke and neighbours' casseroles. Putting the past and future on pause, she was determined to grab hold of the present.

On Tuesday morning, as Noah tucked into his breakfast, he took stock of the last few days. Whilst initially wary of his new environment, he'd learnt that rest was a hospital requirement to allow a patient's body to heal, and everything he needed would be brought to him by an attendant. He was taking great pleasure in the variety of food provided, exploring new and different tastes and textures. Once, a hamburger arrived on a plate for lunch, and Noah delighted in his recognition of the delicacy that Josh and Aaron had introduced to the manor.

Hayley had shown him where the bathroom was on his first day, and he remembered from Maggie's drawing in the dirt, this was where he was supposed to relieve himself. And that he should wash his hands afterwards with water from the tap thing. But he didn't realise he had to close the door behind him. When another patient walked in while he was spending a penny, he greeted them cheerily as he continued his task, and was surprised at the look of shock and embarrassment on the person's face, followed by their hasty departure. He did like the effect of the flushing mechanism, however, and sometimes - when bored - went back to press the button, purely for the entertainment value. In addition, Noah welcomed the relief he was getting from the apothecary, who brought him salves and tinctures to numb the pain. It was beyond anything he could have imagined. But he was well aware that he couldn't stay at the hospital forever, and while connecting with Maggie again and her offer of lodgings, seemed an attractive option, he could feel the fear of uncertainty simmering beneath the surface, like bubbles boiling in a cauldron.

Conversely, Maggie's fears had diminished considerably, giving her a new pep in her step that morning. A problem shared was a problem halved, and Jack had certainly helped her look at things in a different light. Jack, too, was fizzing at the thought of seeing Noah again. He and his mum rode the lift together and said Hello to Hayley. Maggie had previously brought Jack to work a few times during school holidays when he was at a loose end, so Hayley didn't suspect anything out of the ordinary.

They went straight to Room 17 and found Noah sitting up, eating toast.

"I've brought someone to see you. I hope you don't mind," said Maggie as Jack walked in behind her.

"Jack!" cried Noah, elated to see the boy.

"No hugs," warned Maggie, as Jack dashed to his side, "remember his ribs."

"Instead, I can do this," offered Noah, raising his right hand, ready to high-five his young visitor, who exuberantly returned the favour.

"Are you OK if Jack stays with you while I do my work with the other patients?"

Noah nodded avidly, and Maggie could see his eyes light up at the thought of spending time with a youngster who held him up on a pedestal. Conversations with kids could be simple and fun, unlike the complications adults tended to throw in.

Over the next couple of days, Jack took great pride in educating Noah about the ways of the modern world. He taught him how to text, and while he was slow, Jack reckoned all grown-ups were hopeless in that department, so put to good use the patience he usually reserved for his mother's technical incompetence. He showed Noah videos of him playing basketball and throwing a Frisbee to Bronny on the beach. Noah was fascinated with the moving pictures and laughed til his ribs hurt, when he watched Bronny miss the Frisbee altogether and land with a splash in the sea. This small rectangular apparatus really could perform lots of magic tricks.

Satisfied with his patient's progress, Adam said he could leave on Thursday, as long as he promised to rest up, and only go on short walks for the next few weeks. To help Noah assimilate into the real world, Maggie went clothes shopping, while Jack schooled him in the art of contemporary vocabulary;

"So instead of Greetings, you're better to say Hello or Hi."

"Hello or Hi," Noah repeated.

"Or Bro if you're talking to another guy," added Jack, "it's short for brother."

"Like a man of the cloth or a sibling?"

"Like a sibling, but I say it to Josh and my friends."

"Methinks you have said it to your mother, too."

"Yeah, I probably have. I'm a teenager; I'm allowed to," Jack laughed, "And no more 'methinks' or 'tis' or 'twas'. You need to change to 'I think', 'It is' or 'It was'."

Noah nodded, understanding.

"Also, we don't use thou, thee, or thy anymore. It's a lot to remember, but you'll get the gist of it. Besides, you'll be hanging out with people who know you anyway, while you get better, so it doesn't matter if you make mistakes."

Noah smiled at the boy's encouragement.

"Are you staying for good, Noah?" Jack suddenly asked, with no preamble.

"Ah," responded Noah hesitantly, "for that question, I do not have an answer yet."

"But why not?" persisted Jack, "Mum loves you, you know. She was so upset when you didn't come home with us. She's just been on her own for so long, she sometimes forgets how to say things properly when she finds someone she really cares about."

Noah had needed to hear that. Up to now, he hadn't wanted to admit that Maggie's feelings for him were important. But they were, and in a way, he could understand her reserve. He'd also walked alone through life for many years, casting some doubt on whether a romantic relationship was even plausible. Their unique scenario contributed to his apprehension. And this, combined with the way things had gone at the manor, gave him a defensible excuse for keeping his heart safe. As if reading his mind, Jack made an observation,

"You two are quite alike, actually. You both hold yourselves back from falling in love in case you get hurt. Maybe that's part of getting old."

Noah furrowed his brow at the cheeky insult, but Jack wasn't completely off the mark. When you looked at life through young lenses, everything seemed possible, and risks were worth taking. But as you aged, and endured loss and heartbreak, you were more inclined to keep romance at arm's length, for fear of it not working out.

"It's like me and Bronny," Jack elucidated, "I know dogs don't live as long as humans, and one day he'll be gone. But if I chose not to have him in my life, simply to avoid losing him in the end, that would be dumb. We have great fun together and my life's so much better with him in it. You and Mum just need to choose each other, and I think if you stayed, it'd be epic."

Noah was surprisingly moved by Jack's pep talk. There were complexities the boy didn't understand, but he did make a good case.

"Anyway, back to your language lesson," said Jack, "Nay is no. Yea, you only have to tweak to Yeah."

Maggie returned to the hospital and walked to Noah's room.

"Instead of Gadzooks," Jack continued, "try Wow, or Really. And if it's super shocking, there's always 'What the fu..."

"Jack, behave!" interrupted Maggie, nipping that sentence in the bud.

"Spoilsport," Jack pouted.

"I hate to think what he's been teaching you," Maggie said.

"Nay, tis nothing." Noah started, then corrected himself, "No, it is nothing to concern thyself...yourself with."

Jack high-fived him again, approvingly.

"Jack here has been very insightful."

Hearing Noah attempt to grapple with the language, Maggie accepted that her son had been trying to help, and it was lovely to see the two bonding again. She showed them the jeans and tops she'd bought Noah, and they all agreed he was on his way to fitting into society quite nicely.

WEDNESDAY NIGHT BROUGHT WITH it a downpour of rain. Maggie and Jack had spent more time with Noah during the day, and made up the spare room when they got home in preparation for his arrival tomorrow.

Maggie loved the rain when she was cosied up inside. She gazed out the window at the silver-grey droplets piercing the puddles on the ground - punctuating their entrance like Olympic gold medallist divers - and outwardly sighed; the meditative effect of the scene releasing some of her day-to-day stresses.

With her complexion and colouring, she'd never been a fan of the heat and didn't particularly like the freezing cold either; preferring the in-between of autumn instead. But the drumming of raindrops on slate was a sound that soothed her any time of the year. She sat on the couch in her favourite position; legs curled up under her and a glass of Pinot Noir in hand, listening to the calming hum of precipitation overhead. Jack was in the tech room, playing a video game with his mates online, and loudly commentating on their avatar movements:

"Get out of the way, David. You're as big as a freaking elephant!" he shouted into his microphone.

Not so calming, thought Maggie, but she enjoyed the background noise all the same. The place would be unnaturally quiet without it. Just as enjoyable were the texts Noah was trying to send her. She smiled at his first attempt.

'hello or hi'

Very cute. Then a couple of garbled messages. As a virgin texter, he was likely to be all thumbs. She sent him a hug and a heart emoji back and got the response,

'how you do'

That would have to be Jack's next lesson, she chuckled to herself.

A knock on the door interrupted her chat. She opened it to a bedraggled Sam, plainly caught short in the wet weather.

"Sorry, Aunt Maggie, for barging in on you. Mum messaged me asking if I could pop in on the way home from the gallery. She wants to borrow a chair if that's OK, cos we've only got eight, and there will be nine for dinner tomorrow."

Maggie's phone beeped with a message.

"Sure," she said, "why don't you take two to round up the numbers? I'll help you out with them. Did you want to stop for a hot choccie first?"

Her phone beeped again.

"No, I better keep moving. Thanks for the offer, though." Sam nodded towards her aunt's phone, beeping once more. "You seem to be in hot demand, anyway. Arranging a date?" she teased.

"Wouldn't you like to know," said Maggie playfully, as she picked up one of the chairs and passed it to her niece. Wow, thought Sam, was her aunt actually messaging a guy? Nah, unlikely. Then she spotted the picture frame Jack had given Maggie on the dining table.

"Oh, that's gorgeous," she said admiringly.

"My beautiful boy made that for me," boasted Maggie.

"I know this might sound cheeky," Sam continued, "but could I borrow it, please? I've got something in mind that would look perfect with that frame. I promise you'll like it."

"Sure," said Maggie, "I don't have anything myself that fits at present. If you've got a picture that would work, I'd love to see it put to good use."

"Cool," said Sam, and then shouting out to Jack, "Great work, Cuz!"

"What?" he said, not bothering to take his headphones off.

"In the middle of a top-secret operation at the moment," Maggie apologised. 'I'll pass on the compliment. Let's get you home before the shower gets worse."

They dashed through the rain, holding a piece of furniture each - with the picture frame squeezed under Sam's armpit - and quickly wedged the chairs into the back seat of the VW. Not wanting to get completely drenched, they hastily said their goodbyes, and Maggie ran back into the house again to resume her virtual conversation with Noah. A satisfying evening by all accounts.

CHAPTER 18

Thursday 30 December

NOAH GRIMACED AS HE attempted to pull on the T-shirt Maggie had bought him. His whole upper body was black and blue from the recent collision, and although the medication was effectively managing his pain, he still felt fragile and tender. The jeans were easier in terms of his pain threshold, but denim was a foreign material that felt strange. Doing the zip and button up when he only had the use of one hand also proved difficult, but he got there in the end, and stood to inspect the 2000s version of himself in the looking glass on the wall.

Hayley knocked on the door, asking if he was ready to sign the discharge papers. She noted that Ol' Blue Eyes scrubbed up pretty well. He gathered his personal belongings - not forgetting the precious item under his pillow - then walked with Hayley to the lift, where she pressed the button for one floor down. As the moving room descended, Noah found the sensation in his stomach quite alarming, and was thankful when the ride came to a stop.

Maggie stood waiting at reception.

"Noah is leaving today," Hayley said. "He's just waiting for his ride."

"Yes, that's me," Maggie volunteered, simultaneously spinning a quick lie (her story-telling improving). "He's staying at a B and B down the road from us until his family arrives from overseas to help him home, and as I've got the afternoon off, I said I'd be happy to drive him there."

Hayley walked past her to get to the other side of the desk, and in doing so, whispered saucily into Maggie's ear,

"I bet you did, Missy."

Completing his discharge papers and handing them over, Noah said,

"Thank you for your assistance. The facilities here and physician's expertise have been most satisfactory."

"You're very welcome," replied Hayley, amused at his choice of words. "You take care. And Maggie, I'll see you tomorrow, *when I will be asking you a whole heap of questions,*" she continued, muting the second half of the sentence. Despite trying to keep a straight face, the corners of Maggie's mouth curved upwards. She knew what Hayley was thinking, but she'd cross that bridge when she came to it. Putting Noah's belongings in her tote bag, the pair took the lift to the ground floor - he again holding on to the wall as they went - and once outside, mindful of his breaks and bruises, carefully got into her car.

"Hello or Hi," said Maggie, detecting a bit of awkwardness and attempting to break the ice. He smiled in response, but didn't initiate any chit chat. With the safety of the hospital gone, and the reality of the situation dawning on him, Noah's overwhelm seemed to impede any participation in small talk.

Maggie wasn't sure how to deal with his uncommunicativeness. After the initial outpouring of emotions on their reunion, they had both retreated into a place of caution, not quite knowing what the other was thinking. She'd noticed the easy ebb and flow of conversation Noah had with Jack, was more stilted with her, reinforcing her impression that their relationship was still up in the air. Here I go again, she thought: analysing, interpreting, doubting. Reminding herself to concentrate on the moment, she mentally pressed pause on the negative spool in her head; instead, trying to lock in a 'carpe diem' attitude.

"How are you feeling? Do you fancy taking the scenic route? You've only seen the inside of an ambulance and a hospital so far. I could show you around a bit."

"Yes," he said, easing into his seat, "I would like that very much."

"Safety first," she instructed, reaching across his chest and grabbing the seatbelt to strap him in. Her face got very close to his and time stopped for a few seconds. A freeze frame of recollection; of a rainy night, hay bales and horses; isolation and intimacy. The chemistry between them was still blatantly evident, but neither wanted to acknowledge it - yet.

Coming back to earth, Maggie locked the belt into place, started the ignition, and took the handbrake off. Noah watched her every move, clearly mesmerised by the mechanics of the vehicle. She ruminated on the differences between her experience in the past and his in the future. At least going back in time, she'd had a good idea of what life was like then, and could make an educated guess on how to fit in. Especially with Cat's historical knowledge, they'd had the edge in knowing what protocols to be conscious of, and how people thought in days gone by. It was a completely different kettle of fish for Noah. Everything was new and alien to him, and there were things he couldn't possibly have envisioned. She could see his head already spinning, listening to the hustle and bustle outside: the thrum of cars and buses around them; people laughing and shouting; the wail of a siren in the distance; the staccato knocking of a hammer drill as it broke into concrete nearby. She hoped the concise explanation of her world she'd provided when in his, had helped him cope with his first few days, but with the 21st century assailing his senses, he must be overcome with the surrealism of his new existence, and nervous about venturing forth.

On that note, Maggie decided to take him to a place of which he was well acquainted. She drove through the town, pointing out several landmarks but not overloading him with details. Noah kept his window open, feeling a little claustrophobic in the enclosed tin carriage, but he did enjoy the speed of the vehicle and wondered about its horsepower. Which, in turn, made him feel a little homesick, thinking about his animals he'd left in the past. After fifteen minutes or so, Maggie pulled into the school car park, and they disembarked to look across the field he'd walked over so many times. They strolled around the classrooms for a while, then she guided him to an apple tree enclosed in a small courtyard. In tribute to the original Buford Estate, the square paving had been retained and restored to its original condition. When the school had been built, it was on the proviso that the area remained intact and that an apple tree be planted and cared for. Noah, oddly comforted to hear the story, tenderly touched a branch of the tree as if he were still standing outside the manor. After that, she took him to the stone bridge, thinking he may have been there before, as it wasn't too far from the estate.

"We come here quite often," she said. "I thought you might know about it."

"I do," he confirmed, "Tis...it is one of my favourite places in the autumn."

"Really? Mine too. I love autumn: crisp mornings, clear skies, beautiful colours."

"I know. Jack told me," he commented, without expanding further. "This place is still to my liking. Not much has changed."

"You're right. The bridge has been strengthened over the years, but there are still some old bricks. Look."

Maggie showed him the original stonework, still standing in the centre.

"Hah," he said in recognition, reassured to be in familiar territory.

Their conversation took on a more congenial quality, and although the topics were fairly innocuous - the weather and the trees - they began to feel a little more at ease in each other's company. Not wanting to overdo things, Maggie suggested that would be enough sightseeing for the day, and they returned to the car. On arrival at the house, Jack greeted them enthusiastically. He'd shut Bronny out in the backyard, to make sure his goofball clumsiness didn't accidentally cause another unwanted bump. Jack showed their guest to his room while Maggie made mugs of hot chocolate - another novelty for Noah.

"Let's take it easy this afternoon," Maggie proposed. "Going to Tom and Cat's for dinner will be quite an event, so rest until then. Make yourself at home and feel free to take a nap. I'll just be pottering around in the kitchen."

The exertion of leaving the hospital and walking around Pebble Heath had sapped Noah's energy, so he gladly took her up on her offer. She softly shut the bedroom door, giving him some quiet and privacy.

"Is it going OK?" Jack asked.

"I think so," replied Maggie. "It's a big adjustment for him, especially when he's not fighting fit, but he's doing well so far."

Letting Bronny back inside, she enticed the Dane into the kitchen with some dog biscuits, so he wouldn't sniff around Noah's closed door. She found the recipe for a dessert she wanted to bring to her sister's tonight and put it to one side. Needing to clear the decks first, and with her dishwasher still not working, Maggie hand-washed some pots and pans in the sink, leaving them to dry on the draining board. At least this evening's get-together wasn't going to be too late. Harry, for once, was going to stick to the 8 pm curfew at the village, but only because he was planning a humdinger of a night on New Year's Eve. He didn't want to incur Nadine's wrath two days in a row, and thought he ought to pace himself, anyway. That worked for Maggie, too. Her family were going to be flabbergasted to see Noah, and she anticipated the reaction could be overwhelming. She felt very protective towards him, and while she was looking forward to a fun night, Noah's health was paramount.

He woke from his snooze around 4 pm and came back into the lounge. Bronny wagged his tail furiously at the sight of his old friend, and made a low woo wooing sound, to voice his euphoria. As a genuine animal lover, the sight of Bronny helped ground Noah, when he was wrestling mentally and physically to be a part of this new world. He bent down, rubbing the fur on the dog's chest and tickling him under his chin. Feeling refreshed, and with the next dose of paracetamol kicking in, he walked into the kitchen to find Maggie elbow-deep in cake mix. The house was snug and cosy and smelt great, too. He looked around in admiration of the lodgings Maggie had spoken about. Her description did not do it justice. He hadn't been able to conceive of the ingenuity of electricity, nor the luxury of central heating.

"Hey you," she said; that specific phrase always indicating a level of affection in her book. Not that he would appreciate the nuances of modern English, but she felt it appropriate to say, anyway.

"Hello or Hi," he responded, now obviously a running joke between them. It tickled her to think he was being witty, and that they seemed to have created a 'thing.' Their protective walls cracking a bit, perhaps.

Jack came in too, to get some water from the fridge.

"Hi, Noah. You want a bottle?" he asked.

"Ah, this is the chilled water supply you told me about," Noah said to Maggie, and she nodded. Jack held the door open, encouraging Noah to put his hand inside the refrigerator.

"Cold," he announced, amused at the concept.

"And if you think that's cool - 'scuse the pun," joked Jack, "- check this out."

He opened the freezer, gesturing for Noah to duplicate his action. He did so; pulling his hand out again straightaway.

"Freezing!" he shivered.

"That's why it's called the freezer," said Jack, stating the obvious.

Noah looked inside and commented on a frozen chicken.

"You keep poultry in there?"

"And beef and lamb and pizzas," Maggie confirmed.

"And what is that?" Noah pointed to a tub of ice cream.

"That, my friend," grinned Jack, "is nectar from the Gods. It's called butterscotch ice cream and you'll get to taste it tonight with Mum's dessert."

"That I will look forward to, indeed. The gadgets of your time have such innovation."

"Mum, can I show Noah more stuff while you carry on in the kitchen?"

"Sure," said Maggie, "if Noah wants to."

"Lead thy way…the way…young Jack."

Maggie smiled, pleased to see her two guys hanging out with each other.

Jack switched the TV on first, to show Noah more moving pictures, this time on a bigger screen. A football match was on - a sport Noah recognised - but he was astounded by the size and noise of the crowd (chanting I'm Forever Blowing Bubbles), and stunned by the different camera angles. Next, Jack took him to his tech room and fired up the PS5. He found Noah a headset to wear and logged into one of his games. Then he passed a controller over, while keeping one for himself; demonstrating how the buttons made the characters move. Talking into the microphone, he chuckled at Noah's surprised expression on hearing his voice amplified through the headphones. Jack explained this was a fun way to keep in contact with friends who lived far and wide, but did admit to getting carried away by the virtual worlds occasionally, and losing track of time. Noah, already grappling with a new reality, was dumbfounded at the thought of interacting with a fake one. But Jack could see he was curious to try, so switched a few things to make it more user-friendly. Turning Noah's avatar into an archer, he encouraged him to press a few buttons. To Noah's astonishment and mirth, his character made some jerky movements, and with Jack's help, fired a shot. The arrow went vertically into the air, then nosedived to the ground, not hitting anything and scoring zero points. The man and the teenager laughed out loud at the scene in front of them, and Maggie noted that some things appealed to all boys, no matter where they were from.

The rest of the afternoon passed quickly, and it was soon time to get ready. Keeping things casual, they stayed in their jeans, and other than running a brush through her hair, Maggie didn't do much else. She would make more of an effort tomorrow for Sam, she promised herself.

Frankie was already at the Holden house. Having gone a tad overboard on gift purchases, Tom offered the use of his den to keep them tucked out of the way, and fortunately, they'd snuck everything in before Cat got home. Struggling to keep quiet about his good fortune, Frankie waited impatiently for everyone else to turn up. Sam picked up Harry and arrived a short time later; followed by Josh and Aaron, who'd done a hard day's work, and were hanging out for a decent feed.

They all milled around the kitchen until Cat kicked them out so she could baste the turkey again and check on the other components of her belated Christmas feast. It wasn't as extravagant as the Baron's banquets, but not so rustic either. She wiped her hands on her apron and set the table with festive knickknacks; doubling up on Christmas crackers as they'd been on a two-for-one sale. Moving the wreath centrepiece a half inch to the left, and satisfied with the look of the accoutrements, she called on Sam to put nuts and crisps on the coffee table, as pre-dinner snacks. Christmas songs played through the speakers, and talk of chestnuts roasting and treetops glistening got everyone in the mood, even though it was the 30th of December.

Typical for the time of year, the night came early; winter darkness descending upon the Northern Hemisphere like a charcoal-coloured bedspread. Flower petals folded in on themselves, and rabbits scurried to their burrows. Tom had left the front door unlocked and the porch light on, expecting his sister-in-law and nephew to arrive any minute. Sure enough, and punctual as usual, Maggie's car pulled up outside. A second later, Jack burst in, noticeably excited and itching to say something. His mother followed, also looking bright-eyed and bushy-tailed.

"I hope you have room for one more," she said.

Sam jumped up and loudly hissed in her mum's ear,

"I knew it! I knew Aunt Maggie was up to something with some bloke; that's why she gave me the extra chair. I hope it's not that Adam guy from the hospital."

"Err, I don't think so," Cat stammered, pointing to the doorway.

"Oh My God, Noah!!" Sam shrieked, immediately running over to him, only to have Jack head her off at the pass; standing as if on sentry duty with his arms out, protecting his charge.

"No hugs!" he ordered. "He's hurt."

The easy-going ambience of the room five minutes' prior turned into a chaotic scene of disbelief and rejoicing, followed by a machine gun fire of questions. Maggie had warned Noah his entrance might cause a bit of a stir, but he welcomed the enthusiastic reception. After a shaky start and an eye-opening day, seeing Maggie's family and friends was as joyful to him as it was to them.

"Dude!" chorused Josh and Aaron together, clearly thrilled to see him.

"Bro," replied Noah, extending a fist out to be bumped. They cracked up laughing at his response, as did the others. Evidently, Jack had been schooling him on colloquial slang.

"How wonderful you're here," said Cat sincerely, "but what happened? How did you hurt your arm?"

"Well, if you let the poor man in the door," requested Maggie, "we can sit down and regurgitate the whole sorry tale."

They did as she asked, and as the magnitude of the moment settled down, Noah repeated his explanation of how and why he'd come to the future. As if listening to the narrator of a panto, they had to suppress the urge to boo when Sebastian's antics were revealed. Cat and Sam gasped together at the horrific injuries endured by Noah, but he assured them he'd been tended to with great care and competence whilst at the hospital.

"That's where I found him," explained Maggie. "It was such a shock!"

"In a good way," she followed, glancing fondly at him to emphasise her feelings. Apprising her family of the doctor's orders given by Adam, she informed them that Noah would be convalescing at her house for a month or so.

"You're in good hands," said Cat, pumping up her sister's profile. "Maggie was a nurse before she started her own business."

He nodded, but Cat picked up a flicker of apprehension in his eyes and wondered what that was about. Suddenly the timer went off in the kitchen, signalling the turkey was ready.

Cat and Maggie excused themselves so they could dish up dinner. Harry offered to carve the bird, which left Tom and Josh on drinks duties. A few hushed whispers ensued, the knight's unexpected presence still not fully sinking in. Jack stayed glued to Noah's side, hanging off his every word, as he shared his first few days' experience with Sam, Aaron and Frankie - a more than willing audience.

In the kitchen, Cat immediately started the interrogation.

"This is marvellous, Mags. I'm over the moon for you. But what's the story? Are you together now? Is he going to live with you permanently?"

"The jury's out on that," Maggie replied, a little despondently. "He wasn't intending to come here, but the Baron pushed him, as otherwise he could have died. This world might be too much for him; we'll have to wait and see."

"But you're here. And Jack," Cat said earnestly, "surely that counts for something. He's lost his wife and son and thinks the world of you two. Wouldn't he have more to live for in this era?"

"We weren't exactly on the best of terms when I left, and even with the good bits, I think he's afraid the unexpected romance of yesteryear might not be so magical in the light of day here. And I must admit, that's crossed my mind too. Instead of playing games, riding horses and stealing kisses, for us to be a couple in the 21st century means school meetings, paying endless bills and putting the garbage out every Tuesday. Mundane city with a capital M."

"Oh, for goodness' sake," scoffed Cat, "you two are as bad as each other. Too much thinking and not enough snogging. What does Jack say?"

"He says it is what it is, and to grab the moment and get on with it."

"Smart kid. Must be my teaching."

Harry, listening in, contributed his two pence worth,

"Look, love, he's going to be a little unsettled to start with, but give him time. He was pretty rapt with the welcome he received tonight, although he stayed his usual humble self. I'm sure his cogs are ticking over too, about the possibility of life here. Just be yourself. The farce with Sebastian got ridiculously out of hand, and he needs to see the Maggie we know and love."

She appreciated their unwavering support and knew they had her well-being at heart. They were also right about taking one step at a time. Tonight was the perfect opportunity for Noah to participate in her arena, instead of his, and see if the fit was right. As her son would say, she just needed to chill.

The food was scrumptious, as expected. They wore paper hats and pulled the Christmas crackers. Tom insisted on reading out the lame jokes inside, and the little useless plastic toys that fell out were swapped around until people ended up with the one they hated least. Noah found it all very entertaining. After the main meal, Tom poured everyone a glass of champagne to propose a toast (apart from Jack, who had a lemonade instead).

"To friends and family and love and laughter!"

"Hear, hear," corroborated Harry, to the sound of clinking glasses.

"And a very warm welcome to Noah. I expect this is all very strange to you, as it was to us when we were in your time, but we're delighted to have you. Especially as you rescued Maggie and brought her back to us. If we can help in any way, please let us know."

"Hear, hear again," repeated Harry, and another sip of bubbles was taken.

"I'd also like to take this opportunity to wish our gorgeous daughter the very best for tomorrow night. Your mother and I are incredibly proud of you, Sam. We'd say good luck, but you honestly don't need it. We all can't wait to see your exhibition."

Sam got uncharacteristically bashful as a ripple of applause reverberated around the table.

"But before we move on to dessert, I do believe our good friend here might have something to share." Tom turned to Frankie, suggesting it was his turn to talk. Frankie stood up and cleared his throat.

"Well, lovelies, as much as I enjoyed your company in the Middle Ages, I'd rather not do it again. However, as anyone who has ever watched Back to the Future knows, things can unexpectedly change when you return to the present."

There were puzzled looks from around the table.

"It appears that Walter the cooper did very well for himself after his promotion."

Speaking about his colleague from the estate gave Noah an excuse to join in the conversation.

"How so?" he asked.

"On my return...," Frankie continued, pausing for dramatic effect, "...it turns out I have heaps of dosh. Apparently, us Coopers come from a long line of wealth."

He waited for them to connect the dots.

"Dosh?" queried Noah to Maggie.

"Money," she simplified.

"Wait, what?" questioned Jack. "Are you saying you're loaded now because Walter's future changed?"

"Exactly Jackie Boy, you're right on the money. As am I."

"Bruh!!" Jack exclaimed, standing up to give him a high five.

"Bruh?" uttered Noah, again confused.

"Like Bro. Same, same," chuckled his younger companion.

"Frankie, that's incredible news," congratulated Cat. "Is that what you said was strange when you rang me? Has Tom confirmed everything is kosher?"

"Sure has, honeybun. And while tonight has been a highly commendable re-creation of Christmas Day, I do believe there's one thing missing: - presents! If you wouldn't mind, Tom."

Taking Frankie's cue, Tom stood by the den door, ready to reveal its hidden treasures as his friend saw fit.

"Ladies first," Frankie announced. "Lady Catherine, for staying calm throughout a trying time, and in keeping with the pretend life you grew accustomed to, I feel an accompaniment to your handbag would be a fitting addition."

Tom opened the door wide enough to shuffle through a complete Louis Vuitton luggage set, kitted out in a beautiful blue floral pattern. Cat squealed and clapped her hands.

"Oh, Frankie, are you sure? They're gorgeous."

"It's my absolute pleasure," he confirmed. "Your turn, Maggie May. For staying centred and providing an Oscar-worthy performance at the ball, while dancing with the devil..."

Tom pushed open the door further, wheeling out a big square box marked Bosch.

"You got me a dishwasher? That's too much! But very gratefully received. Thank you Frankie, you know us so well - pretty for Cat and practical for me."

Full of merriment, the sisters hugged their friend from either side.

"Now, Marian, my beloved," continued Frankie.

"Hey, watch it you," cried Aaron, claiming Sam as his own.

"And you watch it too," echoed Tom, reminding Aaron that her father was in the room.

"Fair point," laughed Frankie. "How about my partner in crime for a limited time? Anyway, I know you love your Polaroid, but I thought it was about time your equipment matched your talents."

Sam caught her breath as a state-of-the-art camera with interchangeable lenses, tripod, and leather carrying case, materialised from the den.

"And for our intrepid heroes who saved your sorry arse, despite you being a grumpy cow at times..."

"At times?" jeered Josh sarcastically. Sam stuck her tongue out at her brother as Frankie turned to him and Aaron, handing them the latest Apple smart watches and top-of-the-line AirPods. The boys whooped their gratitude, and Sam blew an over-the top-kiss to her previously fake fiancé. Tom closed the door, but the excitement resumed as Frankie retrieved two envelopes from inside his jacket.

"For young Will Scarlett, who is more of a man than that dick, Sebastian."

"Yeah!" said Jack and Noah together, pumping their fists in the air; Noah now fully in the swing of things. Frankie handed Jack one of the envelopes, and the boy's eyes grew wide, then misted up as he opened it. Pulling out first-class train tickets and VIP passes to Wembley Arena, he could barely read the invitation. Frankie made it easier for him.

"It's an exhibition basketball match, Jackie. The LA Lakers are coming here to play against England. So you get to see the real LeBron. You'll have to take an adult with you, but there are four sets of tickets in total, so you can bring two mates."

Jack was speechless. Stretching his hand out like a grown-up, Frankie graciously shook it; patting him on the back before returning to his gift-giving.

"Friar Kenobi, the glue that held us together, solver of riddles and all-around great guy. I wanted to get you something to strengthen the passion you regained in the past."

Harry, like Jack, was gobsmacked at the contents of his envelope: a certificate of ownership and a photo of a stunningly beautiful white racehorse. Harry put his glasses on and read the horse's name on the certificate: - Skywalker.

"You see, I couldn't resist, what with the Star Wars reference and all," Frankie said, tickled pink at the look on Harry's face. Maggie hugged her dad, sensing he was about to crumble at the enormity of the gift.

"You deserve it, Dad. It was you and Tom who brought us home. Frankie, that's so thoughtful."

"Thank you," said Harry hoarsely.

"On that note, can I ask my glamorous assistant to join me, please?"

As Frankie looked towards the den, Tom cheerfully abandoned his position to stand beside the man of the moment.

"Lord Thomas, a true gentleman in every sense of the word, there is something I'd like to do for you. I couldn't very well buy you a treat under your nose, but I have a proposal instead."

Frankie's benevolence had already been astonishing, so everybody sat on the edge of their seats, waiting to hear his next announcement; not least of all, Tom.

"One of the tenants is leaving our building, and as you know, I own it." He brushed imaginary long hair exaggeratedly over his shoulder, in a parody of egotistical pride. Cat and Maggie looked at each other, as if to say, *He does?*

"So... I was wondering if you'd like to pack in your job as an accountant, and head up your own financial services office instead. Free tenancy at Coopers Landing with a bunch of potential clients on your doorstep to start with. And naturally, I want you to manage my money. You showed your fiscal prowess and made things happen in 1380. I'm pretty damn sure you could do it again now, and you wouldn't be beholden to anyone."

Before Tom could reply, everybody else stood up to give him a standing ovation.

"See what putting 'knighthood' on your resume does for your career," joked Josh.

"Will you accept my offer, Sir Thomas?" asked Frankie with mock pompousness.

Amazed and humbled by such a magnanimous gesture, Tom said he would, and bowed to his new landlord in an equally pretentious manner. Frankie curtsied in response. Cat threw her arms around her husband, feeling like the luckiest woman in the world to be married to such a smart man.

"But wait, there's more," Frankie said,

"A set of steak knives?" guessed Aaron.

"Oh God, I don't think we can take any more," cried Sam.

"Buckle up sister, you're going to have to," insisted Frankie, getting a kick out of their reactions.

"Given that our time off for a break turned into something completely bizarre, I think we deserve a proper holiday somewhere normal. So book your leave for Easter, peeps. We're going on a cruise around the Greek Islands."

The room erupted once more.

"It's a bit of a free-for-all," continued Frankie, now shouting to make himself heard. "Harry, please invite Doris. And Jack, you can bring a friend too. Maggie, can I assume for once in your life you have a genuine plus one?"

Your guess is as good as mine, thought Maggie. Obviously referring to Noah, and not being in a position to confirm one way or the other, she diverted the conversation.

"Wow, what a night! A week ago, we were panicking about going through a tunnel; now we're talking about cruising the Mediterranean. Frankie, we're so pleased that your financial troubles have turned around, and completely humbled by your generosity. I think we could all do with a sweet treat to finish off the evening. I'll heat up dessert and be back in a minute."

Picking up on Maggie's deflection, and worried he'd said something out of turn, Frankie backpedalled a bit. But the others had tons of questions about his new wealth, so the discussion easily switched in that direction.

As Maggie vacated her seat, Harry moved next to Noah to check in on him.

"How are you doing?" he asked.

"Thus far fairly well, thank you,' Noah replied, "a little tired and sore, but enjoying the company. The kinship is strong. Of that, I am a little envious."

"Yes, our exposure to your world has brought us closer, without question. Sharing an experience and overcoming adversity does that, I think."

"This is true."

"And you were part of our misadventure, Noah. The bloody best part, in all honesty. Everybody holds you very dear to their hearts, but I understand there's hesitation about staying here permanently? Maggie and Jack are trying to give you space to make up your mind, but I know they'd be devastated if you left again."

"It is not your good selves that beckons doubt. Rather, the lack of clarity with my purpose. It is plain to see that Maggie has a busy life. With Catherine speaking of her nursing career afore, and business commitments now, I fear my presence would be insignificant."

"Ah, I get it," said Harry, finally twigging. "So it's not about you necessarily wanting to go back; you're more worried about what your place is here. I can relate to that. In my day, the man was supposed to provide, and the woman was the homemaker, very similar to your traditions. But I can tell you, my wife didn't subscribe to society's expectations. She was very independent and strong and had her opinions. That's probably where Maggie gets it from. But I loved her for it. I needed someone to challenge me and be my equal. More importantly, though, she needed me just as much. Even though these women seem tough, it's partly because they have to be. Maggie's reticence is her armour, protecting her from being vulnerable; but underneath, she still wants to be cherished by someone special. Once she gets over the shock of having someone she can rely on, it will all fall into place; you'll see. As for your role in this world - well, generally speaking - people carve out their own paths nowadays, but still walk alongside one another. All you need to do is re-discover your passion here, Noah. Seek, and ye shall find."

At that moment, Maggie entered the dining room with oven gloves on, holding a steaming ceramic dish of yumminess. She put it down on the pot holder; the irresistible smell drawing everyone back to their seats. Ducking into the kitchen again, she returned with the ice cream as Sam brought out dishes and spoons.

They all dove in, keen to refuel after the excitement of Frankie's revelations this evening. Noah let out a moan of pleasure,

"Mmm, what is the name of this mouth-watering delicacy?"

"Sticky toffee pudding," came the reply.

"Tis...I mean... it is divinely delicious!"

"Well done," Cat whispered to Maggie. "The way to a man's heart is through his stomach, as they say."

Noah demolished his dessert and asked for seconds. Ditto Josh, Aaron and Jack. They finished with coffee, and Tom brought out the good port for a quick nightcap before Harry turned into a pumpkin. Hugs and kisses abounded as Maggie, Noah, Jack and Harry bid their farewells. On a high, those in the car talked over the top of each other excitedly, as they drove to The Stables first. Too dark for Noah to get a glimpse of his previous home, but Harry assured him he'd see it soon.

As Harry got out of the car and kissed his daughter goodnight, he said,

"Actually, can I borrow your car tomorrow? I could show Noah around The Stables and a few other places while you're at work."

"Sure, I'll pick you up on the way to the hospital and you can take it from there."

"I only need it for the morning. We can regroup at lunchtime."

"What other places?"

"Ah, that would be telling," said Harry, tapping his nose in confidence.

There had been so many surprises tonight, Maggie didn't think she could handle another. She would leave Harry's mysterious venue to him. By the time they got home, even though it wasn't particularly late, she could see Noah was exhausted from the night's shenanigans.

"Thank you, Maggie," he said sincerely. "Tonight was a pleasurable evening, but I have grown weary and must take my leave."

For a minute she thought he was saying he was leaving the house, and going back to the 14th century. Her stomach dropped. Then she realised he was simply saying Goodnight. She nodded and let him go, inwardly breathing a sigh of relief. The elephant was still in the room, however, and neither of them knew how to overcome the inertia they were stuck in.

He walked into the bedroom and took off his T-shirt while the door was still open. She could see his bruises had the beginning of a yellowy/greenish tinge; a telltale sign of healing, but also found she couldn't take her eyes off his well-toned torso. Seeing him in the flesh - as it were - for the first time, it looked like Michelangelo had had a hand in creating Noah's chiselled body. Maggie silently thanked the medieval gods for giving him a life where manual labour was the norm, which had resulted in a physique the polar opposite of a dad bod. His jeans were slung low on his hips - perhaps she'd bought him a size too big - revealing that he probably wasn't wearing any underwear. Old habits dying hard, she surmised. Despite herself, she felt her gut - and other places - churn with desire.

Aside from walking on eggshells since Noah had left the hospital, that didn't disguise the fact that the sexual tension between them was palpable. If they'd been young and unencumbered, they would undoubtedly be ripping each other's clothes off right now. But love and lust were more complicated when you were middle-aged. Getting older diminished the attributes you once showed off, and by extension, your self-esteem. Clearly not in Noah's case, but that in itself shone a light on Maggie's lack of confidence. Compared to him, she felt decidedly past her 'use by' date.

Funny how living in the past had made her feel sexier. Perhaps because then, in comparison to other women of 1380, she was the picture of good health. No missing teeth, deformed limbs, or nasty boils. Skin that glowed by virtue of good nutrition; hair that was thick and lustrous (and still a lovely colour thanks to Loreal Excellence Triple Care). Instead of complaining about her physical imperfections, she'd been grateful for her overall well-being, which she'd attributed to modern-day living. The uniqueness of the situation possibly instilling some bravado in Noah's presence. But also, being away from societal pressures and the day-to-day grind had given her some freedom to be daring in a fantasy world.

Now, in real life, her old fears returned, and she wasn't sure about anything. The romantic aspirations Maggie once had in her twenties seemed so far out of reach at this age. Responsibilities eclipsed spontaneity; candlelit dinners were too much faff; romantic walks along the beach might aggravate a dodgy knee. Throw menopause into the mix, and that added a whole other layer of insecurity. Getting together with someone later in life threw up a minefield of misgivings, and just thinking about it was exhausting.

Frankly, as far as romance went, to have someone sitting beside you, watching telly together of an evening, or to go to the markets with during the weekend, would be more than enough to satisfy her.

But when he looked like that...

Oh God, you've got it bad, girl. You've got it so, so bad.

CHAPTER 19

Friday 31 December

As she rushed around getting ready for work on Friday morning, Maggie's frustration rose to fever pitch. She really wanted to stay home and talk to Noah about his plans. She couldn't stand the uncertainty anymore, and if he intended to return to the Middle Ages, she'd rather rip off the Band-Aid and know now, so she could steel herself for another separation. But her work responsibilities had got in the way of any decent opportunity to chat. Having already taken annual leave - in another century, no less - she needed to be at the hospital today to tidy things up before the end of the year. Maybe they could have a proper discussion after Sam's show tonight.

She told Jack there were leftovers in the fridge for lunch while she threw slices of bread in the toaster. He was up early for a change, expecting David and Liam over soon. Still on cloud nine after receiving Frankie's sensational present last night, Jack wanted to share the news with his friends as soon as possible. Maggie was pleased that Harry had offered to look after Noah this morning. Whatever he had in mind, a bit of male bonding wouldn't hurt either of them.

Noah woke after a solid night's sleep. Getting used to having his arm in a cast, he discovered that if he slept face down with arms above his head - a la Superman - he could find a comfy spot and nod off pretty easily. Stretching slowly and gently (his ribs still giving him grief), he reflected on the last couple of days. Thursday night was splendid. He thought Frankie very funny, and watching everyone's looks of amazement at being recipients of his goodwill had been most enjoyable. Noah had loved getting to know Maggie's family and friends in 1380, but was conscious of the strain the experience put them under. Their demeanour now - home in the 21st century - was one of peace and confidence. It was his turn to feel out of sorts. Living in a time not of his own, the roles had reversed, and he was currently suffering the same strain his friends had undergone. Anxious to fit in, but painfully aware that he spoke differently, thought differently, and had come from a vastly different background, life at the moment was tricky to navigate.

He pulled out the precious object from under his pillow, looking at his sign to take the leap - literally and figuratively - through the tunnel door. And because of the feelings the item evoked, he had done so. But had it been the right call? Yea or nay, the fact of the matter was, he would be here until he recovered from his injuries; likely a month or more. For as much as Maggie needed answers sooner rather than later, Noah too, couldn't remain in no-man's-land for much longer. He hoped his outing with Harry this morning would help untangle his thoughts.

He slipped the source of his dilemma under the pillow again and went to the kitchen.

A sharp bang made him jump, which Jack found very amusing.

"It's the toaster," he laughed.

Maggie chuckled too as she grabbed the toast; hastily spreading butter and jam on four slices. She took one for herself, leaving the remainder on the plate.

"Must fly, sorry," she apologised, snatching the dog leash off the hook. "Dad will be here soon, and I'll be back around five."

Bronny was going to doggy day-care today. They had an overnight option if needed, and Maggie thought this a good idea, as they were planning a late one themselves. Besides, he'd had a grand time mixing with other canines at the manor; a little socialising with his own kind seemed only fair.

"LeBron James!" she yelled out.

The Dane answered her call immediately, stomping heavily down the stairs. Kitchen meant food, paws crossed. He'd already had some biscuits for breakfast, but you never knew who might be a pushover first thing. Wanting to get him in the car without a fuss, Maggie voluntarily offered the bribe. She gave him one of the slices of toast - consumed in two giant gulps - as she attached the lead to his collar. Then together they left, leaving Jack and Noah to themselves.

Bronny took up the majority of the back seat in the car, and unlike most dogs, had a terrible sense of balance. He tried to hang his head out of the window; mouth open, tongue lolling - like videos seen on Facebook reels - but every time they went round a corner, he'd fall sideways.

"You are a hopeless case," said Maggie affectionately, "it's a wonder we didn't get a Border Collie."

Bronny found his footing for a minute, and licked Maggie's ear over the front seat, in appreciation that they hadn't. It only took a few minutes to reach The Stables, and Harry was already waiting outside for her. The retirement village had a rather swanky entrance, with an ornate metal archway opening up to a long, winding driveway; bordered by elegant, established trees. At Christmas time, they were garnished with tiny blue and white lights, making for an enchanting arrival or departure after dark.

As Harry slipped into the passenger seat, he was greeted by a wet nose in his ear. Fortunately, doggy day-care wasn't too far away, and they were able to relinquish Bronny into the hands of professional dog sitters. He wasn't fazed at all, instantly blending in with his furry friends and racing around the yard, mandatory butt sniffs notwithstanding.

Harry moved into the driver's seat at the hospital, bid his daughter adieu, and turned back to Pebble Heath. He picked up Noah as Jack's friends arrived at the house. The three boys waved to them in the car. They were good lads, thought Harry. Hanging out with the right crowd was half the battle when you were a teenager. He knew how peer pressure could influence decisions at that age; with consequences unintentionally affecting the youngsters' futures. He didn't have any worries about Jack, though. Maggie had done a cracking job bringing him up by herself. But a steady male role model coming onto the scene round about now might prove useful. He wondered if he could help make that happen. Harry picked up speed, driving past the retirement village.

"We are not visiting The Stables?" queried Noah.

"Not today, son," replied Harry. "I've had another thought. Sit back and enjoy the ride. We're heading to the country and it'll take about an hour."

Noah felt himself unwind as they left suburbia; taking in and savouring the wide, open spaces of green spreading out around him. He found the occasional advertising on billboards - and Harry's subsequent difficulty in explaining them - very comical. Part way through the journey, they passed a deer farm, at which Noah sat up and took notice; animals again, giving him solace.

At Aldacott Hospital, Maggie picked up her flat white from the café, and walked to Hayley's desk. The receptionist looked up and didn't waste any time.

"OK sister, spill it!' she demanded. "There's no way this was the first time you met Noah."

"Yeah, Nah," admitted Maggie, grinning. "I met him last week during my time off, but he's not from around here, so I wasn't expecting to see him again."

"Well, clearly, you two were chuffed to register on each other's radar again. That was obvious."

"You think? You're right, I do like him. A lot. But I'm not sure he feels the same about me."

"See, this is the problem: you won't go dating for, like, a millennium, and then you don't recognise the signs. You were most definitely floating his boat. Perhaps you ought to think about making some waves."

They giggled together like schoolgirls.

"Anyway, back to work, Cinders; you're going to have a busy day today."

Maggie grinned again. That was the second time recently she'd been referred to as Cinderella. She wondered if she could manifest a Prince Charming moment before midnight.

"First stop is the maternity ward. Sarah had her baby last night!"

"Brilliant! It's about time."

"Mum and bub are doing great. Both parents are smitten already. The new arrival is a little girl named Natalie.'

"That's wonderful! I'll head up there straight away," said Maggie, delighted to hear the happy news. And bundling her handbag, clipboard, and coffee cup together, she started her rounds for the last day of the year.

IN THE MEANTIME, HARRY arrived at his desired destination - Cedarwood Park Racecourse.

"Where are we?" asked Noah, noting the horse logo on the signage; his nose inhaling familiar smells.

"So, the horse Frankie bought for me," Harry began, "is housed here and he races on this track. I thought it would be nice to meet him. Plus, the stable master is an old friend of mine."

"Stable master?"

"Yes, it's a profession that's stood the test of time. As long as there are horses to be cared for, there's always going to be a need for someone to do the caring."

This was all sounding very interesting to Noah, and something stirred in his gut that had been missing since his arrival in the 21st century. He followed Harry into the racecourse grounds and was staggered to see the latter-day version of the arena he'd known from Buford Estate. Towering buildings for corporate events and VIP parties imposed their presence over the humbler grandstands for ordinary spectators. Although 'humble' was not a word Noah would use. In complete contrast to the makeshift viewing stand that had been erected on the estate, these constructions spanned the entire length of the oval-shaped race track. The circuit looked like it went for miles. A white fence surrounded the perimeter of the track with a second, smaller one on the inside. In between the two, the grass was cut short - as if by laser - into dark and light green stripes to distinguish the lanes. All neat, tidy, and finished with such precision; unlike the haphazard, rough-and-ready pastureland he had come from. Noah craned his neck to see a white horse at the far end of the track, switching gears from a canter to a gallop, and back to a canter again; his rider obviously taking the animal out for training. A voice from behind broke his focus.

"Are you the one looking for Skywalker?"

"My friend," Noah corrected, tapping Harry on the shoulder.

Harry turned, and the stranger exclaimed,

"Harry! Long time, no see. How are you, me ol' mate? You're the one who's bought Skywalker?"

They shook hands vigorously and slapped each other on the shoulder.

"George, you rascal, I was hoping you'd be here. This is my good friend, Noah. Noah, this is George, the stable master." The two also shook hands and exchanged pleasantries.

As Harry caught up with his friend, Noah's attention returned to the white horse, now making its way towards them and slowing down to a walk. He strolled over to the fence as the rider dismounted and guided Skywalker to him.

"He's a beauty, for sure," the rider said.

"That he is," Noah agreed, instinctually caressing the horse's muzzle.

At the sound of a friendly snort, the other two men joined them. Harry ran his hand over the animal's withers and down his back. He let out a sigh of admiration, not fully believing this fine beast was his. The rider handed Harry the reins, suggesting he walk him to the stables.

"I think someone else might like to do that," said Harry, not waiting for an answer, and passing them to Noah. Harry and George strolled side by side a few steps ahead, resuming their conversation, with Harry explaining how he'd come to be the proud new owner of a racehorse.

"Did you know they used to race horses on the grounds of your village?" George asked.

"Did they?" said Harry, pleading ignorance.

"Yes, centuries ago. I was reading about it. Baron somebody owned the estate and used to entertain guests with games and races every year. By all accounts, he had a reputation for quality stock. His stable master must have been held in very high regard."

"Mmm, I imagine so," said Harry, discreetly catching Noah's eye.

Noah smiled, flattered at the praise. What would George think if he knew the very same stable master was walking with them right now? They reached the stalls, and Noah drank in the sight of the equine inhabitants - his thirst for normalcy, quenched by a view that instantly made him feel at home. He marvelled at the scope of the facilities and felt his wariness of the 21st century dispel into the ether. Expanding his lungs fully - as much as his ribs would allow, at least - he drew in the scent of hay and manure. Not everyone's cup of tea, but this was the world he treasured, whatever the year.

"So, how long have you been here now, George? It seems like forever," asked Harry.

"Feels like it too, sometimes," his friend chortled. "It's about time I retired, I think. And lived the life of Riley, like you."

"Is that so?" said Harry, "well, if you're looking for a place to settle, there's a retirement village I can recommend. When were you thinking of?"

"In a few months, I would say. Get through the winter, and then maybe new beginnings in the spring."

Noah led Skywalker into his stall.

"I'll be on the hunt for someone who knows the nags too, but it's not easy these days. The young ones are too preoccupied with taking selfies for their Insta Wotsits. I need someone with a bit of maturity and experience who's not afraid of getting their hands dirty."

Noah unsaddled the horse without fuss, lifted the bridle up and over, letting the animal drop the bit himself, and automatically started brushing his coat while making soothing sounds throughout.

"You might say someone who knows horses so intimately, he can tend to their every need with one hand tied behind his back," paraphrased Harry, turning towards the stall, "or perhaps with one arm in a sling."

George followed his gaze, and the two gents watched quietly as Noah and Skywalker interacted together, as if they always had.

"Is he looking for work?" asked George, clearly impressed by Harry's companion.

"He's not sure of his travel plans yet, but I can assure you he'd make an exemplary candidate - or, as you would say, he knows his onions. Leave it with me and let me see what I can do. His arm will need to heal, but I can't think of anyone better to take up the reins, so to speak."

For the rest of the morning, they explored the grounds, including the riding school close by, and Harry could see Noah absorbing everything; wheels turning in his head. Harry had spent many happy times at Cedarwood Park. First in training for his cross-country competitions when he was a younger man. The race track hadn't been developed in those days, but there were miles of open fields, and the stables were already built. That's when he first met George. Then he and Grace had brought the girls here for riding lessons, and later, watched their grandchildren follow in their mothers' footsteps. The apple didn't fall far from the tree, with each generation producing self-assured, skilful riders; their abilities certainly proving useful recently, given the sticky situation they'd gotten themselves into.

Lately, the visits to the track were infrequent. Harry made an occasional outing of it with some of the other village residents, watching the races and having a cheeky flutter from time to time. Now, however, he had a reason again to make the trip on a regular basis. He glanced at Skywalker again, his heart full. Horses had always meant a lot to Harry, as they did to Noah. He understood the way they could anchor a person, providing an oasis of calm when the rest of your life was in turmoil. He'd brought Noah here to give him a taste of the past, and hopefully show him a path to the future.

Thanking George for his hospitality, the two men patted Skywalker one more time, promising to return soon. As they drove homeward to Pebble Heath, Harry noticed a renewed vitality in Noah. Far more vocal than he had been up to now; pointing out places of interest as they travelled, asking questions, and listening to Harry's responses intently. The atmosphere in the car during the drive home was charged with possibility. They arrived at Maggie's house, senses stimulated and souls nourished. Noah conveyed his immense enjoyment of this morning's road trip as he got out of the car. Harry wound down the window, offering a final suggestion to underline his agenda for the day.

"Can I give you a piece of advice, son?" he asked.

"Certainly, you may."

"I know the fear of the unknown is daunting, but I think you need to take on a different perspective.'

"In what way?"

"Instead of fretting about losing your way in our time, understand that the fundamentals are already locked in. You're inherently smart, capable and kind. That will get you a long way in this world. You've got a support crew who are going to top up your oil and change your tyres whenever you need to pull over into a pit stop"

Noah's brows knitted with bewilderment.

"Sorry, bad reference. You haven't a clue what I'm talking about. That's another racetrack for another time. What I'm saying is people are looking out for you, and there are more important things to consider than playing it safe. When Grace was sick and I was scared about what might be around the corner, she said to me, *'Life is not measured by the number of breaths we take, but by the moments that take our breath away.'* Ask yourself, Noah, who leaves you breathless, and why would you want to forfeit that?"

Noah's face registered with comprehension, and he bowed his head in gratitude for Harry's words of wisdom.

"Oh, and there is such a thing as being too much of a gentleman," Harry continued, backing out of the driveway and straightening the car on the road again. Putting his head out the window as he started to drive away, he shouted,

"Kiss her, man. Goddammit!'

Jack was in the kitchen when Noah walked in, heating up leftover macaroni and cheese in the microwave, as per his mum's instructions.

"Perfect timing, Noah," he said. "Grubs up."

A ping indicated the meal was ready, and the mac and cheese came out piping hot.

"The small food box is speedier than the big box," Noah observed, intrigued by yet another display of technology.

"Yep, I'll show you how it works when we make popcorn later."

"Corn that pops? Sounds like a jovial pastime. If not a dangerous one," Noah chortled.

"Dope, Noah, you're making a joke!" laughed Jack. "Did you have a nice time with Pops this morning?"

"That I did, Jack. Your grandfather is pleasant company and very astute. It was a thought-provoking trip."

Jack handed Noah a fork for his lunch, and they sat down at the kitchen table. Noah smiled at the choice of cutlery. Familiar with knives and spoons, he hadn't come across a fork until his stay at the hospital, but had had fun learning how to use it. He liked the scooping and stabbing options, making it multi-functional and certainly useful for today's interesting meal. He turned the utensil over and back again, deciding which action to take. Skewering a piece of pasta, his smile became brighter with every cheesy mouthful. Jack noticed his friend was definitely in good spirits and seemed more animated today. Mum would like that, for sure.

Harry pulled into the hospital car park, locked the car, and took the keys up to the third floor.

"Hi, Harry," greeted Hayley, "Maggie's still upstairs, sorry."

"That's OK. Can I leave her car keys with you, please? I'm getting the bus back to the village. Places to be, people to see, you know. I'll catch her tonight, in any case."

"Sure thing. Did you want to leave a message?"

"Yes I would, thanks. Do you have a Post-it note handy?"

Hayley passed him a bright pink pad, and he hurriedly scribbled down a couple of words, handed it across the desk, and left. Maggie returned to Level 3 shortly after to have lunch, stopping by reception, where Hayley gave her the keys and the message Harry had written. Maggie looked at his note: - *'You're Welcome.'*

"'You're Welcome'? What does he mean by that? I was the one who loaned him the car."

Hayley shrugged. "Dunno. He didn't say anything to me, other than he was catching the bus to the village, and he'd see you tonight."

"He is a man of mystery at the moment. Oh well, I'm sure I'll find out soon enough. You're still coming to Sam's show tonight, aren't you?"

"Absolutely. Adam's coming too, if that's OK. Our first New Year's Eve together and whatnot."

"No problem at all, the more the merrier. I'll see you there."

THE AFTERNOON WHIZZED BY for everyone.

Sam was already at the gallery, putting the finishing touches to her display. One of the staff rushed over with the proof of the banner, showing the final Secret of Love title written on it.

"It's perfect," said Sam, giving the green light for printing. Nothing like leaving things to the last minute, but it had taken her a while to get the wording right. There were five exhibitors in total, each staging their artworks behind thick red velvet curtains, due to be drawn open after the show commenced. High ceilings, hardwood floors, and expertly placed lighting added to the drama of the event. Canapés would be served on arrival, with guests having the choice of alcohol or a hot beverage to drink. It was the height of elegance, and Sam - making an exception to her own rule - wore a dress (still black) to honour the occasion. She was restless with anticipation, and couldn't wait until her family and friends arrived.

At home, in the same state of flux, Tom and Cat were pulling out all the stops for the night ahead. Tom had rented a tux, and Cat, after half a dozen changes of outfit, was in full-on ball gown mode. This was her first opportunity to get properly dressed up since her 50th, and she unashamedly made a meal out of it. Soaking in a bubble bath first, she luxuriated in its warmth and soapiness for an hour; then wrapped herself up in towelling. Sitting in front of the mirror at her dressing table, she used the pre-heated curling iron to create soft waves in her hair, like Frankie had done for Maggie before the masquerade ball, but by way of a much easier process. Sterling silver jewellery lay on her dresser, ready to go with the blush pink dress and matching wrap. Nude-coloured heels completed the ensemble, allowing perfectly pedicured toes to peek out.

Across town, emulating Cat's passion for fashion, Frankie's choice of clothes had also been well thought out. He couldn't do pastels, darling, so was dressing in hues from the other end of the palette. Magenta, indigo and gunmetal grey were woven into a vibrant jacket, oozing a metallic sheen that would have made Elton John proud. Worn over a navy pantsuit, it was ostentatious but stylish - basically, Frankie all over. A singular gold hoop earring finished the look, allowing him to express his true self; a welcome change from the business attire he'd had to get used to since moving up in the world. Before getting dressed, though, he would do what he did best and create the perfect coiffure for his mother. His parents had spent a wonderful time with their son, and were looking forward to a fun party to finish the week. Also opting to dress up to the nines, as the trio left the apartment for an early dinner before the exhibition - arm in arm, synchronising their steps, and looking a lot like Dorothy and her companions on the yellow brick road - it was clear the Coopers were ready to send the year away in style.

At The Stables Retirement Village, Harry and Doris were finally playing the backgammon game they had put on hold ages ago. Harry had confided in Doris about his pre- Christmas escapade, but it had taken a while for her to believe him. He didn't blame her. It sounded like a tall story by any stretch of the imagination. But not backwards in coming forwards, Doris proceeded to probe him with dozens of questions. As he was able to answer each one in detail, and with sincerity, she gradually came around. Finally satisfied he was being truthful, and accepting his descriptions as valid, she told him she particularly liked the resourcefulness of his message on the tree. Returning the compliment, he praised her for seeing the bigger picture and realising something was up. To think there was a secret portal to the past at the end of the garden in the village was quite something.

"Imagine if Esme knew about that," she said, "she'd never let me outside again."

"Speak of the devil," Harry nodded towards the entrance door.

"Oh, yes, she's taking me out for afternoon tea. Not one for staying up til midnight on New Year's Eve, as you can imagine. So this will be as much of a party as I'll get. You'll share a tipple with me this evening, won't you, Harry?"

"That I can guarantee, Doris. Don't be too late with your scones and clotted cream, though. I hear Nadine has organised some entertainment for the village this afternoon.'

"OK, that sounds like fun. I'm sure we'll only be out for a couple of hours. I'll see you soon." She blew him a kiss as she put on her coat to join her daughter. She was glad to have her friend home, even if he wasn't in Esme's good books.

Harry went to his apartment to put his feet up in readiness for a late night and started thinking about Skywalker again. He would take the family on his next visit, but this morning, he was glad it was just him and Noah. They shared an intrinsic understanding and love of horses, and at the very least, it might have planted a seed. Harry dozed off, dreaming about the halcyon days of his youth, when times were simpler and his body was stronger.

At Maggie's house, Jack continued Noah's education on living in modern times. He taught him how to boil a kettle and showed him where the tea and coffee were kept. Noah was growing fond of both drinks. They put a load of dirty clothes in the washing machine, and Jack added the detergent. He pressed the buttons, explaining what they were for, while Noah looked on - fascinated at the garments spinning around in their own whirlpool. To kill time as they waited for the cycle to run through, Jack suggested they make popcorn and watch a movie.

"Yes, I would like to see the corn pop," Noah enthused.

Jack was perceptive enough to realise something had shifted in his friend. Less like a foreigner, struggling with the language and different-looking surroundings, Noah was acclimatising to the Pebble Heath of today, and wanting to know more.

Putting the paper bag in the microwave and setting it for three minutes, the two friends delighted in the sound of the pops; Noah likening the end result to sorcery. They split the warm, buttery snack into two bowls and settled in on the couch together, ready to watch a movie. Feeling comfortable in Jack's company, Noah ardently replayed the events of the morning; his description of Cedarwood Park and Skywalker littered with favourable adjectives, and his eyes sparkling with optimism. A very good sign, thought Jack.

At The Stables, an excited buzz hummed outside the front of the main building. Wanting to do something different for the residents at the end of the year but not sure what, Nadine had picked up a leaflet left under the door earlier on in the week, offering horse and carriage ride hire for special occasions. This was perfect! A little bit of old-fashioned extravagance without being too taxing was just the ticket. She'd booked the service for this afternoon, and right on time, trotting down the driveway, came a magnificent shire horse pulling a glorious open-air Victorian carriage. Sitting atop the small, narrow seat at the front were two moustachioed gentlemen wearing flat caps and tweed jackets. With a gentle Whoa, they pulled the horse to a stop, and one of the men hopped down, introducing himself to Nadine.

"Everybody," she proclaimed, "I'm thrilled to be able to bring a slightly different activity to the village today. A horse-drawn carriage for your enjoyment. You can take it in turns, two at a time, for a lap around the gardens led by your driver, Bill." She indicated the man by her side, who nodded in assent.

"And his colleague...." The man remaining on the seat stood, doffed his hat, and said,

"Ted. At your service, Ma'am."

"Yes, thank you. All right then, Bill and Ted will safely escort you around the gardens when you're ready."

People gathered around, getting themselves in pairs and wrapping up warm, excitedly waiting for the excursion to get underway. Harry, roused by the noise, came out to see what was going on. It was a beautiful sunny day, and the first couple keen for a ride stepped into the carriage with Bill's assistance, sitting themselves down on the generously padded seats. They snuggled underneath the blankets provided; the pattern matching another draped over the sturdy flanks of the horse in front. Grinning like Cheshire cats, the passengers waved to their onlookers as if in a royal parade.

At the same time, Esme and Doris returned.

"Ooh, this looks like a hoot," said Doris.

"Perhaps," said Esme, "but let's sort out your room like we intended. It will be good to refresh it for the new year."

The village was made up of freestanding villas in the north of the grounds, and an apartment block in the south. Harry and Doris lived in the apartments, wanting to be close to the action. Each unit contained an open-plan lounge and kitchen, with a double bedroom next to a fully functional bathroom; fitted out to aid the inevitable ageing process. Those on the ground floor had access to the gardens through an external door. And on the first and second floors, the rooms had balconies boasting picturesque views. Harry and Doris were neighbours on the latter. Both social creatures who enjoyed mingling in the communal areas, they also liked escaping to their sanctuaries upstairs, when they'd had enough. Originally meeting in the lift on their way to dinner some years ago and instantly clicking, they'd become firm friends from the get-go.

The residents were free to decorate their units as they wished, and Esme, as an end-of-year task, deemed today as the day to replace soft furnishings and alternate the pictures in Doris's room. Feeling like she had no choice, Doris followed her daughter to the lift, and as the doors opened on the second floor, they met Harry in the corridor. He was looking out the window at the goings-on below.

"Do you want to try this out?" Doris asked him eagerly.

"Yeah, it looks great," he said, 'but we can leave it until the others have had their go. Esme's been kind enough to help you with your room, so why don't you finish that first?"

Esme looked askance, not used to Harry siding with her, and not entirely trusting his motives. Doris also looked quizzically at her friend, knowing he and Esme rarely saw eye to eye. But she was willing to leave the ride for the moment, and appeasing her daughter in the interim meant she was more likely to be let off the leash later.

"Tell you what, though," added Harry, "why don't we make an event of it and dress up a bit? It is New Year's Eve, after all. You could wear that lovely faux fur jacket Esme bought you."

Again flummoxed by Harry's complimentary comment, but agreeing that her mother should dress up - of the thinking that one should always look one's best - Esme nodded in accord, while Doris remained suspicious of the obvious buttering up going on. She unlocked her apartment door and said to her neighbour,

"Righto then, we'll do our thing first, and then you and I will get our posh frocks on. I'll meet you downstairs in an hour."

Opening the wardrobe door inside his apartment, Harry picked out a dapper midnight blue suit that he hadn't worn for a while. Trying it on, he was pleased to see it still fit. He plucked a tri-coloured tie for a bit of pizazz from the shelf, and skilfully knotted it around his neck, as he'd been taught as a child, when ties were still part of school uniforms. He slipped his feet into the black shoes he'd shined earlier, and slid a neatly folded, crisp, white handkerchief into his breast pocket, then studied himself in the mirror.

"Hmm, sharp as a tack, if I say so myself."

Feeling energetic, he took the stairs to the ground level and joined those outside, making the most of the sunshine that would disappear soon.

MAGGIE WRAPPED UP HER paperwork for the day and gave her reports to Hayley. Today was busy but not too stressful, thank goodness. Hankering to get to Sam's exhibition on time tonight, she wanted to go home as soon as possible. She'd bought Noah another outfit at lunchtime, selecting a jet black shirt and dress pants from Marks and Spencer. Even though still in a cast, he was getting quite dextrous with his left arm now, so she figured he could cope with a jacket too; finding one in a sophisticated smoky kohl to match. She'd always liked the black-on-black look for a guy - like Keanu in John Wick. It reeked of masculinity and style, in her opinion. Satisfied with her purchases and waving goodbye to Hayley, with shopping bags in hand, she caught the lift down to the car park.

THE CARRIAGE RIDES WERE going down a treat at the Stables. Most of those who'd had their turn were warming up inside with a glass of brandy; the room filled with fellowship and lively chatter. Harry, enjoying the celebratory atmosphere, expected Doris to arrive any minute. Esme had rearranged Doris's room to her liking, and even helped her choose what to wear for the upcoming jaunt - her strict personality, softened somewhat by Harry's charm beforehand.

"Why don't you stay up here, love," Doris urged, "you can watch us through the window while keeping out of the cold." Esme agreed, thinking she could make some last-minute tweaks to the apartment while she was at it.

Emerging from the lift on the ground floor in said posh frock and white fur coat, Harry thought Doris looked like a vision. He approached, offering his arm to accompany her outside. Once again, Bill, the driver, assisted his passengers into the carriage.

"Lucky last," he said, shutting the small door behind them.

Off they went at a slow plod around the manicured gardens; ornamental frogs and tortoises poking their heads out of the flowers. Past the rose bushes, under the arched trellis, and down the slope by the oak tree - acorns and holly leaves scattered on the floor. Then they followed the path alongside the old stables. Doris held Harry's hand as they passed by the abandoned stalls, realising the significance, and half expecting a medieval knight to jump out at them. They circled the water feature, admiring the snowdrops flowering against the fence, before slowly ascending the slope again.

"Enjoying yourselves?' the driver asked.

"Oh yes," replied Doris, "this is wonderful."

The carriage gently bounced along towards the main building again, as the walk turned into a trot. Esme, watching from the balcony, had traced the outline of their journey with her eyes. They were nearly back to the beginning of the driveway outside the building entrance.

Whereupon the drivers turned to each other.

"Well, Bill."

"Yes, Ted."

"I think it's time we had an adventure; what do you say?"

"Most excellent."

They turned to those in the back, silently asking for permission.

"What do you think, Doris? Want to come to the art gallery with me tonight?" asked Harry with a sly grin.

Putting two and two together, Doris threw back her head and howled with laughter.

"Yes please," she said, "Forward Ho!"

Esme looked on in disbelief as the shire horse trotted alongside the main building, started to pick up speed past the car park, and unexpectedly began galloping down the driveway with his passengers still on board.

"Hang on to your hats, ladies and gentlemen," instructed Josh, whipping his moustache off. Removing his moustache too, his co-driver Aaron shook the reins and enthusiastically cried, "Giddy up!"

Harry and Doris gripped the sides of the carriage as they made their escape.

"Mother!!" yelled Esme, her body contorting over the railing of the balcony, in a desperate bid to be heard,

"What the bloody hell are you doing?!"

"Having fun, sweetheart," came the cry back. "Don't wait up!"

And sniggering like juvenile troublemakers, the two pensioners rode off into the sunset.

CHAPTER 20

New Year's Eve

MAGGIE ARRIVED HOME TO find Jack on the couch, still eating popcorn and watching A Knight's Tale.

"Yo wassup, Mum."

"Seriously?" she said, questioning his choice of movie.

"Chill - it's for Noah, so he can relate."

"Sure, but I would have thought you'd had enough of medieval yarns. Where is Noah anyway?"

"In the kitchen, making you a cup of tea. We heard you coming up the drive.'

"He is?"

Aside from her father, Maggie couldn't remember the last time a grown man had made her a hot drink when she came home."

"Yep - tutorials for today were kettle, microwave, washing machine and remote."

"Crikey, you have been busy. And what about his outing with your grandad?'

"He went to see a man about a horse."

Realising her son was blissfully ignorant of the double entendre associated with the phrase, and fairly sure Noah hadn't implied that he'd gone to the bathroom, Maggie had to stop herself from laughing. Managing to keep her composure, she said,

"So how is he? In himself, I mean."

"See for yourself," said Jack, observing Noah coming through the door with a mug of English breakfast tea.

"Hello or Hi, Maggie," Noah greeted.

Maggie thought his voice had changed. It sounded more...buoyant.

"Hello or Hi to you too. Sounds like you've had an eventful day."

"Indeed, it was very...fruitful."

Maggie wasn't sure what that meant and he didn't seem inclined to elaborate, but after a busy day, to be welcomed by a handsome man with a smile on his face, handing her a cuppa, wasn't half bad. She took a quick breather to drink her tea and showed Noah the clothes she'd bought him. Jack said the outfit was 'lit', which turned out to mean excellent. Her son was planning to wear some of the gear he'd bought on Boxing Day, so with the males of the household sorted, Maggie thought she better allow some time to get gussied up herself. She wanted to hear about Noah's morning, but they were fast running out of time, so it would have to wait.

"Righto, let's get moving. School's out, work's finished. It's time to party."

They peeled off into their separate bedrooms to get ready. Maggie had a quick shower in her en suite to freshen up, then moved to the walk-in wardrobe afterwards: running her fingers over the hangars and pushing them apart, until she found a garment that interested her. She settled on an emerald green, strapless dress that cinched in at the waist, before flaring out to mid-calf, giving off a retro fifties vibe. She'd had compliments in the past on how well it went with her auburn hair, so tonight, blow-dried her locks and let them flow freely over her shoulders, forgoing the usual ponytail. Deliberately not overdoing the makeup, she applied a light foundation and dark brown mascara, then rummaged around in her drawer looking for the right shade of lippy. Coral coloured should do the trick. She pursed her lips, applying it in two seamless strokes. Next, she slipped her feet into a pair of black, strappy heels that she'd last worn to Cat's birthday party. Maggie didn't wear heels often, but these were exceptionally comfy and her go-to pair for any special occasion. Lastly, in search of earrings, she instinctively reached for a pair of conservative studs. But on impulse, changed her mind and switched to a bolder design that featured a diamond resting against the lobe, with long, dangly threads attached; giving the illusion of sparkling waterfalls cascading down her neck. Go big or go home, she reckoned.

Noah, already in the lounge, looked up the stairs as Maggie came into view. He took a sharp intake of breath as she descended, prompting him to recall the conversation he'd had with Harry that morning. Maggie paused at the base of the stairs, doing her very best to hold it together. Freshly shaved, dressed to kill, and exuding a confidence that hadn't shown itself until now; like a movie star out of Hollywood, Noah looked - there was only one way to say it - hot!

He came towards her and stood so their bodies were only inches apart.

"Beautiful," he murmured huskily.

"And you," she responded, instantaneously hot and bothered.

He smelt fantastic. She hadn't bought him cologne, but maybe Harry had. It was musky and rugged and sexy. His eyes were even bluer than usual: a mesmerising azure like Kingfisher feathers. Miniscule flecks of gold twinkling with temptation drew her in with a promise of untold treasures. The subtlest of smiles crinkled the creases at the corners, inviting her to match his stare. She could feel the heat of his breath on her neck and her pulse quickened. It seemed like a fog had encircled them, blurring the background so they could only see each other. He calmly moved his right hand near her face and tenderly swept away a loose tendril of hair; tucking it behind her ear. He gently touched the back of her diamante threads, pulling them forward a touch; the tips of his fingers accidentally grazing her skin. The electricity between them was so intense, she felt her equilibrium shift off balance.

"Trinkets,' he uttered, looking amused at her earrings, and then languidly back into her eyes.

Whereupon, the moment was completely destroyed by Jack running out of his room and bursting into the lounge. Seeing them standing close - way too cringey for his liking - he acted up in typical teenage fashion.

"C'mon, you two!" he shouted. "No time to be luvvy duvvy now. The car's arrived."

They both took a step back, flustered and awkward, but glowing like embers in a fire beginning to take hold.

Thanks to Frankie, they were being driven to the gallery tonight, giving them the freedom to drink without worrying about the logistics of getting home. Thank God, I could do with a double shot of vodka right now, thought Maggie. She picked up her handbag and opened the door, ushering Jack towards the waiting limousine. About to follow, Noah suddenly held his index finger up, signifying he needed a second. He dashed into his bedroom, slipped something into his back pocket and ran out again, closing the door. Firmly putting his hand on the small of Maggie's back in a guiding, protective manner; his touch fired up another electrical charge within her. She didn't know what had happened today, but Noah had changed. This was shaping up to be quite the night.

In another house, Tom and Cat answered a knock on the door from the chauffeur, who chaperoned them to their transport outside. He opened the car door for Cat, and she scooched over the luxurious leather seat to make room for her husband. The opulent interior included a tray folded into the back of the front seat, that when pulled open, revealed a bottle of champagne and two glasses. In her element, and issuing an exclamation of delight, Cat immediately poured them a glass each. Tom knew he would have to reign in Frankie's spending at some stage, but for now, he was going to enjoy the extravagance on his way to his daughter's big night.

Already at the gallery, Frankie and his parents waited with Sam in the reception area, eager for the others to arrive and for the show to begin. Soon, Harry and Doris walked in - flushed from their afternoon exploits - followed by the boys. Aaron, also in high spirits, wrapped his arm around Sam's waist and swung her around, literally sweeping her off her feet.

"Hello, gorgeous, gifted girlfriend," he said.

"Put me down, you idiot," she semi-scolded in jest. "Hold on, did you say 'girlfriend'?"

"Of course, why wouldn't I?"

He confirmed their status with a quick smooch on the lips.

"Eeew gross," interrupted Josh, "that's my sister. C'mon man, you're ruining Sam's reputation as a brooding artist. Let's go and get a beer."

Aaron yielded to Josh's tug on his arm, but before they targeted the bar, Josh gave Sam a brotherly hug, and conceding to his sibling's hard work, whispered,

"Congrats, Sis, you done good here."

Sam felt giddy. From her brother's compliment; from the kind words drip-fed to her by supporters, but most of all; from Aaron's casual statement of their relationship. It was on. It was definitely on.

Not long after, Tom and Cat turned up in all their finery.

"Sweetie, darling," cried Frankie, hugging Cat and air kissing either cheek, "you look fabulous! Do come and meet my parents."

Introductions were made and small talk proliferated as the room filled up with people. Doris ended up side by side with Tom, while Harry and Cat chatted with Sam. Having gotten to know Harry's family well over the years, there was no need for a superficial icebreaker, and so, taking advantage of a lull in the noise, she leaned into Tom, confessing that Harry had told her the whole story about their time away.

"How did you cope? It must have been so frightening, not knowing if you would get home."

"We were fortunate to have each other, and Harry's stoicism held us together. Plus, there were some lighter moments to distract us from our worries occasionally."

"Yes, he did tell me about LeBron James winning the hound race, and sitting at the Baron's feet waiting for the rest of his burger. That would have been funny."

Tom nodded, and they both chuckled at the image in their heads.

"LeBron James is a bit of a mouthful, though, isn't it?" commented Doris.

"Sure is," said Tom. "I always thought he should be called Prince."

"Like the Prince of Denmark?" suggested Doris, "because he is a Great Dane, after all."

"Doris!" beamed Tom, gratified that someone had finally got his dad joke, "I knew I always liked you. Care for a cup of tea?"

"I should think not," she refused, "it's New Year's Eve; lead me to the champers!"

Maggie, Noah and Jack appeared next. They immediately sought out Sam, extolling their praises, each in their own way:

- A hug from Maggie: 'You rockstar, Sam! This is incredible."

- A smile and small bow from Noah: "Congratulations Miss Samantha."

- A high five from Jack: "Smashed it, Cuz."

Then they joined the rest of the family and talked amongst themselves, counting down the minutes until the show officially opened.

"What do you think, Dad?" whispered Cat. "Maggie and Noah look more..."

"Together?" said Harry, filling in the blank. "I think he's finding his feet at last. I took him to Cedarwood Park this morning to open his eyes. Every man needs a purpose in life. I hope I was able to show him his."

"Well, he certainly has a twinkle in his eye this evening," Cat noted, watching a distinct change in the body language between the two. More people filtered into the reception area, including Hayley and Adam, who walked towards the couple in question.

"Noah," said Adam, "so good to see you up and about. How are the ribs feeling?"

"The pain is diminishing, thank you," replied Noah. "I offer my thanks for your medical skills and attention."

"Not at all," said Adam, feigning humility, and still thinking Noah was a bit of an odd chap. He casually slapped Maggie on the arm and said, somewhat patronisingly,

"Good to see you in your glad rags for a change, Mags. You clean up nice."

Noah turned to Hayley, lifted her fingers with his, and politely kissed the back of her hand.

"Miss Hayley, a pleasure to be in your presence again."

Adam wasn't at all happy with Noah's salutation, nor with Hayley's response; fluttering her eyelashes and smiling coyly. Poles apart in the way they greeted the women, Noah's old-fashioned gesture put Adam on the back foot. He petulantly pulled Hayley closer to him and made an excuse to move on.

"Great work from your niece, Mags. Can't wait to see her pictures. We'll grab a quick drink before the show starts."

As Adam encouraged Hayley to keep moving, she sidled past Maggie with her arm straight down, the palm of her hand turned upwards, and said in a hushed tone,

"You go, girlfriend."

Maggie tittered, and subtly slapped Hayley's hand as she walked on, acknowledging Noah was a catch and looking very fine tonight.

The ambience in the room was effervescent - a mixture of expectation, celebration and bonhomie. Constant toasts of congratulations to the exhibitors and general wishes for good health consolidated into a harmonious agreement that tonight was a special way of seeing the old year out and the new year in. Soon enough, a smartly dressed, bespectacled woman with a look of authority came forth. The curator of the gallery stood on the podium and requested,

"Can I have your attention, please, everybody?"

The din quietened, and all faces turned in her direction.

"I am extremely honoured to host this special presentation, with such superb works of art on display. Every participant should be incredibly proud of their achievements, and I know the audience gathered here tonight will be dazzled by their talents. So without further ado, it's my great pleasure to officially open our New Year's Eve exhibition: 'The Secret to Love'."

She pressed a remote to a round of applause, which opened each exhibitor's curtains, showcasing the best of their work for the project. Sam's contribution had come together beautifully. Capturing the essence of recent experiences, the title of her set of pictures stood out clearly on the printed banner:

'The Secret to Love is...being with people who let you be yourself.'

As her friends and family made their way forward to see her finished pieces close up, she felt her dad's arm around her shoulder.

"This looks fantastic, Sam. Utterly, frigging fantastic!"

She giggled at her dad's uncharacteristic use of profanity, but felt exhilarated her work had warranted such emphasis. Walking unhurriedly, her fans took their time to inspect every detail of every picture, admiring her creativity and execution. In each case, she had pinned the original Polaroid to the side of the picture frame, highlighting the inspiration and thought process that allowed her to recreate the scene, in whatever style she felt most appropriate.

First - Jack playing basketball in the driveway, with Bronny attempting to catch the rebounds. Sam had spent one afternoon watching her cousin shoot hoops; his love for the game and his dog undeniable. Bronny barked throughout, in total adoration of his master and wanting to be involved in anything he was doing. She had heard Jack commentating at the time as he made his moves on the court: "And he zigzags through the opposition... steps back and squares himself up...but, ooh, fakes the shot...instead, driving forward into a windmill dunk...Nooooo...it hits the backboard and falls, but wait...the ball bounces off LeBron's head and goes in! Scooooore!" While Sam couldn't encapsulate the audio, she'd demonstrated the teamwork between boy and dog perfectly, incorporating charcoal swishes and smudges to give the appearance of movement.

Second - Her mum's 50th birthday. Specifically, the moment when her grandad arrived, still dressed up in his Santa suit from the night's hijinks. She'd focused on Harry joining Cat, Maggie and Frankie, already drinking punch and ready to party. Using sharp pencils to sketch intricate facial expressions, she'd laid bare every wrinkle and crease of age. Sam hoped she wouldn't get shit about that from her mum and aunt later, but she wanted the picture to be authentic. A gathering of people comfortable in each other's company. Coloured pencils softened some areas, but she dialled up the red in Harry's suit, and the white on Frankie's halo with a subtle layer of crayon, as a fun contrast to the smaller details.

Third - The incongruous sight of Maggie, Jack and Bronny squished into the back of her VW on their way to the school fair. Dressed in their costumes with her dad in the driver's seat, looking like something out of Blackadder. The Dane's arse parked on the parcel shelf with his massive head chewing on a broom, effectively pinning those on the back seat in an unnatural upright position. It made her laugh then and still had the same effect. She didn't need any special techniques for this one. A car crash of colour and discomfiture, pure acrylic was enough to make her point. Family supported each other, no matter how ridiculous they looked.

Fourth - Her brother Josh and best mate Aaron, a couple of weeks ago when Aaron was no more than her brother's best friend. How things had changed. She'd caught them unaware while at Jack's fair. Having overly exerted themselves in the tug-o-war competition while draped in heavy chain-mail, they'd worked up a sweat and an appetite, and with knight's helmets tucked under their arms, were happily munching on sausages from the barbeque. Joking with each other, they had roguish looks on their faces, belying the true bromance she knew existed. No matter what the future held for her and Aaron, she would never jeopardise the friendship that he had with Josh, knowing how valuable it was to each guy. The boys' mischievous looks featured front and centre of the picture, with Sam deliberately fading out the background.

Fifth - Ivy. Lovely Ivy and her kitchen friends dancing up a storm. Sam felt a pang of regret that she had befriended such a kindred spirit, only for their connection to conclude in such an abrupt manner. The affinity they'd had for each other was instant. Each girl understanding the other; completely nonplussed in relation to their - supposed - different breeding. Little did Ivy know that Sam was as much of a commoner as she. The sly photo Sam had taken prior to Mistress Edith walking in was of the girls facing the opposite wall, practising the TikTok dance she'd taught them; all revelling in a freedom they hadn't been permitted before. The shutter had clicked in the same split second that Ivy turned her head to look over her shoulder, capturing the one pretty face out of a sea of posteriors. Sam had kept this artwork in its photographic form, unchanged other than a vague sepia filter. It looked like a scene from olden times, which, of course, it was, and that's the way she chose to remember it.

Sixth - Inside the chapel on the night they'd told Noah the truth. In amongst the mayhem, and out of sheer relief to have him in the know, Sam had attempted to take a selfie with everyone in the background. Even though a Polaroid doesn't lend itself to that sort of photo, she'd given it a go. It had been a bit of guesswork; holding the camera backwards uncomfortably, in what she thought was roughly the right position. The outcome was pretty cool; she had to say. The sharpness of the shot wasn't up to her usual high standards, but liking the absurdity of the situation and different perspective, she'd turned the picture into a watercolour; allowing the paint to run into itself - creating an image of lightness and free-flowing emotions - reflecting the mood of the evening.

Seventh - How could she resist taking this one? After her dad's knighthood, he'd walked down the stage stairs - shell-shocked to some degree by the experience - and into the arms of his wife. The look of pride and devotion on her mother's face was priceless. How wrong she had been, thinking her parents were dull and boring, when their medieval encounter had clearly shown how courageous and inventive they really were. The importance of the occasion made the theme worthy of an oil painting, so that was the medium Sam had chosen. Keeping her mum and dad in their noble costumes, and emphasising the folds of fabric, decorative brooches, and silk adornments, gave it a Rembrandt feel. Knowing her mum liked a bit of glitz and glamour, she hoped this particular remembrance, decked out in a gilded gold frame, fit perfectly into that category.

Eighth - Slightly different from the other literal portrayals, Sam had worked hard to get this picture just right. On the day the men had gone riding, she'd taken a great shot of her grandad driving a horse-pulled chariot, which would have been a brilliant depiction of his love of equestrian activities. However, it occurred to her that Pops might appreciate something more meaningful. With that in mind, she'd merged photos of Grace, his wife with Perfect Grace, the palomino. It was an inspired combination. The horse's flowing white mane and caramel coat worked in flawless symmetry with her grandmother's silver hair and creamy complexion. Using soft, ivory paint to disguise the photo edges gave it a sublime, ethereal quality. Also employing an L.E.D. frame to illuminate the right areas; Sam's trick of light shone over the two loves of Harry's life.

Ninth - her pièce de résistance! Maggie running through puddles, holding hands with her two men - Noah on one side and Jack on the other. She couldn't recall another instance where her aunt had acted in such a carefree and impetuous manner. Having had to paint by memory, if she said so herself, it was pretty bloody great. Acrylics again; she'd taken the impression of the scene in her mind from the 1300s and transported it into the 2000s. As an homage to her doppelgänger aunt for taking her place at the ball, and as a nod to a few of her favourite things, Sam had changed their 14th-century costumes to contemporary garb, and replaced the background buildings with splendorous trees, dripping with autumn shades of paprika, marmalade, and copper. Jack's self-made maple coloured frame topped it off to perfection. In the picture, Noah looked dashing and assured, and Jack was full of beans. But what she wanted to see more than anything was the unbridled joy on her aunt's face at that moment, duplicated in modern-day life.

On the gallery floor, Sam's family and friends vociferously expressed how impressed they were with her creations. Noah, in particular, stared in awe of the display. Having only seen dark, sombre, religious paintings in Baron Buford's manor, he had no idea such visions could exist. And each presented an insight into the people he had come to know these last few weeks. With his one good hand behind his back, he walked slowly, taking in every brushstroke as if he were an art connoisseur.

Maggie matched his pace, holding hands with Jack; loving Sam's masterpieces and Noah's reactions to them. He found the one of Jack and Bronny humorous, loved the likenesses in the party portrait, and felt sentimental when looking at the images based in his own time. He stood by Harry as they waxed lyrical over Perfect Grace and her namesake, complimenting Sam on her clever idea.

Then he came to the final picture.

At first, he was a little taken aback at seeing a reflection of himself in paint, but that was overtaken by a strong sense of destiny fulfilling itself. Noah stepped back and stood upright, absorbing the image in front of him. Maggie slipped her hand into his, thinking he might be overcome with emotion, but to her dismay, he pulled it away abruptly. She hadn't expected such a sudden rejection when she was sure they were getting closer this evening. The rebuttal stung like a slap in the face.

"I'm sorry," she muttered, wondering how she'd misinterpreted the signs and instantly feeling depleted. She turned away from him, embarrassment coursing through her veins. Harry noticed the stricken look on his daughter's face and glanced in Noah's direction. Jack, too, felt his mother's vibrancy evaporate; intuitively squeezing her hand in support. Maggie wanted to thank him but the lump in her throat prevented it. Her father and son loved her unconditionally; she could attest to that, but she didn't seem able to read other men properly.

See, this was precisely why she shouldn't get her hopes up. Obviously, her instincts for business and practical matters didn't extend to romance. Her judgement was off with the opposite sex. She'd been lulled into a false sense of security today, letting her guard down, and thinking something special was happening, when Bam; the rug had been pulled out from under her. It was clear Noah wanted to keep her in the dreaded friend zone. Every time, she thought. I get it wrong every single time. Even on New Year's Eve, in amongst the positivity and good cheer, Maggie's happy ever after seemed elusive.

Trying to ignore the pain of her disappointment, she forced a smile on her face to commend her niece's artistic skills.

"Sam, you've outdone yourself," she said, her voice edged with a tremor.

"But I believe you are missing a vital piece," interjected Noah.

The hand he'd pulled away from Maggie - which he'd had to do, as he only had use of one - was in his back pocket, trying to regain possession of something important. Successfully retrieving the article he'd kept close to him since his arrival, he moved forward to Sam, who was standing beside the picture.

He handed her the original Polaroid snap of the scene in the puddles.

"It's my photo!" cried Sam in delight. "Noah, where did you get this? I thought I'd lost it."

"You did. On the ground during the scuffle with Sebastian. The Baron found it and gave it to me when I was traumatised in the stables. He felt it may assist me in taking steps towards my healing."

Having no clue of Maggie's turmoil in response to his unintentional slight, he smiled broadly and voluntarily threaded his fingers through hers, as he'd fully intended on doing in the first place.

She was in shock. Firstly, at her misinterpretation of his actions (silently cursing her negative self-talk), and secondly, at the meaning of the Polaroid.

"Wait. This was your sign to come to the 21st century?"

"Yes," said Noah, still smiling and oblivious to her upset.

He took a step to the left, pulling her with him and Jack too, by default, who was still holding his mother's other hand. Guiding his party of three to stand directly opposite the painting, he said playfully,

"Same, same."

"Totally!" confirmed Sam, gleefully watching life imitate art. Although her aunt's unbridled joy had yet to make an appearance.

"But I thought Baron Buford wanted you to come here, so you'd have access to medical advancements," said Maggie, still wrestling with how she could go from elation to devastation to confusion, in the space of thirty seconds.

"That too," replied Noah, finally registering the misunderstanding, and realising he needed to set the record straight. Moving out of their daisy chain stance, he stood in front of her, staring meaningfully into her eyes.

"In truth," he began, "my heart was more broken than my bones."

Jack let go of his mum's hand, leaving her with Noah, but remaining within reach if she needed him.

"So what are you saying?" Maggie asked a little unsteadily, not completely sure she was understanding the context. "The photo of us together, that's what made up your mind? Not the fact that we have hospitals and doctors, but to be here with us? Be with me?"

"This is correct," he confirmed.

By now, the rest of the family - well and truly distracted from the exhibition - had stopped what they were doing. Surrounding the couple, they waited on tenterhooks to see where this conversation was going.

"Maggie," Noah said softly, "I always saw how you would fit into my world. I just didn't know if I could fit into yours."

"And now?" she asked hesitantly.

Those around them held their silence. Cat grabbed hold of Tom's arm, the tension almost unbearable.

"Initially, I was conscious of being a misfit, but young Jack's tutelage allowed me to become comfortable with the language and the gadgets."

Jack grinned from ear to ear at the thought of being instrumental in Noah's decision-making process.

"His invisible friend in the kitchen helped too..."

"He's talking about Alexa," Jack laughed, and a river of giggles undulated in the quiet.

"Then the welcome I received from your kin and companions last night surely made me wonder if staying here for evermore was possible."

Captivated by what they hoped was unfolding, the group's focus remained firmly on Noah and Maggie. Listening to every word, there was no whispering, sipping of drinks, or shuffling of feet. Even Doris waited with bated breath, conscious that this was a make-or-break moment for those involved.

"And then Harry alleviated my lack of direction, by showing me my work on the estate could indeed be transferred to an establishment here..."

Maggie glanced over Noah's shoulder to her father, who cheekily mouthed 'You're Welcome', repeating the message he'd left on the Post-it note at the hospital.

But she didn't want to count her chickens. This could still be a Thank You but Goodbye speech. Noting her hesitancy, Noah continued to reassure the woman facing him.

"Forgive me for not demonstrating my true feelings beforehand, but I thought it necessary to - how do you say - get my birds in a row."

"Ducks," corrected Maggie, unable to stop a smile escaping from her lips, to go with those emerging on the faces around her.

"You have been patient with me and given me time to find my way. To find my path alongside yours."

His hand was still in hers, and she could feel his thumb rubbing her skin demonstratively. Finding it hard to believe this intelligent, considerate, talented man could seriously want a relationship with her, Maggie voiced her doubts for all to hear.

"Noah, I'm glad you're feeling better about being in the 21st century, but there's still a chasm between your day and ours. We've lived in different worlds for over fifty years. You've had protocol and discipline drilled into you, and women from your time have such a different outlook than those in mine. I'm outspoken and bossy and emotional sometimes."

"And vibrant and caring and irrepressible," he soothed.

"Oh," she said, a little stunned by his compliments.

"But it wouldn't be all rainbows and roses, Noah. At this stage of my life, I have obligations, and mood swings and..."

"... sticky toffee pudding," he added.

The others laughed.

"I do not wish for you to change," Noah continued, his eyes crinkling with affection.

"Nor me. Wanting you to change, I mean," Maggie stammered; her argument all but lost in his sincerity.

"The secret to love," he said, looking up at Sam's banner, "is being with people who let you be yourself."

"Love?"

The background noise in the gallery paled into insignificance with the weight of Noah's words. Was he really saying what she thought he was? Noah had had a sign to give him clarity. Now she desperately needed one of her own. As if reading her mind, Harry cleared his throat and said,

"Don't forget the other thing, son."

"As if I could," replied Noah, "it's all I have been dreaming of since I arrived."

His gaze lingered on Maggie's eyes as he clasped her hand tighter, drawing it in an arc towards his mouth and brushing his lips across the rise of her knuckles. Then he pulled it firmly to his chest, removing the gap between them; their faces a hair's breadth apart, and his intentions very clear.

"I love you," he murmured, kissing her mouth with such delicacy and deliberation that all her reservations fell to the wayside. Her protective scaffolding dismantled completely as she kissed him back. Maggie's walls had first cracked, then shot up again moments ago, only to crumble in a heap now as her heart melted, Salvador Dali style. At last, she let herself fall fully for the man in front of her. The man who had consumed her whole being from the moment she'd met him. The man she needed so much to stay in her life.

"I love you too," she said softly.

The onlookers were as enraptured as Maggie, and a joint sound of relieved exhalation sliced through the thick, heavy stillness of the air. Maggie stood motionless, her body tucked into Noah's; without a plan, no thoughts of what happens next, her ducks definitely not in a row. In fact, she didn't even know where her ducks were. At this moment, her life was sublimely out of control, but there was no lip-biting nor indecision. Noah was the antidote to her A-type intensity. The calm to her storm. The ballast to her ship. A flush of colour rushed to her cheeks as bliss set fire to her blood, mirroring the radiance she felt internally, and confirming what she knew in her heart. This was where she was meant to be.

And there it was, noted Sam: the unadulterated happiness written all over her aunt's face. Exactly like her photo and painting.

But there was still a question that had yet to be answered definitively. Cat was the one to ask on her sister's behalf.

"So, Noah, does this mean you're going to stay? For good?"

He looked around and grinned, still holding Maggie tight.

"Well, as a very wise friend of mine once said..." he replied, winking at Jack,

"...I think that would be epic."

THE END

ACKNOWLEDGEMENTS

Many thanks to you, the reader, for being part of Maggie and Noah's adventure. If you enjoyed the story, I'd be most grateful if you could leave a review by visiting https://www.amazon.com/review/create-review?&asin=B0DVGFDP1C

And if you'd like to be one of the first to know about the couple's next escapade, please email me at laura.virgo65@gmail.com to join my reading group.

An enormous thank you to my beta readers – Kerry, Jacqui, Sally, Treena, Marianne, Karen and Sandy - whose input was invaluable; enabling me to turn various dubious drafts into a presentable finished product.

And huge thanks to Kevin Stevens, who took the time to transform a base picture into a stunning book cover, even though he had 101 other things to do.

Lastly, a special mention goes to my 'Bud' Jonathan, who deadass, is the sunshine in my day and lowkey, my favourite human being on the planet. No cap.

ABOUT THE AUTHOR

LAURA VIRGO

Originally from the south of England, Laura emigrated to New Zealand with her family as a child in the 1970s. She now resides in Wellington with her teenage son and two cats, Humphrey and Tilly.

As far as storylines go, she's a fan of well-loved tropes with comedic ensemble casts and is a sucker for a happy ending. When not playing with words, Laura is an avid quizzer, a movie buff, and enjoys walking along the local coastline, and watching her son's basketball games.

Printed in Dunstable, United Kingdom

65942103R00201